It was the height of the season.

At dazzling balls and coming-out parties, the *Ton* gathered to flirt with the latest crop of beauties.

Ambitious mothers displayed their bedecked and bejeweled daughters before the country's most eligible matrimonial prospects.

That year, sophisticated London was maliciously diverted by the love affairs of Lord Byron.

But the whole town would soon be titillated by even more scandalous events!

A
Regency
Scandal

Alice Chetwynd Ley

BALLANTINE BOOKS • NEW YORK

To Elizabeth Stevens,
who has given me so much help and encouragement.

Library of Congress Catalog Card Number: 78-62829

ISBN 0-345-26008-2

Manufactured in the United States of America

First Edition: February 1979

Acknowledgments

The textual sources from which I have drawn information for the writing of this novel are too numerous to be listed here. I would, however, like to place on record my deep gratitude for the assistance received from the following:

D. G. Bompas, C.M.G., M.A. Secretary, Guy's Medical School;

Stephen Green, Curator, Marylebone Cricket Club;

The Staff of Hillingdon Borough Libraries. Eastcote Branch;

and Graham K. H. Ley, who suggested the theme.

PART I

Alvington

1789-1805

"For our time is a very shadow
that passeth away."

Chapter I

THE DAY IN 1789 that Neville, Viscount Shaldon, only son of the fifth Earl of Alvington, attained his majority, the gates of Alvington Hall were flung wide to admit all the Earl's tenants and outdoor staff to an alfresco feast in the grounds.

Alvington Hall was an imposing edifice, as befitted the great house of the neighbourhood. It stood at the end of a long avenue of the beeches for which Buckinghamshire is famous, and about it a pleasant park had been formed by the eminent landscape gardener, Capability Brown. The first Earl had caused the house to be built in the prevailing Jacobean style; but subsequent owners had kept abreast of the architectural whims of their day, so that now the Hall presented a pleasant classical appearance. The windows of the west front looked out onto a terrace from which steps led down to lawns and flower beds; beyond was a view of the two lakes and surrounding parkland. The main entrance was on the north side of the house, while to the east was a large stable block surrounding a courtyard, with the land agent's commodious quarters fronting it. As sometimes happens on large estates which have been in existence for centuries, the church which served both house and village was within the park, separated by a mere fifty yards from the south side of the mansion, a conveniently short distance which enabled the Earl's household to be punctual at their devotions. Fortunately, an early ancestor had

3

caused the graveyard to be removed from the grounds to a more distant site in the village; and though the village people of that time had regarded this as a sacrilegious act which was bound to bring down disaster on the family, so far the prophecy remained unfulfilled.

Every servant, indoors and out, had been up betimes on this bright day in late May, from the stately butler and buxom cook to the humblest kitchen maid and still more lowly bootblack. There had been scoldings in plenty and even boxed ears, in the general fuss and flurry before all was ready, and the long trestle tables, loaded with all manner of tempting viands, had been set out at a discreet distance from the house.

There were boiled fowls; huge rounds of tongue, ham, and beef; and weighty game pies with brown, crisp crust decorated by the hand of an artist. There were great bowls of salamagundy, pyramids of jellies and syllabubs, massive dishes of succulent fruit, and mounds of hot, crusty bread fresh from the oven. Kegs of ale had been brought out ready to fill the tankards which would presently be raised to drink young Master's health; and the crowning triumph of the feast was an ox which was being roasted nearby, well away from the trees, giving off the most mouth-watering smells imaginable.

Eager with anticipation of these delights, the villagers trooped in to join those who worked on the estate, all clad in their Sunday best and with manners to match. Even the youngest child among them knew that the Earl of Alvington, though genial enough today, was an ill man to cross. One word or action out of place could have dire results when everyone's livelihood depended upon the Earl's patronage. They knew well enough, too, that their master's domination extended even to his own family. The Countess was a meek lady who could not say boo to a goose, let alone attempt to oppose her autocratic husband. Pale, languid, almost a shadowy creature, she did her duty at board and in bed without either involvement or complaint. She had managed to bring only this one child

4

into the world, every subsequent pregnancy having ended in miscarriage. To the Earl it was a symbol of her general ineffectualness; but at least she had managed to present him with an heir to the title and estate before her productivity ceased. As for sexual excitement, that was easy enough for him to find in London, where he always had one expensive mistress or another in keeping. Such affairs were a commonplace with men of rank and wealth, and caused no comment among his own circle beyond the usual cynical jest as they laid bets about who Alvington's next ladybird would be.

As for the young Viscount—Master Neville, as many of the older retainers still thought of him—he was no match for his sire. Since he had been trained from childhood in implicit obedience to his father's will, and was still dependent upon him financially, his coming of age today would make no difference to the existing relationship between parent and son. The Earl would still call the tune and Master Neville would dance to it, however reluctantly.

They watched him now, as he walked about amongst them paying civilities with that air of easy charm which warmed people to him momentarily, even though most of them in time came to realise that it meant nothing. The Strattons—the family name of the Earls of Alvington—had always been handsome men, right back to the first Earl in the time of Charles the Second. Neville, Viscount Shaldon was no exception—tall and slim, but with good shoulders, his features almost of a classical perfection, marred only by a slight weakness about the chin. The most distinctive mark of his Stratton heredity was his hair, at present unpowdered and worn tied back with a plain black ribbon. It was of a deep, rich auburn colour that could be seen in all the family portraits hanging on the walls of Alvington Hall. Altogether he appeared a fine figure of a man as he paced beside his father among their humble guests, causing spontaneous murmurs to be heard of "Good health and fortune, m'lud," or more simply, "God bless ye, Master Neville."

5

"Fine day for it," said the Earl, glancing up at the cloudless blue sky. "Good thing. Easier to get the mess cleaned up afterwards. Better for the ball tonight, too, as some of 'em will have a long drive home. Speaking of the ball, I've been turning things over in my mind, thinking about your future."

"My—my future, sir?" repeated Neville, uneasily.

"Yes—your marriage, m'boy." He gave a short laugh as he saw his son's startled look. "Well, got to get hitched some time, ain't you? Thing is, who to choose. Plenty of likely candidates for a young fellow of rank and fortune like yourself—and not too ill-looking a chap, at that, though I say it myself."

"But surely, sir," protested Neville, feebly, "one and twenty is a trifle young to be considering matrimony? I must confess no such thought has so far crossed my mind."

"Let it do so now," recommended the Earl briskly. "No need to press the business on for . . . say a twelvemonth, but time to start looking about you. I collect by what you say that so far your fancy hasn't lighted on any particular gal?"

He paused in his stride to cast a keen glance at his son. The steel-grey eyes which missed nothing detected a certain uneasiness in Neville's face.

"It has, eh? Who is she, then? Come on, out with it!"

Neville shook his head vigorously, avoiding that keen eye. "No, no, assure you, Father! No one in particular. Of course, a man can't avoid noticing a female here and there. Only human," he added, with an attempt at a man-of-the-world air.

The Earl emitted a crack of laughter. "As you say, m'boy. Glad to know there's a streak of the Strattons in you, for don't mind telling you at times I've set you down as a regular milksop.

"Well, if you've no fancy for anyone in particular, so much the better, since I've hit on a very desirable match for you, myself. One of the biggest fortunes in the country, and a considerable land holding. Only child, too, like yourself, so it would all come to you.

6

Don't doubt her father'd be glad enough to settle, for who wouldn't want his daughter to marry into an earldom when he's only a baronet himself? Old family, mind, good name, no drawback there."

Neville listened to this in stunned silence.

"I suppose," he said at last, "you must mean Sir William Cottesford's daughter, Maria."

"Is her name Maria?" asked the Earl. "Known them these twenty years, but never troubled myself to find out. Yes, that's the one. What d'you say?"

"I—well—I scarce know what to say—"

"Fustian! Where would you find a better match, now, tell me that?" retorted his father, forcefully. "Name, fortune, land. What more d'you want?"

"I agree it's a good match from that point of view," replied Neville, hesitantly.

"What other point of view is there?" The Earl's tone was impatient.

"Well, it's just that—Maria Cottesford is not a very personable young lady—"

"What's that to say to anything? She looks the lady, don't she? All you need in a wife, believe me—that, and a strong sense of duty," he added, thinking with satisfaction of his own wife in this respect. "If it's something a bit more fluffy you want, plenty of lady-birds to be had for the asking. Marriage is what we're talking of now, and marriage is a matter of business, not pleasure. Sooner you get that into your head, the faster we'll get on. Eh, what d'you say?"

Neville was obliged to reply to the salutations of some of his father's tenants at this juncture, and so was able to gain time for his reply. A surge of helpless frustration boiled up inside him, almost choking him; yet his face wore an easy smile while his lips uttered the polite words which the occasion required. Would he never be free from his father's tyranny, he wondered, never be able to live his own life, choose his own wife? But even through his inward raging the chill voice of reason warned him that even had he been free to choose, he still could not choose where his inclination lay at this moment.

7

By the time he turned to his father again, he had all but mastered his emotions.

"Well?" repeated the Earl, impatiently.

"I—I suppose you are right, sir. Yes, I will consider it."

"More than that, m'boy, more than that," insisted the Earl. "Push on with the business. Give the gal some hint of how the land lies. Do the pretty to her at this ball tonight. Try to fix your interest with her—or, at least, make a start. We Strattons have always been a success with women. I'll wager you're no exception, if you put your mind to it." He broke off as he saw the stewards directing the crowd to the tables. "No time for more now. They'll be wanting to drink your health. This puts me in mind of my own coming of age, damme if it don't. Ah, well, life goes on in much the same way from generation to generation. Nothing changes, eh?"

The ballroom at Alvington Hall was part of an extensive new wing built onto the original structure some thirty years previously in the style of Robert Adam. Columns of green-veined pink alabaster supported a ceiling decorated with delicate plaster arabesques; the walls were coloured a pastel pink shade, and elegant gilt chairs and sofas were disposed at intervals along them. The brilliant light provided by several magnificent crystal chandeliers was reflected in the highly polished oak floor. It also added lustre to the soft colours of the ladies' gowns and set their jewels sparkling with living fire as they moved about the room in company with gentlemen in knee breeches of snowy white satin and coats of plum red, olive green, cinnamon or blue.

The Earl looked about him complacently, remarking to his wife that nothing was lacking to make young Neville's majority ball a resounding success.

"Everyone's here that matters, m'dear, in this county and the next. All that's wanting now is for the boy to show some interest in that direction."

He nodded his head towards two ladies sitting on a

sofa against the wall at some distance away. As there were several groups intervening, his wife was understandably puzzled.

"In what direction, my love? I'm afraid I don't perfectly understand you," she replied, timidly.

"Don't be more stupid than you can help, Jane. I was speaking to you of it only yesterday—the Cottesford gal."

"Oh—oh, yes, I beg your pardon—of course."

The Countess cast a weary glance in the direction indicated by her husband. She considered the younger of the two ladies thoughtfully. Maria Cottesford was not well known to her, but she had an uneasy suspicion that the girl was scarcely likely to make an instant appeal to such an undoubtedly handsome young man as Neville, who would surely desire—and might reasonably expect to win—a much prettier female as a bride. There was no escaping the fact that Maria was not well favoured. Her figure was trim and neat enough, and her air ladylike. But her nose was too long and her mouth too wide for such a small, thin face; while all the brilliance of the chandeliers failed to draw out any glints in her dull, mouse-coloured hair. The gown she was wearing of a soft apricot shade did what it could for her complexion, but it could not completely disguise a sallow tinge to the skin. There must be at least a score of young ladies in this very room who would be more to her son's taste, reflected the Countess; but she knew it was useless to say as much to her autocratic husband.

She smiled weakly as she said, "I'm sure she's a very nice girl."

The Earl snorted. "Nice? Of course she's nice! Well-bred female, ain't she? Fortune, too. What more's wanting, I'd like to know? Now where the devil's that boy?"

Viscount Shaldon was at that moment talking to a young man of about his own age in another corner of the ballroom.

The Honourable Edward Lydney lived on a neighbouring estate, and the two had been closely associated

9

since childhood, though they had little in common except propinquity. Baron Lydney's son was both physically and temperamentally different from young Viscount Shaldon. He was as dark as Neville was fair, was more stockily built, and gave an impression of greater virility. Although he was half a head shorter than his companion, he seemed in no way over-shadowed. His air of assurance, springing from the knowledge that he was able to order his own life very much as he chose, was more complete than Neville's, which concealed an insecurity engendered by quite a different upbringing. Nevertheless, Edward was the only person in whom Neville ever confided. Lydney would listen to his friend's problems with a mixture of contempt and compassion, afterwards offering such advice and help as he could manage without putting himself to undue trouble. His more vigorous nature would sometimes prompt him to suggest solutions which he realised the vacillating Neville would never find either the courage or the resolution to adopt; but when diplomacy would serve his friend's purpose, he could sometimes find an acceptable way for Neville to resolve his difficulties.

He listened now, as best he could in a crowded ballroom, to the account Neville was giving him of the recent conversation with his father.

"Well, what of it?" he asked, a shade impatiently, at the end of this tedious recital. "It would be a good match, surely? Not that a fellow wants to become leg-shackled too early in life unless he's pinched in the pocket, but you say he don't mean to push the business on too fast. And I think the lady will keep," he added, glancing across the room towards the spot where Lady Cottesford was seated with her daughter, his lips twisting in a sneer. "She's had a couple of seasons in Town, and by all accounts she didn't take there, in spite of being an heiress."

"And pray why should I be saddled with a female whom no one else wants?" demanded Neville, petulantly.

Lydney shrugged. "Nothing against the girl, beyond

10

she's no beauty. I hear she's well liked by other females of her age, which argues a good disposition; for the little dears have sharp enough claws where their own sex is concerned, however sweet and charming they may choose to appear before ours. No, my advice is to take her, dear fellow. I'm sure she's yours for the asking."

"But I don't want her—not if she had twice the fortune!" expostulated Neville. "Fact is, Ned"—he lowered his voice and looked cautiously about him to make sure that no one was within earshot—"there's someone else, someone infinitely more desirable in every way."

Lydney's eyebrows shot up. "Oho!" he said, softly. "And would your father think so?"

The change in Neville's expression gave him his answer.

"Well, then," he continued, "I think you'd best put that lady out of your mind—at least, as far as matrimony is concerned. Of course, if some other little arrangement is possible . . ."

Neville shook his head. "Not with her. She—oh, the devil, Ned, I can't tell you about it now! And there's my father making signs to me to go over to him. I must go. I'll call on you tomorrow, and you shall hear the whole."

This prospect held no particular appeal for Edward Lydney, but he agreed amiably enough as he turned away with relief to claim his partner for the next dance, a lively young lady whom he had been watching out of the corner of his eye during the whole of his conversation with the Viscount.

As Neville expected, his father directed him to lead Miss Cottesford into the dance. Inwardly rebellious but outwardly complaisant, he approached her to make his request.

She accepted with a somewhat shy little smile, which softened her expression, giving her a fleeting attractiveness which her face lacked in repose. They took their places in the set and moved down the dance. Whenever they came together, he addressed a few commonplace remarks to her, which she answered with a lively intelligence they certainly did not merit. He was a little surprised to find her conversation so easy and natural; judging from her appearance, he had expected her to be a dull, uninteresting companion.

Maria was experiencing surprise on her own part, but this was not due to anything in the Viscount's behaviour, which was precisely what she had expected it to be. Her surprise sprang from the sudden quick leap of her pulse as he took her hand, a reaction so new to her that she was hard put to it to answer him in her usual way when he addressed her.

The Viscount, however, though finding his partner less boring than he had feared, was far from being reconciled to dancing with her when there were so many more attractive young ladies present; and it was with relief that he made his bow at the conclusion of the dance, secure in the knowledge that convention would not permit of his dancing with her again for some time, whatever his father might wish him to do. He at once set about finding himself a partner more to his taste, while Miss Cottesford returned to sit beside her Mama.

"Did you find your partner agreeable, my dear?" asked Lady Cottesford, with a complacent smile.

"Why, certainly, Mama." Maria's cool, matter-of-fact tone somewhat affronted her mother.

"I am sure you must have done, for he is without doubt one of the most handsome gentlemen in the room. Not to mention his air and address, which are beyond reproach."

Maria's eyes followed the Viscount as he threaded his way through the crowd in search of a fresh partner. She had no intention of allowing her mother to see exactly what kind of impression he had made upon her; for it had swept over her so suddenly that she was still shaken by it. She was a young lady of high intelligence and strong common sense, and therefore mistrusted such a wild surge of emotion. She suppressed it now as best she could, forcing herself to reply in the same noncommittal tones.

"Yes, indeed, Mama."

"And what did you talk of?" asked Lady Cottesford, reluctant to abandon the subject without securing a more promising reaction from her daughter.

"Oh, the usual topics."

"I must say, Maria," her mother said plaintively, "it is very difficult to gain any notion of your conversation from that remark."

"I beg your pardon, Mama. Did you want a detailed account? Well, then, as far as I recollect, our conversation went something like this. First of all, Viscount Shaldon asked me if I liked dancing; to which I replied that in general I did, unless I happened to be so unfortunate as to get a partner who trod on my toes. To which he replied—"

"Maria! Sometimes your sense of humour may be misunderstood, you know. You may have offended him. Possibly he thought your remark was a reflection on his own performance. Really, my love, was that wise?"

Maria wrinkled her long nose. "Wise? I should think it a waste of time to weigh every platitude one is obliged to utter in a ballroom. At any rate, he seemed not at all put out. He replied that he hoped not to impair my enjoyment on this occasion by any clumsiness of his, and I assured him that I thought it most unlikely. After that, he asked if you and Papa intended to take me to London this season. I replied no; then he said Town pleasures were much overrated in his view, and what did I think? I said I usually enjoyed whatever I happened to be doing at any particular time and wherever I chanced to be. He said I was fortunate in my disposition and I—"

"No!" interrupted Lady Cottesford, pleased. "Did he really say that? How very flattering, my love!"

"Not really," said Maria, reflecting. "He's a gentleman of most accomplished address, as you remarked yourself, Mama, and I'm sure he was merely doing the polite. But do you truly wish to know more of this very commonplace conversation?"

Whatever Lady Cottesford might have replied to

13

this, she was to hear nothing more; for at that moment her husband approached them, accompanied by a group of other guests who were closely acquainted with the Cottesfords. Two of the young ladies were Maria's particular friends, and at once the three started a lively conversation of their own, which was presently broken into by the younger gentlemen in the party insisting that they should all join the set that was forming on the floor.

Maria's partner was Mr. George Tilling, husband of her friend Amelia, who had been married to him for nearly two years. He was a rather grave gentleman in his late twenties, with a square-cut face which gave him a solid, reliable look that did not belie his character. At one time Lady Cottesford had entertained some hopes that he might offer for Maria. The two had frequently been together in company with a group of other neighbouring young people, and Mr. Tilling had seemed then to show a preference for Maria, though not to a degree which could lead to definite expectations. But Amelia Edwardes had returned to the country after a successful season in London, and her blonde beauty had quite cast her friend Maria into the shade.

"The worst of it is, she doesn't even seem to mind," Lady Cottesford had complained to her husband at the time. "She's just as fond of Amelia as ever she was, and entertains no feelings of ill-usage as far as George Tilling is concerned. She treats him exactly as she always did."

"Well, if that don't tell you there was nothing in it, m'dear, dashed if I know what would! What would you have—the poor girl eating her heart out for him? Luckily, it's no such thing; and Maria's got too much good sense to nurse a grudge against a female who's carried off a young fellow she never wanted for herself."

"That's just the trouble—she has too much good sense altogether! I can't think where she gets it from, but she's positively *bookish*. And you know as well as I do, my love, that the way to a man's heart is *not*

14

through his intellect. Most men had by far rather have a pretty, appealing, somewhat helpless little creature—"

"Like you were, eh, when I married you?" he chuckled and tapped her cheek playfully. "Don't worry, Kate, our Maria will find someone in her own good time—and a dashed lucky fellow he'll be, in my opinion!"

But that had been two years ago, Lady Cottesford reflected as she watched her daughter dancing; and in spite of the advantages of two London Seasons, Maria at almost one and twenty had still not succeeded in finding this fortunate man whom her father was confident would eventually appear. It had been most heartening that Viscount Shaldon should have asked her to dance so early in the proceedings. Surely that might reasonably suggest a degree of partiality? The anxious mother shook her head sadly; Maria's comments on her partner had been far from encouraging.

Had she been privileged to understand her daughter better, she would have felt more sanguine. Maria danced with George Tilling and talked with him in her accustomed easy style; but now and then her eyes would stray to the Viscount, noticing his lithe, graceful movements and the charm of his smile as he chatted to his partner. And not for the first time in her life, but more strongly now than ever before, she found herself wishing that she might have been possessed of the dainty features, limpid blue eyes and silken gold curls of that undeniably attractive young woman.

As for Neville, he contrived to find himself a succession of agreeable partners as the evening wore on, disregarding his parent's occasional signals to take Miss Cottesford out a second time. He was confident that he could escape the Earl's recriminations by claiming that it was his duty as a host to dance with as many of their female guests as possible. The fact that there were not dances enough for him to partner any but the youngest and prettiest among the ladies could be trusted to guard him from any reproach on this head. He knew quite well, however, that he would have no chance of escaping Maria Cottesford as a supper partner, so he dutifully presented himself at her side when the time arrived.

Maria was almost too surprised at first to feel the gratification which such a compliment deserved. There were several families present of equal consequence with the Cottesfords, with nubile daughters who had certainly appeared to please the Viscount while the dancing was in progress. There seemed no particular reason why he should single her out from the rest. A raised eyebrow here and there indicated that this thought had occurred to some of the other guests, too, and that they were ready to draw their own conclusions from it. Maria cared nothing for this. She was far too modest about her own claims to attention to allow herself to believe that the Viscount's choice was anything but arbitrary; all she knew was that for a precious hour or so he would be at her side.

But Lady Cottesford was elated. She took particular pains to be extremely charming to the young lady of the golden curls and wide blue eyes who had earlier seemed to appeal so strongly to Viscount Shaldon, telling herself that her previous thoughts about this girl had been uncharitable, to say the least. The poor creature was not, after all, a designing female; or, if she was, her designs had come to nothing. And what else mattered? In the present circumstances, one could surely afford to be magnanimous.

The Earl, too, was pleased. Tomorrow or the next day he would ride over and see Cottesford to give him a hint of what was in the wind. Unlikely that there would be any objections in that quarter, but it might be as well to make the whole business clear from the start. Unless Sir William wanted to get his daughter off his hands quickly, there seemed no reason for an early marriage. He reflected that Neville would be the better for another year over his head, in fact. There was still too much of the boy about him for the Earl's liking. He confided some of his thoughts to his wife in an undertone; and she listened attentively, agreeing with all that he said, as she was accustomed to do. She had almost lost the habit of thinking for herself, and most of her natural emotions had long since been suppressed. But somewhere just below the level of her consciousness, a faint feeling stirred of pity for Maria Cottesford.

Chapter II

THE COTTAGE AT RYE was a modest dwelling in one of the little town's cobbled streets. The front door gave directly on to a small parlour, comfortably but simply furnished; at the back was an even smaller room out of which a door led to a combined kitchen and scullery looking out onto a patch of garden kept bright with flowers. The staircase was concealed behind a door in the parlour and gave access to two bedrooms, from one of which a shorter flight of stairs led to a pair of tiny attic rooms. Everywhere neatness and order prevailed; for the lady who owned the residence was the widow of a Naval officer and liked everything to be "shipshape and Bristol fashion" in the style of her late husband.

In such a simple setting, Dorinda Lathom shone like a jewel. Seventeen years of age, lithe and lissome, with pale gold hair and soft cheeks of pink and white, she delighted her mother's eyes whenever they chanced to rest on her during their quiet evenings together. Until a few months ago, the delight had been untinged by any feelings of misgiving; but now an uneasy frown sometimes settled on Mrs. Lathom's brow as she surveyed her young daughter.

It had all started one showery day in March, when

17

for once Dorinda had gone out unaccompanied to buy some embroidery silk from a shop only a short distance away. As a rule, Mrs. Lathom was punctilious in attending her daughter everywhere, but on this occasion she had been busy with some baking. A girl of fourteen came in daily to help with the housework, but Mrs. Lathom did most of the cooking herself, rarely entrusting it to Dorinda's less experienced hands.

She had just removed her pies and cakes from the oven and the house was filled with the appetising aroma from them, when a loud, urgent knock sounded on the street door. Hastily closing the oven and wiping her hands on a cloth, she went with quick steps through into the parlour to answer it. She opened the door to see a young gentleman standing there with Dorinda clinging to his arm, although modestly, for support.

Mrs. Lathom started, staring helplessly for a moment. Then she saw that Dorinda's cheeks were quite white and quickly put her arm around the girl, drawing her gently into the room and depositing her on the sofa.

"What on earth has happened?" she asked anxiously, bending over Dorinda. "Are you hurt, dearest? Speak, for heaven's sake!"

Dorinda shook her head weakly, but it was the gentleman, still standing on the threshold, who answered for her.

"I think the young lady's not seriously hurt, madam, but she has had a shock. She slipped and fell on the wet cobblestones—most regrettable—I fear my fault, in a way. My horse lost its footing and swerved towards her, and the young lady made a hasty movement to avoid the animal. There had just been a shower and the cobbles were wet—I blame myself very much for not controlling the horse more speedily, but it did not touch her, assure you, ma'am."

Dorinda had by now recovered her breath and was able to say that she was quite all right, but only a little shaken up by her fall. Mrs. Lathom turned to the gentleman.

18

"Well, sir, I think perhaps you'd better come inside," she said, by now satisfied that there was nothing seriously wrong with her daughter. "It's starting to rain again, and there's no sense in your standing there getting wet through."

The gentleman removed his hat and entered. He had to duck his head to do so, and Mrs. Lathom now had time to notice that he was not only tall but well-favoured, with rich auburn hair. She guessed that he could not be much above twenty years of age; both his bearing and well fashioned attire suggested that he was of the Quality. She invited him to be seated while she fetched a cordial for Dorinda. Having administered this, she listened to further details of the mishap until she had the satisfaction of seeing the colour return to Dorinda's cheeks.

"Shall I fetch a doctor to your daughter, madam?" asked the young gentleman, solicitously. "If you will be good enough to direct me—I'm a stranger to these parts and was just taking a look at the old town. Dear me, it's all most unfortunate, and I blame myself very much."

Both ladies disclaimed the need for this, Dorinda blushing a little at having to put herself forward.

"Then if there is nothing I can do, ma'am," said the gentleman, rising, "I will relieve you of my presence. Perhaps you'll permit me to call tomorrow morning to enquire after your daughter's health?"

His civility and easy charm had by now quite mellowed Mrs. Lathom, who felt prompted to offer him some refreshment. He accepted readily, and soon they were sitting over tea and a heaped dish of the freshly baked cakes, chatting amicably together. They exchanged names; he told them his was Stratton, and that he was at present staying with friends in the neighbourhood of Tenterden.

"Being at a loose end today, I rode out in this direction," he said. "And if I may say so, ma'am, although it was an unfortunate beginning, I am very happy to have had this opportunity of making your acquaintance."

19

He bowed as he spoke, and when he finally rose to go he left behind him a most favourable impression.

He called again the next day, as he had promised, and was graciously received. Dorinda was quite recovered; indeed, her mother thought the girl looked more lovely than ever, with a new bloom in her cheeks.

After that, he called on them frequently during a period of several weeks, until his knock upon the door became familiar to them. They were pleased to have a visitor, for so far they had made no acquaintance in the town, having been settled there little more than a year. The inhabitants of most small towns take their time about welcoming newcomers into the community; but this reluctance was more marked at Rye, where there were those with secrets to keep from the Customs Men.

Mrs. Lathom was glad to have the even tenor of the domestic round enlivened by male company. She missed having a man about the house. The late Captain had in the natural course of his profession frequently been absent from home, but his return had always been eagerly awaited by his family. He had seemed to bring with him the fresh, invigorating atmosphere of the sea, stirring everyone and everything around him into activity. Among the many reasons she had for mourning him, this vitality still constituted a major loss. To be sure, young Mr. Stratton was not in the least like Captain Lathom in this respect. He lacked the decisive air which had always marked the Captain as a man of action. But although he talked surprisingly little of his own home background or his interests and pursuits, he gave a welcome change to the direction of their thoughts, which inevitably were centred mostly on domestic affairs.

As for Dorinda, she blossomed out in his company. At first, she had been very shy and retiring, leaving most of the conversation to her mother; but gradually she became more at ease with him. At times, when Mrs. Lathom had to leave the two young people alone together in the parlour for a few moments while she prepared some refreshment in the kitchen, she would

20

smile as she heard Dorinda's light laugh coming through the open door.

And then one day, three weeks or so after the accident which had first brought him to their door, he announced that he was returning to his own home on the following day.

"I've prolonged my visit to my friends beyond what was originally intended," he said, looking downcast, "and so must now return. I cannot tell you how greatly I shall miss our meetings. I trust, ma'am," with a look of appeal in Mrs. Lathom's direction, "that whenever I chance to be in this neighbourhood again, I may perhaps hope to find the same welcome here which has afforded me so much pleasure?"

Mrs. Lathom hastened to assure him that they would always be delighted to see him at any time. "Is there any likelihood of your returning in the near future?" she concluded. "Is your own home far from here?"

He hesitated before replying. "I live in Oxfordshire," he said at last. "As for my future plans, they do depend to some extent on my father's wishes." He sighed, then brightened. "But depend upon it, ma'am, that if it rests in my power to come this way again, I shall most certainly present myself here at the earliest possible moment. After what you have been kind enough to say, I shall feel no hesitation."

She repeated her hospitable assurances, glancing for support towards Dorinda, who so far had said nothing. As she looked into her daughter's face, for the first time an uneasy thought came into her mind. She wondered then that she had never entertained the notion before, and blamed herself for being so blind. But so it was with children; one tended to forget that with every day, every month, every year, they left childhood behind. She had watched Dorinda emerging into womanhood, yet had failed to realise that her little girl now had a woman's emotions.

She began to wish that she had not been so cordial in welcoming Mr. Stratton to return. To be sure, he seemed—now she came to study the matter in that

21

light—to be as attracted to Dorinda as the child was to him. But a man's more volatile feelings were scarcely to be trusted to endure, the mother warned herself, especially on the sketchy foundation of a mere three weeks' acquaintance. Mr. Stratton was young, handsome and almost certainly of superior rank and fortune to themselves. He would return home, see another pretty face belonging to a girl nearer to himself in station, and forget Dorinda. But would Dorinda forget him so easily?

During the weeks that followed, she watched the girl anxiously, and saw that it would not be so. Dorinda tried to be as cheerful as formerly, but the lightness had gone from her step and her laughter was forced. She would often lay aside her book or her needlework and sit staring into space; and once, during a night when Mrs. Lathom was sleeping badly, she thought she heard the sound of muffled sobs coming from the adjoining bedroom. She tiptoed in without lighting a candle and stood for a few moments by Dorinda's bed. There was no further sound, however, and the girl lay still as though in sleep. Nevertheless, Mrs. Lathom returned to her own room dissatisfied. It was possible that Dorinda had heard her mother's stealthy approach and had managed to stifle her weeping.

As the weather improved, Mrs. Lathom began to plan outings, and even talked of a visit to the uncle in London whom Dorinda had never yet seen.

"There has never been time, somehow, to keep up a regular correspondence with my brother since my marriage, and we've always lived so far apart. But I'm sure I'd not find him changed, for we were always happy together as children, and I don't doubt he would make us welcome in his home."

Dorinda showed no enthusiasm for the suggestion, so it was allowed to lapse. The fresh air and exercise on their small excursions about the countryside restored a little colour to her cheeks but failed to bring back her animation. Mrs. Lathom wisely kept her own counsel, not forcing a confidence, but trusting to time to make a change for the better.

And then one day towards the middle of May he returned, after an absence of a month or more. It was Dorinda who answered the knock, rising lethargically to do so and looking as if the caller, whoever it might be, could have no interest for her. The early days, when she had rushed to the door at the faintest touch on the knocker, had long since gone by. Opening the door, she stood for a moment transfixed, then gave a glad cry which made Mrs. Lathom start from her chair.

"Mama! Only see who is come!"

By the time her mother had reached the door, Dorinda's hands were held fast in the young man's, and they were gazing at each other as if nothing else mattered but being together again. They started quickly apart at Mrs. Lathom's approach; Dorinda blushed and Mr. Stratton gave an apologetic cough. The next moment he was bowing and greeting the elder lady with all his accustomed charm.

She tried to respond in the old way; but her recent disquiet had given an air of reserve to her manner which did not entirely escape either of the young people, engrossed though they obviously were in each other. Mr. Stratton explained that he had come down to Sussex for a few days only, and was putting up at the George Inn.

"But remembering your kind assurances, ma'am, when last we met, I made so bold as to look you up without ceremony," he concluded, with the faintest hint of reproach. "If, however, I arrive at an inconvenient moment, pray tell me so at once, and I will call again at some more suitable time."

Seeing Dorinda's eyes also fixed on her with a reproachful look, she at once felt guilty and did her best to dispel the impression she had evidently created. It was impossible to withstand Mr. Stratton's diffident charm for long; and seeing her daughter happy for the first time in a month, how could she do anything to take the sparkle from those speaking eyes? Yet she knew that this state of affairs could not be permitted to continue. Before Mr. Stratton returned once more to

23

his home in Oxfordshire, she would be obliged to have a serious talk with him.

Her determination hardened over the next few days, which he spent exclusively in their company. He had brought his curricle with him and begged earnestly to be allowed to take Dorinda for a short drive, for the weather was fine and warm. Although there was nothing to offend the proprieties in this suggestion, as they would be accompanied by a groom sitting up behind the vehicle, Mrs. Lathom steadfastly refused. Dorinda made no secret of her disappointment, so instead Mr. Stratton hired a carriage to enable Mrs. Lathom to accompany them. They drove along the coast to Hastings, ate a cold collation at a comfortable inn, and returned to the cottage in the late afternoon after a most pleasant outing.

The two young people did not talk at great length to each other and never sought to exclude her from their conversation; yet Mrs. Lathom felt that, as far as they were concerned, she simply did not exist. Their whole world was bound up in one another.

The few days of his visit passed all too soon, and on the morning when he was to call and take leave of them, Mrs. Lathom determined to speak. At the time he was due to arrive, she sent Dorinda, already subdued and listless, into the garden.

"I will call you presently, child, but don't come in until I do. I wish to have a few words alone with Mr. Stratton."

Dorinda opened her eyes wide. "But, Mama—but why? Oh, I do hope you don't wish to say anything unpleasant to him! But how could you? What could he possibly have done to upset you, so kind and considerate as he always is? Dearest Mama, pray, pray don't be vexed with him!"

She looked as if she would burst into tears at any moment, so her mother put an arm about her, holding her close.

"Now don't be foolish, Dorrie. Of course I'm not vexed. What I have to say won't take long, and I'll explain it all to you later. Now run along like a good girl, do, and presently I'll call you to join us. And pray don't cry, for you won't wish to show Mr. Stratton a tear-marked face, will you, my love?"

These last words had the desired effect. Dorinda forced back her tears and obediently stepped out into the sunny little garden at the back of the house. Mrs. Lathom carefully shut the door on her, then went into the parlour to await the visitor.

He arrived promptly and was invited inside. As he took a seat, he looked inquiringly about him, evidently a little surprised at not finding Dorinda present. He said nothing for a time, however, until a few commonplace remarks about the weather had passed between them. Then he ventured to ask after Miss Lathom, saying that he trusted she was well.

"Thank you, Mr. Stratton, Dorinda is in her usual health, if not perhaps in the best of spirits," she replied, gravely. "She will be joining us presently to bid you good-bye, but I wished to see you alone for a few moments."

An uneasy expression came into his face, but he made no remark, waiting for her to continue.

"It is difficult for me to say what is in my mind, sir, but my duty requires me to make the attempt."

She paused, hoping for some help from him, as he must surely see the trend of her thoughts. When he still sat silent, she braced herself to come to the point.

"You have lately been seeing a great deal of my daughter, sir." He nodded, but still said nothing. "She is very young and has never before been in the company of a young gentleman. We live very retired here, as you may judge for yourself. Indeed, my late husband's profession meant that we were often moving from one place to another, so that it was difficult to form intimate friendships. You are the only person whom we can think of in that way, and I have good reason to suppose that my dear child has begun to depend too much upon your friendship."

At last he spoke. "My dear lady, she can certainly depend upon it. I have the highest regard for Miss Dorinda, as I have for yourself."

"Yes, but I think you don't quite see. Oh, dear, it's so difficult to put into words! Can you not understand? Dorinda has come to think of you as—" She broke off, embarrassed, yet realising she must continue. "In short, Mr. Stratton, I think it would be best if you did not see her again."

"Not see her again!"

The exclamation burst from him. It was the first unguarded utterance he had made in the whole interview, and she could see from his expression that he was now in the grip of a powerful emotion.

"No, do not say so!" he went on, with renewed intensity. "I can't do it—I—I love her dearly, Mrs. Lathom, indeed I do"

Mrs. Lathom relaxed, as if a weight had been lifted from her shoulders.

"You do? But, there, I'd guessed as much from the way you both behaved! Well, in that case, my warnings are unnecessary, and there's nothing more for me to do than give you both my blessing—which I do most cordially, my dear Mr. Stratton, for I can think of no one whom I would rather have for a son-in-law! Only wait just a moment while I fetch my darling girl, and you can tell her everything that's in your heart." She rose hastily, almost beside herself with joy. "To think of it—I was feeling so downcast just before you arrived, and now it's all turned out delightfully! Oh, my dearest Dorinda—she little knows at the moment what happiness is in store for her!"

"One moment, ma'am, I beg you."

He put out a hand to detain her headlong rush from the room. She looked at him, surprised, and saw that his face had clouded over with doubt and anxiety.

"What is it?" she asked, sharply. "Is something amiss?"

He nodded. "I need scarce tell you, ma'am, that nothing would give me greater happiness than to make Miss Dorinda my wife. But there is an obstacle in the way—and I fear it may prove a difficult one to overcome."

"An obstacle? What do you mean?"

"I mean that in certain matters—and my marriage would unquestionably be one—I'm not entirely my own master. I am obliged to consult my father's wishes, as well as my own."

"Of course!" she exclaimed, her face clearing. "No right-thinking young gentleman would consider marrying without his father's consent. And since your parents have not yet made the acquaintance of my daughter, naturally their consent can't be expected until they have done so. Perhaps you have already spoken to them about your feelings for Dorinda?"

"No," he replied, reluctantly. "No, so far I have said nothing. I—for one thing, I could not be certain that my regard for her was reciprocated."

She was pleased to think that he had not taken for granted what to her had been so plain.

"Oh, well, that is very natural, my dear Mr. Stratton! But when all is settled between you and Dorinda—and although I should not say so, I know you need have no doubts about the way she will receive your addresses—then you'll be able to inform your parents and arrange for a meeting as soon as possible."

She waited for him to agree to this, pondering meanwhile, womanlike, on what she and Dorinda would wear when the meeting took place. It was obvious that Mr. Stratton came of a good family and most likely a wealthy one into the bargain. She was determined to be well dressed for the occasion, even if the outlay made a considerable hole in her slender savings. There had been a roll of lavender silk in a linen-or draper's at Dover; it would cost a good deal, but set against Dorrie's fair colouring and pale gold hair, what parents would be able to resist the picture she would make? That and, much more, her natural sweetness must carry the day.

She drew back from these reflections to realise that Mr. Stratton had given no answer although several minutes had elapsed. She looked at him enquiringly.

"It's all more difficult than you can well imagine, ma'am," he said, haltingly. "My father's not—an easy man. He's accustomed to having his own way."

She paused to consider the implications of this.

"Do you mean that perhaps he has other matrimonial plans for you, sir?"

"No—that is to say, I don't know, for so far we've never discussed the matter." He hesitated. "But I have an uneasy suspicion that he would expect me to make what is generally thought of as a—as an advantageous match. From a worldly point of view, I mean," he added hastily.

"I see." She sat down again heavily. "Yes, I do see your difficulty. My daughter can bring you no dowry but her own natural endowments, I fear. As to birth, although we're gentlefolk we cannot claim to come very high in the social scale. Both my father and my husband's were of the clergy, with only moderate incomes. We have no genteel connections, either, that I can boast of. You see how we live—in tolerable comfort, but certainly not in luxury." She looked him straight in the eye. "You have never told us much concerning yourself, Mr. Stratton. Indeed, until this moment you've never even mentioned your parents—but I collect that your circumstances must be rather different from ours?"

He raised his shoulders in a deprecating gesture.

"I fear so, Mrs. Lathom—would to God they were not! I am an only son, heir to a title and estate. If I haven't told you this before, it was only to spare you possible embarrassment; but believe me, I have been happier in your cottage than I've ever been in Alv—in my own home."

He remembered in time to suppress the name of Alvington Hall. His last remark had been as sincere as his feelings for Dorinda Lathom were; but he had not yet abandoned all discretion. Mrs. Lathom knew him as Mr. Stratton. That was his family name, and he was practising no serious deception in using what was lawfully his. There was no need for her to know that he was also Viscount Shaldon and heir to an Earldom; indeed, it could be positively dangerous for her to possess that information.

It was her turn to be silent.

"Then what is to be done?" she asked at last, in a despondent tone.

He leapt to his feet. "Only permit me to make my feelings known to Miss Dorinda, and to become betrothed to her! Once we are affianced, I will find the right moment to tell my father, and all will be well, never fear. He could hardly require me to draw back from a betrothal."

"He might," said Mrs. Lathom, dubiously, "if he has not sanctioned it first. Are you—forgive me for asking, Mr. Stratton, but I think the question is needed —have you attained your majority?"

Neville Stratton looked crestfallen for a moment. "Not quite, ma'am. I shall be one and twenty in a fortnight's time. But that's no matter."

She shook her head. "There I cannot agree. How can we expect your father to look with favour on a clandestine engagement entered into while you're still under age? He would then have every justification for thinking me a scheming woman anxious to marry my daughter well. No, sir, I believe that your only course is to go to him and ask his permission—it's the only manly thing to do." Seeing that this had intensified the downcast expression on his face, she smiled encouragingly. "Cheer up, my dear young man. I feel sure that your parent won't stand in the way of your happiness, whatever other ambitions he may have had for you."

"Will he not?" answered Neville, savagely. "I wish I could be as certain of that! He has the most infernal temper, ma'am, allow me to tell you."

"Perhaps so, but once he has recovered from it, he will wish only for what will make you happy, depend upon it. We are all the same, we parents, you know —our bark is worse than our bite."

He made no reply for a moment. How could this gentle, tolerant woman understand the disposition of such a man as the Earl of Alvington? It was useless to try to explain, but at least he would persuade her to let him see Dorinda. That much, he thought resentfully, was owing to him after his honest avowal of his intentions—an avowal brought on by the woman's interference. He stifled his resentment with the ease of long practice, and turned a pleading smile on her.

"But you will allow me to speak to Miss Dorinda of my feelings, ma'am, even if I may not ask her to become betrothed to me? You surely can't be so cruel as to command my silence? I beg you, Mrs. Lathom, don't ask that of me!"

No, she could not ask it, with the image of her daughter's sad little face before her mind. And so Mrs. Lathom sent him out into the garden to bring the waiting girl such tidings as she had scarcely dared to hope for during the past poignant weeks of separation from the man who now meant all the world to her.

Chapter III

"AND SO YOU SEE how it is," Neville concluded, after confiding his story to the reluctant ear of Edward Lydney. "What's to be done, Ned?"

The other pursed his lips consideringly. "There are only two courses of action, as I see it," he pronounced, at length. "Either you give up the notion of marrying this girl—"

"But, damn it, man, I tell you I'm mad for her! And there's no other way but marriage. Her mother's a confounded dragon of a female, who guards her as if she were the Crown jewels. Not that Dorinda isn't a jewel," he added, as a vivid image of her bright presence rose suddenly to his mind, stirring his senses. "She's the most adorable creature—so fresh, so guileless and trusting! Besides being lovely enough to send a man near demented to possess her!"

Lydney suppressed a yawn and tried not to look bored. "Very well. Since you're determined you must have her, the only other thing is to tell your father so."

Dorinda's image faded, to be replaced by one of the Earl after being informed of his son's intentions. With difficulty, Neville controlled a shudder.

"I know; but I tell you I can't face him, Ned! You don't know what it is to have a sire like mine, who rules his household relentlessly. Lord Lydney is more easygoing, more approachable. Besides, you're in possession of your own fortune, whereas I am dependent on my father for every penny. Why, if I go against his wishes, he will most likely cut me off without a shilling! And even though I shall inherit in time, I don't see the old man turning up his toes for some years to come, and how should I live in the meantime? You can have no notion how carefully I have to go with him."

"On the contrary, I have a very good notion, since our acquaintance stretches back almost to the cradle," replied the other drily. "But I fear I can offer no other advice than what I've already given—not that advice isn't a tricky thing, and probably best ignored. You must find your own solution to the problem. It's perhaps a pity that you should have declared yourself to the fair Dorinda before being informed of your father's own plans for you."

"Well, I wouldn't have done so, I daresay, had not the mother forced my hand. Of course, I love Dorinda to distraction, so sooner or later I should have spoken, I suppose. But—"

"But you had rather," cut in Lydney, in an ironical tone, "it had been later than sooner, eh? Oh, well, forget about it now, old fellow. Come and take a look at the latest addition to my stable. A sweet goer if ever I mounted one, and a downright bargain at eighty guineas, as I'm certain you'll agree."

Neville's anxieties were not lessened that evening by a conversation with his father after dinner, when they were sitting confidentially over their wine.

"Saw Cottesford this morning, by the way," remarked the Earl. "Told him what I'd in mind concerning that chit of his and yourself. Seemed surprised, but no objections—at least, none to signify."

"What do you mean, sir?" Neville clutched eagerly at what looked like a straw. "What objections did he raise?"

The Earl drained his glass before replying. "Oh, some nonsense about the gal herself consenting to the match. Wouldn't force her, he said. Well, no need to, if you play your cards right, eh? I told him there was no haste—give you time to win her over, and all that kind of thing. Damme, you wouldn't be my son if you didn't know how to recommend yourself to a female. And on that head," he added, with a laugh, "I've no doubts. No reason to think your mother ever played me false—for one thing, wouldn't pay her to. For another, you're as like all the Strattons as you can stare —only take a look at all those devilish family portraits lining the staircase. Same red thatch, same features; even the eyes are the same colour in most of 'em. Strong strain, undoubtedly." He broke off and seized the decanter. "Fill up your glass, m'boy."

Neville obeyed, wondering if another glass of wine would give him the courage he needed to make his confession.

"So there it is," concluded the Earl. "All fixed up right and tight—only thing you need do now is start courting the chit for all you're worth. Make a beginning tomorrow—take her riding. I collect from her father she sits a horse well enough, and the weather's fine at present. Not doing anything else, are you? I didn't think you would be, so wasted no time in asking you first, but settled that you'd present yourself at the Manor about eleven."

Neville nodded weakly in acceptance of this high-handed treatment, but beneath his calm exterior seethed the familiar feelings of frustrated rage. To have his time disposed of as if he had been the merest schoolboy, not even to have been consulted first! For a moment the wine seemed to choke him, and he set down his glass, spilling some of it.

"Clumsy of me," he muttered, dabbing at the table with his napkin. "Father, I—"

He paused, lacking the courage to continue; but seeing the Earl waiting with raised eyebrows, he made a feeble attempt to say something of what he felt.

"I—I am not at all attracted to Miss Cottesford, as I think I mentioned before. Must she be the one? There are a score of other young ladies whom I would prefer to wed."

"Name one."

"Well . . ." Neville searched his mind for a name that would serve, any name but Dorinda's. "Well, there's Miss Cavendish, for instance."

The Earl snorted. "Cavendish is nothing near as warm a man as Cottesford, let me tell you. And there are three other gals in that family, if I'm not mistaken, whereas this Cottesford chit's an only child, like yourself. D'ye mean to tell me you fancy yourself in love with the Cavendish gal?"

Neville shook his head vigorously. "No such thing, sir. But I only thought I'd prefer her to Maria Cottesford."

"Yellow curls and big blue eyes, that the one? Saw you dancing with her last night. Yes, well, daresay you would prefer her, but we're speaking of marriage, as I said before. Matter of business—do the best for yourself. Love!" The Earl snorted again. "Plenty of opportunity for that outside marriage. Told you so yesterday —if you need telling, but you'll be the first Stratton who ever did, I shouldn't wonder! No, m'boy, I've given some thought to this, and it's the best match for you by a long way, believe me. You'll be a fool if you don't do your damnedest to get the gal."

There was nothing more to say. Neville had selected Miss Cavendish's name more or less as a random example of a young lady whose social and financial standing made her an eligible match for a nobleman's son. If his father considered her a less interesting proposition than Maria Cottesford, then what in the world would he think of a marriage with Dorinda Lathom, who had no worldly advantages whatsoever? Neville recalled Edward Lydney's advice, and thought bitterly that he might in the end have no choice but to give up Dorinda. Supposing he never went to Rye again, walked out of her life as suddenly as he had entered it? Mrs. Lathom did not know who he was or where to find him; he had been careful to keep those matters a secret from her, even telling her that he lived in an adjacent county rather than naming his own.

Characteristically, he pushed a decision away. He had to visit Maria Cottesford tomorrow, and that was a sufficiently gloomy prospect for the moment.

The Cottesfords lived in an ample, stone-built manor house dating from Tudor times and situated about five miles distant from Alvington Hall. Neville rode there through lanes fragrant with May blossom. Birds chirped and fluttered at his approach, and on either side of him stretched fresh green meadows dotted with buttercups and daisies, above which bees hovered, murmuring. Overhead, a cloudless blue sky gave promise of a perfect June day. It was impossible not to catch some of the brightness of his surroundings, to feel his gloomy, morose mood gradually giving way to one of more optimism. Something would turn up to ease him out of his difficulties, he reflected; in the meantime, he must make the best of it and tread warily, as he was quite accustomed to doing.

Maria Cottesford was in her bedchamber, having just stepped into her riding dress. It was in the height of fashion, a pretty cherry-red garment with a bodice fashioned after the masculine style with revers and epaulettes, and a full skirt which allowed freedom of movement. Nevertheless, she grimaced as she considered her reflection in the long mirror, far from pleased with her appearance.

"Something's wanting, Jenny," she remarked wryly to her personal maid. "Now, I wonder what it can be? I know—corn-coloured curls, melting blue eyes, and a nose at least an inch shorter!"

"Go along with you, Miss," scolded Jenny, who had been abigail to Maria for the past eight years and was

34

very fond of her mistress. "If you're not always run-ning your looks down! Reckon you're fishing for com-pliments!"

Maria shook her head. "I don't think there are any fish in those waters, so I'd be wasting my time. But you must know that my governess was always warning me against the sin of vanity. Which is another rea-son," she added, reflectively, "why I always considered her a singularly imperceptive female. If she couldn't see that vanity was the least likely to be my besetting sin, what hope was there for the poor creature to solve my character at all?"

"A Miss Prunes and Prisms, she was!" declared Jenny, with a sniff. "But only see, Miss Maria, how well it will look with this."

She produced a tall riding hat in dark blue velour trimmed with a band and rosette of cherry red ribbon. She placed the hat on Maria's head, tilting it this way and that, standing back to assess the effect of each new angle.

"There!" she exclaimed, satisfied at last. "Now what d'you say to that?"

Maria examined herself critically. "Tolerable," she pronounced presently. "The portrait may not be a masterpiece, but the frame is charming. And thank you, Jenny, for all your trouble."

"No trouble at all, Miss Maria. Do you—" She hes-itated a moment, wondering if perhaps even she was privileged enough to say what was on the tip of her tongue.

"Do I what?" prompted her mistress.

"Do you want to look specially well this morning?"

Maria smiled wistfully. "Do I? Perchance I do, Jenny-penny."

It was the old name she had used in her childhood. The abigail caught her hand for a moment.

"And so you do. Believe me, you *do,* Miss Maria."

She handed a pair of gloves and a whip to her mis-tress, watching her go from the room with the anxious look of a bird for its fledgling.

Maria walked slowly downstairs, trusting that her

measured steps might place a check upon the rapid beating of her heart. She knew he was here. She had watched his arrival from the window of her bedchamber, pressing her face against the glass and thereby temporarily flattening the nose she disliked so much.

Yesterday her father had told her that Lord Alvington favoured a marriage between his son and herself. She had listened almost with incredulity, saying nothing at first.

"What do you think, my love?" Sir William asked gently. "It would be a brilliant match for you—that goes without saying—but worldly advantages count for little without affection. I would be the last to force you into a marriage against your inclinations. But I believe I don't need to tell you that."

"No, Papa, indeed you don't." These two understood one another very well, being cast in a similar mould. "Did Lord Alvington say whether Viscount Shaldon himself wished to marry me? Or is he to seek my hand merely in obedience to his father's wishes?"

"You know enough of the man, I think, to realise that he would approach the subject in a practical manner and say nothing of any feelings involved. So I can't answer that question, I fear."

"Well, I find it difficult to believe that the Viscount has been captivated by my personal attractions," replied Maria, with an attempt at lightness.

"Do you indeed? Well, I do not. Let me tell you that the man who makes you his wife will gain an inestimable treasure. I can say this without any fear of its going to your head—which is more than most fathers could say of their daughters."

She leaned forward to kiss his cheek. "Dear Papa! But you are too partial, you know. For my part, I thought yesterday evening at the ball that Viscount Shaldon was more taken with several of his other partners than with me."

"You can't know that. He chose you for his partner at supper, after all."

"Yes, so he did," agreed Maria, reflectively. "I was quite taken by surprise, I don't mind admitting."

"There you are, you see. But I am not nearly so concerned to discover his feelings at present as yours. Could you care for this young man, do you suppose?"

"Oh, yes. I don't think that would present any great difficulty."

He looked at her sharply, undeceived by the careless tone.

"So you're already favourably inclined towards him," he said, quietly. "Well, Alvington gave me to understand that there was no haste in the matter. He spoke of allowing time for his son to recommend himself to you. It's for you to decide, as I made plain to him. If you truly wish to wed young Shaldon, then the match has my blessing. But think well, my dear."

Maria's thoughts had certainly centred on the Viscount since this conversation, but she could not claim that her thinking was the rational process which her father had meant to recommend to her. She had been in the state of heightened emotion which had swept over her at the ball, so that she was scarcely aware of her surroundings, or even of what was being said to her. Her mother several times reproved her for absentmindedness, guessing at the cause but not the degree of involvement of her daughter's feelings. She tried very hard to induce Maria to talk about the proposed marriage but met with small success.

"I cannot at all understand the girl!" complained Lady Cottesford to her husband. "She should be overjoyed at such a prospect; and here she is, looking as gloomy as if all her hopes were shattered, instead of quite the opposite."

"Leave her alone," he advised. "I've told her that she's free to choose for herself. I expect she wishes to have time to consider."

"Time to consider such an offer? Why, any girl in her senses would jump at it!"

"Maria's not any girl—she's got more sense than most of 'em. Besides, you may say it's a brilliant match, and so it is from a worldly point of view. All the same, I have some doubts about young Shaldon. Don't know him well, of course, but it strikes me there's a lack of bottom in that boy. Plenty of charm and all that, but lacks staying power, I shouldn't wonder."

"You speak of him as if he were a horse! But if you're to set your face against the match—"

"Fustian, m'dear. All I want—and you, too, unless I mistake—is our daughter's happiness. I propose to allow her to be the judge of that, so I beg you won't try to influence her in any way. I shan't myself."

She had to be content with that, and was gratified to notice that her husband's reception of the Viscount when he came to call was not lacking in cordiality. Maria joined them after an interval, dressed for riding. Lady Cottesford looked her over appraisingly and decided that she appeared to advantage; she might not be a beauty, but there was no fault to be found with the trim figure and graceful carriage.

Unhappily for Lady Cottesford's hopes, Neville's thoughts were too full of Dorinda for him to appreciate anything about his present companion except her ability to manage her horse without any assistance from him. As they made their way along little-frequented lanes and bridle paths, they kept up a spasmodic conversation which in no way reflected the inner feelings of either. Afterwards, he could recall very little of what had been said, but it did appear to him that for a female Maria was unusually well informed on the topics of the day. What was even worse, she expected him to have opinions upon them. She mentioned the trial of Warren Hastings, which had begun in February of the preceding year and was still continuing. Did he not think it shameful to pillory a man who had done so much to restore order in India?

Never having given a moment's thought to the matter, it was not an easy question to answer; but with his usual adroit avoidance of controversy, he said that it did seem so, certainly, although one could not judge until all the evidence in the case had been heard.

She flashed him an impatient glance at this remark and looked for a moment as if she intended to dispute

38

the point. But as her eyes rested on him, they softened, and to his relief she changed the subject.

They met frequently during the weeks that followed, though usually in the company of others. The Earl would have ordered matters otherwise, but Sir William held back from causing the neighbourhood to link his daughter's name prematurely with that of the Viscount. He was determined that she should not have her hand forced in any way. The more he saw of Viscount Shaldon, the more he doubted that this would be a happy marriage for Maria, even though the girl herself showed signs of partiality which were plain to an understanding parental eye. A good marriage required affection on both sides, thought Sir William uneasily, and so far he could detect no sign of any such feeling in Shaldon. The young fellow was always attentive and all that, but his civilities lacked the warmth of a lover. Had Maria hit on the truth when she had asked whether the Viscount wished to marry her merely to oblige his father? And if so, what should a responsible and loving parent do in such a case?

It was of no use to try to share these doubts with his wife, whose calmer judgments had been quite overset by the brilliant prospects ahead for a daughter whom she had almost despaired of seeing married at all. She would have agreed with him insofar as Maria must not be persuaded into any marriage, however brilliant, that would be distasteful to her. She might not have been ready to admit this at once, but in the end he knew she would have come round to his point of view. Although she had never quite understood her clever daughter, she had always truly loved her. But once his wife realised, as he did, that Maria was in a fair way to being head over heels in love with Shaldon, his scruples would have seemed ridiculous in her eyes.

It came as something of a relief to Sir William, therefore, when the Viscount announced one morning that he would be absent from home for a few weeks as he was going down to Brighton with his friend Edward Lydney. Maria bore the news with fortitude, wishing him a pleasant stay in her usual calm way. Lady

Cottesford alone looked disconcerted, though she hastened to echo her daughter's sentiments, adding that he could be sure of a welcome at the Manor whenever he returned.

For some time Neville had been searching for an excuse that would be acceptable to his father for absenting himself from Alvington; but it was not until Lydney mentioned that he had hired a house in Brighton for the summer that the opportunity came.

"You've only to invite me to come down with you for a while, and my father can't well refuse. Damn it, he'll scarcely care to make it known that he don't choose to let me out of his sight! And then I'll be free to go to—well, never mind where, perhaps you'd best not know—but, anyway, to Dorinda."

Edward Lydney made no difficulty about acting as a cover for his devious friend; after all, he would be put to no real trouble in the matter. Somewhat to Neville's surprise, the Earl raised no serious objections, either.

"Tired of doing the pretty already? Well, if you want to shake a loose leg for a bit, no harm done, I suppose. Cottesford knows what's in my mind, so he's unlikely to encourage any other suitor in your absence—if there are any others, eh?" He chuckled. "Take the courtship at your own gait, m'boy. As long as we have the wedding round about Christmas, I'll be satisfied."

Neville could only feel thankful that the scheme had succeeded with so little effort on his part, and that now at last he could be reunited with the adorable Dorinda.

Chapter IV

Mrs. Lathom had slipped out to do some marketing, and Dorinda sat alone in the cottage. Her deft fingers were busy with some needlework, but her mind was not on it.

There was a kind of melancholy pleasure in being alone for a while to indulge in uninterrupted daydreams of Mr. Stratton—to recall every word he had spoken to her, every look, every moment in his presence, until she came to those final precious words and looks and the parting kiss that had plighted their troth.

As she let her mind drift along this fair avenue of reminiscence, her heart seemed physically to swell within her as though at any moment it must burst with pent up emotion. Her needlework fell unheeded to the floor as she pressed both hands to her breast to try and quiet the tumult within.

She did not hear the knock upon the door at first, removed so far as she was at that moment from her immediate surroundings. But presently the sound broke through her abstraction, and she moved as one in a trance to answer it.

He was there, standing on the step. It seemed like a miracle, as if she had conjured him up by the very strength of her imaginings. In a moment, he had entered, slammed the door behind him, and gathered her into his arms.

Their lips met with the desperate urgency of lovers who must cheat time, must cram every moment with the outward expression of an inward intensity which can never be fully expressed. There was a singing in her ears; she felt light-headed, so that she scarcely realised when presently he guided her to the sofa and they lay there side by side. With all the strength of her being she wanted to give, give, give. . . .

Afterwards they lay quietly clasped in each other's arms, heedless of time or place. Too heedless to hear the cottage door opening until it was too late, and Mrs. Lathom stood before them, aghast.

The scene which followed soon brought them down to earth again. Mrs. Lathom did not mince her words, spoken in the first shock, and Dorinda punctuated them with sobs which shook her whole body. Neville's first impulse was to escape from the cottage immediately, but he controlled this with difficulty and tried to put the best face on matters that he could.

"Dorinda and I are already betrothed, ma'am, and shall be wed as soon as may be—we but anticipated our union in the fulness of our hearts. Can you not understand and forgive?"

This speech encouraged the outraged mother to hope that Mr. Stratton had already obtained parental consent to the betrothal, and that therefore there need be no delay in contracting the marriage which was now so necessary to make an honest woman of her daughter. She dismissed the still weeping girl to her bedchamber and sat down to discuss matters with the impetuous lover.

She was extremely taken aback to discover her mistake. For the first time, she admitted to herself doubts about his character. But it was too late for these now; the two must marry, and that speedily. What else was to be done? She would have given much at that moment to have had someone at hand to advise her, but the loss of her husband had thrown her entirely on her own resources. With no friends in the vicinity and her only close relative a brother in far-off London whom she had not seen and had

42

scarcely heard of in well nigh twenty years, there was no one to whom she could turn.

The one hopeful aspect of the affair was that Mr. Stratton seemed as bent on an early marriage as Mrs. Lathom herself could be. He undertook to procure a special licence so that the ceremony could take place without delay.

"Depend upon it, ma'am—once your sweet daughter has become my wife, there will be no difficulty in reconciling my father to the match. What's done cannot be undone, and he'll have no choice but to accept the situation. Besides, when he comes to know my adorable Dorinda better, he cannot fail to value her as he ought."

She was as ready to believe this as any mother in her circumstances would be, so she sent him on his way to procure the marriage licence. Any doubts she may have entertained as to whether they would ever set eyes on him again she kept from Dorinda, who passed the next few days in a state of euphoria. In spite of her misgivings, he did return, however; and a quiet ceremony took place in the parish church with only the clergyman, his parish clerk and a verger in attendance. As the small bridal party approached the church door, the quarter-boys of the ancient clock above it struck the half hour. Dorinda looked up and read once again the inscription over the clockface which she knew so well.

'For our time is a very shadow that passeth away.'

She gave an involuntary shiver and the brightness of her face was dimmed for a moment.

The church was a vast building which gave a pathetic appearance to the small party gathered at the altar. How many weddings would have been solemnized there, wondered Mrs. Lathom with tears in her eyes, when so few people were present to mark the event? There should have been a full congregation and a swelling organ, a slim girl coming radiant down the aisle, white-robed and with a floating veil covering her bright hair. And if few mothers could forbear from

43

weeping a little at a marriage ceremony, there should be no bitterness in the tears.

Instead, only two elderly church officers, grave and detached, looked on at a ceremony to which it now appeared that the bridegroom had not even remembered to bring a wedding ring.

The clergyman waited patiently, doubtless used to temporary losses of this most necessary adjunct to the service; but he soon saw from the expression on the bridegroom's face that this was not an occasion when the ring had been mislaid for the moment in the understandable stress attendant on a marriage ceremony. It was plain that this unfortunate young man had actually forgotten to provide himself with one.

Smiling tolerantly, for he understood very well what the bridegroom's state of mind must be when faced with such a dilemma, the Reverend indicated to Mrs. Lathom that she should slip off her own wedding ring so that it might be pressed into use for the time being. Before she understood, Neville quickly drew off his own gold signet ring engraved with his initial, entwined about a poppy head, the insignia of the Stratton family.

He placed this upon Dorinda's slim finger, where it hung so loosely that she was obliged to clench her hand to prevent the ring from falling off.

It was over. For better or worse, they were now man and wife.

After six halcyon honeymoon weeks, Neville reluctantly decided that his father was almost sure to be getting restive at his absence. He must return home; but first it seemed wise to look in on his friend Lydney at Brighton, where he was supposed to have been all this time, in case the Earl had directed any messages to him there. The parting with his bride was painful to both; but he promised a speedy return with, he hoped, news of his father's blessing on the marriage. Mrs. Lathom naturally made some attempt to discover exactly where he lived so that they could communicate with him if need be; but his powers of evasion were more than equal to hers of persuasion, so in the end she learnt nothing and was forced to abandon the attempt, for fear of impairing her daughter's happiness in any way.

It was to this dashing resort of high fashion Neville went from the humbler scenes at Rye. Having called at Lydney's house and been informed that its master was not at present within, he left a message with the servant to say he would be returning later, and then took a stroll about the town. He was within easy reach of the sea front and so took his way there first, standing for a while leaning against the railings which separated the path from the beach, surveying the scene.

The fashionable hour for bathing, which was uncomfortably early by London standards, was long since past; but a group of lads from the town paddled at the water's edge, shoes and stockings clutched in their hands, shrieking with glee as the waves washed up to soak their breeches. Donkeys with riders on their backs cantered past, urged on by the whips of some boys who plied the animals for hire. A fat woman, skirts immodestly billowing in the breeze as she perched precariously on her donkey's back, added her strident yells to those of the lads in the water; while her companions enjoyed her predicament so heartily that they almost fell off themselves.

Farther along the beach, Neville noticed some boats drawn up with fishing nets spread out to dry; nearby, a collier was unloading its dirty cargo. The sea was greyblue today, reflecting the sun's rays; although the white-capped waves were fairly boisterous, driven by a light breeze which set the fishing smacks dancing across them. Gulls swooped screaming overhead, and there was a strong, though not unpleasant, smell of ozone.

Neville lingered a while, finding the scene pleasing, although the crowd here was very different from that which he came upon presently when he strolled round to the fashionable parade in the Steyne. This was a triangular green surrounded by a broad brick path for pedestrians and railed off from an encircling carriageway. Here the people of Quality promenaded daily in fine weather, the ladies in pretty gowns of every hue, chatting with acquaintances or flirting with escorts. The men's more sober garb was enlivened here and there by a scarlet military coat, for officers were quartered in the town from Army encampments nearby.

He had scarcely completed a leisurely circuit of the Steyne when he encountered Edward Lydney in company with several other gentlemen and two or three attractive young ladies, none of whom he knew. Introductions took place, and he continued in their company for the next hour or so, when Lydney took leave of his companions and escorted Neville back to the house.

"What did you think of Miss Barham?" Lydney asked him, when they had walked far enough away for the question not to be overheard.

"Miss Barham?"

"Yes, the dark young lady in the green and white striped gown. She has an air of quiet elegance that you must have remarked."

Neville had no very clear picture of any of the young ladies from whom they had just parted. The image of Dorinda lingered with him still, making other females of little account. He made an effort to be civil, however, and answered that indeed Miss Barham had seemed a most engaging girl.

"I certainly find her superior to any whom I've met so far," said Lydney. "And she has a fortune, too, as I understand."

"Are you thinking of marriage?" asked Neville.

Lydney pursed his lips. "I might do worse, I suppose, although three and twenty is young for a man to think of settling down."

This brought Neville to his own affairs. He had been longing for the opportunity to discuss them, and wasted no time in making his friend acquainted with the story of his sudden marriage.

Lydney heard him out in amazed silence. At the end of the recital he emitted a low whistle.

46

"Phew! That's the devil of a coil!" he exclaimed. "What d'you mean to do now?"

"There's nothing else for it, I suppose," replied Neville, reluctantly, "but to confess the whole. But I'll need to choose my time with care. I don't need to tell you that he won't like it. In fact," he finished, gloomily, "I'd as soon have a limb chopped off—less painful, I dare swear."

"You certainly have a rare talent for getting yourself into scrapes! Was there no other way out but to marry the girl?"

"None that I could see. It's a respectable family. Money wouldn't have served the purpose. Besides, I'm content enough with Dorinda. She makes me precisely the kind of wife I like. She's affectionate and undemanding. She don't always want a fellow to be going out of his way to please her, or expect to be forever squandering money on geegaws and frippery. She lets me order things as I wish, and never thinks of going against me in anything. If only my father would accept her, I might pass the rest of my days with her in tolerable comfort. But the devil of it is that I don't think he will. To tell you the truth, Ned, I'm scared to death to broach the matter to him for fear he cuts me off without a penny! He's quite capable of it, you know—he's got the most damnable temper."

"Well, he can't cut you off permanently," replied Lydney, consolingly, "since the title and estate must come to you on his death, do what he will."

"Ay, that's all very well, but how am I to live in the meantime, I'd like to know? I've no private fortune, only what he chooses to let me have. It's cursed unlucky that none of my wealthy relatives ever thought to leave anything to me! And I was mighty civil to several of the old curmudgeons, too, but all to no purpose. I might as well have let them see what I really thought of them. But so it is. One can never depend on anything in this world."

"Then you'd best retire from it to a monastery, old fellow. Oh, very well, I meant but to cheer you up," Lydney said hastily, seeing that his friend had taken

47

offence. "Come, forget about your troubles for a while. I'll take you to a capital place this evening—cards, wine and women, if you're so minded."

There had never been any strong bond of affection between these two, and by now Lydney was thoroughly tired of his friend's problems. He had come to Brighton to be entertained, not to listen to such sorry stuff as this; neither did he intend to involve himself to any troublesome degree in the other's affairs. Shaldon had made a fool of himself, and he must take the consequences; the more he whined, the more Lydney despised him.

Neville understood quite well what the other young man's reactions were, but he also knew that he could rely on Lydney not to betray his confidence. And since he had a strong need to confide in someone, there was no one more suitable. When he thought the matter over, there was no one else at all. Fear of his father had early engendered in him a habit of keeping his own counsel. Even Dorinda knew only as much about him as he judged it safe for her to know at present. She was still unaware of his title or the whereabouts of his home.

He left Brighton on the following day for Alvington, sleeping one night on the road. He arrived at the Hall in the afternoon of the second day to find his father in an unexpectedly jovial mood.

"Put in an appearance at just the right time," the Earl said, after the first greetings were over. "The Cottesford gal's been away from home, too, on a tour of the Lakes with some relatives or other. Returned two days ago. You can look in at the Manor tomorrow, see how she's managed in your absence, eh? Reuniting of the lovers—affecting, what?"

He laughed heartily, but Neville could manage only a sickly grin. Now that he was face to face again with his father, he began to doubt that he would ever find the courage to reveal his secret.

Maria had been glad to avail herself of an opportunity to escape from home for a while. The house seemed all at once too quiet, the neighbourhood flat, her friends and acquaintances lacking in stimulation. She tried to tell herself that she was out of spirits because she needed a change of air; but in her heart she knew very well that there had been nothing amiss with the air of her native countryside until Viscount Shaldon had left it for Brighton.

She entered enthusiastically into a tour of the Lake District in the company of one of her favourite Aunts and that lady's family. Nature always exercised a beneficial effect on Maria's spirits. The bold austerity of the peaks, the rich green valleys with their gentler landscape and the wide expanse of the lakes offered scenic contrasts to match every changing mood and to remind the onlooker that this alone was enduring, that all anxieties must in time pass away.

She recovered much of her usual tranquillity, returning home with a cheerful countenance which was so suntanned that Lady Cottesford threw up her hands in despair at the sight of it.

"La, my dear, it's a monstrous pity that your Aunt Selina should not have warned you against going out in the sun without your parasol! You are as brown as a gypsy! What's to be done? We must try some lemon juice, or Denmark lotion. It will never do to let Viscount Shaldon see you looking like that!"

"Fustian," said Sir William, inspecting his daughter with a loving eye. "I think she looks charmingly. The tan gives some colour to her cheeks."

This was true. In general, Maria's skin was inclined to be sallow, but sun and fresh air had combined to give it an attractive golden glow which enhanced the brightness of her hazel eyes.

"Thank you, Papa. I can always count on you to make the best of me," Maria replied, laughing. "But truly, Mama, I don't think Viscount Shaldon will notice, one way or the other."

She was right, of course. When Neville called a day or two later, he was as charming and attentive as before; but more than ever, she felt that there was no heart in his performance. As the weeks wore on and

49

they met at frequent intervals, she became more and more convinced of this. It was plain that the proposed marriage would be one of convenience.

By now she was certain of her own feelings and wondered what it was best to do. Could there be any hope of happiness in a match of unequal affection? Sometimes she took comfort in the thought that Viscount Shaldon could not have a fixed preference for any other female, or he would not consent to woo her, even to please his father. If that were so, then there was still hope that she might teach him to love her.

So she set herself to try and win his regard. She dressed with more care than before, studying the fashion plates in *Lady's Magazine,* or *Elegant and Entertaining Companion for the Fair Sex* and choosing those designs which she thought most becoming to be made up for her by her dressmaker. She washed her hair in rainwater and brushed it vigorously in a vain attempt to give it a sheen, and she even went so far as to add a light touch of rouge to her lips and cheeks. She was a naturally lively talker, taking an interest in all the foremost topics of the day; but now she tried to steer the conversation away from subjects which seemed to bore him, concentrating instead upon anything, however trivial, which appeared to arouse his interest.

Most women have a natural ability to recommend themselves to a man by little arts of feminine allure. In Maria, this ability was unfortunately almost totally lacking. Her disposition was so frank and open, her approach so rational, that she failed to realise how to employ such powerful weapons as a fluttering fan, a provocative smile, an arch glance or a seemingly accidental glimpse of a shapely ankle. She might have learnt much from that Miss Cavendish with whom Neville had danced at the ball. But still she persevered in her own way, watching eagerly for any sign of a change in his attitude towards her, and all the time falling more deeply in love with him.

Chapter V

CLOSE ON TWO MONTHS had passed since Neville had parted from his wife, and still he had not found the courage to inform the Earl of the marriage. During this time he had written only one brief letter to Dorinda, giving her no address to which she might reply. He told her that he was unable to leave home at present as his father was gravely ill. It was the only excuse he could think of to explain his continued absence; and, try as he would, he was unable to discover any way of leaving Alvington at present without antagonising his father.

Fortunately, the Earl himself at last provided the much desired opportunity. Early in October, he departed for Yorkshire to join a party of sportsmen friends for several weeks.

No sooner had his father left the house than Neville hastily packed his bag and set out for Rye.

He was rapturously received, and had no difficulty in making Dorinda and her mother believe that he had so far been unable to communicate the news of his marriage, owing to his father's weak condition.

"I waited only to see him out of danger," he said, his arm lovingly around Dorinda, "before hastening to you, my dearest. To stay until he was strong enough to receive my news—which, however much he may welcome it in time, must come as a shock at first—to stay any longer, I say, was more than I could bring myself to do. My one overwhelming desire was to be with you at the earliest possible moment."

Dorinda had no wish to argue with this, and he breathed an inward sigh of relief that everything had passed off so easily. But before he had been in the cottage many hours, he learned that yet another complication had entered his life.

Dorinda was pregnant.

It was only to be expected, of course, yet the news dismayed him. Some absurd notion had lingered at the back of his mind that he might be able to continue keeping his marriage a secret. Now there was small chance of that, with a possible heir to Alvington on the way.

His depression was deepened by a change in his wife. She was still as gentle and loving, as uncritical of him as before, but she was now frequently ailing. The sickness and nausea which sometimes attend the early months of a pregnancy afflicted her sorely. She tried hard to be cheerful, but was forced to spend hours lying down on her bed with her mother in attendance. A faint resentment began to stir in him, the beginnings of regret for his hasty marriage. Why was it that nothing ever seemed to go right for him?

By the time he had spent three weeks in the cottage, he was finding it as much a prison as Alvington Hall had been. He soon made up his mind to go back to Buckinghamshire; in any case, the Earl would return before long, and it would not do for him to find his son absent. It would require some finesse to extricate himself creditably from his present situation, but he trusted to his own ingenuity—and to his wife's affection—to achieve it. Anxiety for his father was the excuse he used; and if Mrs. Lathom felt that a wife's claims should come before those of a parent, however dear, she held her tongue for Dorinda's sake.

The poor girl was extremely dejected and cried for most of the evening before his departure, a fact which made him all the more eager to go.

She tried hard to present a braver face in the morning; but her mother realised the strain she was under, and persuaded her to lie down on her bed for a while, after Neville had gone.

She rested there for some time, racked by a grief that was all the more poignant because she remained dry-eyed. Presently she rose, moving quietly so that her mother would not hear, and went to a special hiding place where she had been in the habit of concealing her most valued possessions. It was a small ledge inside the chimney breast, completely concealed from view and unknown to anyone other than herself.

She put her hand up the chimney and drew forth an intricately worked wooden box which had been brought back from foreign parts by her father as a present for his little daughter. Opening it, she disclosed the signet ring which had been used for the wedding ceremony. Although Neville had since bought her one which fitted properly, she had begged to be allowed to retain this, which she thought of as her true marriage ring.

She lifted it out, pressing it to her lips; and now the tears began to fall. Sobbing, she replaced the ring and drew forth from the bodice of her gown the only letter he had ever written to her. She read it again, although she knew it by heart, then tenderly laid it in the box beside the ring. She replaced the box in its hiding place. Even Mama could not share these precious pledges of his affection.

Meanwhile, Neville thankfully set his course for home. He was relieved to find that his father had not yet returned and was not expected until the following week. He rode over to see Edward Lydney and to acquaint him with the latest news.

"Well, there's no help for it now," remarked Lydney. "You'll be obliged to open your budget to the Earl, no gainsaying it."

Neville agreed grimly. "And there'll be the devil to pay, Ned, I needn't tell you. The fact that I've kept it from him till matters have reached this pass won't help my case, either. What in God's name can I do if he turns me off?"

"Shouldn't think it'll be as bad as that," said the other, judicially. "Not now that there's a legal offspring in prospect—might be an heir, too. A man don't put his heirs in penury."

"You don't know my father," retorted Neville bitterly.

"One thing to turn you off without a penny in the heat of the moment, but quite another to let your brat starve. He'd have to come down with the blunt to provide for the child. Besides, I don't think he'd deprive you of funds for very long—only long enough to get rid of his spleen."

"That might be too damned long for me! No, I tell you I can't face him with it—not yet, at any rate. If you think"— Neville paused, turning over Lydney's words in his mind—"if you really think, Ned, that the birth of a child might make a difference to the old man—well . . ."

Lydney shrugged, already tired of the subject.

"What I really think is that you'd do well to tell him without further delay. There's Miss Cottesford to consider, too. The Earl's bound to try and push the match forward, being in the dark about this other business. Devilish awkward all 'round, I'd say."

Edward Lydney proved right. As soon as the Earl returned home, he urged his son to pursue the courtship in earnest.

"Here we are nearly into November, and nothing settled yet between you," he said briskly. "She's had time enough to know her own mind, so you'd best get round to poppin' the question, m'boy."

Neville tugged at his cravat, which suddenly seemed too tight. "I—I can't do that—that's to say"—his courage evaporated before the fierce glare in those steel-grey eyes—"that's to say, I don't think the time is yet right for a declaration. I—I would rather leave it a while longer—"

"God give me patience!" exploded the Earl. "What a namby-pamby generation this is! Why, devil take it, boy, I'd wedded, bedded and got your mother with child in half the time it's taken you only to strike up a mere acquaintance with this chit!"

54

Neville stammered an apology, but held, if only feebly, to his point of view.

"Oh, very well, I have done! It's no matter, after all, if the wedding don't take place till the Spring, just so long as you don't let the gal slip through your fingers. You're only one and twenty, when all's said, and not half the man I was at your age. But mind you see plenty of her, for how else is the chit to fall in love with you? Fall in love!" The Earl snorted in disgust. "Cottesford's an old woman to insist on such a romantical notion—as though you weren't a devilish good catch for any female, let alone one that's as good as on the shelf."

The months that followed were amongst the most uneasy of Neville's life. Since returning home, he suffered increasingly from feelings of guilt concerning Dorinda. It was bad enough that he could not, through his own lack of moral courage, give her the position to which she was entitled and openly acknowledge her as his wife. It was worse that he had run away at a time when she needed his support and comfort. Selfish though he was, he was not a brutal man; and he loved Dorinda as much as he was capable of caring for anyone except himself. When he recalled the happiness of their brief honeymoon, he knew that she deserved better of him, and the knowledge did nothing to enhance his self-esteem.

He made up his mind to visit her as often as he could find an excuse for quitting Alvington, and enlisted Edward Lydney's help in this purpose. The visits were brief and infrequent, but they helped soothe Dorinda, who was having a difficult pregnancy. Mrs. Lathom felt less satisfied with her son-in-law's lengthy absences, but was obliged to accept his explanation that his father was still too ill to be told the truth; and that moreover many of the duties of the estate now fell upon his shoulders, which meant that he was constantly needed at home. She came to the conclusion that Mr. Stratton's father was most likely on the verge of death, and that therefore it was only a matter of time before Dorinda would have her full rights. They had only to be patient, and all would turn out for the best. This was an essential part of the good lady's philosophy.

Although Neville was able to salve his conscience with these visits, he still had a most difficult part to play with Maria Cottesford. It was not made easier by the fact that he was now finding her a more interesting and stimulating companion than poor Dorinda, who did her best to be cheerful for her husband, but often suffered from sundry ailments which made her feel low. Now that his obsession for Dorinda had faded to a lukewarm affection, he was better able to do justice to the other girl. She was too much of a bluestocking for his taste, but she had a lively sense of humour and frequently made him laugh when he had previously been feeling glum. Although her looks seemed to have improved lately in some subtle way, she was still far from being a beauty; and in her company he never felt the faintest stirring of his senses, although several other females of his acquaintance could produce this effect readily enough. Still, it was no longer quite so tedious to be obliged to pay her the formal attentions required of a suitor, and at least his performance of these civilities kept his father content. More than once he noticed the Earl's eye rest on him approvingly when he had turned a pretty compliment to the lady or had danced with her several times at a private ball in one of the houses of the neighbourhood.

Maria, watching always for any sign from the Viscount which she might interpret as awakening love, noticed the change in him, and wondered how optimistic she could allow herself to be. There was no doubt that he now paid her more heed than formerly, when, at times, he had scarcely seemed to be aware of her presence at all. He had always been punctilious in all those attentions which a gentleman should pay to a lady, but he had performed them automatically; his compliments, though chosen with wit and taste, had been obviously studied and carried no conviction. Now he appeared to enjoy their conversations together, though these were usually light-hearted and inconsequential, since Maria had decided that serious discussion bored him. There could be no doubt that he was at last becoming conscious of her as a personality, but was he falling in love?

She sighed, gazing from her window into the garden where the shadows had lengthened, leaving the trees darkly silhouetted against a sky of grey and opal, in which one star shone high up—remote as happiness, thought Maria sadly, remote as his heart was from hers. What more could she do to win his love? She could think of nothing. Love is not won, after all, she reflected, but freely given—or as freely withheld. Witness how often it was given unwanted; there was poor, simple Phebe in Shakespeare's *As You Like It,* yearning for Rosalind in the guise of a man. That was fiction, of course; but real life offered plenty of examples, one or two of them within her own circle of acquaintance. If he should speak now, would she accept him? She felt there was no real likelihood of a declaration at present, and wondered why he hung back from committing himself. Was it because he, too, wanted to be more certain of his feelings?

Christmas came and went. Maria's grandparents had been staying at the Manor over the festive season, and they now begged her to accompany them for a short stay to their home in Oxfordshire. Reluctant though she felt in one way to leave her own home and the company of Viscount Shaldon, in another she thought her absence at this time might be no bad thing. It was said that absence made the heart grow fonder; perhaps if Shaldon could no longer see her whenever he wished, he might discover how much—or how little —she meant to him. Either way, it might serve to resolve a situation which was growing daily more painful to her.

Telling his father that he intended to take a trip to London in Maria's absence, Neville seized the chance of paying a lengthy visit to Rye, where he had not been since before Christmas. All his former eagerness to go there had now completely vanished; he thought of his visits as tedious duties which he could not escape. His wife was no longer the captivating companion of their honeymoon days. Her ungainly figure, far from arousing his tenderness, only served to repel him; and her constant ailments made the hours he spent with her tedious in the extreme. He would have greatly preferred the visit to Town which was serving as his present excuse for visiting her; there, at any rate, he would have gaiety and diversion.

He found her far from well. Her hands and legs were swollen so that she was in discomfort most of the time, although she tried her best to make light of it. She was a little inclined to be plaintive because he had been absent over the Christmas season, but he won her over with the present of a finely woven Norwich shawl which he placed tenderly about her shoulders. He had brought a fur tippet for Mrs. Lathom which quite mellowed that lady, who nowadays was inclined to receive him with something of reserve in her manner. It was plain that she thought her daughter's marriage unsatisfactory, but for Dorinda's sake she seldom uttered a word of complaint.

He learned that the child was expected at the end of March, and was called on to admire the many small garments on which both women had been working during the past months. He praised everything generously, in particular a beautifully worked white gown with pintucking and insets of lace which he was told was for the child's christening.

"And we must decide on a name, dearest," said Dorinda, laying her head on his shoulder. "What would you like it to be?"

He smiled into her upturned, childlike face, but inwardly remained unmoved. The prospect of fatherhood held no appeal for him; his magical love affair with Dorinda seemed now as remote as a dream.

"You shall choose, my love. What are your favourite names?" he asked fondly.

"Why, Neville, of course—and William, after my poor dear Papa—that is, if you would not object?"

"Don't forget," put in Mrs. Lathom, with a smile,

"that your child may be a girl. You're choosing only boys' names."

"Well, if it should be a girl, then I would like one of her names to be Elizabeth, after you, dearest Mama. But Neville will naturally wish to give her his own mother's name. What is it, dearest?"

"My mother's name? Oh, it's Jane."

"Jane Elizabeth. Yes, it sounds very well, don't you think? And now we have made our choice. It didn't take very long, did it?" Her face changed, grew paler. "Mama, I—I feel unwell—"

Mrs. Lathom, ever watchful, shepherded her out of the room, leaving Neville sitting glumly on the sofa.

Conversations such as this, enlivened now and then by a haphazard game of backgammon or chess, constituted his sole entertainment at the cottage. Without a deep affection to lend interest, these concerns seemed trivial and boring to the young man. After a fortnight, he felt he could no longer endure another day of it. He determined to leave and spend the rest of the time left to him in London, gaming at the Clubs and flirting with the lighter muslin company at Vauxhall.

They were now so used to his comings and goings that they accepted this decision philosophically enough. According to his report, his father was still in very poor health and unable to stand the slightest excitement; and if Mrs. Lathom sometimes wished that the old gentleman would either recover fully or else succumb to his malady, she never mentioned this to Dorinda, who would have been sadly shocked at her mother's seeming heartlessness. The fact was that Mrs. Lathom, although a gentle soul in all matters that did not concern her beloved child, had developed a protective shrewdness since Dorinda's marriage. She had accepted Neville's story of his father's illness without reservation in the beginning; and at that time she had believed it to be a terminal malady which would resolve the young man's difficulties. But lately she had begun to wonder how much credence could be placed on her son-in-law's reports on his parent's condition. Was the old man really in as bad a way as the son represented? If so, how had he managed to survive? It was now four months since Mr. Stratton had first written to tell them the unhappy news; people did linger on, of course. . . . All the same, she had come to know Mr. Stratton well enough by now, in spite of the reserve beneath his surface charm, to realise that he was a vacillating person who always evaded unpleasant decisions. She must do nothing at present, however, to impair Dorinda's happiness, which she sensed was already fragile.

Chapter VI

MARIA HAD often been struck by the different outlook brought about by a removal for a time to another place among fresh company. One had only to travel a few miles away and step into a different environment, and at once all those matters which seemed of so much importance at home receded into the background.

She was relieved to find that her grandparents, unlike her Mama, were not disposed to talk about her matrimonial prospects. They were, of course, well informed on that subject, for anyone related to Lady Cottesford could hardly be otherwise; but they remained undazzled. In their view, a young man who took so long over his courtship could not be as ardent a suitor as they desired for a very dear granddaughter; and privately they considered that her prospects of happiness would be greater with a gentleman of more compatibility of temperament, even though he might lack some of the worldly advantages Viscount Shaldon could offer.

They knew of such a gentleman.

He was the Reverend Theodore Somerby, curate of their parish and the son of an old and respected family friend who was now deceased. Mr. Somerby was twenty-six years of age, a graduate of Oxford University, where he had been a gifted classical scholar, and moreover he was well connected, even if only through a junior branch of a noble family.

"To be sure, he has only a modest private income," said Mrs. Reddiford to her husband, "but what does that signify when Maria has fortune enough already for both, not to speak of what we shall have to leave her, as we've no other grandchild?"

Mr. Reddiford was heard to say that he hoped that would not be for some time yet, as he had no immediate plans for shuffling off this mortal coil.

"Well, no, of course not, my love, but that is beside the point."

"I cannot agree with you there. It seems very much the point to me, however it may affect our granddaughter."

"Oh, you will have your little jest! But pray be serious for a moment—do you consider Theodore's lack of fortune a serious disadvantage? He will obtain preferment in time, you know—he may even become a Bishop."

"Even so, he would be unlikely to enjoy an income anything comparable to what young Shaldon's will be when he inherits," said Mr. Reddiford, smiling at her optimism.

"You really are the most tiresome man! But in spite of Viscount Shaldon's indisputable worldly advantages, I know you think as I do that our darling girl would be better suited with Theodore. I declare I've no patience with Kate! She seems quite overcome at the notion of seeing Maria a Countess one day, so that every other consideration goes by the board. It's very well to be a Countess, I'm sure, but the present Lady Alvington doesn't appear to have much joy of it! And I've managed tolerably well without it, I must say, though of course," with a teasing smile at him, "there didn't happen to be an Earl in the running when you offered for me. Things might have been different if such had been the case."

Mr. Reddiford, remembering the shared youthful passion which had enabled him to carry his lady off from under the noses of several highly eligible suitors, and which had not worn too badly with time, chucked her under the chin.

"Very true, my love. I always knew I was a lucky fellow. Well, if you're determined to set about match-making, I must let you have your head, I suppose. The only thing is"—he hesitated for a moment—"it did seem to me that the girl herself was rather taken in that quarter. Not much to be done, if that's so."

"Well, we shall see. And as Theodore dines here with us frequently in the normal course of things, there will be nothing out of the way in his being invited to join the evening parties I intend to arrange for her entertainment during her stay. Nothing formal, you know, just the kind of neighbourly affair you so much enjoy, only that this time I shall include the younger members of those families who are on visiting terms with us."

Mrs. Reddiford lost no time in carrying out her intentions, and invitations were sent out to four or five families in the neighbourhood, comprising about twenty-five guests. The date given was for the fourth day after the Reddifords' return home with their granddaughter; but barely two hours after a groom had been despatched to the various houses with the invitations, a young lady presented herself breathlessly at the garden door of the Reddifords' house.

Without stopping to knock, she pushed open the door and gave a perfunctory wipe to her soiled half boots of blue jean on the mat provided for that purpose, before rushing along the passage with unladylike haste in the direction of the morning parlour. Having reached it, she burst in, startling Mrs. Reddiford, who was seated alone there at a writing desk.

"Good heavens!" exclaimed the lady, half-starting from her chair. Then, recognising the unexpected and unannounced visitor with pleasure, she rose fully to extend a hand in welcome. "Oh, it's you, Amanda! How very nice to see you! But, my dear child——" taking in the dishevelled state of the young lady's hair, her flushed cheeks, and the liberal daubs of mud on her petticoats and boots, "but what in the world have you been doing to yourself?"

Amanda Paxton, who had been in and out of the Reddifords' house for most of her nineteen years, grinned engagingly, sparing the briefest of glances for her soiled attire.

"Oh, I came across the fields," she said, airily. "It was quicker than bothering to get my mare saddled and coming by the lane, but I forgot how muddy it would be. I beg your pardon, ma'am, for startling you, and I'm afraid my boots," looking ruefully at some marks on the Aubusson carpet, "are not really fit. I do hope——"

She looked doubtfully towards the older woman, but Mrs. Reddiford only laughed and bade her sit down. Amanda, whose manners were good in spite of her unconventional ways, thanked her hostess as she complied.

"You see," she explained, "no sooner did Mama get your note saying that Maria was here, than I simply had to come that very moment to see her! It's an age since we've met, and though we correspond fairly regularly, letters are not at all the same thing, are they, ma'am?"

Mrs. Reddiford agreed that indeed they were not, and informed Amanda that she would find Maria walking in the shrubbery, if she cared to venture out of doors again.

"Like you, she was tempted out by the sunshine, my dear. But if you're tired already by your exercise, I'll send for her here."

Amanda was on her feet in a moment.

"Oh, no, Mrs. Reddiford, indeed I am never tired by walking—at least, not by half a mile across fields, which is all it is! Pray excuse me, ma'am, for I can't wait to see Maria!"

Mrs. Reddiford smiled tolerantly as the girl dashed from the room. What a madcap she was, and yet such a dear girl, too—always ready to do a good turn for anybody, and especially thoughtful for the welfare of the poor in their neighbourhood, assisting her mother in many small acts of charity when she might have been spending her time in the more frivolous pursuits favoured by most young ladies. Not that Miss Amanda Paxton did not have her frivolous side; it was not many years since she had been getting up to all manner of tomboy tricks with those irrepressible brothers of hers, now mercifully—though possibly not for their tutors—away at University.

The two young ladies had not met since the preceding Spring, so naturally there was a great deal of news to be exchanged and anecdotes to be related. But presently Amanda, who was far more perceptive than her ebullient manner might lead people to suppose, saw that her usually lively friend was at present lacking in spirits.

She challenged Maria with this. "You may as well tell me, you know, just what's the matter, because then you'll feel a little better, at any rate. We never *have* had any secrets from each other—that is, not unless you count that time when you wouldn't tell me—oh, you know!" She broke off and turned a little pink.

Maria looked puzzled, but only for a moment. Then she laughed.

"Oh, yes, that! But you are fifteen months my junior, and were still too young at the time. Besides, I would have been in a puzzle how to explain. I'm sure your Nurse made a far better mentor than I could have done, at barely thirteen years of age."

"Well, perhaps so, but I knew there was something you were keeping from me, even then! And I know it now, so you'd best open your budget, as you can't well claim that I'm too young for any confidence at nineteen, now can you?"

Maria acknowledged the truth of this. She had stayed frequently with her grandparents during childhood and adolescence, and Amanda Paxton had been her constant companion during these visits. She had come to regard the younger girl almost as a sister, sharing a closer friendship with her than with any other girl of her acquaintance. Although several of her friends at home were aware that there was some kind of understanding between herself and Viscount Shaldon, she had confided to none of them the exact state of her feelings for that gentleman. It was a relief to be able to open her heart to someone and to be sure of a sympathetic hearing.

"And you say he hasn't yet offered for you?" asked Amanda, at the conclusion of these revelations. "That's very odd, surely, since there's no parental opposition on either side?"

"I think so, too, Mandy. Sometimes I believe it's because Papa insisted that Lord Shaldon must give me time to ascertain my true feelings towards him. That is why I—well, I have tried lately to show him that I'm not indifferent to him." Amanda nodded. "But either I am not very expert in the business of encouraging a suitor, or else he is prodigiously diffident, for it seems not to succeed at all in bringing him to the point. And sometimes I believe"—she broke off and sighed heavily—"that he does not care for me at all, and is only courting me to oblige his father. You've met the Earl during your visits to my home. You know what a forceful man he is, and how all his family is under his thumb."

"Yes, indeed. He's the greatest beast in Nature!" exclaimed Amanda, not mincing her words. "And I must say, from what I recollect of his son when he was a boy—though I haven't seen him for some years—he always seemed terrified of his father. But he is a man now, and things must be very different, surely?"

"I'm not certain of that. A habit of frightened subservience is not so easily broken, and I've observed many signs in Lord Shaldon of a wish to avoid any controversy with his father. To tell you the truth," another sigh, "I don't know what to think."

Amanda was silent for some moments, which she occupied in thoughtfully kicking at a small stone which lay in her path, to the detriment of her footwear. "And the crux of the matter is, that you do not choose to wed a man who don't love you," she stated baldly, at last.

"No—at least, I'm not sure," replied Maria, hesitantly. "Do you think, Mandy—is it possible, do you suppose, that love can come after marriage? If there is affection on one side, I mean. Does love engender love? Sometimes I think that I have enough for both of us," she concluded, in a burst of emotion.

Amanda seized her hand and squeezed it. "No one could live with you and not love you!" she declared loyally. "And if he's as much under his father's domination as you say, then he must have had a wretched time of it at home. It's enough to dry up all one's natural feelings! But once he has his own establishment, with a loving wife and no one to vex him, there's no saying what a difference that will make!"

"Well, you may be right. But it's nothing to the purpose, since he still holds off from a declaration."

"If only you could put yourself in a position of some danger, and he could rescue you!" exclaimed Amanda, who was incurably romantic. "That would do the trick. Now what can we think of?"

In spite of herself, Maria had to laugh. "Oh, Mandy, what a child you are!"

"Well, I'm all for doing something, you know," answered Amanda, a trifle aggrieved. "Not just sitting wringing my hands and crying 'Woe!' like the heroine in one of those dreary Greek plays Mr. Somerby is so fond of. That reminds me," she went on, following a new train of thought, "you haven't met Mr. Somerby yet, have you? He is our new curate. He's been to dine at our house several times, and I like him extremely. He's not in the least bit stuffy, as clergymen so often are. And when I got my sash caught up so that the end fell in my soup, he removed it with the greatest presence of mind and wiped it on his napkin, before Mama could notice what had happened!"

They both laughed heartily over this anecdote, and

66

the previous topic was allowed to lapse for the moment.

Maria did meet Mr. Somerby at her grandmother's evening party and found him every bit as agreeable as Amanda had suggested. He was a tall young man with very blond hair, blue eyes that were for the most part serious but could produce a sudden twinkle, and a smile of unexpected sweetness. He had a wide conversational range, switching from small neighbourhood affairs to topics of more general interest according to the company he happened to be with at the moment, in a way perhaps necessary to a clergyman. His sincerity in all he said was evident; and if he never gave offence, Maria sensed that it was out of consideration for his listeners' feelings rather than because he feared to speak his mind for more hypocritical reasons. Indeed, she thought that had it ever been necessary for him to take a firm stand on a matter of principle, he would not have hesitated to do so. While they were together, they talked chiefly of literature and music; although he spoke once of the recent upheaval in France, and she could see that his imagination had been fired, like that of many another young Englishman, by the ideas of liberty and equality which were abroad. Being of an enquiring turn of thought herself, she found his company stimulating; and it crossed her mind more than once that she could never have discussed such subjects with Viscount Shaldon.

Amanda, too, seemed to find pleasure in his company whenever he chanced to be in conversation with her. Knowing Amanda as she did, Maria realised that the madcap girl had a good head on her shoulders and was quite capable on occasions of sustaining a rational discourse with credit. Her somewhat disconcerting habit of coming out now and then with some frank comment, far from giving offence to the gentleman, seemed to provide him with added zest for their discussion. His smile was much in evidence while Miss Paxton was by his side; and Maria, perhaps unduly sensitive to such things at present, fancied that when the young lady moved away, his expression dimmed for a little while afterwards.

Maria was already well acquainted with most of her grandparents' neighbours, even though she met them at infrequent intervals, so it was not surprising that she found herself invited out a great deal. The season of Christmas festivities was only just over, and no one seemed reluctant to begin all over again. There were morning calls, tea drinkings, dinners and evening parties; and as one followed another, Maria found her former obsessive preoccupation with her own troubles gradually fading for the moment into the background. It was not that she loved Viscount Shaldon any less. At times, alone in her bedchamber, his image would come before her mind's eye, bringing with it a surge of wild longing. But during the day, at any rate, she could forget about him for a space, throwing herself wholeheartedly into the diversions of the moment.

Amanda was of great service in this. She saw her friend almost every day, full of gay chatter about yesterday's evening party at the Mersons' or the Veryans'; or bringing the latest copy of the *Lady's Magazine* to pore over the fashion plates with Maria; or perhaps to walk in the shrubbery, if the day was fine and not too cold, and talk quietly on some of the more serious topics that Maria enjoyed discussing. But they did not speak again of Viscount Shaldon except once, when Amanda asked if her friend had heard from him since being away. When Maria simply shook her head in answer, Amanda said no more. In her wisdom she realised that there could be no profit in returning to the subject unless the initiative came from Maria. All had been said that could be said; and the unburdening had, she knew, brought great relief to her friend.

The relief was so welcome that, as week succeeded week, Maria found herself putting off a return to her own home. Letters from her mother told her of Viscount Shaldon's continued absence; perhaps he, too, was not sorry for a respite from his protracted courtship.

It was after she had been three weeks with her

grandparents that she began to suspect a plot to throw the Reverend Theodore Somerby in her way. He was present at most of the social engagements to which she was bidden in the neighbours' houses, besides being always asked to those held in her grandparents' home. In addition, the Reddifords were most pressing to him to take his pot luck with them at any other time when they chanced not to be dining out themselves; and on these occasions, Maria began to notice how she and the young clergyman were left for long periods to converse together while her grandparents looked on contentedly, saying little or nothing themselves. She had no objection to the arrangement, as she enjoyed his company; but she was puzzled by their behaviour.

Thinking that perhaps she was mistaken in her conclusions, she broached the subject to Amanda one day.

"Is it usual, Mandy, for Mr. Somerby to be so frequently with my grandparents? It seems to me that he is invited here so often, he can scarce have time to discharge his clerical duties in the parish."

Amanda wrinkled her brow thoughtfully. "Well, as you know, he's the son of a very close friend, and they've always made him welcome ever since he arrived. But, no, now you mention it, I don't believe they were used to invite him quite so frequently as lately. Why do you ask?"

"Just a notion that came into my head—quite likely a stupid one," replied Maria, dismissing the subject.

But she had aroused her friend's curiosity now, and Amanda had no intention of leaving it unsatisfied.

"What kind of notion?" she persisted.

Maria shrugged. "The thing is, if I did not know they were fully aware of the way in which matters stand between Lord Shaldon and myself, I would think . . . Oh, but it must be nonsense, of course!"

"What must be nonsense?" There was a sudden sharpness in her friend's tone that Maria was not accustomed to hearing. "Pray, don't be so teasing, Maria! You can surely tell me."

"Why, of course, even if I hesitate to voice my suspicions to Grandmama. It did seem to me that they were deliberately attempting to bring the two of us—Mr. Somerby and myself—together. But that can't be so, for Mama has told them I am as good as betrothed to the Viscount; and you might imagine that she left them in no doubt of *her* strong approval of the match. They would scarce attempt to go against her wishes—no, I must have imagined the whole! I tell you what it is, Mandy—I've reached the state when I suppose everyone about me is busy matchmaking on my behalf! Perhaps it's a delusion which afflicts females who are practically on the shelf," she added, with her usual wry humour.

For once, Amanda seemed slow to respond. She was silent for a moment, a frown creasing her brows and all the animation drained from her face. At last she spoke, as if with an effort.

"No, I believe you are right, even though it does seem a strange way for Mr. and Mrs. Reddiford to act. If it were not for your arranged betrothal—and there is nothing certain about that, by what you tell me—I think Mr. Somerby and you would be vastly well suited. He is exactly the kind of gentleman for you, now I think of it," she concluded, somewhat glumly.

"Unfortunately, one seldom has the good sense to bestow one's affections on the most suitable person," answered Maria, serious in her turn. "But poor Mr. Somerby!" she exclaimed, in a livelier tone. "Is no account to be taken of *his* inclinations? He is not of a disposition to be bent to another's purpose, I am sure. And there are plenty of pretty girls in this neighbourhood from whom he may choose—even if he has not done so already."

Amanda raised her head suddenly. "Oh, do you think he might? But no, I haven't noticed anything like that. Still, one can never be sure. . . ." she added, thoughtfully.

Maria laughed. "Come, we have speculated enough on that subject for one afternoon and shall be guilty of gossiping if we go further. Have you finished Miss

Burney's novel *Cecilia* yet? Do you like it as well as *Evelina?*"

"Not quite—there's less liveliness," replied Amanda, in her old manner. "But these heroines are so *proper,* Maria! I quite despair of ever living up to their standards! One cannot imagine them ever having a hair out of place, or—or leaping over stiles in the way I do! But I dare say," she added, with a sudden return to gloom, "that I behave with less propriety than most girls in *real* life—at any rate, Mama often says so."

"All Mamas are fond of making remarks of that kind," said Maria, consolingly, "so there's no need to let it cast you into flat despair. I like you as you are, Mandy—don't ever change."

Amanda said she doubted if she could, and the conversation took a more light-hearted turn.

The following morning brought a letter from Lady Cottesford suggesting that Maria should return home before long, in case the Viscount arrived back in Alvington while she was still absent. A new mood of defiance seized her, and she wrote back to say that it would do the gentleman no harm to discover that she was not always at hand to be picked up or thrown down like an old glove. She determined to prolong her visit for at least another week or two, in the hope—a forlorn one, she realised in her heart of hearts—of teaching him a lesson.

Meanwhile, she continued to enjoy herself amidst all the entertainment that was offered her. The Reverend Theodore Somerby was almost as constant a companion as was Amanda Paxton, and she saw that her grandmother was pleased at this. But she herself had been observing the young clergyman very closely, and she fancied that Mrs. Reddiford was altogether on the wrong tack.

It was not until late in February that Maria returned home. Her mother was reproachful; Viscount Shaldon had been back a week or more, and had already called several times to ask when she might be expected.

"He looked prodigiously disappointed, too," concluded Lady Cottesford, "when I was obliged to tell him that I could give no certain date. Did he not, William?"

Sir William shook off the torpor which had been slowly creeping over him ever since consuming an excellent dinner, and gave the question careful consideration.

"Well, since you ask, m'dear, I'm bound to say that it didn't strike me quite in that light. Seemed to have something on his mind, certainly, but whether it was disappointment—" He broke off and shook his head. "But there, females are evidently superior to the male sex as thought-readers, for they're constantly at it, so maybe you're right."

When next Maria saw Neville she, too, found him abstracted, though he was civilly attentive as always. After an absence of five weeks, she thought she saw a change in his looks; there was a drawn expression about his mouth and a lack of lustre in his eyes. She wondered if it could be the result of too much dissipation in London, and felt a sharp pang at the thought that among his diversions there might have been one or more females of easy virtue. Although a well-bred girl was not supposed to know anything of such matters, Maria had heard gossip of the way in which the Earl amused himself in Town. With such an example before him, it would be scarcely surprising if the son should follow suit.

The notion gave her pain. Her return to Alvington had brought back all the doubts which had tormented her before, and which she had partially succeeded in putting away from her during her stay in Oxfordshire. If he truly wished to marry her, why did he not speak? And if he did eventually declare himself, what was she to answer?

She was almost relieved when snow fell a few days after her return, filling the lanes calf-deep with its crisp, white mass and cutting Alvington off from the neighbouring villages. As she looked out on trees, shrubs, fences and outbuildings transformed by this unstudied artistry, her weary spirit found a measure of tranquillity. He would be unable to visit her at present; and during his enforced absence, the questions which constantly tormented her might be allowed to rest in abeyance.

For ten days the lanes remained deep in snow. Then the thaw set in, bringing with it slush and mud underfoot which made travelling difficult, even for short distances. March was into its third week and daffodils were dancing in the gardens of the Manor before the roads were back to their normal state, and travelling possible.

But still he did not come.

Chapter VII

THE REASON FOR THIS was that he had set out for Rye a few days after the weather improved. The Earl had for some time been waiting impatiently to pay a promised visit to friends in Leicestershire, and at the first sign of the roads being in a fit state for travel, he had departed, telling his family that they might expect him back when they saw him. This gave Neville the chance he needed—but did not desire—to visit his wife.

Reluctant as he was, he knew he must go. Dorinda was expecting their child in little more than a week from now, and his absence at such a time must certainly bring reproaches and the kind of scene from which he flinched even in imagination.

The journey was subject to tiresome delays, owing to the bad condition of the notoriously difficult roads in Kent at this season. Indeed, he almost abandoned the idea of attempting to get through when he reached Tenterden and was informed that parts of the road through Wittersham were flooded. Having come so far, it seemed profitless to turn back, however; so he pressed on, taking a more circuitous route where necessary to avoid obstruction and arriving in Rye five days after leaving Alvington, weary, travel-stained, and dispirited.

It was dark by the time he reached the cottage, and he could see that inside the lamp was already lit. He hesitated for a moment, unwilling to face whatever awaited him within. How had he come to be entangled in this way, for God's sake? Why were all his decisions forced upon him by others and never the outcome of his own inclinations? Falling in love with a pretty girl was one thing; but why must it entail responsibilities which he decidedly did not want—the responsibilities of a wife and child?

There was no help for it now. He shrugged in a fatalistic way, and raised the knocker on the door.

No answer came for some time, so he knocked again more insistently. He heard a footstep, the door was slowly opened, and Mrs. Lathom stood on the threshold.

Clad in black bombazine, in the dim light she reminded him of a raven or some other bird of ill omen. She stared at him in silence almost as though she did not recognise him at first. When at last she did speak, it was in a hoarse croak which heightened the resemblance that had sprung to his mind.

"You!"

She shot the one word at him and made as if to shut the door in his face. Alarmed, he thrust forward hurriedly, almost pushing her aside as he forced an entry. He closed the door, turning to look anxiously into her face. It was pale with dark rings round the eyes, as if she had not slept lately.

"What is it?" he asked, urgently. "Dorinda? Is aught amiss?"

"*You!*" she repeated, making the word sound like a curse. "What do you care about my poor child?

Haven't you neglected her from the start of this unhappy marriage, making your father's illness an excuse for leaving her alone during long, weary months,
for not giving her a wife's rightful place by your side,
in your own home? As if a father's needs should come
before those of a wife, even if what you told us was
the truth, which I take leave to doubt! Yes!" she continued, seeing from his expression that she had made
a hit with this remark. "Yes, it is just as I thought,
and you were ashamed to own her, too much of a
coward to take the responsibility for your actions!
Well, now it's too late—you can do her no more
harm! My darling—my lamb—"

She broke off and clasped her arms around her
body in an agony of grief.

"Oh, my God!" he said in a whisper. "What are
you saying? What do you mean? Is she—"

Her arms dropped to her sides as the fierce anger
ebbed from her, leaving her cold and drained.

"Yes. She died giving birth to your child. I buried
her two days since."

"Dead!" repeated Neville, sinking heavily into a
chair.

She sat down opposite him, and for a while neither
spoke.

"The child was not due until the end of this month,
or so you told me," Neville said at last, dully.

"It was born prematurely. My poor girl— No, I
can't speak of it, she suffered so much—"

Her lips trembled and she covered her face with one
hand.

"I—I am sorry—"

"Sorry!" She was transformed again into the virago
who had met him. "What good can your sorrow do—
even if you were capable of feeling genuine sorrow
for your loss, which I'm convinced you are not! You
never valued her, or you'd have defied your parent
and kept her by your side, where she belonged! You
desired her, lovely as she was"—her face contorted
—"and you married her because she was too virtuous
for there to be any other way! Don't think I didn't de-

tect your lies in the end, but I kept silent for her sake.
You—there are no words bad enough for what you
are!"

He winced. "You misjudge me, Mrs. Lathom. I did
love Dorinda. As for the rest—you can't know how
difficult my life is, how subterfuge is forced upon me
by an autocratic parent—"

"We all have the strength of mind to act rightly, do
we but choose to exercise it!" she interrupted, scath-
ingly. "You are weak, Mr. Stratton, and your behaviour has been contemptible! Who knows? Perhaps my
poor, darling girl is better out of it. Hers would have
been a miserable marriage, and at least she was taken
before her poor heart was quite broken!"

He stood up. "There seems no use in my staying
longer, ma'am. It's plain that my company brings you
nothing but added pain and grief." He hesitated for a
moment. "You will have been at some expense, which
is properly my affair. You must allow me to—"

She flung out a hand in fierce repudiation. "I want
nothing from you—nothing! But what do you mean to
do about the child?"

Neville stared, his face paling. "The—the child?"

"Yes, the baby—your son." Her tone softened.
"Poor lamb, he is very frail and, I fear, cannot long
survive his mother. But you are wealthy, and can purchase expert care for him, and there may perhaps be a
slender chance . . ."

She shook her head mournfully, then gestured to
him that he should follow her. "But you'll wish to see
him. Come."

In a daze, Neville followed her into the kitchen,
where a bright fire burned, safely guarded from the
wooden cradle which was set before it. Mrs. Lathom
knelt beside the cradle and gently moved back the
covers to reveal the occupant.

Neville stooped, peering inside the hood; and now
he was conscious of a thin wail, only a thread of
sound. He gazed in shocked disbelief at the tiny, wiz-
ened, monkeylike figure of his son. Could this mon-
strosity really be the outcome of his and Dorinda's

76

union? Dorinda had been so lovely; and he himself was always spoken of as a well-looking man. Was it possible that two such personable people could produce something that bore so little resemblance to a human being?

He stood upright, breathing with difficulty.

"It's—it's not very big, ma'am, is it? And—and don't look too healthy to me—though I'm no judge of such matters, of course."

She was busy rearranging the covers as she answered. "No, I fear the poor little mite may go at any time—but there! Who knows, with the kind of care you can provide for him, once you have him at home—"

"But—but—" stuttered Neville, rendered almost speechless for a moment, "but I can't take it home with me, ma'am! What in the world would I do with a —a *baby?*"

She stood up, her face hardening. "What would you do with him? Tend him, care for him, be a father to the poor motherless little creature!"

"You—you can do far more for it than I can, ma'am. There—there's no female in whose care I can place the child—"

"You have a mother, I suppose?" He nodded. "And she is grandmother to your son, just as I am. Will she not order matters for you in regard to reliable nurses and a good doctor?"

"You don't understand. My mother knows nothing of my marriage, let alone of a child. I—she—it would be too great a shock."

She stared at him with so much incredulity and loathing that he involuntarily stepped back a pace from her, afraid of he knew not what.

"You—do—not—want—your—own—child?"

The words came out in a staccato utterance which gave them added emphasis.

Neville gulped. "No—yes—that's to say, no such thing!" he blustered. "Of course I want it, but not now. Later, perhaps, if it lives, when it's older."

The words tailed off as his eyes slid away from the harsh, accusing light in hers.

"So now you'll abandon the child as you abandoned the mother! No matter—better that he should die than live to call such a man father." Her tones were quiet now, grave as a hanging judge's might be. "Go! Leave this house, which was a happy place before you entered it with your blandishments and deceits. Let me never set eyes on you more. Go! And may God forgive you—I never can."

She pointed towards the door. Nothing loth, he turned to obey her; then stopped in his course, clumsily pulling out his pocketbook.

"But you must have money—"

Hastily he extracted a handful of banknotes, thrusting them towards her. "Take this. I will bring more soon, when I come again to see how the child fares—"

"I want nothing from you—nothing! As for the child, you have repudiated him, and that is an end! Should he be spared, he is lost to you for ever. Go, go, I tell you, before I do you a mischief!"

He fled, pausing only to drop the banknotes on a table in the parlour as he passed through.

Once outside, he hurried to the inn to take a post chaise for Tenterden. He would sleep at the White Lion tonight. He could not wait to leave Rye behind him, and everything that had passed there.

Later, when he was sitting down in a snug, low-ceilinged parlour beside a brightly glowing log fire, about to begin on a dinner of mulligatawny soup, saddle of mutton and apple tart washed down with a bottle of claret, he began to feel more his own man again.

He had been greatly shocked at the sudden news of Dorinda's death. She had been a lovely creature, sweet, gentle, yielding; and in other circumstances, she would have made him a most suitable wife. He had loved her for a time with all the affection of which he was capable; but lately, he admitted to himself, the first bright intoxication had faded, leaving him with nothing but a sense of guilt when he was absent, boredom when he was with her, and panic lest his father should come by some chance to learn of the marriage. He had never known an easy moment, he thought resentfully, since he had stepped into that vast church at Rye to promise what he could never hope to perform. The whole affair had been doomed from the start, and he might thank his lucky stars that he was well out of it. The child would die; the woman had said there was scant hope for it, and judging by its appearance, she was certain to be right. That would mean—he poured himself another glass of claret and held it aloft so that the candlelight caught its mellow ruby depths—that would mean that this indiscreet marriage of his could remain for ever a secret.

He drained the glass. His principal feeling now was one of relief that the whole episode was finished.

"There's been more than enough of this damned nonsense," stated the Earl, when he returned from his visit. "The Cottesford gal must know her own mind by now, and if she don't, she deserves to die an old maid. What d'ye think, m'boy? Has she a tendre for you?"

"Well, sir," replied Neville, diffidently, "without wishing to sound too much of a coxcomb—"

"For God's sake, don't mince matters!" snapped his father. "You must know how the land lies. Will she take you or won't she? Because if you don't think she will, draw off, and we'll look elsewhere. It's the best match of the lot, mind, and I'd set my heart on it, but a bird in the hand's worth two in the bush. Eh? What d'ye say?"

"I think that perhaps she is not totally indifferent to me," Neville finished.

"Capital, capital!" The Earl rubbed his hands together as one who has made a good bargain. "Go to it then, boy. Waste no more time, and let's see a betrothal by Easter. And I won't take any more put-offs, mind."

Maria was walking in the garden along a path sheltered by a grey stone wall beside which daffodils and tulips bloomed. She was deep in thought and did not hear Viscount Shaldon's step until he was almost beside her. She turned then, a trifle startled, and spoke breathlessly.

"Lord Shaldon! I—did not expect you. How do you do? Isn't it a lovely day? Spring has come at last, and, as usual, one finds it difficult to believe that only a few short weeks since, all this"—she gestured towards the flower beds—"was covered in snow."

"Indeed it is a beautiful day, ma'am. May I walk with you for a while? There is something I wish to say to you, and we may be quite private here."

She glanced quickly up into his face, then looked away as she felt the colour come into her cheeks. He took her hand and she did not resist, her pulse leaping at his touch.

"Perhaps you know what it is," he continued, with smooth assurance, "for my attentions over so many months must have been plain. Miss Cottesford—Maria! You must allow me to tell you how very much I admire you and wish to make you my wife. Dare I hope—is it possible that—?"

He left the sentence unfinished merely for artistic effect; he knew well enough that indeed he dared to hope, and that it was almost certainly possible that she could love him.

The look she turned upon him was so radiant that for a fleeting moment she almost appeared beautiful. He put out his arm to encircle her waist, but before he could do so, she stepped aside.

"Wait. Please!" Her voice trembled a little. "Do you—can you tell me truly—do you—love me?"

He could tell her anything that was necessary to his purpose, and proceeded to do so with all the eloquence at his command. It was enough. She wished to be convinced, so she allowed herself to believe him.

After so many months of doubt and longing, she was betrothed at last to the only man she had ever loved. That night, she sat down to write a long and slightly incoherent letter to her friend Amanda Paxton.

About a month after his betrothal to Maria, Neville reluctantly made another journey to Rye. He would have preferred to take Mrs. Lathom at her word and never set foot in her home again; but feelings of guilt, combined with fears of what the outcome might be if he neglected to provide her with funds, urged him to return there. He told himself again and again that he had nothing to fear. He had kept the woman in ignorance both of his title and of where he lived. She would not know how to find him, even if she had now changed her mind since the first bitterness of her loss in which she had dismissed him for ever. Still, it was as well to take every precaution; and should he find, as he expected, that the child had since died, then the journey would be amply justified. He would be able finally to put aside all remembrances of that ill-considered marriage and to know for certain that it could forever remain a secret.

He arrived in Rye towards midday and wasted some time in pacing its quiet cobbled streets before he could nerve himself to approach Mrs. Lathom's cottage. As soon as he arrived before it, he knew that no one was within. The shutters were up before all the windows, the front step was dirty instead of being freshly scrubbed, and the whole place wore a neglected air.

In spite of this, he rapped loudly on the door, repeating the knocks several times at intervals when he failed to get any answer. As he at last paused and drew back to survey the outside of the house for a second time, he detected a movement in the window of the adjoining cottage. A woman's head appeared briefly from behind the shelter of a curtain, before being withdrawn.

He paused, debating with himself whether it would be wise to pursue enquiries next door. To his knowledge, Mrs. Lathom had never had anything to do with her neighbours. She had told him that curiosity was not welcomed in the town, but it seemed unlikely that comings and goings could entirely escape neighbourly observation. He decided that there would be little risk

81

to himself to put a few questions concerning Mrs. Lathom's present whereabouts, so accordingly he knocked on the door of the adjoining cottage.

There was evidently some reluctance to answer, although he saw the curtain move again. After he had knocked a second time, he heard a bolt being drawn back and the door opened a few inches to reveal a wrinkled, leathery face surmounted by a mobcap. Its owner viewed him suspiciously without speaking.

"I beg your pardon for disturbing you," he said, with his most disarming smile. "I called next door to see Mrs. Lathom, the lady who lives there, but the house seems to be shut up. I wonder, do you have any notion where I may find her?"

The woman shook her head vigorously and was about to shut the door, but Neville deftly interposed a foot.

"Forgive me, but my business is pressing and I know of no one else whom I could ask. Can you not help me?"

"Folk mind their own business in these parts, young man," replied the woman, in a grating tone that set his teeth on edge. "Pays best. Be off with ye."

"Oh, but—" He was about to explain his relationship to Mrs. Lathom, but thought better of it. "I mean her no harm," he finished, lamely.

"That's as may be. If she'd wanted ye to know where she's gone, reckon she'd have told ye. Shift yer foot."

Neville produced a guinea from his pocket. Her eyes gleamed at the sight of it, and she hesitated just as she had been about to force the door shut.

"Don't know where she's gone, so it's no use for ye to ask. She left about a month back, that's all I know."

He placed the coin in her hand, which closed over it almost before it had left his own.

"Are you quite sure you cannot say where she went? It's a matter of importance."

"Told ye, didn't I? She left in a carriage one morning, and that's the last I see of 'er."

"And did she—can you say if she had a baby with her when she left?"

"Ay, and a trunk and some parcels. Ye're askin' a mort o' questions, young man, an' that's all I can answer. So shift yer foot, afore I do it a mischief."

Neville hastily removed his foot and began to thank her; but his speech was cut short by the door slamming in his face, and a moment later he heard the bolt rammed home.

He turned away, feeling depressed. That Mrs. Lathom should have vanished without trace was of small account to him; in fact, it made matters simpler. It showed that she really did mean to sever the connection between them. He was not so satisfied to learn, however, that the child had been with her. This might only mean trouble in store.

As he returned to the inn to take a post chaise for his homeward journey, however, he found his usual sanguine outlook returning. Mrs. Lathom had assured him that the infant had only the most slender chance of survival; since she had left Rye with it a month since, the odds were that by now it had already expired. He need trouble himself no longer. Everything was at last working out for the best, he thought, even though it had been a devilish close thing.

Chapter VIII

MARIA'S LETTER telling of her betrothal was read by her friend Amanda Paxton with a decided feeling of relief. She would have liked to think that this was entirely for Maria, but she was too honest not to acknowledge that a part of it was on her own account, too. She had felt uneasy ever since Maria had confided her suspicion that Mr. and Mrs. Reddiford were attempting to promote a match between the Reverend Theodore Somerby and their granddaughter. Why this should have made her uneasy was a matter which she shied away from analysing, but she was glad to be free of the feeling. She sat down at once to write an enthusiastic, congratulatory reply. Too impatient to leave her letter to be taken to the post office by the footman at his regular time for dealing with the mail, she determined to walk down with it herself. The post office was only a mile away, just a pleasant distance for a stroll on such a bright morning, she thought, as she hurriedly donned a cloak; for in spite of the sun, there was a chilly wind.

She had reckoned without the treachery of April weather, however, for on her return journey black clouds rolled over the sun. Presently it began to rain, slowly at first, then with increasing violence. She pulled the hood of her cloak over her chip hat, an engaging creation tied with lilac ribbons, and looked about her for shelter. She knew there was little hope of finding any; for she had left the last of the houses behind, and there would be no other building until she reached Hewletts' farm in about another quarter of a mile. She reflected ruefully that by then she would be wet through, anyway, and might as well complete the journey home. Seeing nothing that would serve to protect her from the elements, she shrugged philosophically and went on her way.

She had covered another hundred yards or so in extreme discomfort when she heard the sound of a vehicle approaching from the rear. Turning hopefully towards it, she saw that it was a gig, and the driver was the curate, Mr. Somerby. Thankful that here was someone she knew who could offer her a lift, she raised an arm in greeting, an appeal to which he instantly responded.

Unfortunately, her sudden movement swept the hood back from her head. A gust of wind caught her bonnet, which flew into the air before landing on the ground several yards from where she stood and then went bowling merrily along the puddle-strewn road.

Impetuously, she darted after it, uttering aloud several highly unladylike phrases borrowed from her brothers' sporting vocabulary.

Meanwhile, the curate had reined in his docile old mare and leapt down to join in the chase. Easily outpacing her, he retrieved the bonnet with a lucky swoop and held it towards her.

She surveyed it with repulsion. It was now a sorry sight, limp and dripping, its pretty lilac ribbons covered in slimy mud.

He shook his head sorrowfully. "I fear this will never be the same again, Miss Paxton. But pray let me help you up into the gig, where at least you'll have the shelter of the hood."

He suited the action to the word, assisting her with one hand while retaining his hold on her ruined bonnet with the other.

"Whoa, Brownie," he commanded, as the ancient mare in the gig's shafts moved forward at a sluggish pace. "If you'd be good enough to take the reins, ma'am? Now, the question is, what shall we do with your bonnet?"

"I don't think anyone can do anything with that frightful object!" declared Amanda in disgust. "It's spoilt beyond recovery."

"In that case, shall we inter it decently in the ditch?" he suggested, smiling.

He continued to smile after he had abandoned the bonnet and climbed back into the vehicle to start the mare on its way again.

"I daresay," remarked Amanda, somewhat resentfully, "that you are laughing at me, sir."

He made an effort to assume a more serious expression. "Not at you, ma'am, assure you. I could not be so heartless. But the circumstances, you know . . ."

"Don't think I blame you," she interrupted, quickly. "I must have looked so droll, chasing along after that wretched bonnet!"

Overcome by the thought of the absurd picture she

must have presented, she went off into peals of laughter. He looked at her doubtfully for a moment, then joined in, and for several moments they gave way to uninhibited mirth.

They were recalled to a more sober frame of mind when they were passed by a coach coming in the other direction. Two pairs of eyes glued to the window showed that its occupants were missing nothing of the unconventional scene presented to them.

"Oh, dear," said Amanda, weakly, attempting to wipe her eyes with an already wet handkerchief, "I think that was Mrs. Baydon and her daughter, and they are sure to mention to Mama that I was conducting myself in an unseemly fashion!"

"Let us hope they'll be more charitable," he replied, equably. "But I feel sure that once I've explained the circumstances to Lady Paxton, she will quite understand."

"I don't think you can be very well acquainted with Mama, sir, or you wouldn't be so optimistic!"

"No?" He smiled at her again; and she thought, not for the first time, what an engaging smile he had. "Well, I must hope to improve our acquaintance in time. But tell me, Miss Paxton, do you usually choose to walk abroad in such weather?"

"No, even I am not so stupid! But when I set out, the sun was shining brilliantly, and you must know I'm an incurable optimist. I wanted to post a letter, and could not wait for one of our footmen to take it."

"I see." He said nothing for a moment, speculating a little about a letter that was so important that its writer could not wait to send it away.

Amanda was following her own train of thought.

"I trust," she remarked presently, with a slight blush, "that you didn't overhear my comments when that odious bonnet blew away! I daresay you may know that I have two brothers, and I fear I've a regrettable tendency to make use of some of their expressions whenever I become excited over anything. Mama is always reproving me for it, but it's difficult

86

to break all at once with the bad habits of one's childhood, don't you think?"

"You'll probably be surprised to learn, Miss Paxton," he replied, with a twinkle in his eye, "that there are times when I am afflicted with a purely temporary deafness. Before you commiserate with me, allow me to point out that this disability has frequently been the means of saving an otherwise awkward situation."

She laughed heartily. "Oh, Charlie and Freddy would say you were a right one, sir! How very much obliged to you I am!"

He gave a slight bow. "Yours to command, ma'am. I collect your brothers are undergraduates at Oxford? It is my own University"—as she nodded—"a fortunate coincidence."

"Well," said Amanda, with sisterly candour, "I don't know how fortunate those in authority may find it to have Charlie and Freddy there! They're not precisely scholarly, you know, and are rather given to what they term kicking up larks!"

He shook his head with a mournful expression that was belied by the irrepressible twinkle in his eye. "Dear me—most regrettable. And so unusual, of course, in young men of that age."

Once again, her laughter bubbled over. "Oh, you are the—the most complete hand, sir!"

Sir Robert Paxton's butler was not only a well trained man, but he had also survived service for many years in a household that sheltered three such ebullient young people as Miss Amanda, Master Charles and Master Frederick. He therefore allowed no flicker of surprise to disturb his countenance when Miss Amanda presented herself on the doorstep looking—as he afterwards confided to the housekeeper—as like a drowned rat as anything else he had ever set eyes upon. Lady Paxton was not so stoical, however. She emitted a faint shriek when her daughter entered the parlour with Mr. Somerby in attendance.

"Gracious goodness! Amanda! What in the world have you been doing now?"

"Mr. Somerby will explain, Mama, but as you see I

87

must go up and change," replied Amanda, as she beat a hasty retreat, leaving a wet patch on the carpet from her dripping garments.

The curate did explain in a calm, matter-of-fact way which reassured Lady Paxton that her daughter had not, after all, narrowly escaped a watery grave, which had been the first explanation to occur to her.

"She is such an impetuous child," she complained. "As though her letter could not have waited! But I am most grateful to you, Mr. Somerby, for bringing her home. Dear me, now I come to notice it, you are very wet yourself. Pray let the footman take your overcoat to dry, while I procure some refreshment for you."

The curate protested that there was no need for her to take so much trouble; but Lady Paxton insisted, and after handing over the overcoat to one of the servants, conducted her visitor to the bookroom where Sir Robert Paxton was sitting. The Reverend Theodore Somerby was already becoming a firm favourite with Amanda's father; so the two gentlemen passed an agreeable hour together, at the end of which the curate was invited to partake of a cold collation with the family. Amanda presented herself at table looking fresh and appealing in a primrose gown of Indian calico draped at the neck with a white gauze neckerchief, and with her chestnut curls restored to more seemly order.

"But if only you could have seen yourself when you walked in earlier!" her mother said later, in tones of strong reproof. "Your hair wet and bedraggled, blown about all over your face, and as for your clothes and shoes . . . Well, words fail me! You looked for all the world like some wild gypsy girl! What Mr. Somerby must have thought of you, I can't imagine!"

But Amanda had seen herself in the mirror in her bedroom after she had rushed upstairs, and it had occurred to her then to echo her mother's doubts. To be sure, he had been very pleasant, but *what* had he thought of her?

She was not the only young lady in the neighbourhood to be asking herself this question at that particular time. The comparatively new arrival in their midst was an eligible bachelor with good looks, a pleasing address and, it was understood, creditable connections. Of course, he was no great matrimonial catch—his private income was believed to be comfortable but not large, and he was only one of the minor clergy. But in a neighbourhood where unmarried baronets or peers were remarkably scarce, he was a sufficiently interesting prospect for several Mamas to eye him thoughtfully and include him in their invitations; while, as for their daughters, they were quite ready to follow their parents' lead. Mrs. Baydon, therefore, found receptive ears for her little piece of gossip about seeing Amanda Paxton and Mr. Somerby sharing a gig and seemingly delighted with each other's company.

It earned Amanda several unfriendly looks when she attended an Assembly ball in the local town several days later. She had been escorted there unwillingly by her brother Charles, at present on vacation from Oxford. He was a year older than herself and a young man with a preference for sporting pursuits rather than the more genteel social occasions. His mother had insisted, however, as at the last moment she was unable to chaperone Amanda herself because of a severe headache.

"Well, I'll go," agreed Charles, grudgingly, "since there's no help for it. But I ain't going to foot it round the ballroom with you, Mandy, so don't look for it. Dance with my own sister, indeed! That would be too much of a good thing altogether."

"I'm relieved to hear you say so," replied Amanda, loftily, "since I shall be wearing a gown for which I have a particular regard, and to dance with you, one needs a suit of armour. Believe me, you have only to place me in the charge of Mrs. Veryan, who has kindly agreed to act as chaperone in Mama's stead—"

"Oh, for God's sake, Mandy, stop talking in that missish way. It don't sound natural from you! But tell me"—he seemed struck by a new thought—"will your friend Sue Veryan be there, then?"

"Of course. You don't suppose her Mama would go otherwise, do you, clodpole? And Berenice and Georgie and even Lottie, I think, although she is not quite seventeen yet."

Charles was understood to say that Miss Susan Veryan's sisters were not of the slightest interest to him, being a dull set of girls and one or two of them spotty, into the bargain.

"But if Sue's to be there, it mightn't be so slow, after all," he finished. "Tell you what—I might even stand up with her myself once or twice."

"I'm sure Sue will be vastly obliged to you," replied Amanda, "especially as you're such an accomplished performer, and she is likely to be short of partners."

He grinned. "You're a little cat, aren't you? But that's the devil of it—*she* won't be short of partners, if any girl is!"

The young lady in question was by way of being a local beauty. She was of Amanda's age, with an oval, impish face framed by dark brown curls and a figure that was the envy of her sisters, all of whom were built on more generous lines. She was one of the many girls in the neighbourhood whom Amanda had known since childhood; and, next to Maria Cottesford, Amanda liked Susan best. Although she would not have admitted this to her brother without a struggle, Amanda privately shared his views on the other Veryan girls; but she believed firmly that females should present a united stand against male criticism.

They arrived at the ball a little late, owing to Charles's insistence that the coachman should spring his horses. This resulted in an argument with a farmer who disliked having the side of his gig scraped by the Paxtons' coach, and who took the best part of half an hour to express his views.

Charles eventually settled the matter by telling the injured party to send the bill for the repair in to Sir Robert Paxton, and they were able to go on their way again.

"I wouldn't be in your shoes," said Amanda severely, "when Papa receives that bill."

"Lord, he'll not raise too much of a dust about it," replied her brother, airily. "Well, not for more than a few minutes, at any rate. Old Joseph's past it, really, you know, Mandy. Should have been able to take that bend without getting over on his wrong side. Now if I'd been driving—"

"We'd have done even more damage, or else ended up in the ditch," finished Amanda, unfairly, for her brother was a creditable whip. "It was all your fault for making him go so fast. He's a very steady coachman, and you should allow him to go at his own pace. I only hope Papa won't blame him too much."

"Lud, no, what d'you think I am? I shall tell Father I made him spring 'em, of course. Don't trouble your head over that."

Knowing quite well that this was true, and that he was not at all the kind to shift blame on to another's shoulders, she allowed the matter to rest.

In due course they presented themselves in the ballroom, to find that the dancing had already begun. Casting a quick but searching glance over the floor, Amanda discerned Mr. Somerby partnering Miss Merson, a tall, graceful young lady with dark hair and very soulful hazel eyes, of which she was at present making the maximum use. Forcing a negligent smile, Amanda went to sit by Mrs. Veryan and her elder daughter Berenice; seeing the latter unpartnered, Charles Paxton resourcefully removed himself to the other end of the room and fell into conversation with one or two of his acquaintances.

Towards the end of the dance, he sauntered back again and, contriving to detach his sister from the Veryan ladies, solicited her hand for the next one. She was surprised by this unlooked-for gallantry, but made it clear that she did not wish for the honour.

"What's more," she finished, "I'd like very much to know why you have changed your mind. You made it clear on our way here that the last thing you wanted was to dance with me!"

91

"Well, so it is," he answered, incurably frank. "But I thought it might be no bad thing to put in a bit of practice before I ask Sue Veryan. Not much in my line, dancing, as you well know."

"Thank you very much! I have no intention of allowing you to practise on me!" retorted his sister indignantly.

"Oh, come on, Mandy, be a sport! Tell you what, I'll let you tool my curricle tomorrow, if you do."

"You will?" She was clearly tempted by this offer. The curricle had been recently bestowed on Charles by his father and was his most jealously guarded possession. "Oh, well, in that case, I'll do my best to bear with you for just one dance. Will you let me take the curricle out on my own?"

"No, damme, that's asking too much! You're a pretty fair whip, or I wouldn't risk it at all, but it's no go unless I come out with you."

Amanda accepted this meekly enough, and they stood together waiting for the band to strike up again. At that moment the Reverend Theodore Somerby approached them and, having spoken the usual greetings to both, requested the pleasure of Miss Paxton's hand for the next dance.

Dismayed, Amanda tried to signal to Charles a postponement of their arrangement, but he seemed singularly obtuse. Meanwhile Mr. Somerby stood by, looking a trifle surprised at being obliged to wait for an answer.

"I'm—I'm so sorry," she stammered, at last. "I'm —I'm promised to my brother for this dance."

Mr. Somerby bowed. "Then may I perhaps hope that you will honour me by allowing me to partner you in the next?"

Amanda replied that she would be delighted; but there was a mixture of embarrassment and irritation in her manner which the gentleman sensed without being able to understand. He could not know that the irritation was for her brother, and withdrew wondering what he could possibly have done to give offence.

"Now see what you've done!" exclaimed Amanda,

peevishly. "He thinks I don't wish to dance with him!"

"What, is he one of your beaux?" asked Charles in a teasing tone. "How could I know that? It was Jack Merson during the long vac."

"Jack Merson," replied his sister, loftily, "is only a boy."

He laughed. "I see. Well, don't put yourself in a fidget. He'll scarcely take a huff because you're to partner your brother. Not as if it were some other man, what?"

He swept her into the set and for some time was occupied in watching his steps. Amanda, although a trifle upset still, grudgingly acknowledged to herself that he was performing quite creditably for one who professed to dislike the exercise. It was not until the dance was nearly ended that she had reason to revise this opinion. He allowed his attention to waver for one fatal second when Miss Susan Veryan drifted into view, with the result that he missed a step and trod upon his sister's toe.

She let out an involuntary ejaculation of pain, and he stepped back hastily, apologising. Unfortunately, he caught his foot in the hem of her gown, which was finished with a flounce. At the same time Amanda moved too, tearing part of the flounce from its stitching so that it dangled on the floor.

"You clumsy wretch!" she exclaimed in vexation. "I must go and do my best to pin up my gown now, I suppose, for it's impossible to continue with it like this! Oh, you are beyond anything stupid!"

She gathered up her skirts just as the final notes were being played and headed for the ladies' retiring room. Her speedy exit went unnoticed by the other dancers, who were too concerned with their own affairs to have noticed the mishap, while her brother dropped out with something of a hangdog air to seek consolation in the refreshment room.

Thus it was that when the orchestra began to tune up for the next dance and gentlemen were seeking out their partners, Mr. Somerby was unable to find Miss

Paxton. He approached Mrs. Veryan to enquire for her, but that lady was unable to enlighten him.

"You say she was promised to you for this dance? Well, I'm sure I've no notion where she may be. I believe I saw her dancing the last one with her brother, but she's not returned to me since. Quite likely the pair of them have gone off on one of their mad starts, for they are such droll creatures, those Paxtons, you must know! However, if you are lacking a partner, Mr. Somerby, perhaps you would care to lead out Berenice or Georgiana, for they are not promised to anyone else. Are you, my dears?"

Both Veryan girls confirmed this eagerly; and Mr. Somerby, finding himself in an awkward situation, was constrained to lead out Berenice, who was the elder and therefore had the prior claim. As he guided her into the set that was forming, he did his best to suppress what he judged to be a somewhat unworthy thought that she was a poor exchange for the young lady he had expected to partner. He speculated a little on Amanda's behaviour. When he had first asked her to dance, she had hesitated as though unwilling and then told him that she had promised the dance to her brother. He had thought at the time that an engagement to a brother was of all arrangements the easiest to revoke, and wondered if perhaps she was making an excuse. Her manner as she accepted his application for the honour of the next dance had also seemed reluctant. And now she had absented herself before she could redeem her promise. Did this mean that she wished to avoid his company?

He could think of no cause he might have given her to act in this way. When they had parted a few days ago, after he had taken her home in his gig, it had been on an extremely amicable note. What could possibly have occurred in the meantime to give her a dislike of him? He stifled a sigh as he bent his head to pay attention to Miss Veryan's conversation so that he might make suitable replies to the young lady. Females were strange creatures, after all; but he had thought Miss Paxton more direct in her dealings and less subject to attacks of temperament than most. Either he was mistaken in her, or else he had unwittingly given offence. All he could do now was to keep out of her way until she was disposed to forgive him for he knew not what.

When Amanda finally returned to the ballroom after a protracted tussle with her torn gown, she was extremely taken aback to discover that her partner had not had the grace to wait even a quarter hour for the pleasure of her company. She determined to teach him a lesson by refusing should he have the temerity to ask her to dance again. As the evening wore on and she realised that she was not to have the opportunity of making this gesture, since Mr. Somerby never once approached her, she became by turns depressed and annoyed. She found no shortage of other partners, since she was a popular girl and knew almost everyone in the ballroom; so she danced for the remainder of the evening with a great deal of verve and vivacity, particularly when Mr. Somerby happened to be close at hand.

The only benefit gained by the misunderstanding was that those young ladies who had greeted Miss Paxton coolly on her arrival became noticeably more cordial as the evening wore on and they observed that she had no intention of monopolising the curate. But as Amanda cared nothing for their opinion, it was an advantage which she did not feel.

Chapter IX

DURING THE NEXT FEW WEEKS, she saw the Reverend Theodore Somerby only at church, when nothing but a formal greeting between them was possible. She felt regretful that what had seemed to be such a promising friendship should have petered out in this unsatisfactory way, more particularly as she was at a loss to account for the sudden change in the gentlemen's demeanour towards her.

It was at this point that she received a further letter from Maria, asking if she would be willing to act as bridesmaid at the forthcoming nuptials in July.

And if you could only manage to come and stay with me for a few weeks at present, dearest Amanda, I think it would perhaps assist me in preserving my tottering sanity! I had no notion at all of the prodigious fuss attendant on a wedding! Mama surrounds me with a positive army of milliners, mantua makers, dressmakers, and the like; and I am daily required to inspect yards of material or make a choice from among so many fashion plates that I see them in my sleep. Only your calm good sense can preserve me from being carried off to Bedlam in a straitjacket—which I must own would be a most unbecoming garment for a wedding, besides setting all poor Mama's exertions at naught. So pray do come at once, if you are able, and help me to survive it all unscathed.

Amanda was very much amused by her friend's account of the wedding preparations, and knew Lady Cottesford well enough to realise that it was only a trifle exaggerated. But all the same she wondered at being asked to pay a visit at such a time. Surely lovers would prefer to spend their time together without the encumbrance of a visitor?

For her own part, she was glad enough to go at present, and wrote back to accept both invitations. This time she did not go out to post the letter herself, so there was no chance of again being taken up by Mr. Somerby in his gig.

She remained with Maria for the better part of a month, returning home early in June. While she was there, it surprised her to find how little time the betrothed couple spent entirely alone. They met chiefly in the company of others, so that Amanda had no occasion to feel in the way. She could not help reflecting that these arrangements would not have satisfied her own notions, had she been betrothed; but Maria seemed to find no fault with them, and, indeed, looked so radiant that it was obvious she was happy. As for Viscount Shaldon, he seemed well enough suited, too. Watching him closely at times, however, Amanda would feel a twinge of uneasiness. He was everything that was pleasant and courteous, and he omitted no attention to Maria; yet to Amanda's critical eye there was something lacking. Exactly what it was she found herself unable to decide until one day when she and Maria had been discussing Richard Brinsley Sheridan's brilliant play *The School for Scandal*. And then it came to her in a flash that here was the explanation she sought—Viscount Shaldon's behaviour to his betrothed was a performance, nothing more. She had failed to detect any sincerity in it. She hoped profoundly that she was mistaken, and took herself severely to task for being too harsh a critic of what might well be only company manners. Yet deep down, with an unreasoning presentiment that was often to visit her in later life on behalf of those she loved, she knew that all was not well.

Life at home was soon enlivened by the arrival on vacation of Charles and Frederick, bringing with them a constant stream of visitors, mostly young men of their own age and sporting tastes. Several of these cast a considering eye in Amanda's direction; but although she was quite ready to accompany them on the less hearty of their outings and indulge in light badinage from time to time, she firmly repulsed anything in the way of what she thought of as sentimental nonsense.

As they considered themselves—in their own terms —complete to a shade, they would have been considerably mortified had they realised that to the charming Miss Paxton they appeared little more than pleasant schoolboys. Like her own brothers, she found them still immature. Perhaps it might be because she could not help comparing all the young gentlemen of her acquaintance with one whom she seldom saw nowadays, but of whom she thought more often than she wished to do.

She was assisting her mother in making welfare visits in the village when next she encountered Mr. Somerby alone. Lady Paxton took a compassionate interest in all the sick and needy of the neighbourhood, paying personal calls and conveying comforts to them at regular intervals. In this work she was frequently helped by Amanda; and although the mother's sensible counsel was of great benefit to the sufferers, it was the daughter's cheerful informality which they particularly welcomed. Lady Paxton knew this quite well; so on this occasion she had deputed Amanda to call on Mrs. Joliffe, onetime kitchen maid at Oakley Park, who had recently given birth to her sixth child.

"With five children already, she will scarce require any advice from me on the rearing of this latest addition to the family," said Lady Paxton. "But a visit from you will cheer her up, child, and Cook has packed several nourishing foodstuffs in this basket for her."

Amanda took the basket and set off in the direction of Mrs. Joliffe's cottage while her mother went the opposite way to pay another call. She was admitted to the house by a slightly grubby urchin of six or seven years, who grinned at her engagingly before being hastily adjured by his mother to go and wash himself at the pump before daring to come again into the presence of their distinguished visitor.

"Such a trial they be, these lads, Miss Amanda. There's no keeping them clean for five minutes together! Now, Kitty," addressing a skinny child of about eight-years-old, who seemed to be the eldest, "look alive and place a chair for Miss Paxton. Yes, the best one, with the cushion; that's right. Pray be seated, Miss—ma'am, I should say, but I keep going back to the old days when I was at the Park and you was not much older than Kitty here."

Amanda duly seated herself, made her enquiries as to mother and child's health and delivered Lady Paxton's gifts, which were received with genuine delight and a few tears for the kindness. But before long she was down on the floor playing with the children, having carelessly cast aside her bonnet. Intent on the game, which was causing much childish laughter, she paid no heed to a knock on the door which this time was answered by Mrs. Joliffe in person. She looked up startled at hearing herself addressed a few moments later in masculine tones, and saw that Mr. Somerby had entered and was looking down at her with an amused smile on his face.

"Oh!" She scrambled to her feet, assisted by a hand from the curate. "Oh, how do you do, Mr. Somerby?"

The children began to clamour for more, but were silenced by their mother, who bade Kitty take them out into the back yard for a few moments. She then offered her visitors a dish of tea, but they refused courteously, knowing how scarce such a commodity was in that house.

"I looked in to speak to you about the christening, Mrs. Joliffe," continued the curate. "Perhaps we can settle upon a time and date at present? But if that is inconvenient in any way, I can easily call again tomorrow. I have no wish to intrude upon Miss Paxton's visit."

"Oh, but I was about to go in any case," said Amanda, hurriedly, "as Mama may be already waiting for me in the carriage."

"I think perhaps Mrs. Joliffe and I can conclude our business in a very few moments?" He looked towards the woman as he spoke and she nodded. "That being so, perhaps you will allow me to escort you back to your carriage, Miss Paxton?"

Amanda inclined her head and waited while he made arrangements for the baptism of the latest member of the Joliffe family. It was over in as short a time as he had promised; and after he had emptied his pockets of some sweetmeats for the children, they both took their leave.

Once outside, he offered her his arm. She hesitated a second, looking shyly up at him in an unaccustomed way before laying her gloved hand upon it.

At first they spoke of the weather, of Amanda's recent visit to Maria Cottesford's home in Buckinghamshire and of the forthcoming wedding there.

"To which, somewhat to my surprise, I have been bidden," he said.

"No doubt that's because you are so particular a friend of Maria's grandparents, Mr. and Mrs. Reddiford," she replied. "I am to be a bridesmaid. I do hope I may sustain the part with credit and not do anything too frightful, as I fear I'm only too prone to do!"

His eyes twinkled down into hers. "Are you thinking of what I'm thinking?"

She laughed, feeling suddenly at ease with him again. "Oh, the way I chased my bonnet in the rain that day!" She put up her hands to the creation she was wearing at present. "You know, I have the strongest doubts that this one is not set properly upon my head. Poor Mrs. Joliffe has no mirror in her room, and I was obliged to manage without."

"Well, since you mention it, I must admit that it *is* a trifle askew, ma'am—but nothing to signify, assure you."

She withdrew her arm from his and tried to remedy the defect. "Oh, dear," she said, ruefully. "I don't

100

care a jot, myself, but Mama is always complaining that I pay no heed to my appearance."

"Permit me to assist you, Miss Paxton. The nice adjustment of ladies' headgear was unfortunately omitted from my education, but I think I may claim that I've a tolerably straight eye."

"Oh, if you will, please!"

She turned towards him without the slightest affectation or coquetry and stood patiently waiting for him to adjust the bonnet. A muscle moved in his cheek as his hands untied the ribbons, set the bonnet at the correct angle, and fastened the ribbons again; otherwise he gave no sign of the considerable upheaval which was taking place beneath that calm exterior.

"There, I think that will pass muster," he said, stepping a cautious pace away from her.

She thanked him in a rush of embarrassment, for the experience, slight though it was, had not left her unmoved.

They walked on in silence for a little while, then he turned towards her in an impulsive way that was not characteristic of him.

"Dare I hope I'm forgiven now, Miss Paxton, for whatever unwitting offence I committed on the night of the Assembly ball last month?"

She started, for she, too, had been thinking of that night.

"I did think you might have waited before leading out someone else!" she exclaimed, in her usual direct manner. "My odious brother had stepped on my gown and torn it during the preceding dance, so I was obliged to go and pin it up—and there you were, when I returned to the ballroom, dancing with Berenice!"

His face lengthened. "Oh, dear, so that was it! But, you know, I thought you were reluctant to dance with me at all. Your manner when I first applied for the honour—you hesitated over accepting—"

"Because," broke in Amanda, "I was trying to make that stupid boy Charlie understand that I wished to be let off from dancing with him, that's all, but he wouldn't take my hint, because he was set on having a practice dance with me before taking out Sue Veryan—and you see what came of it!"

Mr. Somerby did see, and he looked at her in such a very meaning way that Amanda held her breath. But before he could make any further explanations, Lady Paxton's carriage drew up beside them and they were obliged to terminate the conversation at what each felt to be its most interesting point.

Unfortunately, opportunities for resuming it did not present themselves for some time. The two met at frequent intervals in church or at evening parties attended —so it seemed to both—by the whole neighbourhood, so that there was no chance at all of being private. And although Theodore Somerby often at this time paid calls at Oakley Park, he was such a welcome visitor to Sir Robert that the squire gladly monopolised his company without once realising that perhaps the young clergyman came there for some other reason than to enjoy a comfortable masculine chat.

It was gradually borne in upon Mr. Somerby that desperate measures might be needed before he could gain the private interview with Miss Paxton that he so much desired. Although he was a gentle person, much given to reflection, he could act resolutely when the occasion required it; but one thought gave him pause. Had he mistaken her? When he came to review all their dealings together, he could not positively state that she had ever given him reason to suppose that she felt anything warmer for him than friendship. She was such an artless girl, so apt to say the first thing that came into her head, that a man might well draw false conclusions.

Thus his natural diffidence held him back from contriving a private meeting, and the weeks went by until he could bear the waiting no longer. So it was that when next he presented himself at Oakley Park, he was less calm than his outward appearance suggested. He had come with the fixed intention of seeing the master of the house, and inwardly he had misgivings. He knew that he could not be considered a brilliant match

102

for the squire's daughter. He was certainly of good birth and education, and in possession of a moderately comfortable private income; but he had neither title nor lands to his name and was at present an obscure clergyman with a meagre stipend. It would not be surprising if Sir Robert wished to look higher for a son-in-law.

Once closeted with Sir Robert in the bookroom, he lost no time in making his position clear to the squire. Sir Robert stared in amazement, pushing up his spectacles on to his forehead in a way he had when he was taken aback.

"God bless my soul! Amanda—little Mandy! And does she return your sentiments, Somerby? What does she say—eh?"

The curate lost colour a little. Sir Robert's amazement did not seem to promise well for his cause.

"I have not taken the liberty of addressing myself to Miss Paxton without first obtaining your permission, sir."

"Very proper—quite right." Sir Robert nodded. "Only sometimes, you know, impulse outruns discretion in such cases. But you've acted just as you ought, my dear fellow, and it's what I'd have expected of you. Well, now, and has the dear girl not given you just a hint? For she's one to rush in where angels fear to tread, our little Mandy, and for all the notions of propriety her Mama has tried her best to instil, I wouldn't be at all surprised to learn that she'd done the wooing herself, dashed if I wouldn't!"

He laughed, and all at once Theodore Somerby felt more relaxed.

"What am I to answer to that, sir?" he asked with a smile. "To say that your daughter has given me any positive encouragement is to pronounce myself nothing better than a coxcomb. To seek her hand in marriage without being persuaded that she will not be totally averse to hearing me must be the action of a fool."

"Answered like a true academic!" chuckled the older man. "Well, Somerby, you'd best settle the matter with my daughter, for she's the prime judge in this affair."

"And I can take it, then, that you would have no objection, Sir Robert?"

"Not the least in the world, my dear fellow. If Amanda has had the good sense to fix her affections on you, I shall be prodigiously glad of it, for she might have chosen a much stupider man whose conversation would have been a penance instead of a pleasure. Off you go, then, for I'm sure you'd be wishing me at the devil were it not for your cloth."

It was a fine, warm day and Amanda was in the garden cutting some roses. A trug lay at her feet half-filled with blooms of velvety red and yellow shading to amber. Their fragrance wafted up to him as he halted beside her, a scent that was often to come back in memory across the years which still lay before them.

She started as he came up to her, pricking her finger on a thorn.

"Oh!" She looked ruefully at the spot of blood appearing, but only because she did not choose to look directly at him. "You startled me."

"I am sorry. May I look?"

He took her hand, inspecting the tiny prick for a moment before dabbing it with a clean handkerchief which he drew from his pocket.

"It's nothing," said Amanda, smiling as she attempted to draw her hand away.

He retained his hold upon it, and she looked half-shyly, half-expectantly into his eyes.

"I wish to keep this hand, Miss Amanda. Will you not give me leave? I think you must know already how deeply I admire and respect you, but now I have your father's permission to tell you openly of my feelings. I cannot know what your own may be, whether you can at all reciprocate my love. I can only hope that you are not totally indifferent to me, that you will not reject one whose whole happiness is bound up in you—"

"Oh, no, indeed I won't!" exclaimed Amanda,

breathlessly. "That's to say, dear, dear Mr. Somerby, indeed I do love you most sincerely—and, oh, I thought you were never going to speak! I was quite at my wits' end!"

She paused to look at him meltingly with her soft hazel eyes, wondering if he would think it quite proper to embrace her, which was at that moment the thing she most desired in the world. But a clergyman in love is very much as other men are; and Amanda, finding herself suddenly crushed in strong arms and kissed most delightfully, was profoundly glad of this.

Chapter X

MARIA COTTESFORD and Viscount Shaldon were married in July, on a sultry day with storm clouds threatening on the horizon. As they stood before the altar, the first peal of thunder sounded, followed by a flash that gave an eerie light to the interior of the church. Amanda Paxton, who was one of the bridesmaids and looked charming in a gown of soft pink lawn with a white frilled neckerchief, started so violently that she dropped the bride's bouquet, which had been handed to her at the start of the ceremony. It was retrieved for her quickly and without ostentation by the Reverend Theodore Somerby, who was seated close at hand.

The bride remained calm throughout the ceremony, although the storm rumbled overhead, at times almost drowning the words. She looked a trifle pale in her ivory satin gown, but perhaps that was the fault of the colour, which did not become her. The rain beat mer-

105

cilessly down upon the congregation as they left the church and hastened to their carriages.

"Happy the bride that the sun shines on!" commented one dowager, acidly, as she thrust her daughter before her into their waiting coach. She had permitted herself at one time to have some hopes of the Viscount for her daughter, and therefore felt entitled to a small show of malice. "And if there's anything in the old saying, my dear, she'll have little enough cause to rejoice, even though she is a Viscountess."

It did not occur to Maria that she had little cause to rejoice until some months after her marriage. At first, the expression of her own deep love concealed from her the lack of any but a mere physical response on her husband's side. They were together, and that sufficed to make her happy. If he showed no particular urge to stay in her company but frequently passed his days and evenings apart from her, she told herself with her characteristic tolerant common sense that it would be a great mistake for husband and wife to live in each other's pockets. It was natural that a man should prefer sometimes to have the company of others of his own sex, rather than to devote all his time to riding, walking, or sitting at home with his wife. So that he might have no feelings of guilt in leaving her alone so often, she cheerfully resumed her old interests and friendships, reflecting how fortunate she was that marriage had not removed her to any great distance from her parental home.

She did feel, however, that it was a pity they were obliged to live at Alvington Hall. She would have preferred a home of their own, away from the Earl's domination. Now that she was within the sphere of his influence, she realised how much Neville was under his thumb; and she sometimes wondered a little uneasily how long she could keep a still tongue in her head, or whether there might not come a crisis when she herself would find it necessary to have a confrontation with the Earl. She hoped sincerely that by the exercise of tact and diplomacy she could avoid this;

but she was not the young woman to allow herself to be intimidated when any issue of real importance was at stake. Meanwhile, Alvington Hall was sufficiently large for the married couple to have their own set of apartments, so at least they were not obliged to be always in company with the Earl and Countess.

The first doubt which Maria felt about her marriage came when, in October, she had news to impart to her husband which she was sure must give him joy. They had dined with the rest of the family that evening and afterwards retired to their own private withdrawing room, which had been decorated in the bride's taste with a grey-blue damask paper and hangings of rose coloured silk. Neville sprawled in an upholstered satinwood armchair with a copy of the *Gentleman's Magazine* while Maria seated herself before her embroidery frame. After a while, she looked across at him.

"My love," she said, quietly. "I've something to tell you, if you should not be too engrossed in your magazine just at present."

He raised his head and tossed the book aside.

"No, devilish dull, if you must know. What is it you want to say?"

His tone was not inviting, but Maria pushed her work aside and moved over to a chair close beside him.

"Perhaps you can guess," she continued, smiling softly at him.

"No, damme, Maria, don't set me to guessing games after dinner! If you've something to say, then for God's sake say it, and have done!"

This was worse; for a moment she considered delaying the communication until he should be in a more receptive mood. But she was so excited by her news and understandably eager to share it with the one other person most concerned, that she decided to persevere.

"Oh, you *are* a bear," she said, with a rueful twinkle in her eye, "but I fancy you will be as delighted as I am myself when you know."

"Which is likely to be never, at this rate," he returned in a surly fashion, evidently not catching her drift.

"Oh, dearest! But perhaps I have teased you enough, only I felt sure you would guess. We are to have a child, Neville. I waited to tell you until I was quite sure. There! Is not that wonderful news?"

He sat up straight in his chair. "A child?"

She laughed softly. "Well, don't look so amazed. It does happen, you know."

He made no reply for a moment, but started to pace up and down the room, while she watched him in surprise.

"A child," he repeated, at last. "Well, so long as it's a boy, I'm sure my father will be pleased. In fact, he's been asking lately if there were any signs."

"Never mind your father!" Her voice trembled between indignation and distress. Are *you* not pleased?"

He paused in his pacing and gave her a long scrutiny. There was no warmth in his eyes.

"To be sure—oh, certainly. I will go and tell my father at once."

And before she could say any more, he had gone from the room.

For several minutes she sat quite still, staring into space. Presently, she felt a salt taste on her lips and realised that the tears had been trickling unheeded down her face. He had shown no delight, no involvement even, in her news; worse still, he had uttered no word of tenderness.

From that moment, she began to realise that she had failed in her attempt to make her husband love her as she loved him. Just for a while, the future seemed bleak indeed, and her wonderful news of no account. But she was a courageous young woman, and too proud to show how deep the hurt went. There was a child within her; boy or girl, it mattered not to her, for was it not his—and hers? A child to think about and plan for eagerly during all the long months of waiting, a child who might perhaps for a few short years return some of that affection which its father had rejected.

The Earl certainly was pleased at the news. He increased his son's allowance yet again—it had been augmented on the marriage—gave orders for the nursery to be refurbished and put in readiness, and presented Maria with a heavy old-fashioned necklace set with diamonds and rubies, which she disliked, though she thanked him politely.

"Belonged to m'mother," he said, "but the Countess never wears it, and you may as well have it now as wait for it when she's gone. But mind, m'dear, it must be a boy. Set your thoughts hard on that, and you'll bring it off, right enough. An heir for Alvington, eh? Well, that son of mine may be more of a man than I supposed, after all!"

The Countess said little; but occasionally when Neville was absent and Maria had no other company, she would go and sit with her daughter-in-law for a while. Hers was not an intrusive presence; she liked to listen while Maria played on the new pianoforte which had been a wedding present from her grandparents, or to sit quietly working on her own embroidery while Maria, too, plied her needle. Only once did she pass any opinion of her own on the forthcoming event.

It was when Maria said, half-serious, half-laughing, "They've quite made up their minds, ma'am, that it will be a boy! It never seems to occur to either of them that it may just as easily be a girl."

"Well," replied the Countess, slowly, "I daresay you wish for a boy, so that you may please my husband and your own. But you know, my dear, there's more comfort to be had from a girl—boys are so soon lost to you." A look of alarm crossed her face. "But there! I should not say so, and I beg you won't repeat it to Neville—nor, indeed, to anyone. Pray, pray do not, my dear!"

Maria reassured the shrinking woman, reflecting how sad it was that she should go in such terror of her husband that she dared not even pass an innocuous comment such as this.

"Of course I will not, if you don't wish it," she said gently.

Then, thinking to change the subject so that Lady Alvington might not dwell on her indiscretion, she began to talk about Edward Lydney's recent marriage to a Miss Sophia Barham, a young lady of fortune who lived near Brighton.

"Such a pity that they are to take up residence in London," she remarked. "That is, a pity from my husband's point of view, as Mr. Lydney is his closest friend. But I daresay they will contrive to meet fairly frequently, after all."

The loss to Neville was greater than Maria realised. Edward Lydney had been his only confidant, and now there was no one to whom he felt able to speak freely. His wife, the natural successor to this role, was debarred from it both by the nature of the secret which he must guard and from his own indifference to her.

Had his character been different, he might have learned in time to return her love, and then they could have shared all the secrets of the past and met the future together. As it was, though outwardly united they went their separate ways and could glean no comfort from each other.

The months passed, and on a bright day in May their child was born. It had been a long and difficult labour for Maria, and the Nurse carried the lustily yelling infant from the room almost before its mother had time to see it. The Earl, waiting impatiently with his own family and Maria's parents, stepped forward eagerly as the swathed bundle was borne into the room.

"A boy?" he demanded. "Is it a boy?"

The Nurse proudly displayed her burden, still loudly complaining at its eruption into a cold, unfeeling world

"Yes, m'lord, a boy, and a healthy one."

"B'God, we'll wet its head, Cottesford, what d'you say? Neville m'boy, you've brought it off. Congratulations!"

110

The ladies gathered round the infant, admiring and tracing likenesses in its tiny features, after the manner of grandmothers. Just then, Maria's personal maid burst into the room.

"My mistress wants the child," she announced.

"Not now," the Nurse answered, firmly. "She must rest. Did not the doctor say so?"

"She won't rest until she has it in her arms," persisted Jenny, firmly. "Give it to me, if you please."

"Best humour her," said the Earl, tolerantly. "Hand the infant over, Nurse, and for God's sake have a care with it."

This earned him a dark look, but Nurse could do no other than obey, and Jenny took the precious bundle from her, carrying it back to the bedchamber.

Maria extended her arms to receive her baby, and gazed down in wonder at the tiny, perfect features at present distorted with yelling.

"There, my darling, there," she soothed. "Should he be red like this, Jenny? Is there anything amiss with him?"

"Bless you, Miss Maria—milady. I should say— they're all red when they're born. And the doctor says he's as stout in health as can be. He's a fine boy, and you've no cause to fret. Now give him to me like a good girl, and get some sleep."

But Maria shook her head. "Not yet, Jenny-penny. Only let me hold him for a while."

As she bent over the infant, he fought one tiny arm clear of its coverings and seized one of his mother's fingers in a surprisingly firm grip. A wave of tenderness swept over her, bringing a throbbing to her breasts. Instinctively she gathered the child close. His wailing ceased abruptly as his mouth found the sustenance and comfort he had been seeking.

"My son," she murmured. Tears of joy blurred her vision. "My own sweet child!"

Maria was to experience now the testing period which she had always foreseen must come about if she and her husband continued to live at Alvington Hall.

The Earl had quite made up his mind that the future heir of Alvington was his exclusive property, and that he would determine the child's upbringing without reference to the parents. Maria was equally determined that she would not allow this to happen.

The first clash came early

"What shall we call our baby?" Maria asked Neville a few days after the birth, when he had looked in to see her. "He must have a name to answer to, bless him, even though he won't be answering us intelligibly for a while as yet! Do you know, I think I would favour the name Anthony. It's Papa's second name, and I've always liked it. But not if you have another preference, of course."

Neville shrugged. "As to myself, I've no objection, but my father's already decided what the child's to be called."

"Indeed?" Maria infused both surprise and indignation into her tone. "And may I ask what the Earl's choice happens to be?"

"Now don't bristle up, Maria, for you know it can do no good! He thought Pelham should be the first name—after himself, you know—and then Neville for myself, and after that Charles, as it's been a family name for generations. I suppose he would have no objection to your tacking on any other names you fancy, though he didn't actually mention that."

"I see. And didn't you point out to my lord that we might reasonably expect to have a say in the matter?" asked Maria, coldly.

"Oh, Lord, Maria, don't put yourself into a taking! You know as well as I do that it never pays to argue with my father. Besides, what does it matter if the child goes by one name or another? We shall soon accustom ourselves to it, whatever it may be, and never think of him under any other. Now pray don't make a stir, but let him settle it as he pleases. It's the only way to keep the peace."

"I do *not* like Pelham, and I *do* like Anthony! And as I bore the child, I think I have some rights in the naming of him." Her tone had been aggressive, but

112

she softened suddenly, stretching an imploring hand towards him. "Oh, my dear, is it always to be like this? Will you never face up to your father in anything? We cannot—*must* not—allow him to manage the whole of our lives in this way!"

"That is a gross female exaggeration," retorted Neville. "In what way is he seeking to manage the whole of our lives, as you put it? We live pretty much as we please, in my opinion."

"But we do not, my love," she said, still gently. "Would you not prefer to go away from Alvington, and have a home of our own somewhere?"

He considered this for a moment. "Well, I might perhaps care to have a house in Town, later on. But at present I think Alvington suits me well enough, and I can always pay a visit to London from time to time."

She noticed sadly that he did not speak of her accompanying him on these visits, but she made no comment on that.

"I was not thinking of London. I meant somewhere in the country, suitable for our child—perhaps Oxfordshire or one of the adjacent counties."

"That would be scarce worth the trouble and expense of setting up a separate establishment. Since I am to inherit Alvington, we may as well make our home here. I have a fondness for the place, and, besides, it pleases my father for us to remain."

"That is precisely what I mean. Everything is to be ordered to please your father!" Her indignation rose again. "Well, you may tell him that I will not please him in the matter of our son's name—I insist on Anthony!"

"I tell you what it is, Maria," he replied, his colour rising. "You will become a nagging wife, if you don't take care! It's your duty to obey me, and I must ask you to remember that."

"Obey you, yes, but I've taken no vow to obey your father."

"It comes to the same thing, since I desire to comply with his wishes in this regard."

"And what of mine? Do they count for nothing with you?"

She did not mean to provoke him, but she was still a trifle weak, and the tears came in spite of her efforts to keep them back.

"Oh, for God's sake!" He had a natural masculine dread of a woman's tears. "Very well, then, I'll do what I can. But I'm not prepared to have a scene with him, and so I warn you! If he won't come round, you must make the best of it."

He mentioned the matter tentatively to the Earl, tactfully representing it as one of those whims which might be expected from a female who had recently been confined. Somewhat to his surprise, his father was pleased to be indulgent.

"Ay, ay, very likely, Neville, and she's done her part, after all, in producing a boy. Anthony, eh? Well, it's not so bad a name. There was a Stratton who was an Anthony, too, now I think of it, though only a younger son. Anthony Pelham Neville—yes, it will serve. Very well, m'boy, Anthony it is. I'll tell her myself."

Neville breathed a sigh of relief, hoping that his troubles were now at an end. But in a day or two, another crisis occurred when it came to the Earl's ears that Maria was suckling her child.

"Never heard such damned nonsense in my life!" my lord exploded. "No lady of Quality ever gives suck to her brats. Get the housekeeper to find a wet nurse —plenty in the village, I'll be bound."

Neville promised that this should be done; but he had reckoned without his wife, who once more opposed him, gently but firmly.

"No, I don't wish for a nurse for him—at least, not yet, until he's a little older and I am obliged to go into company once more. But at present we're both so content in the arrangement. He's thriving, and I'm happy in being of use to him. It forges a bond between us—I'm certain of that."

In vain did he put forward his father's views; she was adamant. The Earl went so far as to remonstrate with her himself, but she artfully stressed the fact that young Anthony had put on weight; and in the face of this welcome news, he decided to let well alone.

"I'll tell you what it is, though, m'boy," he said afterwards to Neville; "you'd best have a care with that wife of yours. She's got a devilish contrary turn of mind, and you'll be under the cat's thumb for the rest of your natural if you don't teach her who's master without delay. Take a leaf out of my book, and stand no nonsense—firm line from the start."

The last thing Maria wanted was to oppose her husband; she realised that already they had drifted apart, and she had no desire to increase the breach between them. But where their child was concerned, she felt strongly that the Earl had no right to impose his will; and since her husband would not make this clear to his father, she was obliged to take the task on herself. She was convinced that the whole difficulty arose from their living under the same roof as Neville's parents. In a house of their own, Neville would be master. She was no bread-and-butter Miss to sit meekly by while someone else took charge of what she rightly considered to be the affairs of her husband and herself. She had respected her father's authority because it had never been unreasonable; but the Earl was an autocrat who took no heed of any other opinion save his own.

As time went on, such minor crises became a commonplace. The Earl was always interfering in little Anthony's upbringing, and Maria was resolute in opposing him where she believed this to be in the child's best interests. Neville, doing his utmost to avoid any unpleasantness with either side, drew farther away from his wife and took no interest at all in his son, whom he was beginning to dislike as a source of unwanted trouble.

In these rather bleak circumstances, Maria did her best to remain cheerful. Increasingly, she fell back upon her own resources, drawing unfailing comfort from her child.

Chapter XI

THE UNEXPECTED DEATH of his father elevated
Neville to the Earldom when little Anthony was only
three years old. The fifth Earl was thrown from his
horse while hunting and was killed instantly. Although
no funerary observance was lacking from his obse-
quies, no one truly mourned his passing. To Maria,
who blamed his constant interference in their domestic
concerns for the alienation of her husband from herself and the child, it brought hope of an improved relationship for the future.

The dowager Countess decided to remove to Bath
to share the home of a widowed sister. Maria was
sincere in pressing her to remain with them, but her
mother-in-law unexpectedly stood firm.

"You are mistress here now, my dear, and will go
on much better without me. You've had but a sorry
time of it so far, but once you and Neville can be
alone together with your dear little boy, I'm confident
matters will mend. As for me, I like Bath. The air suits
my constitution, and my sister will be delighted to
have me with her. So long as I may see my dear grandson from time to time, I shall have no regrets."

Maria noticed that she made no mention of seeing
Neville, and felt all the sadness of this omission.

It was scarcely surprising that Neville should at
first find himself at a loss without his father's guiding
hand. He had seldom been permitted any say in the
conduct of his personal affairs, and now he was
abruptly confronted with the management of a large

estate with its usual complement of tenantry and staff. It was fortunate that he had two capable allies in his attempt to enact the part thrust upon him. One was his land agent, a shrewd, conscientious man called Harrison, who had been in the family's service for close on twenty years, and had all the business of the estate at his finger tips. The other was Maria herself.

In her desire to establish the loving relationship with her husband which she knew was lacking, Maria was eager to aid him in any way which he would permit. He realised that she was a well-balanced, rational young woman, and her judgment was generally sound. A prey to indecision himself, he frequently took her advice on what ought to be done; but far from having the effect of drawing him closer to her, this only fostered resentment in him.

To the world, outside, theirs appeared to be a normal enough marriage. They took part in neighbourhood activities and entertainments, were visited by and visited their relatives, appearing always in company with each other on these occasions. But in the privacy of their own home they passed very little time together; while once or twice a year Neville would take lengthy trips to London or Brighton, leaving his wife and child to their own devices. The pattern of the first years of their marriage continued, and as time passed, it was gradually borne in upon Maria that she was powerless to make any change for the better.

She was wise enough to make herself content with what she possessed—loving relatives and friends as well as a never-failing source of interest and affection in her lively, intelligent young son. She would have liked to provide Anthony with brothers and sisters for companionship; but after several miscarriages, she was forced to abandon the hope of more children.

She was glad therefore, both for his sake and her own when in 1795, a year after Neville became the sixth Earl, Alvington Rectory was occupied by the Reverend Theodore Somerby, his wife Amanda, and their three-and-a-half-year-old son, James. The living at Alvington had fallen vacant that year; and as it was in the Earl's gift, Maria managed to persuade her husband to bestow it upon Theodore Somerby. He had done so grudgingly—not out of any doubts as to Mr. Somerby's suitability, but because he knew how greatly Maria wished to have Amanda near her. As he could think of no other suitable candidate at the time, and moreover wanted, as usual, not to have too much trouble over the business, it was finally settled to Maria's satisfaction.

Besides bringing the two friends together, the move was of material benefit to the Somerby family. As Rector of Alvington, Mr. Somerby would enjoy a comfortable stipend and occupy a commodious, well equipped house in the village instead of the rather cramped quarters to which he had originally taken his bride on their marriage five years before. Amanda was in ecstasy. She darted from room to room on the day when they first came to look over the Rectory, deciding which would be the parlour, the study, or the nursery, and exclaiming over the view from the upper windows at the rear, which looked out across the park of Alvington Hall.

"How nice and open it is, dearest," she said, drawing him to the window. "And only fancy, we are in a direct line with the Hall! That is, as the crow flies."

"But you're not a crow, my love."

She wrinkled her nose at him. "No, but just look. We've only to go through that little wood at the end of our garden, and the park paling is on the other side! No doubt Maria could have a gate put in it, if there isn't one already, but I can't be sure from this distance. Then there's only a short strip of ground to cross before reaching the drive. It's all on an incline— why, I could be there in ten minutes or so, and it would take more than twice as long to walk 'round by way of the road and all up the length of the carriage drive."

He hugged her, laughing. "And you're so impetuous, my love, you could never tolerate such a delay! But it occurs to me that Lord Alvington may have objections to putting a gate in his fence merely for our convenience."

"No, why should he? I'm sure it would be the easiest thing in the world to do, and he need not consider the cost, after all, for he's as rich as Croesus! It would make it so easy for us to visit each other whenever we wished. Besides, it would be pleasanter for our little boys, too. Maria agrees with me that they should play together as much as possible, seeing that they are only children and would otherwise lack companionship." She paused a moment and a shadow crossed her face, but the next moment she went on again in her usual lively way. "It would be so much quicker and more convenient for them than having to trudge along the dusty road, or go cooped up in a stuffy carriage. You know what my views are on fresh air and as much freedom as possible for children."

"I am perfectly acquainted with your views on that and on several other matters about which you feel strongly," he replied with a teasing smile. "You don't scruple to keep me informed of them, and I must be stupid indeed if I could plead ignorance."

Amanda pouted. "Oh! You are saying that I am a monstrous bore, Mr. Somerby!"

It took some time to reassure her on this point, but he managed the business with enthusiasm and skill.

"I'm so happy," she murmured, drawing away from him presently. "We have a pleasant house, a playmate for little James, and I shall be situated close to dear Maria. What more could I wish for?"

The momentary sadness returned again to her eyes and he gathered her close, not wanting her to brood over the little daughter, a stillborn infant, whom they had lost two years ago.

"Well, I must confess it will surprise me if you're not demanding a new gown or bonnet, or some such matter, before the month's out," he replied, with a creditable attempt at lightness. "But possibly I do you an injustice, ma'am. Tell me, shall we paint the panelling in the parlour white, or do you prefer it as it is?"

He was rewarded by seeing her face light up once

119

more as she plunged animatedly into plans for their new home.

They were soon comfortably settled in; and as Neville, if somewhat ungraciously, acceded to his wife's request to have a gate placed at a strategic point in the park fencing, Amanda was able to visit her friend informally in the way she had done so often in the past during Maria's girlhood visits to Oxfordshire. Indeed, there were few days when the two young matrons did not meet; and their sons derived much benefit from the companionship, sharing their toys and amusements and in general becoming just like brothers.

Like siblings, too, they occasionally had their tiffs; but as both mothers wisely agreed to interfere as little as possible, instructing their respective nursemaids to pursue the same policy as well, these clouds on the relationship soon blew over.

There was one occasion which the two friends often recalled afterwards, when the ownership of a brightly coloured ball was in question. Each young man firmly declared that the ball was his and in consequence claimed a prior right to bounce it. The argument grew heated, and Anthony reinforced his point of view with a push which sent James, the younger by seven months and therefore lighter in weight, into collision with a table. James was picked up in floods of tears, and a small bruise rapidly appeared on his cheek.

Anthony, stricken by what he had done, stood stammering that he was sorry, that he had not meant to hurt his friend; but his Mama turned a deaf ear to his protests, dismissing him to the nursery in disgrace.

When Amanda pleaded for him to be allowed to return, he came into the room with a dejected air clutching something tightly in his hand which he held out to the other child.

"What is it?" asked James, now quite recovered and bearing no animosity. "Oh, it's your blue marley, the one with white bits in it! Are we going to play with it?"

120

Anthony shook his head. "You can—it's for you. To keep. To make up, 'cos I hurt you."

James stared in disbelief. The marble was the most attractive one of a set presented to Anthony by his grandfather on a recent visit, and the little boy knew how much his friend valued it. Suddenly overwhelmed by this generous attempt at reparation, his lip began to tremble.

"No, Tony, no, I won't take it! You like it, I know you do! Oh, Tony, I haven't *deserved* it, 'cos I was horrid, too!"

Amanda was hard put to it not to laugh, moving though she found the scene; she had often heard her husband use this expression to his young son during James's occasional lapses from grace, and now here the child was, using it of himself.

With the unselfconsciousness of the very young, the two little boys flung their arms about each other, and were soon playing contentedly with the marbles, the controversial ball quite forgotten.

Shortly thereafter, there was yet another arrival in the neighbourhood. Edward Lydney returned to Buckinghamshire with his wife and young family to take up residence at Askett Hall with his father, now a widower. The arrangement suited all parties concerned. Sophia Lydney had not been in the best of health, and it was thought that country air and a quieter pace of life would suit her better than the racket of London. As Askett Hall lacked a mistress, Baron Lydney was glad to have her installed there and pleased to see his son taking some interest in the property which he would one day inherit.

Mrs. Lydney was a fashionable woman with a languid, reserved manner which gave an impression of boredom, and she evidently felt that in quitting Town she had left civilisation behind her.

One of her early visits was to Alvington Hall. Maria, trying in vain to engage her in conversation on a number of varied topics, confessed later to Amanda

121

that never had a twenty-minute morning call seemed so long.

"She looked exquisite, you know, in a gown of white lawn in the first stare of fashion and a hat of pink and white striped sarsenet. She has glossy black hair and small, delicate features"—Maria sighed, then smiled ruefully—"very different from my own! But she was for all the world like an animated doll, and I should own myself surprised if I managed to drag more than a dozen very brief replies from her during the whole visit. She showed not the slightest interest in any of our concerns in the neighbourhood, nor did she seem anxious to become acquainted with people. Of course," she added, fair-mindedly, "she may improve when one knows her better. Sometimes those who are reserved at first turn out to be the most interesting on further acquaintance. I did suggest that she might like to send her elder child, Henry, who is much of an age with our two, over here sometimes to play. The poor little fellow will be missing his London companions, I dare-say."

"And what did she say? Is he to come?"

"Well, as to that, I'm not perfectly certain. She said she left all such matters to the child's Nurse, which made me feel that perhaps I ought to do so, too. She seemed to have a little trick," added Maria, reflectively, "of putting one in the wrong, you know. But I should not be prejudicing you in this way, Mandy. You will see her for yourself, and then you may judge."

Amanda was obliged to wait for an opportunity to do this, however, as Mrs. Lydney did not do her the favour of paying a call at the Rectory. Possibly she considered the Rector's wife beneath her touch. As Mrs. Somerby was everywhere received in local society, the two did meet before long, and Amanda then found no cause to disagree with Maria's verdict on their new neighbour.

Evidently young Henry Lydney's Nurse had been given Lady Alvington's invitation, though, and approved of the notion; for she presented herself at the

Hall a few days later with her charge, freshly scrubbed and resplendent in a pair of yellow nankeen trousers and a snowy white frilled shirt. His appearance put Anthony's own Nurse, a sensible young woman trained by Maria's Jenny, to the blush; for her two charges had just been playing one of their favourite games, that of rolling down the grassy incline at the side of the terrace steps. As a result, their clothing and persons were liberally daubed with earth and grass stains, while James had lost one of his shoes.

They eyed the newcomer warily after the manner of young children. Then Anthony, who already showed a tendency to combine his father's charm with his mother's more genuine friendliness, took a step towards the other child.

"I'm Anthony and this is James. What's your name?"

"Master Henry, you should make your bow," prompted his Nurse before the boy could answer. "This young gentleman is Viscount Shaldon, and the other is Master Somerby."

Recalled to a sense of social duty, all three little boys sketched a bow as they had been taught, then fell silent again, overawed by the adult pressures put upon them. It was Anthony's Nurse Meadows who saved the situation by drawing her colleague away to a bench at a short distance where they could keep an eye on the trio without obtruding their presence. In a little while, the new arrival had been initiated into the game and was rolling merrily downhill with the others; though not without giving rise to some doubts on the part of Master Henry's nursemaid, who was accustomed to exercising her charge in a much more sedate manner in the gardens of a London Square.

In a very few weeks, the metamorphosis was complete, and Master Henry Lydney was accepted into the society of his local contemporaries with far more enthusiasm than had been accorded his Mama.

It was not many months later that Amanda discovered to her joy that she was pregnant again. With

123

all her heart, she longed for a girl to replace the little daughter she had lost. This time, all went well; and on a fine October morning in 1796, Helen Somerby was born.

Chapter XII

SUNLIGHT DAPPLED the wood, bringing the golden glow of honey to the little girl's hair as she wandered among the trees, intent on her play. She was not really supposed to come here unless she was accompanied by her brother or the other boys who came to Papa for lessons; although the wood was too small for even such a young child to get lost in it, and moreover it was situated immediately at the bottom of the Rectory garden, quite close to the house. But it was dull for Helen when the boys were at lessons in Papa's study and Cynthia Lydney did not come over to the Rectory to play. At such times she would try to evade her nursemaid and wander among the trees which she loved, to indulge in the solitary games suggested by a lively imagination.

That little mound by the chestnut tree was a castle, and the chestnut 'candles' were lights glowing in its windows as a guide to the Fairy Prince who would surely come to rescue his Princess, locked in a turret room by her horrid, cruel guardian. The interlacing branches of some nearby beeches formed a shady bower where the two might sit when once the Princess had been released. For Helen's Papa had a copy of Charles Perrault's Fairy Tales on his shelves and would sometimes read these to his little daughter, who would listen wide-eyed with rapt attention. The child had very expressive hazel eyes which changed with her moods; now brimming with laughter, now bright with intelligent curiosity or softened by feeling. She had a small featured, oval face, and people often said that her smile put them in mind of her Papa. Amanda Somerby would sometimes feel her heart turn over as she watched this miracle of Nature's duplication. Perhaps Helen was a trifle small for her age, which was at present a few months short of seven; but her air of fragility was deceptive, for she had the buoyant energy and spirits of a healthy child.

At present, she cradled a doll in her arms, a recent acquisition of which she was very proud. Her previous dolls had been carved out of wood, but this was an up-to-date model with a painted waxen head fastened to its rag body. The arms and legs were of wax, too, and the carved shoes on its feet were coloured a bright red. It had yellow hair, a pink and white complexion and staring blue eyes which James—horrid boy!—said made it look for all the world as if it would go off into a fit at any moment. It was modishly dressed in a blue gown of finest silk finished with a white lawn neckerchief. Helen thought it was the most beautiful doll in the world and would seldom allow herself to be parted from it.

When Grandmama, who had made the gift, asked Helen what she intended to call her doll, the little girl had replied without hesitation that it was to be named Peggy.

"Peggy! Isn't that a plain name to choose for such a vastly fine lady, my love? Do you not think she deserves a grander one?"

But Helen, who could hold firmly to her opinion when she was convinced it was right, shook her head, saying that Peggy was a very nice name because it belonged to the girl at the farm who brought the milk to the Rectory every day.

"She's got yellow hair, too," said the child, "and she's my friend."

She made this statement with a certainty that took

no account of differences in age and station. Almost everyone was Helen's friend, from the stable boys at Alvington Hall to its young master, Anthony, Viscount Shaldon. She shared her Mama's outgoing disposition, and had yet to learn the melancholy lesson that not everyone might be trusted.

She was standing by the little hollow near the oaks when she heard the first sounds of the boys approaching. A light of mischief came into her eyes, and she was about to conceal herself in this familiar hideout used by all the children when they wished to avoid the seeking eye of Authority; but she thought better of it, and instead ran gladly to meet them.

Two of them came crashing into the wood from the Rectory garden, shouting at the top of their voices, flinging sticks into the air and leaping over obstacles in their path. Lessons were over for the day, and some relief was necessary for muscles long cramped from sitting at a desk and voices hitherto hushed to a seemly pitch. Bertram Durrant came first, a good-looking boy of twelve who was the stepson of Lord Alvington's land agent, Mr. Harrison. The boy's own father had been a lawyer; and conscientious Mr. Harrison was anxious to see that Bertram should have as good an education as could be afforded for the boy so that he might be eligible for entry to a similarly clerkly occupation. Knowing this, Mr. Somerby had three years ago kindly offered to tutor Bertram alongside the other three boys whom he was preparing for public school. His own son James, now eleven and a half years old, was one of these; the others were the young Viscount Shaldon and Henry Lydney, both the same age as Bertram Durrant.

Helen's face clouded with disappointment when she saw that Bertram Durrant was followed only by Henry Lydney, and that the two she valued most were missing.

"Where's Tony? Where's James?" she asked.

"Still with Mr. Somerby!" yelled Henry, although she was only a couple of paces away. "Doing some extra Latin—better they than me!"

126

Then, ignoring Helen, who was after all only a girl and five years younger at that, he shouted, "I say, Durrant, what shall we play at?"

"Let's play at Revolutions," replied Durrant promptly. He was a decisive boy who knew what he wanted and usually how to set about getting it. "You know, Mr. Somerby was telling us all about the Revolution in France. They chopped people's heads off, even their King's."

"That sounds a horrid game!" exclaimed Helen, but no one took any notice of her.

"I should like to chop off someone's head!" Bertram went on heartily.

"Gudgeon," said Henry, scornfully. "It may be all very well for the Frogs to chop off each other's heads, but you don't think we'd be allowed to do it, do you? Besides, whose head would you want to chop off, anyway?"

"Yours for a start, you great show-off!"

Henry cuffed him, but without much force. "Button your lip, or I'll teach you to mend your manners," he warned. But the idea of the game had caught his fancy, and he asked, "How do we play this game, Durrant? Should we wait for the others?"

Durrant considered, frowning. "We need one side to be the sans-culottes."

"What's that?" queried Helen.

"Well, they're the mob—the common people, y'know," said Henry.

"What's common people?" asked Helen, who had been listening with one ear while the other was alert for the approach of James and Anthony.

"Oh, the labouring folk," replied Durrant impatiently. "But it can't interest you to know, as you're not going to play."

"I am! Why shouldn't I?" protested Helen, laying down her doll carefully on a mossy patch and seizing Henry by the arm. "You'll let me play, won't you?"

"Well, if we're just to stand here, I'm off home," said Henry, ignoring her question. "Are we going to play this game, Durrant, or aren't we?"

"Yes, but we'll need Shaldon and Somerby to be on the other side, the noblemen," explained Durrant.

"I'm a nobleman," stated Henry. "My father's a baron."

"It's the noblemen who go to the guillotine," Durrant reminded him, with a sneer.

"Then I shan't be one," replied Henry, promptly. "And I daresay Shaldon won't want to, nor Somerby, neither."

"That only leaves the girl, then."

"What about you?"

Durrant shrugged. "I'm going to be the leader of the Revolutionaries. Besides, I don't come of a noble family, like you others."

There was a tinge of bitterness in his tone.

"That don't signify. It's all playacting, ain't it? What shall we do for a guillotine?"

"I've got something," replied Durrant, "hidden under those brambles. I picked it up at the farm a day or two ago, and thought it might come in useful."

The other boy emitted loud whoops and rushed eagerly to the spot indicated, with Durrant close behind.

"Out of the way!" he ordered, pushing past his friend to burrow cautiously beneath a patch of brambles. He straightened up, triumphantly displaying a very rusty hoe, which had obviously been discarded as useless by its original owner.

"How shall we fix it?"

"Like this." Durrant produced a ball of twine from his pocket, fastened one end to the hoe, then suspended it in midair by passing the twine over one of the lower branches of a beech tree. He cut the twine to a suitable length, made a loop in it which he secured to a twig near the base of the tree, and stood back to admire his handiwork.

"There!" he exclaimed, in satisfaction. "Now we have only to release this loop—so—"

He suited the action to the word, grasping the loop in his hand and lowering the hoe to the ground. There was a satisfying crack as it landed on a small, dry twig and snapped it.

"Famous!" yelled the other boy.

He insisted on trying the device for himself, and for a time both became totally absorbed in this aspect of the game. Helen soon lost interest and wandered away to the edge of the trees looking for her brother and his friend. She espied them at last coming across the Rectory lawn and ran joyfully to meet them, her hair swinging about her face, for she had lost her ribbon.

"It's not very satisfactory," said Durrant, standing back at last and surveying his handiwork critically. "It don't stay rigid enough to come down with the cutting edge foremost, as it should. More of a bludgeon than a guillotine, I'd say."

"I daresay Somerby can fix it. He's a dab hand at making things work," replied Henry. "But anyway we can't use it properly in our game, can we? Leastways, not on any of us! There'd be the devil to pay and no pitch hot if someone got hurt. It's a pity we can't find anything to behead, though," he added, a trifle crestfallen. "Something that don't matter, I mean."

"Who says we can't?" said Durrant, his eye lighting on the doll which Helen had for the moment abandoned. He strode over and lifted it from its bed of moss. "What about this? She looks a truly aristocratic lady, wouldn't you say?"

Henry whistled, awed. "You'd never dare! There'd be no end of a dust if we broke it!"

"Pooh, I doubt we could. This wax is as hard as a bullet and not at all brittle, you know," replied Durrant, examining the doll. "And the hoe's not heavy enough to crush it, either. But it'd be rare sport to have a victim that looked the part, don't you think?"

Henry looked troubled. "But Helen's very fond of Peggy," he objected.

"There ain't anything else half as good," said Durrant, crushingly. "It can come to no real harm—and if it does, we can say it was an accident. Helen's sure to have lots of other dolls, besides. Girls always have."

"Ay, and if anything does go wrong, we can buy her

129

another," decided Henry, with the assurance of a boy whose pocket money was not stinted. "Come on, Durrant, make haste before she gets back!"

Durrant stooped to arrange the doll face down over a large stone with its head dangling over the edge. In this position, it presented a suitably dejected appearance.

"You can work the guillotine, Lydney," Durrant offered, not without the thought that if anything did go wrong, it might be as well to avoid responsibility for wielding the offensive weapon. He stood up, struck an attitude and declaimed, "She's an enemy of the Republic and must die! Death to all aristocrats!"

Henry released the cord and the hoe descended with some force, bludgeoning the doll's head, which jerked forwards in what seemed a most satisfactory manner to the executioners.

Before they could fully grasp what had happened, an agonised shriek rent the air. Helen, arriving on the scene a moment too late with the other two boys, leapt forward like a wildcat to the rescue of the hapless Peggy.

"My Peggy!" She snatched up the doll to clasp it to her; but she let out another yell, this time of anger, as the doll's head lolled forward on its chest, severed at the back from its cloth body, although the front still held.

"What have you done to her, you horrid, *horrid beasts*? Oh, look, James. Look what they've done!"

Trembling with emotion, she held out the doll to her brother. He took it, studying the damage thoughtfully. Characteristically, his first interest was to consider how it might be repaired. But Helen's was to avenge the wrong. Hazel eyes flashing, she flung herself upon Henry Lydney, heedless of his superior age and strength, and began to pummel him with all the force of her small fists.

Henry, half-laughing at her fury, tried to hold her off, saying he could not fight girls. Anthony strode over, seized her round the waist and lifted her to one side.

"No, Nell, he can't, but I'll attend to this for you. Now Lydney, put up your hands!"

"All right, Shaldon, I'm ready when you are, but it was Durrant's idea."

"Durrant, eh?" Anthony, too, had stripped off his coat, but now he turned to survey Bertram Durrant through narrowed eyelids. "It seems you'll have to wait, then, Lydney. I'll settle accounts in this quarter first!"

"By all means," replied Durrant, swiftly casting his coat aside. "That's to say, if you think you can!"

Without more ado, the two boys squared up to each other, the tawny head and the mid-brown one on much the same level. In build, too, they were evenly matched, in spite of Durrant's four months seniority over Anthony. Boxing was not among the accomplishments which the Reverend Theodore Somerby endeavoured to impart to his pupils, but it was a national pastime enthusiastically followed by Lord Alvington's stableboys, from whom the young gentlemen had gained a certain amount of expertise. Mr. Somerby turned a blind eye to the occasional sparring match, knowing that boys will be boys and that physical prowess was a necessary part of the wider education for life.

They fell to at once, cheered on by the Lydney boy, who soon forgot the origin of the quarrel in his enthusiasm for what he termed "a mill."

James alone took no interest in these proceedings. He was still studying his sister's damaged toy. He was as keen a sportsman as any of the others, but his overriding interest had always been in setting things to rights—a broken toy or a bird's damaged wing were alike regarded by him as a challenge to his ingenuity and skill. He could never turn his attention to anything else until he had put forth his utmost efforts to repair any damage.

Helen, her anger spent, had burst into tears and stood watching him through blurred eyes. Presently he put an arm about her.

"Don't cry, Nell. I think I can mend Peggy for you.

See, the wax head has been forced away from the body, here." He had removed the doll's neckerchief and pulled back the garments to reveal the cloth body. "It's been fixed on with glue, and it still holds at the front. I have only to glue it again at the back, and it will be as good as new, I promise you. Dry your eyes, there's a good girl. It's no great matter, after all."

Reassured, for her faith in her brother was bound-less, she obediently took a handkerchief from a pocket in her blue and white print dress and mopped her face with it. Then she pulled at James's sleeve.

"Bertram and Tony are fighting. Please stop them," she urged.

He gave her an incredulous look. "Stop them—not likely! But I tell you what—I've a good mind to teach Henry Lydney a lesson! Here, take your doll back to the house, and mind no one sees it, or the fat will be in the fire! You'd best take it straight up to the nursery and hide it in a cupboard, and then I'll smuggle it out to the carpenter's later on. He'll give me some glue to mend it. Off you go, now, and no tale-tattling, mind."

"You know I wouldn't!" Helen was indignant. Her association with the boys had soon taught her to avoid this notoriously feminine habit. "Only I wish you will not fight, nor Tony, for you might get hurt."

He shrugged this off, dismissing her again in a way that brooked no contradiction. Taking the doll from him, she ran off.

She entered the house by the back way, creeping cautiously up the servants' staircase and hoping de-voutly that Martha, whose business it was to care for her needs, might chance to be absent from the nursery at that moment. She was fortunate in this and man-aged to conceal poor Peggy in a toy cupboard just before the nursemaid entered the room.

"So there you are, Miss!" Martha greeted her. "And a fine pickle you're in, too, and little Miss Cynthia downstairs with Lady Lydney and your Mama, wait-ing to see you. Come along now, quick, and tidy your-self! I suppose you've been off with those rough boys again. Why Mistress allows it I can't think, for a proper little hoyden it'll make of you, and no mistake! And there's little Miss Cynthia always so pretty-behaved, and never a hair out of place!"

She was bustling about while she delivered this speech, pouring water into a basin to wash the child, then scrubbing her dry with a towel before finally brushing out the tangles in the golden brown hair.

"There, now you look fit for company! Come along downstairs."

Helen entered the parlour timidly, bobbing a shy curtsey to Lady Lydney, of whom she was always in awe. Cynthia, a few months younger than Helen, was sitting beside her mother on an embroidered foot-stool, her hands demurely folded. She was a pretty child with a heart-shaped face and glossy blue-black hair, which curled naturally; and when she smiled, twin dimples showed in her cheeks. She was her father's darling, and young as she was, had already learnt how to cajole him into giving her anything she desired.

Although she had now been residing in the neighbourhood for seven years, Lady Lydney seldom visited the Rectory. She had lately permitted her little daughter Cynthia to come there accompanied by her Nurse, so that the two girls might play together. There being no other little girls of a like age and sufficient gentility in the neighbourhood, the Rector's child must do for the present, until Cynthia would be old enough to be sent away to one of the more select Young Ladies' Seminaries.

The arrangement was all the more convenient because her son was attending the Rectory as a pupil. She did deplore the fact that Mrs. Somerby, a somewhat unconventional female in her view, allowed her own daughter to run wild with the boys; but as long as it was made quite clear that such conduct was not approved for Cynthia, she felt that not much harm could come of the association. Helen was in her turn occasionally summoned to Askett House, where the large, well fitted nursery—so different from the haphazard room at the Rectory which masqueraded under that name—was efficiently supervised by a highly trained Nurse with several reliable underlings. Helen's Martha was not at all in the same category, being nothing more than a motherly housemaid promoted to the post because the children had become fond of her. It could not be claimed that Helen particularly enjoyed these visits to Askett House; but she did like playing with Cynthia, and philosophically made the best of restraints to which she was unused at home.

On this occasion, it was not long before Amanda Somerby wisely dismissed the two little girls to the nursery and Martha's care. They went with relief, for even Cynthia did not find it much fun to sit quietly, as children should, without speaking unless addressed first by the adults. Martha, having seen them installed in the nursery, withdrew to an anteroom to busy herself with some sewing, leaving the communicating door open so that she could keep an eye on her charges.

"Your Mama says you have a new doll," began Cynthia. "May I see it? Do let me."

Helen looked uneasy. "Not now. Wouldn't you like to play with my new picture puzzle? It's very pretty."

"No, thank you," replied Cynthia, obstinately, "but I would like to see your doll."

"Well, you see, she's poorly today," said Helen, putting on a motherly little air that would have charmed an adult, had one been present. "I've put her to bed."

"Poorly!" exclaimed Cynthia, laughing. "A doll can't be poorly!"

"Peggy is, I tell you. I'll show you her when she's better, another time."

"Do you mean you've broken her?" demanded Cynthia, with a child's uncanny instinct for the truth.

Helen's hesitation was answer enough.

"You have, you have!" exclaimed Cynthia, triumphantly. "Oh, won't your Nurse be vexed! I daresay she may tell your Mama, and then you'll be punished."

Helen shook her head. "Martha won't be vexed, 'cos James is going to mend Peggy for me."

"My Nurse would be vexed, but Papa wouldn't let her punish me. How did you break your doll?"

"I didn't break it, not myself."

"Then who did? Was it James?"

"James doesn't break things. He tries to mend them," replied Helen, indignantly.

"Who was it?" persisted Cynthia. "Was it my brother?"

Helen's mouth set in a firm line. "It's no use asking, 'cos I shan't tell you."

"I don't care if you don't. I shall ask Henry. He's sure to tell me."

Helen felt momentarily downcast. She was not too young to understand, if only subconsciously, that her playmate took a perverse pleasure in stirring up trouble. Now that Peggy was in a fair way to being made as good as new again, Helen, never a vindictive child, wished to forget the unfortunate incident. She certainly did not want anyone to be punished for it.

"Let's play with my picture puzzle," she said decisively, rising from her stool to fetch it from a cupboard.

Cynthia, knowing there was a point beyond which her playfellow could not be coerced, shrugged dainty shoulders and capitulated.

When the two young voices ceased, Martha peered into the room. She always acted on the principle that if children were quiet, they were usually up to some mischief or other. She smiled as she saw the two little heads, one fair and the other dark, bent together over the puzzle. It was a good thing, she reflected as she withdrew to the other room again, that Miss Helen would have little Miss Cynthia for company now that she was so soon to lose Master James and the other boys. Miss Cynthia might be a trifle overindulged, and she had a spiteful side to her nature at times—no gainsaying that. But at least she would help to fill the gap left when the boys went off to school in the autumn; for Miss Helen, with her affectionate nature, would miss her brother sorely, no doubt about that.

Chapter XIII

WHEN ANTHONY WAS SENT off to Eton in that autumn of 1803, Maria could not help feeling that the main purpose of her life had come to an end. After so many years of loving guidance and encouragement, of sharing in his triumphs and vicissitudes, she was no longer needed by her son. From now on his horizons would widen, and he would move into that exclusively male world where she could not follow.

This was in the natural course of things; and Maria was far too intelligent not to have anticipated such a contingency and to be in some measure ready to accept it as being in the boy's best interests. The trouble was that she could not feel herself to be really necessary to anyone else. As the mistress of Alvington Hall she had duties and obligations, but the discharge of these brought her no sense of fulfilment. Her relatives and friends, though always loving and pleased to have her company, enjoyed independent lives in which she could play no major part. The one person whom at this time she might have looked to for comfort and support had become little more than a stranger to her.

Over the years, Neville had drawn more and more into his protective shell. With Mr. Harrison's aid he had come to understand the affairs of the estate, and he now occupied himself chiefly in this direction. He hunted, fished, or shot with his neighbours and occasionally dined with them, too; but he had no intimate friends. Even his former association with Edward, who was now Baron Lydney, had dwindled since the latter's marriage.

He continued to visit London and Brighton at intervals on his own; and from gossip which from time to time drifted her way, Maria guessed that like his father before him, he had one mistress or another in keeping. She had long since given up resenting this or even making any more efforts to right the situation. She saw now that she had made a mistake in marrying Neville with the thought that she could, by the strength of her own love, kindle an answering spark of feeling in him which would bring comfort to their lives together no matter what might befall. She had never been able to reach him through his unaccountable reserve; sometimes she wondered what secrets this masked, for at home he was often broody and irritable, occasionally giving way to unreasonable spurts of temper.

She sometimes watched Amanda and Theodore Somerby with wistful eyes, thinking how different was their marriage, but there was no resentment in her thoughts. She did not begrudge these two dear friends their happiness, only wishing that her own marriage might have been similarly blessed.

She strove hard against this growing feeling of futility, but her struggle was not helped by poor health. She was suffering at this time from female disorders which seemed beyond the skill of even the fashionable London doctor who had been summoned to Alvington at great expense for a consultation. After recommending her to keep up her strength with a diet in which underdone beefsteak and port wine figured prominently, he attempted to console her by saying that the underlying cause of her trouble must in the course of Nature be removed within a few years.

"By then, of course," said Maria to Amanda, trying to make light of the matter, "I shall be firmly addicted to the bottle, and will most likely develop gout as well."

Knowing how much her friend missed Anthony, Amanda often took Helen with her to the Hall, and

137

was rewarded by seeing Maria's face light up as she chatted to the child.

"What a little creature of quicksilver she is!" remarked Maria, smiling. "Now dreamy, now lively, by turns. Does she miss James much?"

"I think she misses all the boys. There is Cynthia, though I can never feel that her Mama quite approves of her coming to us."

"She's a pretty child," said Maria, thoughtfully. "So is your Helen, of course, but she's quite unconscious of such matters. I feel that Cynthia, young as she is, not only realises her own power to charm, but is prepared to exploit it. But perhaps that's a harsh judgment to pass on a child of seven years."

"I think it's her father's fault. Lord Lydney dotes on her, and isn't averse from allowing her to see that she can twist him around her little finger. Theo is just as fond of Helen." She smiled, remembering the look in her husband's eyes at times when they lighted on his little daughter. "But though he is a kind and affectionate father, as you well know, he would think it very wrong to allow her to have all her own way."

Maria nodded. "Very true, and you are sensible, too, my dear. Do you mean to find her a governess when she's a little older, or shall you send her to school?"

"We've already discussed this, and we both think that it would be best for her to go away to school, though we should miss her sorely. If she had sisters, a governess would do very well; but an only child kept always at home, with few opportunities for mixing with others of her age and sex, must be lonely indeed. Besides, it would restrict her outlook to be always here in Alvington. She must know something of the world outside."

"Your views are very much those of Mary Wollstonecraft, the authoress of *A Vindication of the Rights of Woman*. Her notions are considered prodigiously shocking, but I find they contain a good deal of common sense."

"I do not know the work," Amanda admitted.

"Perhaps one would hardly expect to find it on a

138

clergyman's bookshelves, even such a liberal-minded one as Mr. Somerby," replied Maria. "But in brief, the author finds the dependence of women a matter to be deplored. She advocates educating boys and girls together in similar courses of study, so that females may be equipped to take a part in the work of the world and develop a healthy independence."

Amanda considered this in silence for several minutes. "Certainly Theo agrees that girls should develop their intellects besides acquiring the more usual feminine accomplishments, and so he intends to give Helen a grounding in the Classics, later on. He says there's no finer mental discipline. And I try to allow her as much freedom as possible, myself, for I always detested to be too much constrained—but I don't need to tell you that!" she added with a laugh. "All the same, I would not wish her to grow up without any feminine graces, or entirely to flout acceptable social behaviour. I think perhaps your Mary Wollstonecraft's notions would require a vastly different world from the one in which we live, don't you?"

Maria sighed. "I daresay you are right. But I sometimes think that I would have fitted better into that kind of world."

In spite of all that could be accomplished by doctors and a trip to Bath to take the waters and at the same time visit her mother-in-law, Maria's health continued to deteriorate over the following two years. She made a strong effort to rally on the brief occasions when Anthony was home from school for the holidays; but she always paid for this afterwards by renewed spells of fainting fits and general weakness. Amanda became seriously alarmed, and even went so far as to urge Lord Alvington to attempt something more to aid his wife.

"What would you have me do, ma'am?" he asked impatiently. "Already Maria has consulted the foremost medical practitioners, and to no purpose. They say she must not overtax her strength, and yet every time that boy comes home, she is constantly exerting herself to please him! There's no sense in it, none whatever!"

Yet another medical consultation took place, however, with no better result. Commenting on this one day at the breakfast table when James was home from school, Amanda noticed that the boy was listening and she fell silent.

"Mama," he said presently, "did you say that none of the doctors can cure Lady Alvington?"

"You shouldn't be listening to my conversation with your father," she reproved him. "It was not intended for your ears."

James reddened.

"I beg your pardon, Mama. I don't listen in general, you know, but that subject is especially interesting to me, because I mean to be a doctor myself one day. And then perhaps I may be able to make Lady Alvington well again."

Amanda sighed, between a tear and a smile. But Maria was unable to wait for the day when her young friend might perhaps come to her aid. She sank lower and lower, until in the autumn of 1805 she died in the arms of her faithful Jenny. Her son's name was the last word on her lips.

The boy stood among the mourners at the graveside, his bright auburn hair accented by the sombre hue of his funeral garb.

He had been fetched from school yesterday. His father had not bothered to come, but Mr. Somerby had been waiting for him in the Headmaster's room. That sudden summons to the sanctum had set him feverishly going over in his mind any recent offences for which he might be called to account. He had been late for chapel a few days ago, and there had been a mill with Smythe minor to resolve some dispute; but these were minor peccadillos which had already been dealt with at a lower level, not of sufficient seriousness to warrant an appearance before the Beak. Otherwise, things had been going rather well this term. His classics tutor had expressed satisfaction with his work, and the man was not easy to please. Anthony racked his brain but could think of nothing.

And then, surprisingly, the Beak had spoken to him

kindly, saying that he feared Mr. Somerby had some
bad news to deliver. After that, it was all blurred.

He could not believe it was his mother in that box
they were bearing to the freshly dug grave. He knew
he had lost her, would never see her more, would never
again find an affectionate welcome at his home. But
surely a bright, lively mind and a loving heart did not
die with the body? There must be something that would
live on, somewhere. The Rector said she lived on in
Heaven. Where was Heaven? Could he believe there
was such a place? Mrs. Somerby said that his mother
lived on in the mind and heart of her son. Anthony
found that less difficult to understand. But for the moment everything was too difficult; he needed to get away
on his own somewhere, to think out these things.

After the service was over and the mourners had returned to the Hall for the customary cold collation, Anthony was missing. His grandparents enquired for him
with loving concern; and when they learned that he was
nowhere to be found in the house, sent a message over
to the Rectory to see if he had gone there. Amanda,
her heart too full to face the family gathering, had returned straight home from the churchyard; and they
knew that Anthony had always regarded the Rectory
as a second home and Mrs. Somerby in the light of a
special kind of Aunt.

The young Viscount was not at the Rectory, however, and Mrs. Somerby was unable to suggest where
he might be. Wherever it was, she felt convinced that
for the present the poor lad would do better to be left
alone. She reflected with tears in her eyes what a dreadful shock it must have been to the child—yes, he was
a child still to her, even though he had now attained
his fourteenth year—to receive a summons of such
gravity in the familiar hurly-burly of what had until
then been a normal school term. His loss was great indeed, all the greater because he had no affectionate,
understanding father to share and soften his grief. So
if he chose to creep away to nurse his hurts in solitude
for a while, she would not be the one to force him

141

back. Later, he might come voluntarily to her; she rather thought that he would.

But if her mother did not know where to find Anthony, Helen did. Creeping into the kitchen, which was at present deserted, she went over to the box where Bess lay with her four puppies before the fire. They were only three weeks old, soft, warm, roly-poly creatures with moist noses.

She took up one of them, wrapping it in a soft shawl which she had brought with her for the purpose. Bess looked up anxiously for a moment, but she did not make a fuss. She trusted Helen, knowing that the puppy would be safely restored presently.

With the little creature clasped tenderly in her arms, Helen stole quietly from the house and through the garden into the wood. Lightly as she trod, the fallen leaves crisped beneath her feet, a carpet of yellow, red, gold, and brown. They were still fluttering down from the trees as she passed, lighting for a moment on her hair or brushing against her cheek.

Presently she came to the spot she sought, the hollow near the oaks which in happier times had been the children's hideout. And there was Anthony, as she had known he would be.

He lay curled up in the hollow, silent and motionless, his bright hair blending with the autumn leaves scattered around him.

He did not stir at her approach, and she stood still for several minutes, surveying him doubtfully. Then she climbed down to him and twined an arm about his neck. She spoke no word, but she laid her soft, cool cheek against his with infinite compassion.

He flung away from her with a quick movement, burying his face deeper into the leaves, and striking at the ground with clenched, impotent fists. She saw that his shoulders were shaking.

She knew then that there was no more she could do for him. Presently, perhaps, he would come to Mama and Papa, and they would help him. But now she must leave him alone with his sorrow.

She stood up, turning to go.

Then she hesitated. She pressed a kiss upon the puppy's soft, warm head, gently laying her bundle down within the shelter of Anthony's outstretched arms.

PART II

London

1815-1816

"Yet heavens are just, and time
suppresseth wrongs."
—WILLIAM SHAKESPEARE
Henry VI

Chapter XIV

ON A WARM AFTERNOON in June, 1815, Helen Somerby was walking with three of her schoolfellows in the secluded gardens of Mrs. Cassington's Select Seminary for Young Ladies in Kensington.

Kensington was a pleasant, healthful village which had originally consisted solely of farms, riverside inns, and cottages; but in the days when King William III had moved his court there, new houses had sprung up suitable for occupation by the Gentry. Although Kensington Palace had since fallen out of favour with Royalty, King George III preferring Buckingham House as his London residence, the village remained a fashionable locality for the aristocratic and wealthy.

A young lady needed to be both of these to gain admittance to Mrs. Cassington's superior establishment. The fees were one hundred and fifty guineas a year, with a long list of extra subjects. In her advertisements, the Principal undertook to provide Board and Lodging for Young Ladies of Refinement together with instruction in English Writing and Grammar, Arithmetic, History and the use of the Globes; in addition, they might acquire Proficiency in the French and Italian tongues, the Art of the Dance, playing upon the Harp and the Pianoforte, Drawing, Painting, and Needlework. She also promised that Parents and Guardians might depend on the Utmost Care being taken of the Young Ladies' Manners and Deportment, and that a Particular Tenderness would be shown to their persons. How far her educational claims were justified might perhaps have been judged by the gratifying number of young ladies who left her care to enter upon the London social scene and eventually to make advantageous marriages. And as this was undoubtedly the aim of most parents who placed their offspring in Mrs. Cassington's establishment, there could be no doubt that, in spite of the high fees she charged, the lady performed a most valuable service.

As far as the physical well-being of her pupils was concerned, Mrs. Cassington's establishment was undoubtedly superior to most others of the kind. Visitors to the school, who were led by a liveried servant to an elegant sitting room with damask draperies and fine lustres fitted to the walls, and furnished throughout in the style of a wealthy private home, at once formed a gratifyingly favourable impression; this was further enhanced by a conducted tour of the school. Many other boarding schools crowded their pupils into cramped, airless dormitories, frequently requiring them to sleep two in a bed. At Mrs. Cassington's establishment separate dormitories were provided for each age group, with no more than eight beds a side, every girl having a bed to herself. Each dormitory was under the supervision of a schoolmistress who slept in the same room. Moreover, in the senior girls' dormitory personal privacy was ensured by white curtains draped around each bed to form a kind of cubicle.

The food was good, wholesome fare. Breakfast consisted of porridge, tea and toast; a light nuncheon of cold meats, bread, and fruit was offered at noon and a substantial dinner in the evening. Since children will always find something to grumble at in school meals, the complaint most often voiced here concerned lack of variety. Even the youngest among them soon learned that Monday would bring roast beef, Tuesday broiled mutton, Wednesday pork, Thursday roast mutton, Friday stewed beef and dumplings and Saturday cold beef or mutton with pickled walnuts. Sunday was poultry day and usually looked forward to by all, if only as a change from meat. The range of puddings was even more limited—either boiled suet, with or

148

without currants, or else plain rice pudding, rarely a favourite. The Principal always insisted, however, that young ladies' likes and dislikes should not be taken into account at mealtimes. Unless a girl was genuinely unwell, she would be expected to eat most of what was set before her. Another of her rules was that meals must be eaten in strict silence, unless it was necessary to ask for anything on the table to be passed; such requests were to be made in low tones, and any girl voicing them too frequently would be suitably reprimanded. It was scarcely surprising that as a result of this rule, some of the more timid girls developed a life-long abstinence from certain condiments and sauces, which had habitually chanced to be placed out of their reach during their first year at the Seminary.

As Mrs. Cassington preferred to think of her Seminary more as a Finishing School for Young Ladies than an establishment for the elementary education of little girls, she never accepted a pupil, however highborn, under the age of eleven. Although most of her pupils had left her care by the time they reached sixteen, some few remained with her longer. These were the "parlour boarders," accorded the special privilege of being permitted to take their meals with the teaching staff in the private parlour, instead of sitting down with the rest of the school in the communal dining room. The parlour boarders enjoyed other privileges, too; discipline was somewhat relaxed in their favour, they were able to have more free time and occasionally even to dine elsewhere, provided they were in the company of an approved escort, such as a close relative.

Even for those who never claimed this last privilege, the parlour dinners were a distinct improvement on the general school meal. This was not so much because of the food provided, which was unchanged in essentials, but because of the greater social ease prevailing. Guests were often present, and conversation of the kind suitable at an elegant dinner party was encouraged. Once a week Mrs. Cassington decreed that nothing but French should be spoken over the dinner table, thus ensuring that her young ladies should eventually enter the Polite World sufficiently versed in the tongue of that nation—with which regrettably the country had for many years now been engaged in warfare, but which had in the past contributed much to culture.

The strident dressing bell at seven o'clock was the signal for the girls to embark on the day's activities. Dashing the sleep from their eyes, they made haste—especially in winter, for the dormitories were unheated even in this superior establishment—to wash and dress in the brown cambric muslin considered practical for everyday wear. Their toilet completed, they assembled downstairs for prayers before going in to breakfast at eight o'clock.

The meal over, lessons began. Much of the work consisted in learning by rote or copying extracts from approved textbooks. The teacher in English Grammar relied a great deal on a book by Miss Murry entitled *Mentoria, or The Young Ladies' Instructor*. This took the form of educational conversations between Mentoria and two of her highborn pupils on such oddly assorted topics as Elocution and Geography, the Use of Grammar, or Politeness and Gratitude.

Another publication much in favour was Miss Richmal Mangnall's Question and Answer book, especially the one dealing with History. Doubtless, it was hoped that by learning the answers to the questions posed, the pupil would gain a sufficient knowledge of the subject to sustain her throughout the intellectual rigours of a London Season.

After nuncheon there would be a walk in nearby Kensington Gardens if the weather proved suitable, or a period of needlework and Improving Conversation, should it be inclement. Afternoon sessions consisted of music, drawing, dancing and the all-important lessons in manners and deportment. These aimed to instruct a young lady in such vital matters as how to enter and leave a room with decorum; how to sit, rise, and make a curtsey gracefully; how to greet an acquaintance either in the street or the drawing room; how to pay and receive calls in the approved style and to write gracious letters of compliments, condolences, or thanks.

150

A coach was available in the stables so that the young ladies might learn how to enter and dismount from a vehicle without any awkward movements or an immodest display of ankle.

From four until five o'clock, a period was set aside to enable them to complete their preparation for the following day's lessons or to fulfil any tasks set them as disciplinary punishment. By the time the clock struck five they were all thankful to conclude the day's work and change into their regulation white muslins in readiness for dinner. The day ended with prayers, and candles were extinguished in all but the senior dormitory by eight o'clock.

The four young ladies at present taking exercise in Mrs. Cassington's gardens were shortly to leave the lady's care for good, this being their final term. They were all about eighteen years of age, dressed similarly in simple white muslin gowns with sashes of different colours to give a note of individuality.

They made an attractive group. Cynthia Lydney and Helen Somerby had fulfilled the promise of their childhood and become pretty girls, each in her own way. Cynthia was tall, dark, and elegant with provocative eyes that would later wreak havoc in the London ballrooms. Helen had a slim, well proportioned figure, and her delicately boned face held all the liveliness and charm of her earlier days.

The third girl, Melissa Chetwode, was shorter than her companions and at present inclined to be plump, a fact which caused her much heartburning in spite of Helen's friendly assurances that it was merely "puppy fat" and would fine down before long. She had a round, piquant face, melting brown eyes and a crop of rich chestnut curls. Catherine Horwood, on the other hand, was a trifle angular. Occasionally she expressed a wish for some of Melissa's "comfortable padding," but her lack of it did not detract from the pleasing impression made by her candid blue eyes and good-humoured, intelligent countenance.

"So we're to have company at dinner again this evening," remarked Cynthia in a cynical tone. "Nobody under the age of forty, I daresay, exactly as usual. Lud, how sick I am of Old Catty's odious dinner parties! Thank Heavens, we shall soon be done with all that and may look forward to entertainments of a vastly different stamp—balls, routs, shopping in Bond Street —I can hardly wait!"

"Oh, I don't know," said Helen, with a twinkle in her eye. "Surely you'll miss the games of backgammon, Cynthia?"

The others laughed. It was well known that the Vicar, a frequent visitor to Mrs. Cassington's dinner parties, always preferred to secure Miss Lydney as a partner at backgammon, one of the few games allowed on these occasions. This was not because her play was superior to that of the other young ladies, but on account of the secret delight he took in her way of indulging in the mildest and most discreet form of flirtation with him. It did not go unobserved by her preceptress; but Mrs. Cassington looked on with a tolerant eye, thinking that the Honourable Cynthia Lydney, daughter of Baron Lydney, could scarcely be judged to do anything improper.

Cynthia gave a reluctant smile. "Well, the Vicar's a male creature, after all, and as such, a rarity in these quarters. One must make shift with whatever offers." She cast a malicious glance at Melissa. "Now, if only one had the same opportunities with Monsieur Falaise! What say you, Melissa?"

The other girl blushed, trying in vain to conceal it by putting up her hand to pat her curls into place. Monsieur Falaise was the dancing master, an émigré from Revolutionary France whose Gallic charm, in spite of his forty-odd years, had produced a devastating effect on several of the senior girls at the Seminary. Mrs. Cassington was far too experienced in the ways of young ladies not to be very well aware of the hazards attendant upon employing a personable gentleman to instruct her pupils in the art of the dance. On the other hand, she was too good a businesswoman not to take advantage of the fact that Monsieur Falaise's fees were as modest as his expertise in his subject was great. She continued to employ him, therefore, but took care that a responsible teacher should be present at all his lessons, and that at no time did any of the young ladies have an opportunity to be alone with him even for a second.

Melissa Chetwode was at this stage of her life somewhat prone to attacks of hero worship, and she had early fallen a victim to the attractions of Monsieur Falaise. Unlike some of her schoolfellows, who suffered from the same malady and took a delight in languishing for him openly before their friends, she did her best to conceal her feelings. The attempt was abortive, however, as such things are in a close-knit community; and everyone knew poor Melissa's secret, though few were unkind enough to tease her about it, respecting her reticence.

"I suppose you'll make your come-out in London next season?" Helen asked Cynthia.

She was not really interested in the answer, which she could guess at already; she was merely making an attempt to distract Cynthia's attention from Melissa.

"Oh, yes, of course," replied Cynthia, promptly relinquishing her prey. "Mama complains that it will be prodigiously fatiguing to give me a season, but she knows her duty. Nowadays she seldom goes to the town house in Berkeley Street, even though Papa spends most of his time there since he took his seat in the House of Lords. She doesn't like the country, precisely, but I think she's become accustomed to it now, and finds London too rackety. But that's all one to me, so long as I may go there." She broke off and looked enquiringly at her companions. "I daresay the rest of you will be having a London season, too? Certainly I'll expect to see you there, Melissa, as your parents have a house in Cavendish Square."

Melissa, who had recovered by now, said that there had been some talk of it at home.

"And Papa means to hire a house in Town to bring me out," put in Catherine, adding with a laugh, "He says he has great hopes of getting me off his hands at last, for with three other girls in his household, he'll soon be driven either mad or bankrupt, else! He's so droll, is Papa, but he's prodigiously fond of us all, really, you know."

"I'm sure he is," said Melissa, warmly. "So we shall all meet again in London next Spring, it seems."

"All except perhaps Helen," corrected Cynthia, with a sideways glance.

She knew that Helen owed her place at the Seminary to the generosity of her grandparents, as the Reverend Theodore Somerby could scarcely have afforded to send her there. It seemed unlikely that she could expect to enjoy the same advantages as her friends in the future.

Melissa and Catherine exclaimed in dismay, casting compassionate glances at their friend, but she only laughed in an unaffected, light-hearted way.

"London's not the only place where one may enjoy balls and parties," she reminded them. "I dare say I shall contrive to have my share of entertainment in Buckinghamshire."

"Oh, as to that, if you like rural society!" scoffed Cynthia.

"Some of our rural society is most exalted, you may recall, Cynthia. There's the Earl of Alvington, not to mention your own family, for instance."

"Alvington—oh, you must know you can have no hope of balls there! The Earl has become practically a recluse, so Mama says, and suffers much from the gout. As for Shaldon, he lives in Town and rarely visits the Hall. I haven't set eyes on him myself since I was a child. Henry says that he's become a regular dasher, much sought after by the Town belles, but it seems"—she lowered her voice mysteriously—"he has *other interests* than matrimony."

"What kind of other interests?" asked Melissa, innocently.

"Oh, aren't you a Bath Miss!" scoffed Cynthia. "Do you really not know what I mean?"

"And if she does not, I hope you'll have too much delicacy of mind to inform her!" said Helen.

"I shouldn't depend upon *that,*" put in Catherine.

154

"Naturally, you two are always such models of propriety," retorted Cynthia.

"Catherine, perhaps, but as for me—well, I try, though Old Catty doesn't appear to think so," laughed Helen, determined not to allow the conversation to de-velop into a schoolgirl squabble. "Only yesterday she reproved me for an improper display of my ankle as I sat down at the pianoforte!"

"That's because you will skip about so," explained Catherine, "instead of walking in the decorous manner suited to a young lady of Quality."

They all laughed over this, and harmony was restored as each girl recalled occasions when her conduct had fallen short of their Principal's required standard. The incidents they related were harmless enough, but the recollection of Mrs. Cassington's shocked reactions caused so much general merriment that soon Catherine, with tears in her eyes, was begging them to stop before she quite went into hysterics.

"Yes, and if we're not more careful we'll be heard from the house, and then the fat *would* be in the fire!" gasped Melissa, herself helpless with laughter.

This sobering thought produced a lull in which it was possible to hear that some kind of commotion was taking place in the street on the other side of the high wall enclosing the gardens. They stood still and listened. Excited shouts came to their ears, the sounds of running feet, the constant blowing of a post horn which gradually drew nearer, and finally the clatter of fast galloping horses.

"What in the world can it be?" they asked, looking in amazement at one another.

"Well, there's only one way to discover," said Helen, running over to the wall at a spot covered by a thick creeper. "We must take a look over into the street!"

"Oh, no, Helen, think of your dress!" warned Catherine. "There'll be no end of trouble if you should get it soiled!"

This went unheeded. Helen grasped a thick branch of the creeper, found a foothold on a lower one, and succeeded in hoisting herself up so that her head was just above the wall and she could see down into the street. Melissa, not to be outdone, found herself another spot where the ascent was so easy that she was soon sitting triumphantly right on top of the wall.

The other two girls made no attempt to follow suit, but contented themselves with uttering scandalised exclamations interspersed with impatient demands to be told what was happening in the street.

"There's a tremendous crowd!" Helen cried back to the others. "Yes, and there's a Mail coach coming along the street, all decked out in greenery! They're all shouting something. I can't quite hear what—"

Her voice was completely drowned then by a loud fanfare blown on the yard of tin by the guard of the Mail coach as the vehicle reached the point where the two girls were stationed. As the sound died away, a great shout went up from the crowd.

"A famous victory! The Duke has routed Boney! The archfiend's conquered. The war's over! Victory! A battle won on the plains of Waterloo! Victory! God bless Wellington!"

At the same moment, the church bells rang out in a wild carillon of joy. The coach swept past, the crowd running after it, shouting, laughing, dancing, breaking out into the National Anthem.

"Did you hear that?" cried Helen. "Did you hear that the war is ended—that the Duke of Wellington has defeated Napoleon?"

Melissa turned excitedly to corroborate this, forgetting her precarious perch. She wobbled, lost her balance, grabbed frantically at the wall to try to support herself, then tumbled igominiously over into the street.

Providentially, her fall was broken by a young gentleman who had not rushed away after the rest of the crowd, but was still standing almost beneath the spot where Melissa had been perched a moment before. He had not until then noticed the watchers on the wall, being too taken up, like everyone else, with the spectacle in the street; but he was alerted by the scream she gave as she felt herself falling, and with great presence of mind rushed forward to grab her.

He succeeded in breaking her fall, although the impetus of it sent them both sprawling on the ground with Melissa uppermost. The crowd was now so intent on racing after the coach that no one took any notice of the incident, so they were left alone to scramble to their feet.

"Are you hurt, Miss?" asked the gentleman, curtly. "Here, let me see. Walk about a little. Come, come, do as I bid you! That's right. No, there's no injury—perhaps a bruise or two later. What of your arms and wrists? Move them about, will you?"

Melissa, breathless and dishevelled, obeyed.

"Nothing hurting?" She shook her head. "Good, good. And now, young lady, what the devil d'you mean by jumping off that wall? It would have served you right if you'd broken every bone in your body."

"I did *not* jump off!" cried Melissa, indignantly. "I lost my balance and fell—and I think you are vastly uncivil, sir, even if you did save me!"

At this moment the gentleman heard a strangled sound from above his head and looked up to catch sight of Helen.

"Well, of all things!" he exclaimed, in disgust. "Nell! I might have known this would be one of your freakish starts! And what do you think you're doing up there?"

"Oh, Melissa, you're really not hurt, are you?" asked Helen, anxiously. "It gave me such a fright when I saw you fall! You're sure you're all right?"

"Only a trifle shaken up," answered Melissa, beginning to regain her composure. "I was saved from the worst by this—this gentleman here," she added, in a frigid tone. "He appears to know you."

"It's my brother—oh, dear, it's not a very propitious moment for making introductions! Miss Melissa Chetwode, Mr. James Somerby. But what in the world are you doing here, James?"

From force of habit, Melissa gave a curtsey, though she could not help feeling it was a slightly ridiculous gesture in the circumstances. Mr. Somerby answered it with an inclination of his head, then stooped to recover

157

his hat from the ground. He dusted it over with a handkerchief, afterwards performing the same office for his blue coat and riding breeches. He looked up at his sister again, and they both burst into laughter.

"Impossible girl!" he said, severely, when he had recovered. "Why the deuce did you have to clamber up there?"

"Because we wanted to see what was going forward in the street, of course! We heard all the commotion, and it was so frustrating not to be able to see the cause of it."

"But, my dear sister, why not step out into the street to look in a civilised manner?"

"Because we can't. The garden gate is kept locked, and we would need to go through the house and leave by the front door. In any case, we're not allowed on the street without an escort."

"Very proper, of course. But since matters stand as you say, there will be a certain difficulty in restoring this young lady to your side of the wall," he pointed out. "That is, unless she would not object to my escorting her to the front entrance?"

"Oh, no!" chorused both girls, in dismay.

"You can't have thought, James!" added Helen. "Mrs. Cassington will learn of it if Melissa enters the house by the front door, and how can she excuse herself for breaking the rules? She can scarcely say that she climbed on the wall and fell off!"

"Mm," said the young man, thoughtfully, rumpling his blond hair in a way he had when wrestling with a knotty problem. "Yes, I do see it might be awkward. There's no other way in, is there? What about the stable entrance?"

"It's completely shut off from the gardens," Helen informed him. "We might as well be in a nunnery cloister! But, I say, James," as a sudden idea struck her, "if you could procure a ladder from somewhere . . ."

"Nothing easier, assure you. I always travel with a stock of 'em," he replied, sardonically. "No, I see only one thing for it. If I should hoist you back on to the top of the wall, Miss—er—"

"Chetwode," supplied Melissa, in a small voice.

"Quite. Well, do you think you could then contrive to climb down on the other side with my abominable sister's assistance, and without injury to either of you?"

"I—I think so," said Melissa, dubiously, for she felt all the impropriety of being hoisted up, as the gentleman put it. At the same time, she could see no other way of returning to the premises without alerting the Principal.

"Oh, yes, she could do that easily," put in Helen, "as there's a sturdy creeper growing this side and three of us to help her climb down by it. It's a capital notion, James! But can you put her safely up, do you think?"

"I wouldn't have suggested it, else. This wall's barely a foot over my own height, after all." This was true enough, for he was a little over six feet. "Now, Miss, if you're ready."

He turned purposefully towards Melissa. She shrank back, her modesty outraged for a moment at the thought of what was to come.

"For Heaven's sake, don't be missish!" he recommended her, sharply. "I promise to turn my eyes away once you're safely seated atop. It won't take a minute, you know, and should prove far less of an ordeal than facing your schoolmistress."

She could not help but acknowledge the truth of this. She blushed a fiery red as he grasped her firmly in his strong arms and swung her up so that she found herself sitting securely on top of the wall, but facing away from him with her feet dangling over the other side. They were now within easy reach of the creeper by which she had clambered up; and with a host of garbled instructions and a certain amount of giggling, her friends soon assisted her to find a footing and climb safely down to join them.

Apart from a few scratches and a snag or two in her white stockings, Melissa seemed none the worse.

"You'd best go and change your stockings, though, Mel," recommended Helen. "Old Catty has the most uncanny knack of noticing such things, even though your skirts should conceal the damage."

"Besides which," remarked Cynthia, scornfully, "she looks a complete fright."

Thus adjured, Melissa went off at once, hoping that she might manage to reach her dormitory unobserved. She was fortunate in this, and hurriedly set about making herself tidy again. As she dragged a comb through her hair before the mirror, her cheeks burned at the recollection of what had just passed. It was the first time she had ever been clasped in a male embrace, if one discounted those permitted by close relations; and she felt all the impropriety of it, even if the gentleman's manner had been far from amatory. Indeed, when she considered the matter calmly, he had shown no more interest in her than if she had been a sack of coals. She was a little ashamed to discover in her maidenly bosom a certain measure of regret for this. To be sure, he was a most personable gentleman. . . .

Meanwhile, Helen had reported Melissa's safe landing to her brother; and she discovered that he had in fact been on his way to the Seminary to pay her a visit.

"I'm hoping to persuade your Principal to allow you the indulgence of dining out with me this evening at the Red Lion," he said. "I've already engaged a private parlour."

"Oh, I do hope she will!" exclaimed Helen.

"Not if she gets wind of this, so you'd best follow your friend indoors and freshen up a trifle," he replied, giving her a critical glance. "There's a smut on your face and your hair's all anyhow. I'll continue round to effect an entrance by the more conventional method, and hope to see you later."

"Oh, but, James, isn't it splendid news about the victory in Brussels? No wonder the whole village was in such an uproar!"

"Famous! Wellington's a brilliant man in the field. Only he could have brought this off! I'd give much to have a full account of the battle."

She waved her hand airily at him before vanishing from sight behind the wall. James duly presented himself at the front entrance of the Seminary and was shown into the visitors' parlour, where he was graciously received by Mrs. Cassington.

The Principal made no difficulty about giving permission for Helen to dine at the nearby inn with her brother, provided he would undertake to return her pupil to her care by nine o'clock; this he readily promised to do.

Later, when they were seated together in the private parlour at the Red Lion, they exchanged their news. He had just returned from a visit to the Rectory, so was able to fill in details which had been sketchily dealt with in the frequent letters Helen received from her parents. He told her, too, about his plans for the future. For the past five years, ever since he had left school at eighteen, he had been serving as an apprentice to a Dr. Gillies who had a thriving practice in Paddington, a rapidly expanding village on the outskirts of London. Now he was to go in the autumn to walk the wards at Guy's hospital in Southwark, where Dr. Gillies himself had trained as a medical man.

"I am to be a dresser to the great Astley Cooper," he informed her, his eyes alight with enthusiasm.

"It sounds famous, James! But what precisely is a dresser? I thought it was a lady's maid!"

He laughed. "A fine abigail I should make! No, Nell, a medical dresser's a man who assists surgeons at operations, does dressings and so forth, and sometimes has accident cases confided to his care in the absence of his superiors. I shall learn something of surgical matters, you know, to add to the experience of physic and general practice that I've studied under Dr. Gillies. I'll be attending lectures on Anatomy and the Practice of Physic, and at the end of my six months' training I shall hope to become a Licentiate of the Society of Apothecaries. Then I'll be a fully fledged medical man, and Dr. Gillies has offered to take me into partnership."

"Oh, Jamie, I'm so glad for you!" She pressed her hand affectionately. "It's what you've always wished to do. And will you reside in the hospital?"

161

"Not permanently, only when it's my periodic week as dresser on duty. A bedroom and sitting room are provided in the hospital for that purpose. Otherwise, I shall need to find a lodging close by, so that I can be fetched quickly when needed. I may probably share rooms with one of the other students."

They continued talking on this interesting topic for a while longer; until James, who was by no means self-centred, said it was time Helen told him of her own concerns.

"You're leaving school at the end of this term, Nell, and I daresay you'll not be sorry to be home again. You may miss your friends at first, though. The plump little girl's a nice creature, isn't she? Now I think of it, I realise that she's the daughter of Father's old Oxford friend, Sir George Chetwode. Been staying with you at times during the holidays, hasn't she? Though we've never chanced to meet before, since I've so rarely been at home."

"Oh, James, don't refer to poor Melissa as plump!" Helen pleaded. "She's prodigiously sensitive about it."

"Well, I wouldn't do so to her face, naturally. It's a pretty face, too, and she's not all that plump, after all. Nothing that won't fine down in a year so so, mark my words."

"So I'm for ever telling her, but she won't believe me. We intend to keep up our friendship by correspondence and visits, though. Talking of keeping up friendships, do you ever see anything of Viscount Shaldon these days? Cynthia Lydney was remarking earlier today that she hadn't set eyes on him since she was a child, and I believe I was about twelve when last we met. But that's scarce surprising, seeing how rarely he has visited Alvington Hall during the years since he first went up to Oxford. Mama says he always calls on them whenever he does chance to go there—but, of course, I've been away from home most of the time."

"Yes, we've met occasionally, though not very recently, I fear. My work with Dr. Gillies occupies me constantly, so that I can rarely get up to Town. But I've dined now and then with him at his rooms in

Clarges Street, where he's been living for the past three years, ever since he came down from Oxford. Now and then, we've been together to watch a cricket match or a mill, too."

"Is he"—she hesitated, then went on—"is he just as he used to be?"

James pursed his lips. "Difficult to say. We're still on easy terms together, if that's what you mean."

"Well, no, not precisely. You see, Cynthia said"—Helen paused, finding it a little difficult to repeat exactly what Cynthia had said. "She implied that Lord Shaldon had become—something of a flirt."

"You females!" exclaimed her brother in disgust. "Must you prattle gossip even in the schoolroom? I should have supposed Mrs. Cassington might have found you something better to do with your time! As for Miss Lydney, you should know by now that she was always a rare one for stirring up mischief, and most likely she hasn't changed. Gives her the excitement she craves, I daresay," he added, percipiently. "You'd be a gudgeon to pay any heed to what she has to say."

"Oh, I do realise that, of course, but I just wondered if there might not be a grain of truth in it?"

"Well, don't exercise your curiosity. Always one of your strong points, Nell. Let the poor chap be. Small wonder if he did turn out all nohow, with a father who's never shown the slightest interest in him, not to say positively disliking him, God knows why! But Shaldon ain't a bad hat as far as I can tell, and I reckon I know him better than most." He paused, then added reflectively, "He's a trifle withdrawn perhaps, nowadays, and takes a cynical tone. A man don't wear his heart on his sleeve, of course, but I reckon Tony's is in the right place—metaphorically, as well as biologically," he finished, with a laugh.

"I'm glad to hear that for old times' sake, though it's extremely unlikely that he and I will ever renew our acquaintance."

James could not but agree with this, and the conversation drifted into other channels.

Chapter XV

In the early Spring of 1816 a group of four gentlemen stood in the bow window of White's Club gazing idly down into St. James's Street. They represented the very Pink of the *ton,* dressed in well fitting tail coats of superfine fashioned by the most modish tailors such as Weston or Schultz, with light coloured waistcoats and extremely tight fitting pantaloons in yellow, buff, or grey. The effect of elegance was enhanced by the high starched shirt points framing their cheeks; supported by a broad, tightly wrapped cravat in snowy linen tied in one of the many intricate styles prevailing, chosen in accordance with the individual taste of the wearer.

These four gentlemen were distinguished not only because of their elegant attire. They were sprigs of the nobility with fortunes to match their pedigree, and bachelors into the bargain; as such, they were among the most sought after of all eligible gentlemen by the Town's matchmaking Mamas.

From this point of view, Viscount Shaldon was undoubtedly considered the cream of the quartette, for none of the others could lay claim to an Earldom. Close on five and twenty, tall and well formed, with the Strattons' classical features and rich auburn hair, he was a man to stand out from the crowd at any time. But his air of aloof cynicism gave little encouragement to young ladies determined to attach his interest in spite—or perhaps because—of the rumours that the Viscount was not a marrying man, but was scandalously

164

addicted to less permanent liaisons such as that with the notorious courtesan, Harriette Wilson. He had been on the Town ever since coming down from Oxford four years since, so that every season represented a recurring challenge to hopeful mothers of nubile daughters. Occasionally he condescended to attend their various social functions, to dance with their offspring, and even now and then to indulge in a mild, short-lived flirtation with one of them. But although hope would inevitably rise in the breast of the young lady concerned and even in that of her more experienced parent, it was soon dispelled. No doubt about it, Shaldon was lamentably capricious. The girl who seemed to have caught his interest at one social function would be more or less ignored by him at the following one which he deigned to attend. And though there were a few original spirits who had essayed the different approach of trying to pique his interest by a pretended show on their part of indifference, this gambit, too, failed to counter his cool detachment. If a young lady appeared to wish to ignore him, it was all one to Viscount Shaldon. He could really manage quite well without any of them. Most of them were attractive enough, and he was far from being impervious to feminine attractions; but in his view they all bore the stamp of having been schooled for their purpose, like racehorses, and had nothing else in their pretty heads but winning the matrimonial stakes.

The Honourable Henry Lydney was considered by many female aspirants to be a more likely catch, for there was no doubt that he was impressionable enough. A dark, virile looking young man of much about the same age as the Viscount, his roving eye constantly lighted on fresh objects of interest among female society, to whom he would for a time pay consistent court. But just when the young lady concerned was beginning to feel that her suitor might at last be brought to the point, she would find herself cut out by a new arrival on the scene. It was exasperating, but as her Mama would be sure to explain, it was one of the setbacks in the game which must be taken philosophically. Gentlemen of Mr. Lydney's stamp were common enough; they were not yet ready for marriage, but were looking about them. At some point they would see that a decision must at last be made; and when that time came perhaps Mary—or Jane—or Augusta—would reap the benefit; always supposing that another eligible suitor had not presented himself in the interval, which was more than likely. Thus soothed, the rejected ones would do their utmost to conceal injuries which for the most part were only to their vanity.

The other two gentlemen in the group were Sir Jeremy Linslade, a wealthy baronet of three and twenty whose entire interest at present seemed focused upon sporting pursuits; and Mr. Philip Chetwode, eldest son of a baronet and known to be inclined, like his father Sir George, to be bookish. This presented a little difficulty, as few daughters were sufficiently in the bluestocking line to be able to interest him in their conversation; but the intrepid Mamas did not entirely despair. Every normal male must eventually think of marriage, however reluctantly he might reach that stage in his development.

"You going to Newmarket, Jerry?" asked Henry Lydney.

Linslade nodded. "Got a filly running—not much hope, though. The devil's in the Turf, lately—I've dropped a packet. Still, the luck's bound to change, sooner or later."

"I hear Brummell's run aground," put in Philip Chetwode. "All to pieces—he'll most likely have to clear out of the country."

"Who is Brummell?" asked Viscount Shaldon in his most languid tone.

Lydney laughed. "Doing it too brown, Tony! You can't pretend not to know Beau Brummell, the onetime arbiter of fashion. Devil take it, if it hadn't been for him, we wouldn't all be wearing starched neckcloths now!"

"And a deuced good thing, too," replied Shaldon.

"Trouble was, he got too big for his boots, didn't he?" demanded Philip Chetwode. "Not very clever to make an enemy of Prinney, first by criticising the cut of his coat and then by following it up on a later occasion with a highly personal insult."

"Oh, you mean the occasion of that ill-fated ball at the Argyle rooms to which Prinney had been invited by Brummell, Alvanley, Mildmay and Pierrepoint?" said Lydney. "Highness greeted two of 'em but ignored Brummell and Mildmay, whereupon the Beau called out loudly to Alvanley, 'Who's your fat friend?' My father told me of that—said at the time it would finish the Beau for good. Well, mean to say"—he lowered his voice—"a Certain Person may not be very popular in some circles, but he is the First Gentleman, after all."

"I fancy Old Moore must have told us that this is not a propitious month for those whose surnames begin with the letter *B*," drawled Shaldon. "I saw a devilish scurrilous cartoon of Byron in one of the print shops yesterday."

"Well, no wonder," said Jeremy Linslade. "Byron's always set the Town by the ears. Trouble is, fellow's an exhibitionist. There was all that dust about Lady Caroline Lamb, then worse"—he lowered his voice—"with his half-sister, Mrs. Augusta Leigh. And now his wife's left him and is considering a legal separation. Damned if I can understand what the women see in him, let alone in that poetry of his—devilish stuff, in my view."

"No, I can't agree with you there," put in Chetwode, decidedly. "He has great energy of expression and a lyrical eloquence at times, particularly in his admirable pictures of the elements—"

Linslade suppressed a yawn. "Oh, Lord! I'm not a literary man, Phil, so spare me your transports. Are you going to Newmarket, Tony?"

Shaldon drew a gold and enamelled snuffbox from his pocket and thoughtfully inhaled a pinch of its contents.

"Possibly. But I'm off to Alvington first."

"Don't often go there, do you?" asked Lydney, incuriously.

"I can generally resist its charms, certainly. But on

this occasion, my parent has particularly requested the pleasure of my company."

His tone was heavy with irony.

"My father's there," Lydney remarked. "Bringing m'mother and sister back with him shortly. Cynthia's making her come-out this season. Lord, what a fuss these females make over the business! I'm thankful I'm not living under the same roof, give you my word."

Baron Lydney's town house was in Berkeley Street, but his eldest son had taken rooms for himself in Bruton Street when he had come down from University.

Chetwode nodded glumly. "You may well be. Truth to tell, I'm considering looking for a snug lodging for myself, now that my sister Melissa's about to be launched into society. It was all very well while she was away at school, but things aren't the same now there's a young female to turn the house upside down."

In spite of this speech, the others knew Chetwode too well not to be aware that he was very fond of his young sister. Lydney was another matter; there seemed little love lost between him and Miss Cynthia Lydney, with whom so far no one except Viscount Shaldon was acquainted.

The topic was soon put aside in favour of speculations about the chances of Linslade's horse in the forthcoming meeting at Newmarket; and before long the Club betting book was produced to record each gentleman's degree of optimism concerning a successful outcome for their friend.

On the following morning, Shaldon took himself off for Alvington, driving his curricle drawn by four well matched bay horses.

He arrived in mid-afternoon, having paused on the way to eat a nuncheon and rest his cattle. As he pulled up his team while the lodgekeeper opened the gates of Alvington Hall to admit him, a horseman approaching along the road drew rein and doffed his hat.

"Good afternoon, my lord."

Shaldon looked round to find himself addressed by a personable man of about his own age dressed with care and taste, but without ostentation, in a brown coat and buff pantaloons fastened with a strap under the instep so that they were suitable for riding. He recognised the rider at once, even though they had not met for some years.

"Good God, Durrant! How d'you do?"

"Very well, I thank you, Lord Shaldon. And you— I trust I see you well?"

Shaldon made a suitable reply, adding, "I daresay your errand is much the same as mine. You'll have come down to visit your stepfather. How does Mr. Harrison go on these days?"

"He's pretty stout, my lord, considering all things. But I'm not here solely on his account. I came down a few weeks since with Lord Lydney." He paused. "I daresay you may know that I have been his secretary for the past few years?"

Shaldon nodded, gathering his team together as the lodgekeeper set the gates wide.

"Yes, I did. Well, I'll hope to see you again before I leave, Durrant. Good-bye."

Bertram Durrant removed his hat again, bowed and rode on. Shaldon continued on his way down the drive pulling up before the door and handing his reins to the groom, who jumped down from the perch behind the curricle. Shaldon himself alighted, mounted the steps and plied the heavy knocker.

His knock was answered almost at once by the butler, a well preserved, superior looking man of sixty, who greeted his master's son with the restrained enthusiasm proper to one of his lofty position. He at once summoned his minions to deal with my lord's luggage, privately deciding that the present stay was clearly not intended to be long, as this consisted only of one portmanteau.

"Is your man following, my lord?" he asked respectfully.

"No, I didn't trouble to bring him, Peters. The fact is, I may not be staying overnight, but my plans are uncertain at present."

Reflecting sagely that the one certain thing about the

young Master's plans would be a removal from the Hall as soon as possible, Peters conducted the Viscount to the small salon where the Earl usually sat. On the way, Shaldon asked after those members of the staff whom he had known as a boy and who had not yet withdrawn to an honourable retirement.

"He'll make a good master," Peters confided later to Mrs. Broadbent, the housekeeper. "He don't forget those who served him once, and isn't too puffed up in his own conceit to send them a kindly remembrance. He even gave me a message for his old nurse, Meadows, and she's been pensioned off I don't know how many years."

"Ay, he was always a good boy, Mr. Peters," answered the housekeeper, shaking her grey head. "But small comfort he's ever had from his father, and that's a fact. What kind of father sends his only child to spend the school holidays with his grandparents, I'd like to know? But there, least said soonest mended—only no one can blame young Master if he don't trouble to visit here as often as folk might expect."

The Earl was sitting in a wing chair, with one leg, much swollen and bandaged, extended before him on a footstool. The once bright colour of his hair had dimmed to a mottled grey and there was a drawn look about his face, but the resemblance to his son was still marked. The only differences in their features were that Anthony's nose was longer, more in the style of his dead mother's, and there was a firmer, more resolute set to his chin.

"I'm sorry to see you in this case, sir," said Shaldon, taking the Earl's hand for a moment. "Gout, I collect?"

"Can't get rid of the devilish complaint," growled the Earl. "Damned quacks are no good—tried enough of 'em. Sit down—over there, where I can talk to you without turning round. Well, you've been long enough in coming! Thought you couldn't have had my letter. I wrote to you three weeks since. Where the devil have you been till now?"

Shaldon murmured something about pressure of engagements.

"Don't try to gammon me," returned his sire, irritably. "You could come soon enough if you wanted to, I'll be bound."

"Since you're so certain of that, sir, I won't presume to contradict you," said Shaldon, coolly. "Was there any particular reason why you wished to see me?"

"Particular reason!" echoed the Earl, petulantly. "What particular reason should a man have for wishing to see his own son, I ask you? If you had an ounce of family feeling, you'd come to Alvington a damn sight more often, instead of giving all your time to those damned seditious friends of yours in Town!"

Shaldon raised his eyebrows. *"Seditious* friends? I'm afraid I don't follow you."

"Yes, seditious friends—and worse," repeated the Earl, his face turning a pale purple shade. "There was that good-for-nothing poet fellow, Shelley, who got sent down from Oxford while you were there for writing blasphemy—and he was a particular friend of yours, by all accounts—still is, I daresay. Not content with that, I hear you're forever dining with that damned Whig set, the Hollands. Why, they even supported Bonaparte, and if that ain't treason, I don't know what is!"

"It seems you're singularly well informed about my movements," remarked Shaldon, drily. "Since you don't go up to Town yourself nowadays, and seldom receive visitors, one wonders how you manage it."

"Ay, hipped you, that has, hasn't it?" replied his father, in a tone of satisfaction. "Well, I have my sources of information—I don't mind admitting that."

"Lord Lydney, perhaps? But I'm flattered to think that he takes so much interest in my concerns. As a member of Parliament, I should have supposed he might have had weightier matters to occupy him."

"So he has. But he's served by those who still retain sufficient interest in me to visit me now and then and recount to me some of the things which I ought to know about my own son."

"Ah," said Shaldon, softly. "If I mistake not, you must mean his secretary, Durrant."

171

"Ay, Durrant—Harrison's stepson, and I've yet to meet a more grateful young man for all the advantages that have been offered him."

"Doubtless. But surely he owes you no especial marks of gratitude? It was Mr. Somerby who tutored him as a boy, his stepfather who paid for his schooling, and Lord Lydney who gave him his present post."

"The boy grew up on my land, housed in the comfortable, not to say luxurious, quarters which I allotted to his stepfather as my land agent, didn't he? Certainly he owes me a duty, and I'm pleased to see that he makes some endeavour to pay it. Unlike some I could mention, whose connection is nearer, but who are too taken up with their damned Whig friends!"

Shaldon gave a frosty smile. "It might surprise you to know, sir, that the conversation at Holland House is not entirely concerned with politics. One may meet there all the foremost literary and intellectual figures of the day, and the ideas discussed are often, in a sense, above politics. This is what I find fascinating. I've always been interested in listening to new ideas."

The Earl snorted. "You are like your mother in that."

Shaldon's grey eyes took on a hint of steel.

"You could not pay me a finer compliment."

"Well, I don't mean to pay you compliments, and so you must know," replied the Earl, irascibly.

"I had collected as much. If not to pay me compliments, sir, what was your real purpose in desiring me to attend you? Was it solely to give me the benefit of your opinion on my friends?"

"A damned fool I'd be to bring you here for that, as I can see very well that my opinion goes for nothing with you! No, there was another matter."

Shaldon waited expectantly. Typically, the Earl was reluctant to begin, and there was a pause of several minutes.

"You know Ned Lydney's been down here at Askett House for the past few weeks, I daresay?" he went on, presently.

Shaldon nodded. "I learned as much from Durrant,

whom I met as I was turning in at the gates. We exchanged a word or two."

"Yes, well, when Ned returns to Town he's taking
his wife with him for the girl's come-out. He took a
notion into his head—came to see me about it. Must
say, I think it's a sound scheme."

Shaldon waited again; but his father seemed reluctant to continue, pulling out a handkerchief with some
deliberation and blowing his nose with unnecessary
force.

"I imagine," said Shaldon, at last, "that all this must
have something to do with me in some way?"

"Yes, well, of course it does," replied the Earl tes-
tily, seeing that he could scarcely avoid making a plain
tale, and disliking the task. "You had any thoughts
about marriage yet?"

Shaldon looked up alertly. He saw now where all
this was leading, but perversely he had no intention of
giving his father any help in explaining matters.

"It's a subject I always take care to avoid," he answered smoothly.

"Ha! Well, don't say I altogether blame you. I myself was married too young—but that don't signify
now. The thing is, you're in your mid-twenties, and
that's a good time for matrimony. Can't leave it much
longer, y'know. We must have an heir for the estate."

He paused, hoping that he had already said enough
for Anthony to take the point; but the grey eyes turned
on him were glinting with mischief. And suddenly the
Earl was reminded uncomfortably of an interview on
the same topic long ago between himself and his own
father, and of the difference between his reactions at
that time and Anthony's now. The memory sharpened
his resentment.

"Oh, quite," replied Shaldon, calmly. "I will give the
matter my attention at some time, when I'm not too
taken up with more pressing concerns."

"I'm saying you're to give it your attention at once—
at once, d'you hear?" shouted the Earl, turning purple
again.

"Have a care, sir," said Shaldon, soothingly. "I would not wish you to do yourself a mischief."

"Much you care, you good-for-nothing, you! It must be plain to the weakest intellect what I'm trying to say, but you take a positive delight in affecting not to understand me! Don't tell me—I'm up to your knavish tricks, right enough!"

Having no desire to see his father work himself into an apoplexy, Shaldon decided to abandon his fencing.

"I collect that all this roundaboutation is to do with the notion Lord Lydney took into his head, and which you approve? Could it by any chance concern a match between Miss Cynthia Lydney and myself?"

The Earl sighed in relief, his colour subsiding.

"Ay, that's it. We've been friends since youth, Ned and I, our estates march side by side, and an alliance there would be suitable on all counts. What d'you say, Anthony?"

"I don't wish to marry at present, sir."

"Why not? What can be your objection? There ain't anyone else you've in mind, is there?"

Shaldon shook his head.

"Then what's wrong with Ned's girl? She's as pretty as a picture, not like—well, never mind that," he added, hastily. "And she's got winsome ways, too. I declare when Ned brought her here the other day, she made me feel young again! You ought to jump at the chance of such a girl—birth, breeding, fortune, and good looks, into the bargain!"

"And also—unless she's changed a great deal since childhood—a malicious tongue," added Shaldon. "That's not among the endowments I desire in the lady whom I shall one day make my wife."

"How long is it since you've seen her?" demanded the Earl, working himself up again.

Shaldon meditated. "Let me see . . . It was sometime when I chanced to be here during the holidays from Eton. I suppose I was fifteen or sixteen—that would make Cynthia about ten years old. Shortly afterwards she went to school herself, I believe, and our paths have never crossed since."

174

"Well, the chit's close on nineteen now, and a woman grown, so there's no reason to suppose she'll bear the slightest resemblance to a child of ten! Why don't you suspend judgment until you've met her again? I can easily arrange with Ned to bring her over here, if you're staying for a few days, as I daresay you will."

"You are very good, sir, but I believe I need not trouble you to make any arrangements for my benefit," replied Shaldon, firmly. "Since Miss Lydney is to have a season in Town, I must inevitably meet her there among the scores of other young ladies who are making their debut. I can then judge how much—or little—she has changed."

"And what kind of answer do you expect me to give Lydney in the meantime?" demanded his father, angrily. "Am I to say that you will look the girl over and decide if she'll do, as though she were—were—"

"A piece of merchandise?" supplied Shaldon, cynically. "Isn't that precisely what you intend to make of her, between you?"

"You know well enough that such arrangements are a commonplace between families of consequence. Why, my marriage to your mother was one such."

Shaldon gave him a straight look. "Yes, I am aware of that, sir, and it does nothing to diminish my dislike of arranged marriages."

The Earl uttered an incoherent cry, and thumped his fist on the arm of his chair.

"You dare to defy me, boy!" he raged. "Let me tell you that when my father directed me to marry, I durst not have answered him as you've done, for my life! It's a pity that you are not dependent upon me, as I was on him, and then we would see! This all comes of the Reddifords settling their estate upon you after your mother's death. You now have a house and a fortune in your own right, and can cock a snook at me, knowing that I am powerless to force your hand!"

He paused for breath. His son sat silent; everything germane to the issue had already been said, and there was no point in enraging his father to the verge of hysteria. To Shaldon's surprise, however, suddenly the

Earl's frenzy abated, and a look of triumph appeared on his face.

"Don't you be too sure of that, though, my lord Viscount—just don't be too sure!"

Chapter XVI

THE GATE IN the park paling which had been so convenient to Amanda Somerby during the lifetime of her dear friend, the Countess of Alvington, was seldom used nowadays. It squeaked dismally as Viscount Shaldon pushed it open to step through into the wood beyond.

He did not know what sudden impulse had made him go on foot by this half-forgotten route to the Rectory instead of calling in at the house on his way as he drove out of the village; but once inside the familiar wood he found himself assailed by memories. It was very quiet here now. The silence closed about him as if this were a secret place and he an intruder. Yet he could remember it ringing with the shouts of children intent on some game or other, scrambling up the trees like monkeys to snatch down autumn's glossy brown conkers, or gathering greedy armfuls of the bluebells that in spring grew there in profusion. Did they grow there still? He looked down at the ground around his feet, and detected the first green spears appearing. Of course, it was too early for them yet, but there might be primroses.

In those days, the weather must always have been fair; for his memories were of sunlight shining through the foliage, warm upon his back, and glinting on the bright hair of a little girl. Quick upon this recollection came another memory, long pushed to the depths of his consciousness. Memory of an agony so sharp that for a second he felt it again, new sprung, dragging him down with the chains of the past. And almost in the same moment, he could feel a soft cheek pressed against his own with the wordless sympathy of a child who had left him one of her treasured pets for consolation.

These were sentimental maunderings, he told himself, shaking the unaccustomed mood from him and striding purposefully forward. That boy—all those children—had vanished long since. Life moved on and people changed. There was nothing quite so certain as change.

He became aware that he was no longer alone in the wood. He heard the scurrying of animal feet through the undergrowth and the intermittent high-pitched barking of a dog. In between the excited yelps, there was the sound of someone calling, evidently trying vainly to bring the recalcitrant wanderer to heel. A few moments later a brown and white terrier puppy came bounding past him, pulled up abruptly in a flurry of paws sliding over vegetation, then raced off again, tail wagging furiously. After him came a girl, breathless and dishevelled.

"Oh, Patch, you wretched creature—stop! Stop, I say! Patch! Patch! Come here at once!"

She had almost run into the Viscount. She pulled up hurriedly on seeing him, a look of dismay crossing her face.

"Oh, dear, I do beg your pardon!" she panted. "I was chasing my dog, and I'm afraid I didn't see you!"

Shaldon removed his hat. "No need for apologies, ma'am. Can I be of any assistance?"

"You are very good, but I must not trouble you," she began, then broke off, staring at him with a fixity that seemed scarcely civil.

Her gaze lingered particularly on his auburn hair. He put up a hand to smooth it down, thinking that it must be in disorder and wondering cynically why she

177

should take exception to this, considering the dishevelled state of her own.

"Oh!" she gasped, as one who has had a sudden revelation. "You are—surely you must be—Viscount Shaldon?"

He bowed. "The same. But I fear you have the advantage of me, ma'am."

"Well, I daresay I may, for it's not at all likely that you would recollect me from all those years ago, especially—"

She paused, blushing as she realised that there were briars clinging to her skirt, and that her hair, which had been caught up by twigs once or twice in her recent flight, must be tumbling about her face.

"Especially not looking as I must do at present," she finished, lamely.

"Enchanting, if I may say so," replied the Viscount promptly, with considerable address. "But I fear I can't quite . . ."

He considered her appraisingly. Her hair, which had pulled loose from its pins and was floating about her face and the collar of the somewhat shabby cloak she was wearing, was of a light brown colour—honey gold, he told himself. Apart from a smudge on her face, no doubt gained in passing too close to the trunk of a tree, the effect of her delicate features and lively hazel eyes was decidedly pleasing.

It was her expression, friendly yet slightly rueful, which finally became familiar. He snapped his fingers in triumph.

"Of course! What a dolt I am! It's Helen—Miss Somerby, I should say. And how are you, ma'am after all these years?"

"Out of breath," she replied, laughing. "And almost out of temper! I brought out my wretched puppy to exercise him, and only see how he serves me, running away the first moment I allow him off the lead!"

"Móst reprehensible," he agreed, gravely. "But I daresay he'll return now that you've ceased to chase him. There's positively no fun in running away without a pursuer, you know. And look—there he is."

She turned her head to see the puppy standing only a few yards away, looking at her with its head on one side, expectantly.

"You odious creature!" she scolded. "How dare you!"

The puppy greeted this reproach with a wild orgy of tail wagging and excited yelps, then turned to dash off again.

"Come here, sir!" commanded Shaldon, in his sternest tones.

The puppy's tail stopped wagging and sank between its legs as it crawled abjectly forward towards the recognised voice of Authority. Shaldon stooped and held its collar with one hand while he took the lead from Helen with the other, fastening it securely in place.

"Well!" she exclaimed in disgust. "If that isn't the outside of enough! Here have I been shouting at the creature to come to heel until I was hoarse, and at one word from you—a stranger—he capitulates! Shame on you, Patch!"

"I daresay it's because I am a stranger, and the little chap has no real hopes of a game with me. Whereas I'm quite sure you are always romping with him."

"Very true. Well, thank you, sir—not least for saving my face! Shall I take him now?"

"As I was about to stroll over to visit your parents," replied Shaldon, retaining the dog's lead, "I may as well relieve you of the responsibility. How old is he?"

"Only seven months. I daresay he'll settle down in time, but he's the most lively handful at present. Only last month, he chewed poor Papa's slippers to shreds! Papa threatened that he would have to be handed over to one of the farmers, so that he could take out his hunting instincts in their barns; but I managed to propitiate Papa by working an extra handsome new pair of slippers for him. So all is forgiven for the present, until Patch does the next dastardly thing."

She chattered on in this way for several minutes, while Shaldon enjoyed watching the changing expressions on her mobile face. The more he looked, the

179

more memories came to him of the lively child who once had been his companion in this wood.

"Are you on a visit to the Earl?" she asked, as they came to the gate leading into the Rectory garden.

He nodded. "A short visit only. I arrived but a few hours since and have the intention of leaving as soon as I've visited your parents."

She looked up alertly at his dry tone. "Oh, dear! I collect he must have been a trifle in his crotchets? He suffers much from the gout nowadays, so that may have been the reason."

"In part, no doubt. But I believe you know my family affairs too well, Miss Somerby, not to be aware that my father and I don't deal well together. That is why I'm not a more frequent visitor to Alvington. In point of fact, he summoned me here on this occasion."

"He did? That sounds as though he might have wished for you to be better friends."

He gave a short laugh. "If so, he chose an odd way of going to work. He began by ringing a peal over me on account of what he termed my seditious friends."

"Oh."

It was plain that this remark had aroused her ever lively curiosity, but good manners prevented her from pressing for an explanation. He seemed to understand as much, for he regarded her with a twinkle in his eye.

"Pray don't restrain your natural interest, ma'am. One of my seditious friends is Percy Bysshe Shelley, the poet. You may not be aware that he was sent down from Oxford while I was there, for publishing a pamphlet entitled *The Necessity of Atheism*. I daresay that may shock you, as you're a clergyman's daughter, what?"

She paused to consider this. "I should suppose that the main purpose of a University education is that young men may have an opportunity to examine ideas. And a poet will not see things quite as other men do, after all."

He looked at her with dawning respect. "You speak your mind with admirable certainty for a very young lady, Miss Somerby."

"I am not so very young," she protested, half indignantly. "I am turned nineteen."

"A great age, indeed."

She gave him a saucy glance. "Now you're quizzing me," she accused. "I've not forgotten that you're my senior by five and a half years—I suppose you mean to patronise me on that account!"

"Assure you I wouldn't dare to do so! I must not quarrel with you as soon as we have met again after a lapse of so many years. Besides, I've had enough of wrangling for one day."

"I expect you have," she replied, her mood changing. "Was it only for that you and the Earl came to cuffs?"

Shaldon raised his eyebrows ostentatiously at this slang expression, and she laughed.

"Now you're treating me as James does, and it's a great deal too bad of you. One brother is enough!"

"I daresay. But no, my father's animadversions on my friends were not the only cause of our disagreement. He was also bent on planning my marriage."

"Oh. I did not know. That is, my brother had not mentioned that you were intending to marry. But possibly you haven't informed him."

"I am not. Nothing is further from my mind, at this present. But the matter seems to be occupying my father's a good deal, and he took it amiss when I refused to consider the subject with the seriousness which he believes it to merit."

"I see. And did he recommend the state in general to your notice, or—" She broke off, dismayed at her temerity, and blushed. "Oh, dear, I really should not ask!"

His eyes twinkled down at her. "No, perhaps you should not, were you not very nearly my sister. But since you've succeeded during this past ten minutes or so in re-establishing that relationship, I may as well tell you. He would like me to marry Miss Lydney."

They had reached the door to the house some moments since and were lingering on the threshold, absorbed in their conversation. He saw that a momentary shadow crossed her face, and raised his eyebrows in an unspoken query.

"Cynthia," she said, slowly. "I suppose it would seem to be a suitable connection."

He shrugged. "But not one to which I aspire. I said as much, and brought a scene about my ears. Indeed, I had the gravest fears that he would go off into an apoplexy! All things considered, it seemed wiser to relieve him of my presence."

"I daresay you did right." Helen pushed open the door. "And now pray do come in and see my parents, while I relieve you of the charge of that tiresome hound."

Recognising instantly this reference to itself, the puppy, which had been behaving with surprising docility while led by Shaldon, at once pricked up its ears and emitted a short, sharp yelp.

"Yes, well, that will be quite enough," said Helen severely. "I daresay there'll be some titbits for you in the kitchen. Will you take him, Sally?"

She took the lead from Shaldon and handed it over to a housemaid, whom Patch greeted as an old friend. Then she conducted Shaldon to a small, oak-panelled parlour furnished with an air of comfort rather than fashion, where her parents were sitting.

"I've brought you a visitor," she announced.

The Rector pushed his spectacles up on to his forehead as he glanced up from his book, but his wife at once jumped to her feet.

"Anthony!" she exclaimed. "Oh, what a delightful surprise!"

She came impetuously towards him, hands extended. Amanda Somerby's hair was streaked with grey nowadays and her waist had thickened a little, but she was still an attractive woman. He took her hands, carrying one to his lips in a courtly gesture.

"I found Lord Shaldon in the wood," said Helen, "when I was exercising Patch. At least," she added, laughing, "I'm not sure that it wasn't the other way about, and that Patch was exercising me! If you will

182

forgive me for a few moments, I really must go and tidy myself."

The Rector, who had risen in his turn to greet their visitor, gave her a quizzical glance.

"Yes, my dear, I scarcely think anyone will disagree with that."

She wrinkled her nose at him and went out of the room. When she returned about ten minutes later, her hair was pinned neatly back into a chignon with only a few soft tendrils escaping onto her face. She wore a plain dark blue Kerseymere gown with a high neck and long sleeves buttoned at the wrist. Shaldon thought that she looked very different now from the madcap girl who had burst through the trees in pursuit of her dog. He felt a little regret for the change, and found his conversation with her a shade more formal because now she looked so much the young lady. But as the Rector and his wife had a great deal to say to him, there was less opportunity at present for him to talk to their daughter.

Evidently he had explained to her parents in her absence how matters had gone at the Hall, for soon her mother was pressing him to stay overnight at the Rectory.

"You won't wish to begin a journey to London without first taking a meal," she urged. "And you will be doing us a great service by enlivening our dinner table, for we are to be on our own this evening. Now do say that you'll take pot luck with us! There's no need of formality, for you were always used to be quite one of the family. And if you're thinking it will put me to any trouble, you are wrong, I assure you."

He hesitated. Before leaving the neighbourhood he had planned to spend a few days with his maternal grandparents at Kenton Manor. Although the Manor was only five miles distant, he had previously decided against going there this evening. The Cottesfords were getting on in years and, moreover, were not expecting him until tomorrow. It had seemed kinder not to present himself prematurely and unannounced, but to stay at the local posting house overnight. The prospect of a solitary dinner at an inn now appeared bleak, however, in comparison with the warm hospitality offered him by the Somerbys.

Mrs. Somerby saw his hesitation and renewed her persuasions, calling on her husband and daughter to second them. They soon overcame his polite diffidence, and a servant was sent over to the Hall to fetch his luggage and deliver instructions to his groom to bring the curricle round to the Rectory in the morning.

It was a long time since he had passed such a pleasant yet uneventful evening. The dinner set before him was as Mrs. Somerby claimed, a plain family meal; it consisted of chicken soup, fish with an egg sauce, roast beef and cabbage, with a syllabub to follow. But it was well cooked, attractively served and seasoned by entertaining yet easy conversation. Helen sat beside him in a simple white muslin evening gown that set off her fair skin and gold-brown hair. He found himself once again watching with pleasure the changing expressions on her face, or the set of her head as she turned to speak to him. Certainly she had grown into a lovely girl, and her attraction was enhanced by the fact that she seemed unconscious of her own charm.

"You can have no notion," she said, smiling up at him, "how delightful it is to be able to speak freely at mealtimes. I am becoming accustomed to it now, but at first when I came home from the Seminary in Kensington I fear I was a great trial to my parents! I was always trying to entertain them with the kind of elegant conversation permitted there at table."

They all laughed over this.

"It's very necessary, though," said Mrs. Somerby, "to know how to manage that kind of civil small talk, even though your own family do not wish for it. And I daresay it will stand you in good stead, Helen, when you go to Town next month."

Shaldon raised his eyebrows.

"Are you then to make a visit to Town?"

Helen nodded. "I have been invited to stay with

184

one of my friends, Melissa Chetwode, who lives in Cavendish Square."

"We're very well acquainted with the family," put in Mrs. Somerby; "otherwise we might have hesitated to accept the invitation, even though Melissa was so set on having Helen there. Sir George Chetwode has been a friend of Mr. Somerby's since their Oxford days. I first met his wife soon after their marriage, and we became firm friends, too. We were used to see a good deal of them at one time, when they lived in Oxfordshire, but since they took up residence in London we've met less frequently."

"I too am acquainted with the family, in particular with their eldest son, Philip," said Shaldon.

"An agreeable young man," remarked the Rector. "And interested in literary subjects, I recall from our infrequent meetings."

"Oh, yes, Phil's a trifle in the bluestocking line," agreed the Viscount.

"Dear me!" exclaimed Helen. "It looks as though I shall need to polish up my elegant conversation to include some literary allusions!"

Her father smiled at her. "I venture to think that you will acquit yourself sufficiently creditably, my dear, without any scholarly burning of the midnight oil. But we must allow for your nonsense."

"Well, Melissa isn't at all a bluestocking, at any rate," said Helen. "And we know each other so well that I may be as nonsensical as I like with her."

"She's devoted to you," Mrs. Somerby remarked, with a smile. "She once told me that but for your kindness to her when she first went to school and felt so dreadfully homesick, poor child, she would have begged her Mama to take her home again."

Helen looked embarrassed for a moment. "Oh, well, all of us felt like that at first, Mama, but it soon passed off, and then we had no end of fun, in spite of Old Catty and her rules! But," she added, looking apologetically at their guest, "we mustn't bore Lord Shaldon with such talk."

"Not at all. I am fascinated. But you mustn't think

that my friend Chetwode is at all stuffy, for all his bookish leanings. Nothing could be further from the truth, assure you. I shall hope to see you, then, ma'am, when you are staying with the family in Town. That is, if you don't find yourself too occupied, for the London season is a rackety business, you know."

Helen glanced a little ruefully at her father, and Shaldon wondered if perhaps he had said the wrong thing. However, the Rector made no comment, but smiled tolerantly as his wife and daughter rose from the table, the meal being concluded, to leave the gentlemen to sit over their wine.

"It must be more than five years since you last saw Anthony," said Mrs. Somerby, as they seated themselves in the drawing room. "What do you think of him now, Helen?"

"He seems to be everything that a gentleman should be—handsome, amusing, and with considerable address," replied her daughter, carelessly. "He's a regular dasher, or so I'm told."

Amanda Somerby frowned. "I must say I don't quite like such a description of him. Who told you so?"

"Oh, Cynthia. She also hinted that he was— well . . . " Helen's voice trailed off as she met her mother's indignant glance.

"Cynthia! I suppose you know how much credence you can place in anything she says!" Her tone changed. "He was telling us while you were upstairs that the Earl wishes him to marry that girl. I must say I sincerely hope he doesn't! We've known Anthony since he was a child, and he's almost like another son to me, little though I've seen of him since he came to manhood. He's not in the least like his father in disposition, but takes after his dear Mama. Marriage with such a girl as Cynthia would totally wreck his happiness. Of that I'm convinced!"

"But, Mama, what can you really know of him nowadays?" protested Helen. "Surely one needs to be constantly in company with people to judge? I'll confess that when he told me the Earl had decided upon

186

Cynthia as a wife for him, I was dismayed for the moment. But that was a foolishness—a kind of echo from my childhood, when I, too, thought of him as one of my own family. He and I are strangers, now, meeting as if for the first time."

"Well, that may be true, my love, but I think we can never quite cast off our childhood associations," persisted her mother.

"Oh, Mama, you must have forgotten what it's like to be young!" laughed Helen. "At my age, that's the very thing one tries hard to do! At any rate, I haven't the slightest intention of concerning myself with Lord Shaldon's marriage. He may wed whom he chooses, for my part!"

The entrance of the gentlemen naturally put an end to this conversation; and it was only later, in the privacy of her bedchamber, that Helen was able to consider the day's events and speculate further on the subject of Viscount Shaldon.

He was certainly most agreeable, and she had found a great deal of entertainment in his company. Was he really the kind of man Cynthia's dark hints suggested? She surprised herself by discovering a hope that he might not be. But that was absurd. What could it possibly matter to her, one way or another? In London she hoped to meet many agreeable gentlemen, besides other interesting people of both sexes. So far, she had never been much in society, and the prospect of new places and faces excited her eager curiosity. Viscount Shaldon would be only one amongst many, if indeed he did take the trouble to renew their acquaintance once he had returned to his own circle.

Mama, of course, felt differently about him, for she was emotionally involved. Mama, bless her, like most of her generation, lived chiefly in the past. To Helen, avid for the new experiences that life might offer, it was the present that mattered.

Chapter XVII

"Good God, Neville, I think you must have run mad!"

Baron Lydney faced the Earl of Alvington in consternation.

"Have you paused to consider what a pretty scandal you'll be bringing about your ears—and your son's too, come to that! Why, that damned fellow Bryon's affairs will be nothing to it!"

The Earl's face took on a mulish look. "What should I care for scandal? I live out of the world here, so they can say what they will and never trouble me. As for Anthony, he must take his chance. Time he learnt that everything ain't going to fall into his lap."

"You never liked the boy, did you?" asked Lydney, curiously. "Can't quite think why. He's a pleasant enough chap, by what I've seen of him. Don't visit you much, but then none of 'em want to hang about the parental home once they come to manhood. A good thing, too, I'd say. And in any case, you only seem to come to cuffs whenever you are together, so mayhap he's wiser to stay away."

"I never got the chance to stay away from my own father, and well you know it," growled the Earl. "Why the devil should he be able to go his own road without so much as a by your leave? Tell me that!"

Lydney shot an acute glance at him. "Jealous of the boy, are you?" he asked. "Don't care to see him independent when your own case was so different?

All the same, no need to play him such a shabby trick as this."

"You don't mince your words, b'God, do you?"

"We've known each other too long for that." Lydney changed his tone to a persuasive one. "Be guided by me, Neville, and let matters stand as they are. No point in bringing out your dirty linen to wash in public for everyone's amusement. Especially as it must be pointless. Depend on it, the child died years ago, as the woman told you it must."

"She could have been mistaken," replied the Earl, obstinately.

"Stands to sense it can't have survived, my dear fellow, or you don't suppose she'd have allowed you to remain in ignorance of its continued existence?"

"She told me she'd take nothing—ordered me off."

Lydney smiled cynically. "Yes, in the first emotional high flight, very likely. But afterwards, as the child grew older, needed food, clothes and so on, do you suppose for a moment that her rancour would have withstood her cupidity? She'd have been after you like a shot."

"Ah, but she couldn't." A look of cunning crossed the Earl's face. "You may have forgotten, Ned, but I told you at the time that I was careful—very careful. She never knew my title or so much as the county where I lived, let alone the actual residence. There was nothing by which she could have traced me."

"You went through the marriage ceremony in your family name. It would not be impossible for a determined person to trace you through that."

"Pshaw! She was without friends or connections who could have helped her in that regard, and she was not the kind of woman to tackle such a task on her own. Besides, if she had ever been able to make any such enquiries, she would surely have done so during my long absences while I was wedded to her daughter. She trusted me little enough; I could see that."

Lord Lydney reflected that in this the unknown

woman had showed great common sense, but he wisely suppressed the comment.

"Well, even if you feel secure on that point, you may easily have left other clues that you've forgotten —letters, for instance, or small items of personal property?"

"The only letter I ever wrote to the girl—my first wife—I took good care not to put any heading on it, I can tell you. As for items of personal property—" He broke off, looking discomfited for a moment. "I'd forgotten until now, but she did keep my signet ring. I had made use of it for the marriage ceremony, because like a fool I forgot to procure one beforehand. She begged to retain it afterwards, and I couldn't well refuse. Besides, I saw no harm in that. It bore the initial *N* and the flower of the Stratton crest—a poppy. But how many people could identify that, I ask you? And of the few who could, none would be at all likely to have any acquaintance with Mrs. Lathom."

"No, but if she took it to a lawyer, as she well might do if she wished to trace you, it would not have been beyond his powers," Lydney pointed out. "And that's why I feel confident that the child could not have survived. So why not let things be, and save yourself from stirring up a nasty scandal that can achieve nothing?"

"I've already told you I care nothing for being the subject of one of the London on-dits! I never go to Town nowadays. This damned leg," he groaned as he moved the bandaged member to what he hoped might prove a more comfortable position. "How can a fellow get about with an encumbrance like this? What have I got to lose? I daresay I shan't last much longer, so I may as well set matters straight before I go."

"Well, if you're not scared off by the thoughts of a scandal for yourself or even for Anthony, surely you have some regard for the family name?"

"Devil a bit! The Strattons were never Puritans, as my father always reminded me. Besides, who's going to be shocked? With adultery and bastards abounding in high society, not to speak of incest, if what they

190

say of that chap Byron is true, who will exclaim over a secret marriage? Didn't Prinney himself contract one? Bah!"

"There's far more to it than a secret marriage," Lydney reminded him caustically. "If the full facts became known, they wouldn't look pretty. While you were married to one woman, you were courting another under the guise of honourable intentions. Moreover—I am sorry to be blunt, but I'm endeavouring to show you what will be said by others—you not only neglected your first wife, but you abandoned your child."

The Earl's face suffused with anger. "Damn you!" he roared, following this with a vivid oath. "You think to preach to me now, do you? You know very well how matters stood—how helpless I was in the face of my father's insistence that I should wed Maria—"

"Yes, yes," Lydney replied, soothingly. "*I* know how matters stood, right enough. I was merely trying to show you how the facts would appear to others."

"Then don't, damn you! And damn them, too, for a set of scandalmongering, whited sepulchres!"

Lydney shrugged. "It's the way of the world."

"Yes, well, thank God I'm out of it!"

"But I'm not," retorted Lydney, deciding to play what he hoped would prove to be his trump card. "I feel bound to inform you, Neville, that if you persist in dragging all this out into the light of day, any thoughts of an alliance between our two families must be at an end."

"You mean your daughter Cynthia and my son? Well, that's as you choose, of course. But who says," demanded the Earl, in a milder tone, "that anything need be made public at present? A discreet inquiry by my family lawyers was what I had in mind, as a beginning. Afterwards, if it proves that the child died, no one need be any the wiser. And since you seem strongly of the opinion that matters will turn out in that way, there can be no occasion to call off the arrangement between us for the time being."

Lydney considered this for a few moments in silence. He was very set on a marriage between Cynthia and Viscount Shaldon. Even with her advantages of beauty, birth and fortune, there could scarcely be a more brilliant prospect for her. It would be a pity to abandon it without a struggle. But he had done his utmost to persuade Neville against this harebrained notion of his, without success. The Earl had become obstinate nowadays and opposition only made him worse. Supposing, though, the investigation could be carried out with the utmost discretion, so that not a word about it ever leaked out? Lydney felt convinced that the child of that secret marriage had died long since, and that therefore Anthony's position would remain secure as the rightful heir of Alvington. Since the Earl was undoubtedly determined to carry out an investigation, the only way to save the situation was to make quite sure that it should be done by someone completely trustworthy, who would not talk.

"Not your lawyers, Neville," he said, aloud. "You know how it is in such a case. They employ clerks to assist them, and in the end a score of individuals are privy to your secrets. And who's to say that one of 'em won't blab to one of these damned scandalmongering journals that circulate in the Town? No, I've a far better notion than that. Entrust your inquiry to one man alone—a man who's dependent on our patronage, yours and mine, for a living; who already owes us a great deal, and can be relied on to consider our interests. Moreover, I can tell you confidently that he's a devilish clever fellow—shrewd enough to be a match for any sharpster, and well up to snuff in everything."

He saw at once that this time he had made some impression. The Earl hesitated for a moment, then nodded.

"Well, you may be right about the lawyers," he said, a shade grudgingly. "I might instruct Watson to handle matters himself, but there's no guarantee that he wouldn't pass some things over to an underling to deal with, hoping I would never know. If we could keep it to one man for the time being, it would certainly be an advantage, but whom have you in mind?

I must confess I don't quite follow you. Someone who depends on our patronage for his living, you say? Oh," as illumination came, "I suppose you mean my agent's stepson?"

"Exactly—my secretary, Bertram Durrant. He's the very man for the job. But you will be obliged to tell him the whole, keeping nothing back."

The book room at Askett House was very quiet, its silence broken only by the faint sound of a pen travelling industriously over paper. The young man who wielded the pen looked up from his work for a moment as the door opened, then sprang to his feet as he saw who the intruder was. Miss Lydney, the soft folds of her stylish green morning gown swishing about her ankles as she entered, smiled at him apologetically.

"So sorry for disturbing you, Mr. Durrant. I left my book from the circulating library in here somewhere, I think."

"Permit me to help you find it, Miss Lydney. Pray, what was the title of the book?"

He stood poised helpfully, awaiting her answer. She moved over to stand beside him at his desk, lifting one or two books lying there and glancing carelessly at them.

"Oh, I'm not sure," she answered, laying the volumes down again with a shrug. "Some tedious novel or another."

She was standing very close to him and now she looked up into his face, her dark eyes provocative. He tried to prevent his own from following the white curve of her neck beneath the transparent muslin which formed the yoke of her gown, but without complete success. She was a lovely creature and he found her nearness disturbing, a fact which she knew very well. Life was dull at Askett House, and baiting Bertram Durrant provided a welcome diversion.

"Do you read novels, Mr. Durrant?" she asked. "Or do you find your entertainment in real life?"

His cravat, which was faultlessly arranged, suddenly seemed too tight. He put up a hand to loosen it. She smiled bewitchingly, revealing twin dimples in her cheeks.

"As to that, ma'am, I fear I cannot devote very much time to the reading of fiction."

She gave him a deprecating smile. "A pity. And so you're obliged to look for your romance elsewhere, is that it?"

"I—er—"

She laughed, a low musical sound that he found entrancing.

"Oh, pray don't be too bashful to confess it! Even a studious gentleman such as yourself must have some diversions. I venture to think that beneath that sober exterior beats as warm-blooded a heart as any to be found in the pages of the most romantical novel!"

He took a firm grip on himself, moving back a few paces in the pretence of arranging some papers on his desk so that he could avoid the challenge of her eyes.

"I am no match for your ready wit, Miss Lydney."

"Ah, I see you mean to be odiously discreet, sir. But you may trust me with your secrets, you know."

Her tone was still one of light raillery, but he felt more in control of the situation now that he had increased the distance between them.

"You do me too much honour, ma'am," he replied with a bow. "Nevertheless, I have no secrets of sufficient interest to disclose, I fear."

"No?" Her eyebrows arched in a pretty gesture of surprise. "Oh, dear, I find that prodigiously sad! What a dull life it must be, with nothing to be gloated over in privacy, no circumstance which may not be freely revealed to the world at large! I most sincerely commiserate with you, Mr. Durrant."

"You need not, ma'am. I consider myself most fortunate in my situation here."

"You mean as my father's secretary? Ah, but that is *work*, sir, and I was speaking of *diversion*. You know the saying, 'All work and no play makes Jack a dull boy'? You would not wish that to be true of yourself, surely?"

"I should be sorry to think that you considered me

194

a dull dog, indeed, Miss Lydney," he retorted, with some show of spirit.

She smiled complacently, and he saw she knew that she had scored a hit at last. Damn the girl, he thought, why must she choose to flirt with him, knowing full well that he was not in a position to take his part freely in her game? If he were once to step out of line, say one ill-chosen word, his livelihood would be in jeopardy. She knew this as well as he did; no doubt it added spice to her performance.

"A dull dog? Oh, no. How could you ever impute anything so uncivil to my account? Indeed, if you must know, I consider you to be more interesting than most of the gentlemen of my acquaintance."

He looked up quickly at that, an unguarded expression in his eyes for a second. Then he lowered them again to his papers. When he spoke, his voice was carefully controlled.

"I am indeed honoured, Miss Lydney, but I fear the compliment is undeserved. I cannot suppose your male acquaintance to be very extensive as yet."

"Oh, how odiously reserved you are, to be sure!" she exclaimed, pouting. "I say something which I hope will please you . . ."

"As it does, assure you, ma'am—"

". . . and you can do nothing but turn my poor compliment this way and that, saying it is not much of one, after all! Bah! I am out of all patience with you, Mr. Durrant!"

He could not restrain himself from looking up into her eyes again. Seeing the mischief in them, he averted his gaze.

"I am very sorry to hear you say so, Miss Lydney. Possibly I should try to redeem my character in your eyes by helping you to find the mislaid book? I can at least be of some small service to you."

He moved away from the desk with a purposeful air, beginning to search the room. She was about to join him when the door suddenly opened to admit her father.

Lord Lydney paused just inside the door, a frown

gathering on his brow as he saw Cynthia in the room.

"And what the devil are you doing here?" he began, ominously.

She ran to him, taking his arm in hers and looking up appealingly into his face.

"Oh, dear Papa, you do sound most odiously cross! I beg your pardon for intruding, but I came to find a book which I've mislaid, and Mr. Durrant was so good as to assist me in the search. But it isn't here after all, so I'll go away at once if that will make you happy."

He smiled down at her fondly. "Silly puss, you know I can never be cross with you, but you really mustn't waste Durrant's time on trivialities. You could have sent one of the housemaids in to look for your book. And now run along, dear"—he patted her hand—"as we have certain business matters to discuss."

He shepherded her to the door, closing it firmly behind her. Then he motioned Durrant, who had remained respectfully standing, to a chair.

"I have a most delicate commission for you, Durrant," he began, seating himself. "It requires the utmost discretion, as it involves no less a personage than the Earl of Alvington, but I am confident that no one could handle it with greater tact and skill than yourself. I think I need scarcely emphasise that no word of the story I am about to relate to you should ever on any account be divulged to any other person? I have guaranteed his lordship the utmost confidentiality."

"I am grateful for your good opinion, my lord, and shall put forth my best endeavours to serve you."

"Splendid, my dear fellow. Well, now, let me give you the gist of the matter and make plain what is required of you."

Some time later Durrant was walking along the main street of Alvington village as Viscount Shaldon swept through in his curricle. Shaldon raised his hand in a cheery salute and Durrant responded by removing his hat respectfully. Once the vehicle had passed in a swirl of dust, however, his mouth twisted in a sardonic

196

smile. Viscount Shaldon, indeed, heir to the Alvington estates—or was he? It would be a fine take-down for that self-assured young man to find himself only a younger son, after all, to lose both his title and his primogeniture. And not only to lose that, but also his chance of marriage with the lovely Miss Cynthia Lydney. Durrant knew all about the arrangement which had been made between his employer and the Earl for this desirable match—desirable only if Anthony remained his father's heir. But if not, if this mission with which he, Durrant, had been entrusted perchance should end in the discovery of one with a prior right, what then?

He gave some thought to this as he strolled along, unconscious of his surroundings. Presumably Lord Lydney would look elsewhere for a husband for his daughter, settle upon some other sprig of the nobility. Whoever it was, Durrant thought resentfully, it certainly would not be himself. That would be to indulge too high a flight of fancy. Yet he had strong hopes of being able to improve his position in time. Lord Lydney had hinted at a seat in Parliament for him as the Earl's reward for undertaking this investigation; and once there, among men of wealth and influence, he could trust himself to find the means of material advancement. He knew how to get on in the world, if any man did, for the simple reason that he possessed neither birth nor wealth and therefore must rely solely on his wits. He could outwit them all, he thought, and laughed aloud at this reflection.

The next morning he had sobered again. These plans were all very well, but they would take time. While they were coming to maturity, his lovely girl would have been married to someone else. His jaw tightened at the thought. He wanted her more than he had ever wanted anything in a life clouded always by envy of those better born and wealthier than himself. Even when the Lydneys and Shaldon had played with him as equals in boyhood, the rancour had been there. He had never been able to forget their differences in station; James Somerby, too, though not of equal rank and wealth with the others, had still been at a social remove from Bertram Durrant, who was a mere nobody. He thought with contempt of his stepfather Harrison, content to be the Earl of Alvington's agent, happy in his work for the estate, his modest home and income and now equally contented in his retirement. He had never sought or even desired anything better, thinking himself fortunate to have so much. He had told his stepson this many times in the past, adding that it was a great thing to be cock on one's own dunghill; and so he had been, for the Earl had left the management of the estate largely in his hands. To which Bertram had replied that he had no wish to manage some other man's estate, but to possess his own.

There had been no time for women in Durrant's life, but he was a man of strong feelings. During these past weeks he had been privileged to be a good deal in Miss Lydney's company, and her provocative beauty had quickly fired his senses. He was far too shrewd not to realise that she was merely amusing herself with him to pass away the tedium of her stay in the country. Once the family returned to Town, it was unlikely that she would seek out his company in the same way. But at present scarcely a day passed without her coming on some pretext or another into the bookroom where he was working, to flirt with him in the most seemingly innocent way possible. It was becoming almost more than he could bear, lately, to keep his place and behave as if he were stuffed with cotton wool, instead of having hot blood coursing through his veins. Perhaps it was a fortunate thing that he would be obliged to go away for a time now, in quest of the Earl's lost heir. No advertisements, no noise about the business, Lord Lydney had instructed him. That would mean retracing the incredible story from the point where it had started, at Rye in Sussex.

Cynthia was becoming an obsession with him. Her bold dark eyes, her inviting mouth, the curve of her breasts beneath the thin material of her gown, her shapely ankles—all these delights when brought, as so frequently, at close quarters to him, made his senses swim. He must have her. How, he could not at present conjecture. But if he could prevent Shaldon from having her, that, at any rate, would be one step forward on the way. He promised himself grimly that he would spare no possible effort to trace this firstborn son for the Earl of Alvington.

He heard someone addressing him and came to with a slight start, to realise that he was at that moment going past the Rectory and that Miss Helen Somerby was standing at the gate bidding him good day. He paused, responding civilly.

"I won't say a penny for your thoughts, Mr. Durrant," she said with a friendly smile. "Judging from your expression, they were too sober to be worth the price. But then, as Lord Lydney's secretary, you must carry a deal of responsibility."

"I fear so, Miss Somerby, at times. I passed Viscount Shaldon a little way back, tooling his curricle along as though he hadn't a care in the world, and thought how fortunate he was."

"Oh, did you?" asked Helen brightly. "He has been staying overnight with my parents and has just parted from us. As for not having a care in the world—well, I cannot say about that."

"How should you, indeed, ma'am? I suppose nowadays you and he are comparative strangers. But a man in his position can have few cares."

She shook her head. "I scarcely think a man's position makes any difference in that regard. But whatever problems are vexing you at present, sir, I hope you may soon resolve them."

His mind was still partly occupied by the thoughts which he had been revolving before she spoke to him, and for once he made an unguarded remark, speaking in the bitterness of the moment.

"Oh, I will, ma'am, never fear. But I've a matter in hand at present which may bring some far more inflexible problems to Viscount Shaldon's address."

He stopped suddenly, realising his indiscretion.

"Why, what can you mean?" Helen's curiosity was

on the alert at once. "What problems—what is this matter which you have on hand?"

He made a deprecating gesture.

"Merely a general observation, Miss Somerby. Pray pay no heed to it. Good day to you."

He bowed and passed on, but she remained standing at the gate looking after him for some time.

He might pretend that he meant nothing, but she knew better. His tone had been vindictive.

She turned to walk up the path towards the house, a worried frown on her brow. There was some kind of trouble approaching Lord Shaldon, and Durrant not only knew of it, but was taking a spiteful pleasure in the knowledge. Somehow or other, she must try to discover what all this meant.

Chapter XVIII

MEANWHILE, Viscount Shaldon went on his way with no slightest thought of impending trouble. His grandparents were delighted, as always, to see him; they seemed to have aged a good deal since his last visit, especially his grandfather, who was now looking very frail. They asked after his father as a matter of civility rather than interest, and were not at all surprised to learn that the visit to him had ended in a tiff.

"He would like to be able to rule you as his own father ruled him, I daresay," remarked Sir William. "Fortunately, you are not dependent upon him, Anthony, since the Reddifords left you the bulk of their estate. We didn't want it, you know. We told them we would far rather it came to you. And, of course, when we are gone, you are our heir, too."

"And that, sir, will not be for a very long time, I hope," replied Shaldon, with a gentle smile.

Sir William sighed. "I don't know, my boy. One gets very tired, sometimes. But this is dull stuff to be talking, when you have only a few days to stay with us. And so you visited the Somerbys on your way? We see them occasionally. Your mother was very attached to Mrs. Somerby, you know. I find her little altered, except that like all of us, she has grown older."

"She is one of the most charming women of my acquaintance," replied Shaldon. "And as far as I can judge from our brief reunion, her daughter bids fair to be just such another."

"Little Helen? Yes, she was always a delightful child —but I suppose I mustn't call her so, now that she's a young lady full grown and about to step out into the world."

Shaldon laughed. "Indeed not! I was reproved only for saying that she spoke her mind plainly for so young a female."

Sir William's lined face lit with an answering smile. "Were you, my boy? But when one is young, one doesn't wish to be reminded of the fact. Strange, since thereafter females seem intent on appearing younger than in fact they are! But come and entertain your grandmother with some of your Town gossip, Anthony. You can always make her laugh."

Shaldon remained several days at Kenton Manor, afterwards going on to Newmarket, where Sir Jeremy Linslade's mare acquitted herself to the satisfaction of both jockey and owner by winning her race by a comfortable two lengths.

After a short stay in Cambridge with some of his racing friends, Shaldon returned to Town to find a neat stack of correspondence awaiting him on his writing desk. He flipped quickly through this, as most of it consisted of invitations to one entertainment or another —a ball at Lady Malmesbury's, the Duchess of Gloucester's rout, a musical party, a dinner at Holland House—until he came to a letter written in a lady's hand which he knew only too well. He lifted it to break the seal; as he did so, a lingering, familiar perfume drifted to his nostrils.

Since you are as yet the only man who has had the power to make me remember you in absence, do not, I entreat you, forget me utterly. I shall look for you in my box at the Opera on Tuesday, and you may accompany me home afterwards, if you still desire my society.

Yours ever affectionately,
Harriette.

As he read, a cynical smile twisted his lips. His connection with Harriette Wilson had started some years before, when he had first come upon the Town. The lady was an elegant courtesan who had started life as a humble clockmaker's daughter, but had decided that it would be foolish to waste her beauty and talents on marriage to a man in a similar sphere to that of her father, when she might follow the example of her elder sister Amy by making a career for herself in the demimonde. Accordingly, she had embarked on a liaison with the Earl of Craven at the tender age of fifteen, and since then had enjoyed the favours of a distinguished succession of noblemen, among them the Honourable Frederick Lamb, son of Lord Melbourne; the Marquis of Lorne; and Lord Worcester, son of the Duke of Beaufort.

Shaldon had made her acquaintance largely as a matter of bravado, in response to a wager made one evening at White's when the bottle had been circulating freely.

"To the fair Harriette!" one of his companions had said, tossing off a glass.

"Harriette?" Shaldon had queried, for he was still new to the Town and not yet apprised of all the gossip.

"Good God, here's someone who doesn't know who Harriette is!" exclaimed Sir Percy Dunton, a young man whose residence in London antedated Shaldon's by a bare six months. "Why, dear boy, she is the Queen of the demimonde, a peerless barque of frailty who can only be attained by those of the highest rank, the longest purse, and, need I add, the most experience?"

"Which, I suppose, places her beyond your reach?" Shaldon queried, politely.

The other flushed. "Damme, and yours, too, I'll be bound!"

Shaldon's eyes glinted. He had imbibed freely enough to be reckless and he was still barely one and twenty.

"Would you care to lay any odds on that?"

In a moment their companions had gathered round and the wager had been ceremoniously made amid much laughter, encouragement, and advice on how best to storm the lovely citadel.

The following day had brought, besides a slight hangover, a less assured mood. Exactly how did one set about scraping an acquaintance with an acknowledged leader of the demimonde? Shaldon confided his difficulty to Henry Lydney, who happened to call round at his rooms.

"Lord, you'll never have a touch at that one!" Lydney exclaimed, incredulously. "They say she's even been Prinney's mistress, in between his more serious affairs!"

"I don't mind admitting," replied Shaldon wryly, "that I'd liefer it had been an easier bet. It wasn't altogether a sober evening, you understand; otherwise I wouldn't have embarked on an enterprise of the kind. Having done so, however, what's the best way of approaching the female? A bouquet, a handsome geegaw of some kind? I bow to your doubtless superior experience in this field, Lydney."

Lydney laughed. "Such quarry's above my touch," he confessed. "No difficulty about the ordinary little bit of muslin, of course—but I daresay you manage tolerably well yourself in that quarter. I've heard she's surprisingly literate. Why not write her an intriguing letter? Say you're dying to make her acquaintance—all that kind of thing."

"Good God, no! If there's one thing I do know, it's that a man should never put pen to paper in such a case—unless he wishes to pay handsomely at some later date for the doubtful pleasure of obtaining repossession of his own maudlin scribblings!" He broke off, grinning, as an idea suddenly occurred to him. "I have a notion, though, by Jove! Let's see how far sheer impudence will serve me!"

That same evening when Harriette Wilson entered her box at the Opera with two dazzling female companions, she found a young gentleman already sitting there. He rose to his feet with lazy grace; and she saw at once—for she was a connoisseur in such matters—that not only was he a singularly well-looking man with unusual auburn hair, but also that he was undoubtedly a member of the *ton*. Nevertheless, she favoured him with a haughty stare.

"There must be some mistake I fancy, sir," she said, coldly. "This is my private box, and you may see my name on the outside of it."

He bowed, giving her one of his most disarming smiles. "No mistake, assure you, madam. I must confess to having deliberately thrown myself in your way because I most ardently desired to make your acquaintance."

"If that is so, you should have found someone to present you to me in due form," she replied, very much on her dignity.

"How could that be?" He spread his hands out in a rueful gesture. "Can you suppose that any man so fortunate as to enjoy the friendship of La Belle Harriette would be willing to present to you another? No, you must see that it would be asking too much, madam."

"Come, Harriette," pleaded one of her companions, as fair as Harriette was dark, and therefore a perfect foil for her. "Surely you can relent a little towards so gallant a gentleman?"

Dignity satisfied, Harriette allowed herself to be persuaded. Fixing her saucy dark eyes on the intruder,

204

she first demanded to know his name and then gave permission for him to remain with them in the box. Now that he had leisure to study her, he saw that she was attired in an expensive gown of rich figured French gauze over white satin. Her dark hair was dressed in ringlets, and she wore a pair of very long earrings ornamented with diamonds, rubies, and turquoises which must have cost someone a very pretty penny, he reflected. Her companions were dressed in similarly expensive gowns, with rather more adornment than Harriette favoured, for neck, arms, and fingers glittered with jewels.

He was not to enjoy his monopoly of their company for long, as from time to time other gentlemen entered the box, some looking in for a short time and others remaining there. A good deal of gay chatter continued throughout the performance, for it was plain that no one was present in the box for the purpose of listening to the opera.

So far, so good, thought Shaldon, but he was still a long way from fulfilling the terms of his wager. He accepted with alacrity an invitation to take supper after the performance with the three females at the house of Harriette's sister Amy, another notorious member of the demimonde. He found the drawing room crammed, and recognised many well-known male members of the *ton* amongst the crowd. Beau Brummell was there in his elegant though unostentatious evening attire, passing to and fro with his usual supercilious air, as if he conferred a favour upon everyone by his own presence. Presently supper was served, a sumptuous meal of cold chicken and other delicacies washed down with champagne and claret in generous supply. By now the assembly was becoming rowdy, with all the guests talking and laughing at the top of their voices and the temperature of the room rising to an uncomfortable height. Shaldon eased himself out into a narrow passage leading off the drawing room, so that he could take a breather for a few moments.

"You are finding it uncomfortably hot and noisy, my lord?" asked a soft voice at his ear.

He turned to find Harriette Wilson beside him.

"Yes, devilish, ain't it?" he replied. "And I've scarce passed a single word with you, divine creature, since I came here."

She moved closer to face him, so that his eyes were attracted irresistibly to the decolletage of her gown, which just revealed the swelling curve of her breasts.

"La, sir," she said, mockingly, "if you came here for conversation . . . !"

He had drunk a quantity of champagne, which heightened the heady effect of this generous display of the lady's charms. With fingers that shook slightly he traced the neckline of her gown, pausing when he came to that seductive cleavage.

"No," he muttered, hoarsely. "B'God, no!"

She laughed softly as she led him upstairs.

Thus began a liaison which had lasted during the past four years, though by no means continuously. On both sides it was a casual affair, untroubled by any emotional overtones. Harriette had a series of acknowledged protectors who monopolised her during the term of office, so to speak, and were extremely jealous of any outsider who attempted to share the lady's favours. She always claimed that she was completely faithful to whichever man happened to be paying her bills at present, but Viscount Shaldon had good cause to know that these claims could not invariably be upheld. As his knowledge of the social set in which he moved increased, so did his cynical amusement in this situation. Most of them were playing the same game, but few were fortunate enough to remain as emotionally uninvolved as himself.

As for those other very different females who inhabited the beau monde and who every season flocked to the Royal drawing room and such unexceptionable places as Almack's Assembly rooms and the *ton* parties, he had scant interest in them. Frequently they were pretty and he would enjoy a mild flirtation with them until he chanced to see their Mamas eyeing him speculatively, when he would draw off hurriedly before he should find himself committed. For, pretty or plain, they seemed to Shaldon to be fashioned to the same pattern, like the expensive set of Wedgwood ware that appeared on his grandparents' dining table at meal-times. They were all highborn, elegant, and models of propriety. The business of their lives was to achieve a creditable marriage, and all their behaviour was regulated to promote this object. `

With the example before him of his own parents' marriage, Shaldon was not disposed to think of matrimony as a desirable state. It was easier to tie a knot than to untie it; and what could marriage possibly offer to compensate for the benefits it would remove— the freedom to go where one pleased and the sense of being one's own man, instead of a puppet manipulated by some female? Of course, if he should ever chance upon a woman like his mother . . . but that was impossible, he told himself. The heredity and circumstances which had moulded Maria Cottesford into a loving and compassionate, yet intelligent and lively woman were unique to herself.

He had allowed the letter to fall from his hands as he sat meditating. Now he swept the papers aside from the top of the desk and drew a sheet of paper towards him. On it he penned a single short line.

I will be there.

S.

In spite of Helen's determination to discover what lay behind Bertram Durrant's dark hints of trouble in store for Shaldon, she could think of no way of doing this other than by paying a visit to Cynthia Lydney to see if anything could be gleaned discreetly from her.

Although the two girls had been living in the same neighbourhood ever since leaving the seminary in Kensington last summer, visits between them were rare. Neither cared very much for the other; and their respective parents had never had any close association, although naturally the families were bound to meet

207

when taking part in the various neighbourhood activities.

Cynthia therefore was somewhat surprised when Helen was announced to her one morning soon after Shaldon's departure.

"Why, Helen, it's an age since I saw you," she said, inviting her visitor to be seated, and subjecting her to a searching scrutiny. "Pray, how do you contrive to become so brown at this season of the year? Never mind, as you are naturally of a fair complexion, it shouldn't be too difficult to rid yourself of that country look before you appear in Town. My dresser makes up an excellent lotion for the purpose. If you like, I'll let you have some of it."

Helen laughed. "You're very good, Cynthia, but pray don't trouble, for I could never bear to be daubing my face with lotions! If it will not do as it is, I fear I must resign myself to being stared at. How is your Mama, and all the rest of your family?"

This civil enquiry being answered and reciprocated, the two girls fell to talking of their forthcoming visit to London—a discussion which on Cynthia's part involved a minute description of all the various morning gowns, walking dresses, carriage dresses, ball dresses and other adornments to her person which she intended to take with her. Suspecting that Helen's wardrobe would not be nearly so extensive or fine, she was hoping to raise envy in the other girl. In this she was disappointed, however. Helen merely remarked that it was wonderful how many clothes one was supposed to require for a few months in the Metropolis.

"My own mother has gone to a deal of exertion over the business. Indeed, I felt obliged to protest that I could never hope to wear the half of what she thinks necessary! But I believe she's enjoying all the fuss of preparation every bit as much as if she were going herself, so I haven't the heart to discourage her, poor darling."

"I daresay Mrs. Somerby never had the advantage of a come-out in London herself?"

"No, but I believe she had a grand ball at her home in Oxfordshire, with most of the county present."

Cynthia smiled pityingly. "Then it's no wonder that she should take a vicarious pleasure in your debut. Of course, it may be a little uncomfortable to be obliged to accept the patronage of the Chetwodes. After all, Melissa will naturally be their first concern."

"Naturally. But their kindness is such that I know they will treat me as if I were a very close relative—otherwise my parents would not have dreamt of accepting their offer. I am quite at home with the family, you know. Melissa and I often used to exchange visits during the school holidays, though I never went to their town house."

"Ah, but this is different. This time, you and Melissa will be rivals."

"Rivals? I don't think that likely."

"But surely, my dear Helen, since you will both be on the catch for eligible husbands?"

Helen wrinkled her nose with distaste for Cynthia's phrase. "I can't speak for Melissa, of course, though I doubt if she would view the matter quite in that light. As for myself, I have no thought of husband catching! I hope to go amongst agreeable company and to enjoy a whole host of new experiences. In short, I wish to be thoroughly entertained, and not to spend my time scheming for an advantageous marriage, which seems to me a dreary waste of a splendid opportunity!"

"Well, you were always an original. But in truth, my own plans are something akin to yours, since I, too, mean to give up the whole of my time in Town to pleasure. My case, of course, is different from yours, since I am already certain of an eligible match. That is all arranged."

Helen saw no point in pretending that she did not understand what was meant, so she nodded.

"You know?" Cynthia seemed a trifle surprised. "Oh, but Shaldon was recently with you, was he not, and I suppose he must have mentioned it?"

"Yes, he did say that the Earl desired a match between you."

"And did he favour you with his own views on the subject?" asked Cynthia with some curiosity.

"Only to state that he had no thoughts of matrimony at present," replied Helen.

Cynthia shrugged. "Scarcely flattering! But then, he has not seen me lately, so I need hardly feel offended! In any case, his views meet my own. I've no wish to marry immediately. Shaldon will keep. Like you, first I wish to sample all the delights that a season in Town can offer."

The next quarter of an hour passed in an enthusiastic review on both sides of some of these delights, Helen pronouncing in favour of the theatre, sightseeing, and even Astley's circus, while Cynthia's heart was set on balls, rout parties, and fashionable shopping.

At the end of this spirited dialogue, Helen rose to go, feeling that she had failed in her original enterprise. She made one last attempt to retrieve the position by casually mentioning that she had seen Durrant in the village a few days since.

"Very likely," replied Cynthia. "He's been here with my father for some weeks, and I wonder you should not have run across him before. What do you think of him nowadays? He's a well-looking man, don't you agree?"

"Oh, yes, quite handsome, I suppose. He seemed somewhat preoccupied when we met, as though he had some problem on his mind."

Cynthia gave a knowing smile. "I fancy he admires me," she said, complacently. "I've looked in on him once or twice in that fusty old book room of ours, while he's been down here with Papa. Well, one must do something, and there's so little that's entertaining going on in the country! It's quite amusing, really. You should only see how hard he tries not to reveal his admiration. For, of course, he dare not, you know."

The smile left Helen's face. "I must say, Cynthia, I think that's the outside of enough!" she exclaimed, forthrightly. "Oh, yes, I know of old that you can never resist flirting; but to take advantage of a man in Durrant's position is surely carrying levity too far!"

Cynthia shrugged. "You always were a prude—but what else can be expected from a clergyman's daughter, after all? Don't trouble yourself over Durrant's misfortunes, however. I'll warrant he knows very well how to look after himself! In any event, he and I will not be meeting until after I am settled in Town, for he has left suddenly for Sussex and, as I understand, will not return here but to our town house when his business shall be concluded. And I need scarcely trouble to inform you that *I* shall be far too occupied than to bother my head with Durrant. There will be more interesting things in prospect!"

"I don't doubt that," Helen replied, coldly.

"I did wonder, you know," remarked Cynthia, thoughtfully, "whether Papa had sent him off on purpose, because he has caught us chatting together on one or two occasions and looked displeased, though I soon brought him round my thumb again. But I discovered that it was no such thing and that Durrant had been despatched on some errand for Lord Alvington. You may be sure I did my best to ascertain exactly what it was, but Papa was not to be coerced into revealing anything. Men are so tiresomely secretive! But I do wonder what Durrant can procure in Sussex that is vital to the happiness of Alvington, do not you? Sea shells, do you suppose?"

Helen was obliged to laugh at this, and the two girls parted with the appearance, at any rate, of reasonable amity. But as she took her way homeward she wondered if Durrant's errand to Sussex for the Earl could be the matter in hand of which he had spoken, and which was to bring trouble to her childhood friend.

Chapter XIX

UNLIKE MANY GIRLS of her age, who preferred to observe a certain reticence towards their parents, Helen was in the habit of confiding most of her doings to her mother; they were so alike in temperament, that she was always certain of a sympathetic hearing. She told Mrs. Somerby, therefore, of her uneasiness about Durrant's remark and what she had managed to discover from Cynthia.

"Oh, my dear, I fear you're too like your misguided Mama, always intrigued by the least hint of a mystery!" exclaimed Amanda Somerby, laughing. "But depend on it, Durrant meant nothing in particular by what he said about Anthony. There was always some envy on his side, you know, even when he was quite a child."

"Yes, I do know, of course. But his tone was more than malicious, Mama; it seemed to suggest to me some actual knowledge of impending trouble for Lord Shaldon. And don't you think it odd that Durrant should have been sent off to Sussex on the Earl's behalf? After all, he is not in the Earl's employ, but Lord Lydney's—and surely the Earl has sufficient staff of his own to perform his errands?"

Mrs. Somerby frowned. "Yes, that is very true, and it certainly does seem an odd circumstance. Sussex?" She frowned thoughtfully. "To my knowledge, Alvington has no property or connections in that county. Still, there's no saying what may arise in matters of business," she went on, in a more casual tone, "so

I should put it out of your mind, my love. What else did Cynthia have to say to you? I suppose she is busy getting ready for her trip to London?"

"Oh, she had a good deal to say about the clothes she will be taking, and all that kind of thing." Helen gave an attractive little chuckle. "I fancy she meant to overawe me, but if so, it didn't answer, for I told her how busy you've been in seeing that my wardrobe is adequate! She seems to think that Melissa and I will both be 'on the catch,' as she put it, for eligible husbands."

"Well, one can't deny that most girls do embark on a London season in the hope of meeting some eligible young men." Mrs. Somerby hesitated. "On that subject, my love, I suppose I ought really to offer you some maternal advice."

"What kind of advice, Mama? If it concerns the proprieties, I assure you Mrs. Cassington schooled us all thoroughly in that regard. And if it's"—she looked a little self-conscious, removing her candid gaze for a moment from her mother's—"well, of a more—intimate—nature, I think perhaps you may safely spare yourself the trouble of explaining. One cannot live in the country amongst animals, you know, without gaining a pretty good notion of how nature regulates such matters. Besides which, one gains a surprising amount of information from reading such unexceptionable books as the Bible and the classics. I don't think you need have the least uneasiness in that quarter."

Mrs. Somerby placed an arm about her daughter. "Oh, no, I should scarcely allow you to venture forth into a wider world unless I felt secure in your understanding of such matters. But even though I have the utmost confidence in Lady Chetwode's protection, you will still need to be upon your guard. You see, Helen, you have yet to fall in love, and to understand how that state can often overset one's judgment."

"Oh, Mama!" Helen sounded impatient.

"What you must bear in mind is that young gentlemen of fashion are very addicted to flirting. Yours is a candid nature and an affectionate one, and you may quite easily fall head over ears in love, as I did with your Papa." She smiled reminiscently for a moment. "When that happens—and I'm certain it will, sooner or later—we must hope that you will be as fortunate in your choice as I was. But do not, I beg you, be too ready to trust to appearances, and think yourself secure of a man's affection only because he pays you all manner of attentions and makes pretty speeches. You have nothing to fear from fortune hunters, as your dowry will be a modest one compared, say, with Cynthia Lydney's or your friend Melissa's. On that head, we may be easy. The very fact that you lack fortune, however, may make you the target for attentions from young men who do sincerely admire you—as what young man could not?—but who have no intention of marriage, reserving that for some wealthier girl. If you should allow yourself to feel in earnest about any one such gentleman, you could suffer a broken heart. And that," exclaimed Amanda Somerby, vigorously, "I shall not allow to happen through any lack of a warning on my part, however little I know you relish it! Try to forgive my motherly croakings my love, and believe that I mean them for the best."

"Oh, yes, certainly. What you're saying, Mama, is that I may not fall in love until I have a signed guarantee from my suitor that his intentions are strictly honourable?" asked Helen, with a twinkle in her eye. "I suppose it will be quite admissible for me to *flirt* with as many gentlemen as I choose, however?"

"Wretched girl! You make a jest of everything! Well, I have done my duty, and I daresay you'll pay as much heed to my warning as I did to anything my poor dear Mama said to me on such a subject. And most likely," concluded Mrs. Somerby, in her more usual optimistic vein, "you will manage the business very well without advice, just as I did myself."

They both laughed and dismissed the subject. But although Helen had seemed to dismiss her mother's counsel frivolously, she had not totally disregarded it.

A few weeks later, Helen set forth on her journey to London accompanied by her brother James, who had come down to Alvington especially to escort her. Although the Rector possessed a smart new Dennet gig for his parochial duties, the only closed carriage in his stables was an ancient vehicle now unsuitable for long distances but used occasionally to convey the family on local excursions to neighbours' houses or shopping in the nearby town. The brother and sister therefore travelled by post chaise; and as only a limited amount of baggage could be taken on this vehicle, a large trunk containing the bulk of Helen's wardrobe was sent on to London by carrier.

Their postillion seemed determined that the chaise should live up to its familiar title of 'yellow bounder,' and sent it along at a rattling pace which soon ate up the miles. Several drivers of other vehicles which they passed on their way, and who were often obliged to draw in uncomfortably close to the ditch, found other less complimentary terms for the equipage, and speculated bitterly on the ancestry of its driver. These comments amused James Somerby a good deal, and regrettably did not shock his sister nearly so much as perhaps would have been proper. While the horses were being changed at Berkhamsted, they took some refreshment and seized the opportunity to stretch their cramped limbs; but they were soon hurtling onwards again through pleasant country, where lambs sported in the meadows and trees were putting out the first green of Spring. As they raced along Watling Street, which had been built by the Romans and which would eventually bring them down to the Hyde Park Corner turnpike, James consulted his watch and saw that it was only half past eleven.

"I say, Nell, would you mind if we turned off to Paddington village just before we reach the Tyburn turnpike? I would like to look in on Dr. Gillies. It's an age since I went there, because I'm not often that way, and you know how my work at the hospital keeps me constantly occupied. But he and his sister were very good to me during the years of my apprenticeship, and I wouldn't want to neglect the old fellow. I may not have so good an opportunity again for some time."

"Well, if you think they won't object to me in a crumpled pelisse and looking a trifle dishevelled," said Helen, dubiously.

"Oh, no, they're capital people, and not in the least stuffy, just the kind whom I know you'll like. Besides, if you feel you're a trifle out of point after the journey, you could freshen up there, you know, and present yourself in Cavendish Square looking more the thing."

"Thank you. Now I know that I do indeed look dishevelled, after that remark," said Helen, with a rueful grin.

"Fustian! Didn't you say it yourself? But that's just like a female, twisting a fellow's words into something he never intended. Very well, since you've no objection, I'll give the postillion his orders. He can bait at the Red Lion there, while we pay our call. I don't intend to stay very long."

Accordingly, they entered the village a short time later, crossing an ancient stone bridge over a stream and pulling up outside the half-timbered inn. A farm waggon stood in the forecourt; the carter was watering his horses at a trough while he chatted to one of the ostlers, but the latter hurried forward on seeing the post chaise, and opened the door to allow the passengers to alight.

"It's just around the corner from here," said James, as he handed down his sister.

Taking her arm, he led her under the swinging inn sign through some white posts into the village street. The house they sought was only a few doors from the inn, a grey stone two-storeyed building with a roof of thatch in which some sparrows had evidently set up a home, judging by the frequent comings and goings of the birds, and the twittering in the eaves. A small patch of garden surrounded by a white fence fronted the house, which had a well kept air, with shining windows draped in spotless white dimity and a well polished brass knocker on the front door.

James rapped and waited. There were sounds of a scurrying in the hall, then the door opened to reveal a diminutive maidservant standing behind it. James gave his name; but before the girl could either invite him to enter or retreat to convey the information to someone in authority, whichever she had in mind, a female voice called out from inside one of the rooms.

"Who is there, Sally?"

The next moment, the speaker herself appeared. She was a little woman of neat appearance, in her early sixties but slim and spry, with grey hair arranged tidily under a white lace cap with lappets, and a friendly expression on her face. At sight of James, she exclaimed with delight.

"Why, Master Somerby! And how is our Jamie? The doctor will be monstrous glad to see you, that I can tell you! But come in, my dear young man, and bring the young lady with you, do."

She looked enquiringly at Helen as she ushered them both into the house, evidently uncertain as to who she was. James soon enlightened her, and she pressed Helen's hand warmly as she remarked that Master Somerby had always been a favourite pupil of her brother's.

"How is the doctor?" asked James, as they followed her through the hall.

"Tolerably well, I'm thankful to say, though a trifle plagued by the rheumatics. He's looking forward to the time when he'll have you to assist him." She pushed open a door and announced, "I've a delightful surprise for you, Andrew! Here is Jamie Somerby come to see us, with his young sister."

A well built man with white hair and a wrinkled, tanned face rose to greet them, placing a hand in the small of his back and grimacing with pain as he did so. The next moment, his features relaxed into a broad smile as he extended a hand in welcome.

"Deuced rheumatics!" he grumbled, in a deep voice. "Ah, well, Anno Domini, I suppose—catches us all in time. How are you, my dear boy? And how do you go on at Guy's? But, bless me, I am neglecting this charming young lady—your sister, I collect? Yes, she has a look of you. How d'ye do, miss? Sit down, now, both of you, and Mistress Betty will bring us some refreshment. Have you come far?"

James explained that they were on their way to Cavendish Square from Buckinghamshire, and that their visit must necessarily be brief.

"Only I couldn't bring myself to pass so close to you without looking in," he concluded. "I knew you'd forgive the lack of formality."

"I should hope you might. But since you've both come a good way already, perhaps you'd care to freshen up a little before partaking of some refreshment? My sister will take care of Miss Somerby, and you can go into the surgery."

Helen was conducted up a short flight of stairs to a bedchamber with old-fashioned, well polished furniture and a small dressing room beyond. Here she was able to wash off some of the inevitable dust of travel and to make herself presentable again. As she was arranging her hair before the mirror, her hostess picked up a heavily chased gold locket which was lying on the dressing table.

"Oh, now there is someone to mend this for me!" she exclaimed. "Master—I should say *Mister,* but old habits die hard!—Somerby was always quite a hand at this kind of thing. It is only the split ring which fastens it onto the chain which has become forced so that the locket slips off, but my brother's eyesight is no longer equal to the task of setting it right. Though of course," she addd, doubtfully, "I can scarce ask your brother to see to it now, as he has so little time to stay. Perhaps on another occasion."

She laid the locket down again.

"Nothing of the kind," Helen assured her. "James will fix it in a trice and be very glad to serve you in such a small way, I am sure. Let us take it downstairs with us, ma'am. It's a pretty trinket, and it's a shame that you shouldn't be able to wear it."

"Yes, for I've been used to wear it for nigh on thirty years, and one misses such things, you know. Well, if you're quite sure that your brother will not think himself imposed upon, I'll venture to ask him."

James at once expressed his willingness to oblige, and with the aid of a small pair of pincers soon repaired the ring which held the locket on its chain. Afterwards they all partook of wine and cake, the two doctors talking away at a great rate on professional matters; while Helen and Mistress Betty maintained the less lively conversation of those who have only just met, but who nevertheless feel a great deal of goodwill towards each other.

Presently, the Somerbys were obliged to take their leave, James promising that he would look in again before very long.

"And if ever you should manage to get down to Guy's, sir," he concluded, with a vigorous handshake for the doctor, "I shall be delighted to take you round the wards and show you one or two interesting cases."

When he and Helen were seated once more in the post chaise to resume their journey, he enlivened the way with reminiscences of his years as an apprentice in Dr. Gillies's household and the maternal kindness he had always met with from Mistress Betty, as everyone called the doctor's sister.

They arrived in Cavendish Square in the early afternoon to find the family assembled to give them a warm welcome. Lady Chetwode was a small, rather plump woman with a round face, somewhat vague brown eyes and a kindly expression. She was wearing a high necked, long sleeved gown, of green velvet fashioned with that simplicity which is always expensive. Sir George, her husband, had the long, thin face of the scholar; and anyone acquainted with the Reverend Theodore Somerby would not find it difficult to understand why these two gentlemen had been close friends in their youth. Indeed, Sir George rarely knew what was going on in his household, as for most of the time he was shut up in his library, reading. His son Philip had something of his father's cast of countenance besides inheriting Sir George's bookish tendencies; but he was a personable young man, tall and slender, fashionably attired in a well tailored dark blue coat, fawn waistcoat, and grey stockinette pantaloons.

Melissa, who had thankfully shed several pounds in weight since leaving Mrs. Cassington's seminary, looked charming in a gown of pink muslin decorated with sprays of white flowers, her chestnut hair dressed demurely in a chignon. She had not forgotten her previous encounter with Helen's masterful brother, and as he bowed over her hand, her face coloured just sufficiently to match the tint of her gown.

"Dear me," he murmured in a tone which did not carry beyond her own ear, "can this be the little schoolgirl I had the privilege of assisting not so many months back?"

She was not displeased in spite of the mocking light in his very blue eyes; and when he made his excuses and rose to go after a short interval, she felt disappointed. This was soon dispelled, however, at the prospect of seeing him again before long, for Helen reminded him of his promise to accompany her to Astley's Circus.

"That is, if you will permit, ma'am," she added, turning to Lady Chetwode.

"Oh, certainly, if you would like it, my dear," her hostess agreed. "And your brother will be the very person to accompany you there, as I should not care for it, myself. The first positive engagement I have made for you is an evening at the Opera next Tuesday, for you must hear Catalini. But otherwise nothing is fixed upon for the next few days."

"And may Melissa go with us, too?" asked Helen, correctly interpreting her friend's pleading look.

"If you would have no objection to extending your party to include myself," intervened Philip Chetwode, addressing James, "I should very much like to accompany you. I haven't been to Astley's since I was a boy, and the equestrian feats there are very fine."

James readily agreed to this, and Lady Chetwode was quite content to fall in with an engagement for the day after tomorrow, when he chanced to be free.

As soon as James Somerby had departed, the two

girls found an opportunity to slip away to the bed-chamber which had been prepared for Helen, in order to enjoy a private chat. As they had seen nothing of each other since quitting the seminary last July, there was a good deal of news to exchange; and so eager were their tongues that scarcely any one topic was pursued to a conclusion.

"And did it take you long to recover from your partiality for Monsieur Falaise?" asked Helen, with an arch glance at her friend. "I recall you were quite in despair at the prospect of parting from him for ever!"

"Oh, that was a mere schoolgirl's fancy," replied Melissa, with dignity. "You know how it is when one is young. Why, I am almost a year older now, and have very different notions!"

"Have you indeed?" teased Helen. "Don't tell me that you've fallen in love again!"

"What nonsense you do talk, Helen! But when I compare our late dancing master with—with other gentlemen whom I've met, he does seem a frippery fellow, and I wonder at myself for ever thinking him anything at all out of the common way!"

"And have you met a great many other gentlemen?"

"Well, some," replied Melissa, avoiding her friend's observant eye, "though of course since I am not yet out, I haven't been to any but family parties so far. But Philip brings his friends here sometimes, though in general they meet at the clubs or in the gentlemen's chambers which most of them occupy."

"Have you ever met Viscount Shaldon? I collect he is a friend of your brother's."

"Yes, he did come here once, some months back, and I thought him prodigiously handsome—but, of course, you must know him well, Helen, since you live on his estate. And Cynthia Lydney does, too. I remember how she mentioned him when we were at school, and said that he had Other Interests than matrimony. I didn't understand her at the time, but now I think I do. It is very shocking, of course, and a great pity, but Mama says one must beware of him, as he's a monstrous flirt even with girls of his own Quality."

"And yet when he came to call on us at Alvington a few weeks since," remarked Helen, reflectively, "he didn't seem at all dangerous, nor in the least disposed to flirt with *me*, at all events. But then he thinks of me as a sister, so he says. That would account for it. Evidently I have no need to beware of him. It's a lowering thought," she added, mischievously.

Melissa forgot herself so far as to let out a schoolgirl giggle. "Oh, Helen, you aren't a bit changed, and I'm monstrous glad of it! Do you know, in spite of all the excitement of my come-out, things have seemed so *dull* here lately? But with someone of my own age to share in my activities and to laugh with me, everything will be different—we shall have such fun together, won't we?"

"Indeed we shall. And I quite pity the Polite World to have two such madcaps descend upon it in one season! But you've grown delightfully slender, Melissa," concluded Helen, in a typical non sequitur.

This remark was all that was needed to make her friend's day complete.

Chapter XX

SURPRISINGLY CLOSE to the magnificence of Westminster Abbey and the pleasant verdure of St. James's Park lay a district of a vastly different nature called Tothill Fields. The only field in evidence here was a rubbish dump that served to fatten pigs after the local inhabitants had picked it over for possible additions to their own meagre diet. The principal buildings were an ugly Bridewell as full as it could hold with felons, a row of dingy almshouses and a charity school where both the charity and the schooling were of so grudging a nature that recipients of these blessings might have fared little worse in the streets from which they were drawn. These same streets were narrow and dirty, with dark alleys and courts leading off them crowded with filthy hovels and dingy tenements. Here London's poorest inhabitants found some kind of shelter by stuffing rags into cracked walls and boarding up broken windows; even if no remedy could be found for the prevailing damp from a leaky roof or the icy cold in winter caused by an ill fitting door—sometimes no door at all—and the lack of fuel for a fire.

What trade there was in the district took place in the many seedy taverns and gin shops, where for a penny the miserable inhabitants could purchase a short period of forgetfulness of their wretched state. A few disreputable pawnbrokers and rag dealers also eked out a paltry living in unsavoury premises. Occasionally a street cry would be heard, offering the humbler kinds of merchandise or demanding old iron, but few customers were forthcoming.

The inhabitants were frowsty women, made prematurely old from childbearing and malnutrition, and men brutalised by their environment, earning a precarious livelihood as road crossing sweepers, chimney sweeps, coal heavers, scavengers, and the like. In spite of the high infant mortality, the alleys and courts were filled with filthy, half-naked children playing among the mangy curs and lean cats that prowled in the gutters and garbage heaps.

In one of these miserable hovels in a place which rejoiced in the name of Star Court lived a woman who called herself Mrs. Dorston. In spite of its name, the inhabitants of Star Court were never privileged to gaze on the stars, as their light was completely blocked out by the crowded buildings. Mrs. Dorston occupied a small, cheerless room in one of the tumbledown, neglected tenements. She was one of the few people in the Court, or indeed in the whole area, to enjoy the privilege of a room entirely to herself; most of her

223

neighbours were obliged to crowd a family of as many as ten or twelve members of varying ages and both sexes into a similar space. It was not a place where people were curious about their neighbours' antecedents, for the endless struggle against poverty and disease demanded all their energies; but it was generally supposed that Old Peg, as they familiarly called her, had once seen better days, had perhaps been a servant in one of the grand mansions in the brightly lit squares and wide thoroughfares which were not so far away in distance, though as remote from their way of life as another world. This supposition was based on the fact that when she had first come among them, some years ago, she had been more gently spoken than themselves, although she had long since acquired the slovenly idiom of the neighbourhood. At that time, suspecting that she might have money or valuables concealed on the premises, they had made several raids on her room whenever she chanced to be absent. The results had proved disappointing, however, and soon she was taken for granted as being one of themselves.

Moreover, it did not pay to quarrel with Old Peg, as they soon discovered. She was a useful woman at a lying-in, a not infrequent contingency in a neighbourhood where the only pleasures were those of the flesh and the gin shop. The fine ladies of London might have their accouchers or fashionable man midwives to attend on such occasions; in Tothill Fields, females counted themselves lucky if they knew of a neighbour who would oblige.

On certain days of the week, Mrs. Dorston arrayed herself in the most presentable garments she possessed, an old rusty black cloak and a shapeless bonnet acquired for a few pence at the local rag shop, and set out for Westminster Abbey. She was acquainted with a flower seller who had a pitch close by the magnificent building, and who paid Mrs. Dorston a meagre fee to act as her deputy on occasion. It was neither a very brisk nor a remunerative business, but it made some small contribution to Old Peg's subsistence.

She was just about to start on this errand one afternoon when she was hailed by one of her neighbours, a scrawny female with lank hair hanging about her unwashed face and neck, and clad in a tattered garment which barely concealed her emaciated bosom.

"Hi, Peg, gi' us a penny for a dram," she said, in a mendicant's whine.

"Ain't got it," replied Mrs. Dorston, shaking her head firmly.

"Garn! Bain't for me, 'tis for Moll. 'Er's near barmy wi' the pains. Reckon she'll be needin' yer soon, too."

But Mrs. Dorston had lived here too long to be taken in by this moving tale. She knew that to hand over money to anyone was only to invite a host of similar applications from others; moreover, the wretched Moll most certainly would not be the recipient of her beneficence. So she shook her head again, slammed her door and locked it firmly, then pushed unceremoniously past the other woman on her way to the street. The unsavoury female as a matter of course gave vent to a few choice Billingsgate expressions, but she bore Old Peg no real malice. It was always worth a try to get something out of the old bitch, but there had been no serious expectation of success. She shrugged and went back to her evil-smelling room in the basement, where five or six unwashed, semi-naked young children were creating Bedlam.

Mrs. Dorston continued on her way until she reached the road fronting the Abbey, where she paused for a moment to draw a breath of air. It was clean and fresh compared to that of Star Court, in spite of the dust raised by a constant stream of traffic. She saw her friend the flower seller standing in the usual place, only twenty yards or so away, and raised her arm in greeting. As she did so, she lost her balance for a moment and stumbled out into the road directly in the path of an oncoming post chaise. As usual, the vehicle was being sent along at the gallop; and though the postillion pulled up his horses in time to avoid actually running over the unfortunate woman, she was hurled to the ground and lay there motionless.

Earlier on that same afternoon, Helen had set out with her brother and the Chetwodes for Astley's Amphitheatre in Westminster Bridge Road. As they were to pass so close to the Abbey, she had pleaded that they might spend just a little while in looking over this famous burial place of so many of Britain's great men.

"If you should not object, that is?" she asked diffidently, addressing Philip Chetwode. "For you must have often been there before."

"Not for some years," he confessed. "And I know my sister had never set foot inside, so I am sure she will find it interesting. By all means let us stop on our way. We will set out in good time."

Two days in the company of Melissa's friend had given Mr. Chetwode a strong inclination to try to please her. Undoubtedly she was an attractive young lady both in looks and personality, but so were several others of his acquaintance. What made Miss Somerby appear superior to these others, to his way of thinking, was the lively, intelligent mind which made her capable of holding a rational conversation. He was too calm a young man to fall madly in love at first sight, but there was no doubt that he did feel himself strongly attracted to Miss Somerby.

So Helen had her way, and the visit to Astley's Amphitheatre was preceded by a short tour of Westminster Abbey. They had just completed this and were leaving the building to walk across to their waiting carriage, when they were halted by a loud scream and the sound of horses being pulled up suddenly.

"Oh, Heavens!" cried Helen, looking in the direction of the noise. "Someone's been knocked down—poor thing!"

She darted away to the scene of the accident, where a woman lay prostrate on the ground. At once, Helen went down on her knees to see what could be done.

"Don't move her, Nell!" ordered James, who had been as quick in arriving at the spot. "Here, let me take a look!"

"Oh, my Gawd!" exclaimed the postillion, who had dismounted and stood looking at the woman in dismay. "She bain't dead, is she, guv'nor? T'weren't my fault, not nohow, as Gawd's my judge. She stepped out suddenly right afore the nags, and 'ard work of it I 'ad not to go clean over 'er!"

By now a crowd was gathering, among them the flower seller, who made her way through to James's side.

"Be she badly 'urt, sir?" she asked. "Can ye tell?"

"I'm a doctor," he replied briefly, continuing with his examination. "Concussion and a fracture of the left tibia," he murmured to Helen, a few moments later. "Nothing more, though that's enough to be going on with, for one of her age and state of health."

He stood up, addressing the crowd authoritatively. "Stand back there, and let her have some air. Procure me a hackney, one of you, quick."

A street urchin from among the crowd ran to do his bidding.

"Will she be all right, sir?" It was the flower seller again. "I know 'er, ye see. She 'elps me in my trade."

James looked at her compassionately. "It's hard to say at present, but I should think so. Do you know her well? In that case, you can furnish me with her name and other particulars, and perhaps inform her relatives that I'm taking her to Guy's Hospital, in the Borough."

The woman shook her head. "I don't know 'er that well, sir, though I knows 'er name's Peg Dorston, an' she lives in Star Court in Tothill. There's no relatives that I knows of. Leastways, she lives alone."

While all this was happening, Melissa and her brother had been standing on the edge of the crowd, uncertain what to do. At that moment, the hackney drew up; James signalled to Philip, who came forward, the crowd parting to admit him.

"Will you take the ladies on to Astley's, Chetwode? I'll follow as soon as I've seen this unlucky female installed at Guy's."

"Very well, but won't you need help in putting her into the hackney?" asked Philip, as he assisted Helen to her feet.

"Yes, but one of the men standing about here can

assist me—no point in all of us turning up at the circus looking the worse for wear. I'll try to get there in time to see some of the show, at any rate, but don't trouble if I fail to appear."

At this point, a head poked out of the window of the post chaise.

"How much longer are we to spend here, postillion?" demanded its owner, red in the face with anger. "Surely there's been enough fuss made over a low female who hasn't even the sense to keep out of the way of traffic! As for you, my good sir," addressing James, "permit me to say that you're wasting your talents on such a patient, for there'll be no fee!"

James gave an ironical bow. "I thank you for your warning, sir, but beg leave to remind you that all rewards do not come in the shape of coin. Take him to the devil, postillion, or wherever else it is he happens to be off to in such haste."

The crowd raised a cheer at this; and the postillion hastily remounted to convey his passenger away before it should turn ugly, as crowds sometimes did. A sensible man helped James to place his patient carefully inside the hackney, and that, too, drove off, leaving the crowd to disperse now that there was nothing further to be seen.

Having given her gown a shake to relieve it of some of the dust gathered from the road, Helen accompanied her friends back to the coach.

"Was not your brother splendid?" exclaimed Melissa, her eyes glowing, as they settled themselves in their seats. "The way he took charge, and in particular the way he depressed the pretensions of that odious man in the post chaise! I have never been half so glad of anything!"

"I'm afraid I wasn't of much assistance," said Philip, ruefully, "but to tell the truth, I couldn't think of anything useful to do."

"But of course you were!" Helen insisted. "James could not have left us without an escort, you know. As for his part in the affair, his profession enabled him to know just what ought to be done. I am glad the

228

poor woman was not even more badly hurt. For a moment I feared the worst, when I knelt beside her and saw no sign of life."

Philip was grateful for the kindness which attempted to restore his confidence, but it could not entirely prevent a feeling of inadequacy. He knew that he was not, unfortunately, one of those men who showed up well in a crisis; and at present he would have given much to be able to impress Miss Helen Somerby with the kind of masterful competence which her brother had displayed so unconsciously. However much his reason bade him laugh at such instinctive masculine feelings, which he told himself were akin to the mating displays of animals, he could not shake off their effect upon him.

Fortunately, by the time they arrived at the Amphitheatre and had settled themselves in their seats, he forgot his chagrin in sharing the uninhibited enjoyment of the performance experienced by his two unsophisticated charges. The first part of the programme consisted of songs and dances against appropriate scenes such as a Dock Yard with several Artists at work on a large ship, ending with a spirited rendering of a Hornpipe; and a Tempest, which inspired a graceful Water Ballet.

"Now what is to come?" Melissa demanded excitedly of Helen, leaning over her shoulder to consult the programme. "Oh! 'The Theatre of Florence, representing several Frontispieces of beautiful Fireworks, which have been displayed in different Parts of Europe.' Do you suppose they will be real fireworks? But no, only pictures, of course."

There was a short intermission between this part of the performance and the next, which promised to be even more exciting, as it would consist of horsemanship, juggling and acrobatics. Helen suggested that they might go and see if there was any sign of James, so they all strolled out into the passage leading to the foyer, glad of an opportunity to move about for a while. There was quite a press of people here, and presently Helen became separated from her companions, caught up between the wall of the passage and a jostling group who would not allow her to pass. An unmannerly push sent her against a door marked 'Private'; it opened, evidently being insecurely latched, and she found herself partly thrust through into a long, narrow passage beyond.

Curious, because she guessed that this must lead backstage, she took a good look before attempting to regain her rightful place on the public side of the door. She saw two men at the far end of the passage, so deep in conversation that they remained oblivious both of the open door and the intruder. With difficulty she held back a startled exclamation as she recognised instantly that one of the men was Bertram Durrant.

The other man she had never set eyes on before. She had just enough time to notice that he was tall with auburn hair similar to Viscount Shaldon's, and that he was dressed in a clown's red and white striped costume with large white bobbles down the front of it, although his face had not yet been made up for the part. Fearful that at any moment Durrant might look that way and recognise her, she hastily stepped back into the crowd, pulling the door shut behind her.

"Oh, so there you are, Miss Somerby!" exclaimed Philip, in relief. "I shouldn't have brought you both out here, for I never saw such a rag-mannered set of people as these! I think perhaps we had best try to resume our seats, and leave Somerby to make his own way to join us, as I'm sure he's quite capable of doing. Will you take my arm, ma'am?"

Helen acquiesced, and they made their way back to their seats without too much difficulty, carried along in a stream of others with the same intention. But during the next few turns, which were juggling and vaulting, her mind was not completely on the entertainment before her; and when three tumbling clowns appeared —and in spite of the makeup, she recognised one as the man to whom Durrant had been speaking—her attention was even more distracted.

What interest could Durrant possibly have in a

230

clown at Astley's Circus? Could he in any way be connected with the management of the place? It seemed hardly likely that, even if Durrant had somehow managed to acquire business interests, he should involve himself in such a business as a circus. Was it then some undertaking of Lord Lydney's, and Durrant was acting on his employer's behalf? Or—more unlikely still—had this any connection with the errand for the Earl of Alvington which had taken Durrant down to Sussex some weeks since? And had any of it a possible connection with Durrant's dark hints about trouble in store for Shaldon?

Helen drew her thoughts up with a jerk, softly laughing out loud at the absurdity of them. As the scene being enacted before them at that moment was supposed to make the audience laugh, this caused no surprise to her companions, who readily joined her. What in the world was she at, she asked herself mockingly, to let her curiosity and imagination run away with her like this? Durrant might need to talk with many unexpected people in discharging his duties as secretary to a Member of Parliament. As for Shaldon, as Mama had said, he was very capable of looking after himself.

Ah, and here was James at last, making his way past the disapproving spectators to gain his seat. Melissa's speaking eyes shone as he quietly slid into it, and Helen was momentarily distracted from her previous train of thought to speculate on yet another possibility. It was beginning to look as if her impressionable friend had found a successor to the once adored Monsieur Falaise. Well, it can do her no harm, thought Helen philosophically, and settled down with an undivided mind to enjoy the brilliant display of horsemanship which was the chief feature of Astley's.

The male riders performed the most difficult feats, of course, but there were two equestriennes who gained their share of applause. One of these was a strikingly pretty young female with golden hair and a slender, agile body. She rode astride, bareback, then stood up on the horse's back, balancing on one foot as the animal charged round the ring.

"You're not a bad horsewoman, Nell," remarked James. "How'd you like to try that trick, though?"

Helen laughed. "No, thank you. I fear I should only make a sorry mess of it, and injure myself into the bargain."

"But then you would have the very best of attention afterwards, you know," Melissa said, looking shyly up at James.

He smiled at her, but shook his head. "If you mean me, I'm naturally flattered, Miss Chetwode. But it don't do to doctor one's own family."

"I suppose not, but it does seem a waste to call in another doctor whom one may not like—that's to say," she amended, hastily, "does not know so well."

"That's the point, ma'am. People don't pay any heed to the advice of their relatives. Besides, who's to say a doctor might not abuse the situation, and poison off some wealthy connection?"

"No, what a dreadful suggestion! But of course you're funning," she added, seeing the twinkle in his eye. "That is just what Helen does to me, sometimes."

"Then I won't do so again, for we can't have you positively persecuted by our family, what d'you say, Chetwode?"

"That I can't imagine Miss Somerby persecuting anyone, in the first place. Secondly, I'm certain my sister can do her own share."

"Well, of all the positively *brotherly* things to say!" exclaimed Melissa, in feigned indignation.

"Hush, we've come to the Finale," warned Helen.

As the cast bowed before the thunderous applause, she noticed that the auburn-haired clown had joined hands with the pretty equestrienne, who was looking up at him with very much the same expression that had been on Melissa's face while she talked to James.

Chapter XXI

THE FOLLOWING DAY, Lady Chetwode decided that they should go shopping.

"For once you have been presented, my dears," she informed the girls, "there will be no end of invitations to balls, rout parties and the like. And although Melissa's wardrobe is not precisely *scanty,* one must be beforehand in such matters. Besides, I daresay Helen will be glad to see some of our fine Town shops, will you not, my dear?"

Helen readily assented, and the carriage was sent for to convey them first of all to Messrs. Clark & Debenham's premises in Wigmore Street.

"If we don't find anything to our liking there," said Lady Chetwode, "we will try Grafton House or Layton & Shears. Indeed, it may be as well to look in at all of them, you know, for one cannot make up one's mind in a minute over such an important matter as the material for a gown."

The truth of this maxim was abundantly illustrated in the course of the following three or four hours. Helen was completely dazzled by such an abundant display of twills, bombazines, sarsenets, muslins, silks, satins, and velvets as the willing assistants laid out before them. As roll after roll of cloth appeared, a choice of any particular one became increasingly difficult for Melissa, never the most decisive of females; and her Mama, also inclined to be vague, was obviously not the best person to guide her daughter's wavering inclinations.

"The pink muslin is very pretty, Melissa, though I think yellow becomes you better. No, not lilac, my love; that would suit Helen monstrous well. What do you think, Helen? Would you like a length of this made up? I know your Mama has already provided you with a most extensive wardrobe, but one cannot have too many gowns for a come-out, you know." Before Helen could reply to this, she was off again. "Oh, but that aquamarine silk is exquisite! And that silver gauze would look so pretty over this blue! I'm sure I don't know. Perhaps we should try somewhere else, for I quite despair of your ever making up your mind here."

Helen looked with some compassion at the two seemingly tireless assistants who had been busy reaching down bales of material, often from high shelves, for the customers' inspection; but they seemed quite unruffled, and made low bows as the three ladies left, thanking Lady Chetwode for her lack of custom with as much enthusiasm as though she had just placed a very expensive order. Helen could not help passing a comment on this to her hostess, but Lady Chetwode only smiled knowingly.

"Ah, but then they know quite well that next time I go into the shop I may well give them a large order, so it's worth their while to show me every attention. Besides, if one serves in a draper's, one must expect to pull out several rolls of cloth whether or not the customer eventually makes a purchase. Depend upon it, they are quite accustomed and feel no hardship."

Helen would have liked to be more certain of this; but she said no more as they resumed their seats in the carriage to go on to Grafton House, which was the nearer of the other two shops favoured by Lady Chetwode. By now Helen was becoming a little more accustomed to London's traffic, but at first it had made her stare in surprise. Smart town carriages, phaetons, curricles, and other sporting vehicles made their way with difficulty among brewers' drays, stage- and Mail coaches, carriers' carts, hackney coaches, waggons with hay for the markets, and horseback riders. Even the pavements were always busy; in the fashionable quarters with modish strollers, and towards the City with scurrying clerks, tradesmen shouting their wares, postmen in scarlet coats going from door to door, grimy chimney sweeps carrying brushes, milkmaids with pails suspended from yokes across their shoulders, and sellers of lavender or other flowers in season. Noise and confusion seemed the lot of Londoners of every degree, she reflected, but one soon became accustomed and ceased to regard it.

They had barely entered the doors of the emporium in Grafton Street when an excited exclamation drew their attention to a young lady in a smart cinnamon velvet pelisse who was standing before one of the counters with an older lady, looking at some shawls.

"Helen, Melissa! Oh, how splendid to see you!"

It was Catherine Horwood. Although the three girls had kept up a lively correspondence with each other since leaving school, this was the first occasion on which they had all met. They broke out at once into animated chatter, almost forgetting to perform the necessary introduction between Lady Chetwode and Mrs. Horwood, who were not known to each other.

"Papa has taken a house in Bruton Street. It's so vastly convenient for everything. Oh, you must come and see me. Mama, they may come, mayn't they?" said Catherine, all in a rush.

Mrs. Horwood, a tall woman nearly as slender as her daughter and modishly dressed, smiled at Catherine's eagerness. "Of course, Kitty." She turned to Lady Chetwode. "I hope we may have the pleasure of a visit from you and the young ladies very soon, ma'am."

Lady Chetwode caught a pleading look from Melissa, and bowed. "Thank you, ma'am. But I am wondering if perhaps you might permit your daughter to return home with us today, when you shall have finished your business in Town? That is, of course, if no prior engagement prevents it? I fear," shaking her head and smiling, "that they are all three so eager for a good cose, they will scarcely endure to postpone it until another day."

There was such a chorus of approval for this scheme that Mrs. Horwood had the utmost difficulty in making herself heard to agree to it; but it was eventually decided that they would separate for an hour in order the better to do their shopping, and that Catherine should then accompany her friends to Cavendish Square.

It was rather a squeeze in the carriage, for in the end several parcels and a bandbox had to be accommodated as well as an extra passenger; but it was all managed with so much goodwill and enthusiasm that only Lady Chetwode had the least consciousness of not being completely comfortable.

As soon as she was back at home again, she wisely left the young people to themselves, and retiring to her bedchamber, thankfully shook off her shoes and put up her aching feet on a stool.

"Now, tell me everything that's happened since last we met!" demanded Catherine, as soon as the girls were alone. "Oh, yes, I know we've exchanged letters, but that's not at all the same thing as a long chat, is it?"

Helen and Melissa enthusiastically agreed; and for the succeeding couple of hours their tongues were never still. At last Catherine said reluctantly that she supposed she ought to go, as her Mama would be expecting her.

"Oh, but you'll take some refreshment first, will you not?" urged Melissa, belatedly recalled to a sense of the proper duties of a hostess. "That will give us a little longer, at any rate."

Catherine demurred but was not difficult to persuade, so Melissa sent for some tea. This had just arrived in the drawing room and she was about to dispense it to her friends when the door opened to admit her brother Philip, accompanied by Viscount Shaldon.

For a moment both gentlemen were taken aback;

they had evidently expected to find the room unoccupied.

"What, you here, Mel?" asked Philip. "I quite thought you would still be out shopping. Pray excuse us. We've no wish to intrude."

They made their bows, prepared to quit the room instantly.

"No, pray don't go," said Melissa. "I should like to present you to my friend Catherine Horwood, whom we encountered in Town."

The presentations were duly made, and the gentlemen bowed again. Catherine blushed a little on being confronted with two such personable gentlemen at once, for she was rather shy.

"Miss Somerby is, of course, already known to you," Philip Chetwode said to Shaldon.

"To be sure," replied Shaldon, smiling. "Our acquaintance is of very long standing, is it not, Miss Somerby?" He turned to Melissa. "And how d'you do, ma'am? I trust not too fatigued by your expedition?"

"Oh, no, it was most diverting," she replied. "But pray be seated. Will you take tea with us?"

The gentlemen exchanged a brief glance which indicated to Helen, at least, that tea was not their favourite beverage. Nevertheless, they politely accepted a cup and tried to look as though they were enjoying it. Shaldon took a chair beside Helen, while his friend seated himself between the other two young ladies.

"And how is that rascal Patch?" enquired Shaldon, having first asked after Helen's parents. "I daresay he misses you sadly."

She laughed. "Oh, he is well up to form, I fear! Mama tells me in her latest letter that he is in Cook's bad books for stealing a mutton chop from right under her nose the other day!"

Shaldon shook his head gravely. "Tut, tut, a most abandoned creature, evidently. But time may tame him, as it does with most of us. And how are you enjoying your stay in Town, ma'am?"

"Oh, prodigiously, I thank you! Today we have

been making a tour of some of the shops, and yesterday we paid a visit to Westminster Abbey and Astley's Circus."

"Two vastly different diversions. I will not ask what you thought of the Abbey, but do tell me how you enjoyed the Circus?"

"Well, the day was somewhat marred by a sad accident which befell an elderly woman who stepped in front of a coach just as we were leaving the Abbey," replied Helen, her hazel eyes solemn. "But James took her off to the hospital, and later he was able to give us a fairly optimistic account of her condition. As for the Circus"—her face lit up again with animation—"I never enjoyed anything half so much in my life!"

She proceeded to give him a lively account of all that they had seen at Astley's. Philip Chetwode, who was watching the pair while at the same time conducting a conversation with Catherine and his sister, was surprised to see that man of the world, Shaldon, apparently deriving so much entertainment from such unsophisticated chatter. The fact was that Shaldon was once more yielding, as he had done during his brief visit to the Rectory, to the influence of Helen's infectious laughter and the enchantment of watching the changing expressions on her lively face.

She sobered suddenly and lowered her voice.

"The oddest thing, sir," she said. "I saw Durrant there, in conversation with one of the clowns. Not in the public part of the building, though, for inadvertently I entered a door marked private."

He raised an eyebrow. "Durrant? And with a clown, you say? That's certainly unexpected. I would not have supposed him to be a follower of the motley."

"No more would I. And I did very much wonder—"

She hesitated, while he regarded her quizzically.

"Cynthia Lydney told me some weeks since, while I was still at home, that Durrant had been down to Sussex on some errand for my Lord Alvington," she went on, impetuously. "And that made me wonder, too. You see—"

"An errand for my father—in Sussex?" he asked incredulously. "That's deuced odd! But I fail to see any connection between that and Durrant's friendship with a clown from Astley's circus. It seems there exists some such connection in your mind, however, Miss Somerby?"

He sounded amused, and she coloured a little but determined to pursue her theme.

"Well, I daresay you may think me an impertinent busybody, but—but forgive me for asking—you're not in any kind of fix, are you?"

"Fix?" He repeated the word in some astonishment. "What on earth can you mean, ma'am?"

"Only that"—she hurried on now, obviously embarrassed as she realised that her tongue was running away with her, yet she was powerless to stop it—"that I saw Durrant after you'd been staying with us at the Rectory last month, and he told me that you would soon be finding yourself with some unpleasant problems to face. I did not at all care for his tone! You must remember how he used to speak in that way when we were children together, as though he knew of something to the disadvantage of one or other of us and was glad of it? So, you see, putting two and two together—"

"You made eight or nine of it!" he exclaimed, laughing. "Oh, my dear N—Miss Somerby, how refreshing you are! I think I may safely promise you that if Durrant does know of something to my disadvantage, I don't care a rap for it. I daresay my credit will survive."

Her eyes flashed with sudden indignation. "I am glad you find it amusing, my lord," she said, with frosty dignity. "I can only beg your pardon for what may seem to you an impertinence. It was kindly meant, however."

He bent closer to her, a contrite expression on his face. "No, it is I who should beg your pardon, Miss Somerby. Believe me, I do appreciate your kindly concern for my welfare—it's a deal more than I deserve.

But if I venture to tease you a little, it's only because I cannot entirely put by the habit of years gone by, when we were almost as brother and sister. Say I'm forgiven?"

She gave a reluctant smile and had just time to murmur an assent to this plea, when they were interrupted by Philip. He had not quite liked to see them talking so intimately together, and determined to break in on the conversation.

"Oh, Miss Somerby, I've just brought back a set of volumes from Hookham's which I'm confident you'll wish to read."

She looked up, a little flushed and disordered, and not altogether sorry for the interruption.

"Indeed? But you must tell me what the work is, Mr. Chetwode, for I cannot hazard a guess, I fear."

"It's a new novel from the pen of the author of *Pride and Prejudice,* the lady whom we know is a Miss Jane Austen," he said, smilingly. "Now confess yourself intrigued, ma'am!"

"Indeed I am, and cannot wait to read it."

"If only it may be as lively as *Pride and Prejudice!*" exclaimed Catherine, with shining eyes. "I enjoyed all three of the novels Miss Austen has already published, but that is my favourite, so far!"

"Oh, dear," said Melissa, humbly, "I must admit I haven't read any of them. I'm not such a prodigious reader as you two."

"I also must plead ignorance," interposed Shaldon. "I don't read many novels."

"Never say that you despise them!" Helen said, accusingly.

"Not if you forbid it, certainly," he replied promptly, a twinkle in his eye.

"Oh, I am not to be forming your taste, I hope," she said quickly, a trifle disconcerted.

He laughed softly. "A formidable setdown, ma'am."

She judged it wiser to ignore this. He seemed to be trying to flirt with her now, yet only a moment ago he had spoken of their brother and sister relationship. She recalled what Cynthia had said of him, and wondered if he could not help trying to flirt with every young lady he met. She, at any rate, would offer him no encouragement in this direction. She turned to Philip.

"But you haven't told me the title of this new novel, Mr. Chetwode."

"It's called *Emma,* and I have great hopes of it," he replied promptly. "By the way, it may amuse you to hear an anecdote concerning the author that was recounted to me by someone acquainted with the Prince Regent's librarian, a Mr. Clarke."

He paused diffidently, fearful of boring his audience; but the young ladies at once urged him to continue, while Shaldon appeared interested.

"This same Mr. Clarke is rather a prosy fellow," he continued. "It seems he suggested to Miss Austen that she might like to write a historical romance illustrative of the House of Cobourg for her next, and dedicate it to Prince Leopold. I wonder can you guess at her answer?"

"No, but I'm certain it would be vastly amusing!" replied Helen, laughing.

"For my part, I hope she refused," said Catherine, decidedly. "I prefer the kind of novel which she writes at present, and I wouldn't have her change her style for the world!"

"Which is precisely what the lady did reply," said Philip, amused by this vehemence. "She told Mr. Clarke that she could never write a book of that kind under any other compulsion than to save her life; and that if she could never relax into laughing at herself or other people, she was sure she'd be hanged before she'd finished the first chapter! She saw nothing for it but to keep to her own style, even though she might never succeed again in that."

"So you may both congratulate yourselves on having guessed aright," remarked Shaldon, smiling at both Helen and Catherine. "Evidently you've managed to learn a good deal of the author's own character from the pages of her novels—but so, I suppose, one might." He glanced at the clock and rose to his feet.

"And now I hope you will forgive me, ladies, if I take my leave of you, though reluctantly. I fear I have another engagement."

Philip, too, was obliged to make his excuses, and the two gentlemen quitted the room together.

"Oh, dear, and I must go, too!" exclaimed Catherine, with a dismayed glance at the clock. "I hadn't intended to stay so long. Mama will be wondering what can have become of me."

"You'll be home in a trice," said Melissa. "I'll ring for the carriage. Mama said I was to do so when you were ready. Oh, and I tell you what—Catherine, Helen and I will go with you for company. Pray let us go up and ask Mama."

Lady Chetwode, still seated in her bedchamber indulging in a pleasant forty winks, roused herself sufficiently to give the required permission and bid Catherine good-bye; and presently the three girls were seated in the carriage chattering away as though they had only just met. The distance to Bruton Street was all too short for them, and they parted with many expressions of regret and resolutions to meet frequently in the future.

"I shall be driving in the Park with Mama tomorrow afternoon," Catherine said, as she left the others. "Do come, if you can. I'll look out for you."

They promised, and with a final wave of the hand, she mounted the steps to the house.

The coachman took them back by way of Berkeley Square. As they were turning from Berkeley Street into Piccadilly, Helen suddenly uttered an exclamation and sat forward in her seat, gazing earnestly out of the window at the crowd which thronged the pavement.

"What is it?" demanded Melissa. "Have you seen someone you know?"

"Yes—no, not precisely," Helen replied at random. "Melissa! Pray desire the coachman to set me down!"

"Set you down?" repeated Melissa, amazed. "Here, in all this crowd? Besides, he can't stop here, you know. It's by far too busy! What in the world can you be thinking of?"

"I've just seen someone. Quick, or I shall lose sight of him, and I most particularly wish to see where he goes! Melissa, please!"

Melissa, a softhearted girl, could not withstand the urgent pleading in her friend's voice. She gave the order to the coachman; but almost before the coach had time to pull up, Helen had flung open the door and leapt out. Melissa started to follow her, but was waved back.

"No, no!" said Helen, in an urgent undertone. "You stay there, or better still, go home and I'll make my own way back."

"But whatever will Mama say?" almost wailed Melissa. "It's most improper to walk about unattended, and—"

"Wait for me in the Square—the carriage can stand there—I may not be long! Don't worry."

So saying, Helen dashed off into the crowd. Her friend stared anxiously after her for a moment, then shrugged her shoulders, directing the coachman to return to Berkeley Square. There was no use in trying to argue with Helen when she was in the grip of an impulse, thought Melissa philosophically; but all the same it would never do for this escapade to come to Mama's ears.

Meanwhile more than one person in the crowd stared in shocked disapproval at the young lady in a fashionable cherry velvet pelisse and bonnet with curled feathers who was pushing her way past them with ill-bred haste, and who, moreover, appeared to be completely unescorted. One or two bucks ogled her hopefully; but Helen was oblivious of all this as she quickened her steps until she had all but come up with the man whose red hair had first attracted her attention from the carriage, and who she felt convinced was the clown she had seen with Durrant at Astley's.

Suddenly, he crossed over towards the Green Park. She darted after him, narrowly avoiding a Stanhope gig which was being driven by a very dashing buck who shouted a protest, and a hackney whose driver favoured her with a less inhibited opinion of her be-

243

haviour. Reaching the other side of the road safely through good fortune rather than judgment, she followed her quarry into the Park. With deer and cattle grazing beneath the trees, this presented a pleasing rural scene in sharp contrast to the road she had just left; but she had no eyes for anything but the man she was following. He walked purposefully on for a little way, then stopped suddenly and looked about him. She just had time to conceal herself behind the solid trunk of an old oak before his glance travelled in her direction; but she could tell from his lack of interest that he had not noticed her. Nevertheless, she had obtained a sufficiently good look at his face to know that she was not mistaken. This was certainly the man in clown's attire whom she had seen with Durrant at Astley's Amphitheatre.

Even as she confirmed this, she saw another man approaching the spot where her quarry was standing, fortunately from the opposite direction. And as the new arrival came up with the other, she was not at all surprised to recognise Durrant himself.

But now for the first time she began to wonder what she had achieved by this discovery; and what in the world would happen if perchance they should come in her direction and Durrant should recognise her, as indeed he must. At the moment, the two men seemed too taken up with each other to have leisure for looking about them. Durrant was addressing himself earnestly to the other man, who seemed somewhat reluctant to listen. Now, if ever, was the time for her to make a strategic withdrawal. She glanced around her, but there were few other people about; it would have been simpler in a crowd.

The luck was on her side, however. After a few moments spent in conversation, the pair turned their backs upon her and walked off in the opposite direction, Durrant still talking volubly. Helen breathed a deep sigh of relief and hurried back by the way she had come.

This time, she was more circumspect in crossing over; and being fully conscious now of her surroundings, she was mortified to realise the amount of un-welcome attention she was attracting. She quickened her steps, anxious to regain the carriage and respecta-bility—with the result that, as she crossed the bottom of Clarges Street, she almost collided with a gentleman in evening dress.

He stepped back a pace, raised his hat and apolo-gised, then gave a perceptible start.

"Good God! Miss Somerby!"

She, too, looked startled. "Lord Shaldon! What are you doing here?"

"I live here, ma'am—nearby, in Clarges Street. But what is more to the purpose is, what are *you* doing here?" He looked about him. "Who is in attendance on you?"

She blushed. "No one. That is to say, Lady Chet-wode's carriage is waiting for me just around the cor-ner, in Berkeley Square."

"You don't mean to tell me that Lady Chetwode has permitted you to step into Piccadilly without an escort?" he demanded, with a heavy frown.

"Oh, no! That's to say, she knows nothing about it for she's at home. Melissa and I were returning from seeing Catherine Horwood back to their house in Bruton Street, and—and I saw someone from the carriage whom I recognised, so I asked Melissa to put me down, and I—well, I ran after—that person," she finished, lamely.

He looked at her in some surprise. "Was this—er—person a gentleman, by any chance?"

"No. Well, not precisely." She glanced up at him a little timidly, and went on, "Oh, it isn't a bit what I can see you're thinking!"

"I am sorry to be so obvious. Do you say the car-riage is awaiting you in the Square? Then I'll do my-self the honour of walking there with you. We cannot stand gossiping here for everyone to gape at."

His tone was stiff, and she noticed his grey eyes had a steely glint.

"No, indeed, you need not trouble," she said, hast-ily. "It is only a step—"

245

"I feel sure that both your parents and your brother would prefer me to accompany you, nevertheless. Besides, I am going that way myself, as I am dining with the Lydneys in Berkeley Street."

She said nothing, but meekly accepted his arm.

"And now," he said, as they began to stroll along, "perhaps you won't object to explaining this extraordinary conduct to me."

She took fire at that. "You have no right to use that tone to me! I am *not* your sister, you know, whatever our past relationship may have been! I am not accountable to you for my conduct!"

"Very true." He smiled down at her, softening unexpectedly. "All the same, won't you please explain? I am so very curious, and I'm sure that is a feeling with which you will readily sympathise."

She could not remain impervious to the charm of that well remembered smile. Her sudden spurt of anger evaporated.

"Oh, very well, since it really concerns you, in a way. You remember I told you earlier of the clown I saw talking with Durrant at Astley's Circus?" He nodded, giving her a quizzical look.

"Well, he was the man I noticed from the coach. I daresay it was foolish, but—but I suddenly felt that I simply must go after him to see where he went," she finished, lamely.

"Oh, Nell!" Unconsciously he fell into the old style of address, as he shook his head and smiled down at her. "What a little madcap you still are, to be sure!"

"Yes, you may say that, and I suppose it's true," she answered defensively. "But all the same, I followed him into the Park and saw him meet Durrant there, which you must allow was something to the purpose."

"To what purpose? You're letting that vivid imagination of yours run away with you, my dear girl. Why shouldn't Durrant possess a friend who's a clown? I knew plenty of fellows at Eton—yes, and at Oxford, too—who would have graced the profession, had they chosen to adopt it."

"Well, you might not mind having a showman for a friend, but I am very sure that Durrant would," retorted Helen, refusing to smile at his quip. "It is several years since either of us had much to do with him, but you cannot have forgotten that he thought only of what could give him consequence in the world or contribute to his advancement! Mama, who knows more of him than either of us, says he hasn't changed."

"Very well," conceded Shaldon. "This unknown chap isn't a friend of Durrant's, but a business acquaintance. Does that satisfy you? And since we have no means of conjecturing what manner of business they are engaged in—even supposing it could remotely be considered any of our concern—"

"But it might!" she insisted, earnestly. "There was something else Durrant said to me on that occasion when he was being spiteful—something I forgot to repeat to you when we were talking earlier. He said"—she screwed up her eyes in an effort of concentration—"he said that there was 'a matter he had on hand.' And he spoke those words immediately after talking of your being faced with problems. Yes, and what is more," she finished, triumphantly, "it was not long after he'd said this to me that he went off on an errand to Sussex for your father!"

For a moment Shaldon looked thoughtful, then he laughed softly. "I'm sorry, but it really does sound a farrago of nonsense. Even you must admit that, my dear girl."

"Oh, well, if you think so." Her tone was frigid. "And may I remind you again that you are *not* my brother? You have no right to address me as 'my dear girl.'"

He smiled ruefully at her. "Oh, Lud, I see I'm in the suds! I beg your pardon most humbly, Miss Somerby, ma'am. How absurdly formal that sounds when not so many years ago we were simply Nell and Tony! However, since it is your wish that we should put by old associations and meet as strangers—"

"Oh, you are absurd!" exclaimed Helen, bursting into laughter.

247

By now they had reached Berkeley Square and saw the carriage waiting, Melissa's head poked anxiously out of the window.

"Oh, thank Heavens you have come back!" exclaimed that sorely tried young lady, as they came up to the vehicle. "I was in quite a worry—oh! My lord Shaldon!"

He assisted Helen to alight, bowed to both young ladies and sauntered off without further delay.

"Well!" said Melissa, as they started on their short journey home. "Of all things! Never tell me it was Viscount Shaldon whom you chased after in that monstrous improper way!"

Helen shook her head. "No. I met him on my way back, and he insisted on escorting me." She wrinkled her brows thoughtfully and added, "No, it was not Lord Shaldon, Melissa, but someone not so *very* unlike him in appearance."

Chapter XXII

SHALDON CHUCKLED as he continued on his way to Berkeley Street. Really, it was too absurd of the chit to build such a house of cards on a few chance remarks made weeks ago, and by Bertram Durrant, of all people! Anyone who had been acquainted with them as boys would know very well that Durrant had always felt spiteful towards his playmates simply because they belonged to a more elevated sphere than himself, and most of all towards Shaldon, as the heir to a great title and estate. Knowing this, who in their senses would heed a few cryptic utterances, no doubt tossed off as a relief to Durrant's spleen?

Only Helen Somerby, he thought, smiling as he recalled the vivid imagination that had peopled the wood where they played as children with fairy-tale figures, gallant Princes rescuing beautiful maidens from wicked ogres and the like. Evidently she had not changed so completely as her outward appearance—and vastly charming, too!—might suggest. But she was now trying to reverse the time-honoured formula of the fairy story in making the beautiful maiden come to the rescue of the Prince. He must remember to quiz her about that when next they met.

Arrived at the Lydneys' house in Berkeley Street, he was shown up into the drawing room, an elegant apartment in white and gold with crimson hangings. Lord Lydney and Henry were already sitting there and invited him to join them in a glass of sherry wine while they awaited the arrival of the ladies. Although Henry Lydney and Shaldon were frequently together, it was seldom that they met in Baron Lydney's town house, the younger men naturally seeking the society of their contemporaries. On this occasion, Shaldon suspected that he had been asked to dine there so that he might meet Miss Cynthia Lydney informally before she emerged upon the London social scene in all the glory of a coming-out ball. It was only to be supposed that his father had made some tentative approach to Lord Lydney concerning the possibility of a match between Miss Lydney and himself; and no doubt, he reflected cynically, the lady wished to look him over.

Which she did, very prettily, when she and her Mama entered the room a while later. She saw some resemblance to the schoolboy she remembered in this tall, personable gentleman with the Stratton features and auburn hair; but the coltish look had vanished with the years, giving way to an air of easy assurance that at times bordered on the cynical. There was nothing cynical at present in the look he bestowed on her as he made his bow, a look compounded of surprise and approval. Cynthia Lydney had been a pretty child, but she had developed into what he would unhesitatingly have declared a stunning girl. He had seen plenty of pretty girls in his years on the Town, but there was a striking difference in this one. Those dark, provocative eyes, that seductive way of moving as if she never for a moment lost consciousness of her femininity, belonged more to the females of the demimonde than to a gently reared young lady of Quality.

The usual polite nothings passed between them until the small party went into the dining room, where he found himself seated beside her.

"By the way, I was in company with some friends of yours earlier today," he remarked, as the soup was being served.

She raised her brows. "Male or female, sir?"

"Oh, young ladies. Miss Somerby, Miss Chetwode, and one whom I had not previously met—a Miss Horwood, I believe."

"Oh, those friends." Her tone was a trifle disparaging. "I haven't seen them since I came to Town, although I was aware that Helen Somerby had arrived to stay with Melissa Chetwode. But then, one is so busy, don't you find?"

He agreed shortly, and turned to address a remark to Lady Lydney, who sat on his other side.

"And which of them do you admire the most?" asked Cynthia with an arch smile, when he could give her his attention again.

"Like most young ladies one meets, they are all prodigiously charming."

"Do you find me charming, sir?"

"But of course. How could it be otherwise?"

His tone was cool and amused. She saw it as a challenge and determined to alter it before she had done with him.

"I am flattered." She gave him one of those provocative glances which men found hard to resist. "Tell me, did you find Helen Somerby much changed since last you met? Oh, but I forget. I believe you saw her when you were in Alvington a month or so since."

"That is so. She's certainly changed in appearance, of course, for she was only a schoolgirl of thirteen or so on the previous occasion when our visits to Alvington chanced to coincide. But in disposition, she is very much what she was as a child—or so it seemed to me."

"She's quite a well-looking girl, is she not?" asked Cynthia, with an air of magnanimity. "Though I did caution her about allowing her fair skin to become too weather-beaten—she's careless in such matters."

"No doubt that's because she likes outdoor pursuits such as walking and riding. But in any case, I think that light suntan becoming to her."

"I do trust you told her so," replied Cynthia, with a laugh. "I'm sure she would be vastly gratified."

"I scarcely see why she should value any opinion of mine," he said carelessly.

"Do you not? Then you must have forgotten how she used to toadeat you when we were children. It was vastly touching to witness."

He glanced at her with a hint of steel in his grey eyes. "I would not put it in quite that way," he said, bluntly. "The two Somerbys and myself were brought up almost as one family. But all that is a long time ago, in any event."

"Yes, of course, and no doubt you've quite lost touch with her brother—a medical man moves in a vastly different world from ours."

"On the contrary, I value my association with James Somerby, as I do with all his family. We meet as often as he can spare the time. Regrettably, that is not very frequently."

She looked a trifle incredulous at this, as though she believed him to be offering excuses for a lapse in friendship which anyone in his social position would naturally find expedient. A member of the peerage could scarcely be expected to remain on terms of intimacy with a humble doctor; it was the way of the world.

"You did not honour us with a visit when you were in Alvington," she said, reproachfully.

"Unfortunately, there was no time. My stay was limited to one night."

"Then I must forgive you, which I do most readily." She flashed an enchanting smile at him which

251

somewhat abated the hostility he had been feeling at her recent remarks. "And I daresay you were much occupied in business affairs with your father at that time, for a day or two afterwards Lord Alvington despatched Durrant on some errand to Sussex, which was no doubt connected with them."

She was every bit as curious as Helen about this errand; for in spite of her easy contempt of Durrant, she could not altogether avoid taking some interest in the secretary's concerns. But if she had hoped to learn something from Shaldon about it, she soon saw that she was to be disappointed; for he turned the subject neatly, and afterwards the conversation became general.

When the ladies presently rose from the table to leave the gentlemen with their wine, Shaldon's eyes followed Cynthia to the door. Undoubtedly she was the most provocative female he had ever met in his own social sphere; a woman whose eyes invited and who knew to a nicety how to employ all her physical attractions to endorse the invitation. She was feline, he thought suddenly, with a cat's warm, seductive movements and purrings—yes, and with a cat's cruel claws. She would make the most delightful mistress—but a wife? Heaven forbid!

Lord Lydney, watching his guest narrowly for his own reasons, saw without surprise that Shaldon was exhibiting signs of some attraction towards Cynthia. It would be a cold fish indeed, reflected the father, who could not feel the girl's magnetism. This was all to the good, since a match was being planned between the two. But there was that other matter, about which so far Shaldon knew nothing; and which might—though for his part, Lydney did not seriously believe it would come to anything—throw a hitch in the way.

Durrant, when questioned about his progress in the investigation, had been reticent—admirably, Lord Lydney reluctantly conceded, since the fellow had promised to proceed with the utmost discretion. He did admit to having unearthed some faint clues as to Mrs. Lathom's destination when she had quitted Rye twenty-

252

six years ago, but had stated that so far he was still following these up without any definite results. It was to be hoped, thought Lord Lydney fervently, that the results would remain negative and the whole affair be buried once more in oblivion.

He would have been prepared to wager that by now Alvington himself was echoing these sentiments, and almost ready to abandon the quest. Neville had never been retentive of any purpose for long, and more sober reflection must have shown him that nothing but unwanted trouble for himself could come of this one. He had been motivated solely by spite against his son. It was possible that should Anthony return home and attempt to make his peace with his father, Alvington would call Durrant off and allow the investigation to lapse. But before that could occur, Anthony would need to be warned; at present, he was in total ignorance of what was happening.

All these thoughts passed through Lord Lydney's mind while he talked smoothly on various topics with his son and their guest over the wine, for he was not a politician for nothing. Gradually the determination came over him to drop some kind of hint to Shaldon, though how much ought to be said was a point on which he felt uncertain. It was not so much a matter of his reluctance to break confidence with Alvington; he considered there were times when a sensible man must decide to overlook these finer points of honour. But to relate the whole story to the son might prove to be but another way of ensuring that the investigation was continued. From what Lord Lydney knew of Shaldon, he was not likely to take a pragmatic approach, and would insist on discovering the truth even though it should work out to his own disadvantage.

Not the whole truth, then; but some hint, something to make the boy attempt a reconciliation with his father.

His opportunity came when Henry left them alone together for a few minutes as they were about to go into the drawing room. He laid a hand on Shaldon's arm to detain him; the other looked at him inquiringly.

"I understand from your father, my dear fellow, that when you two last met, you did not part on very good terms?"

Shaldon shrugged ruefully. "Afraid so, sir. We always do seem to come to cuffs, and the gout doesn't help my father's temper."

Lord Lydney inspected his nails thoughtfully, then nodded. "Just so. And in a moment of passion, one often performs actions which are later regretted. I have known you almost all your life, my boy, so may I presume to offer you some advice?"

Shaldon raised his eyebrows, but nodded.

"I believe you should go at once to Alvington and use your best endeavours to make your peace with your father," Lord Lydney continued, in a grave tone. "I do not put this view forward for the usual moral reason of filial duty, but for the more worldly one of self-interest. If you remain estranged from him, I fear the outcome for you both."

"Fear the outcome!" repeated Shaldon, in a puzzled tone. "What can you mean, sir? Pray, give me a plain tale!"

"Unfortunately, I am not in a position to do that. Any further information must come from your father. But I trust you will heed my advice."

Shaldon thanked him, and would have tried to press the subject further, had not Henry rejoined them at that moment; although he could judge from the finality of Lord Lydney's tone that there would have been small chance of success.

As he walked home later to his rooms in Clarges Street, he pondered on this strange communication. Coming as it did so close on Helen Somerby's warning, it really did begin to look as if something was afoot at Alvington which might cause him some trouble. He had discounted Helen's story as the fabrication of a romantic, imaginative mind which must always try to find an interesting explanation for incidents which seemed at all mysterious. But Baron Lydney was a very different case—a hard-headed politician, and one, moreover, who knew the Earl as few people did.

Was it conceivable that his own father could be plotting something to his disadvantage? He had to admit that it was. He knew his father to be a weak man; and in moments of spite, weak people sometimes lash out unexpectedly. What the Earl could possibly do, though, to harm his son in any way, was more than Shaldon could envisage. He was independent financially, so the traditional measure of cutting him off with a shilling did not apply. The estate was entailed, and he was heir to it. So what remained? Brewing scandal broth? Bah, there was nothing that had not already been whispered in the London drawing rooms and circulated in the Clubs—the affair with Harriette Wilson, flirtations, and the like. The *ton* made light of such matters; they were a commonplace. He had never run into debt, put his name to vouchers he could not meet, or cheated at cards. His life was an open book for those with a taste for such literature, and for his own part he did not give a damn who should read it. As for Sussex, though he had passed a few months at Brighton now and then, he had left no secrets there; Durrant's errand to that county could not possibly concern him. He could not deny, though, that it was certainly odd for the Earl to have sent Durrant on business to a county where the family had neither property nor connections. And why Durrant? The Earl had plenty of trustworthy staff of his own to employ on any business he wished to execute. Lord Lydney must have given his consent, too, or Durrant could not have been employed by the Earl. This was surely strange, in view of his warning tonight? Or perhaps the visit to Sussex was unconnected with the outcome which Lydney said he feared, an irrelevance capable of a simple explanation.

Hell and the devil! thought Shaldon, impatiently. He disliked mysteries. To solve this one, he must obviously confront his father, and that meant a visit to Alvington. He might go tomorrow. But he must certainly return to Town by the following day, for he had a very important engagement to keep in the evening.

The morning after his visit to the Lydneys' house, Shaldon accordingly set off for Alvington. He was impelled by curiosity rather than the motive of self-interest which Lord Lydney had suggested. He had no intention whatever of submitting to his father's domination, either in the matter of his marriage or of any other personal concerns. He could feel no affection for a parent who had never shown him any; a close association now was impossible after so many years of neglect and indifference on his father's side. Nevertheless, he would have preferred not to have been constantly at loggerheads with the old man—to have met, on the rare occasions when they did come together, with civility and a reasonable amount of forbearance. But the mere sight of his heir always seemed to arouse in the Earl a mood of bitterness that found vent in criticism and reproaches which, thought Shaldon wryly, even a saint would have found difficult to endure for long. He had never quite been able to account for his father's unnatural antagonism towards him, but so it was. Any paternal interest and affection he had known had been supplied by his grandfather, with whom he shared an excellent relationship.

He was to be disappointed in his hope of discovering what lay behind Baron Lydney's veiled warning, however; for when he reached Alvington Hall, the butler informed him that the Earl had departed for Bath in the preceding week.

"His lordship is still much afflicted with the gout and hoped the waters might alleviate his condition," said Peters. "We don't look to see him back for some weeks, but if your business is urgent, my lord, I will furnish you with his direction. Will you be staying? If so, I'll instruct the housekeeper to have your room made ready."

"No, don't trouble, Peters. I'll be leaving almost immediately," Shaldon replied, as he settled himself in an armchair. "Can you manage a cold collation, do you suppose? And I'll take a glass of madeira."

"Very good, my lord."

The man withdrew, to reappear presently with the

256

liquid refreshment and a promise of something more solid to follow in a few minutes.

Shaldon meditated as he sipped the wine. He had no desire to make the long journey to Bath, a place he disliked at the best of times. It would mean staying overnight, and he had several engagements tomorrow, one of which at any rate he was determined to keep. Was this little mystery worth so much effort? He was inclined to think not. One thing he could do, he resolved, was to have a word with the Earl's land agent. If there was anything brewing that concerned the estate, he was the man who would know of it.

Mr. Harrison had been replaced some five or six years ago by a younger man called Fowler, whom Harrison had carefully instructed in all the affairs which would henceforward be in his charge. Harrison himself, then in his late sixties, had gone into an honourable retirement in a small house in the village, leaving his previous quarters to the new man. After Shaldon had eaten his nuncheon, he strolled over to the house fronting the stableyard to hold a lengthy interview with Fowler, who was very glad of this opportunity to discuss estate matters with someone who was ready to take a keen, intelligent interest. Of late years, the Earl had been somewhat lacking in this regard; and privately Fowler considered it high time that the Viscount, as future heir to Alvington, should begin to take the reins into his own hands. Without the assurance of long service, he did not like to say as much, instead contenting himself with hints.

"I'll look in upon you for a chat from time to time," Shaldon conceded, tacitly acknowledging his understanding of this technique. "By the way, do you know if my father has any business interests in Sussex, or has lately acquired any property there?" he added, in a careless tone.

"Sussex?" Fowler sounded as though the Viscount had mentioned the moon. "No, my lord, most certainly not. Why do you ask?"

Shaldon nodded. "Just a notion—I see it was absurd. Think no more of it. Well, my thanks to you,

Fowler, for acquainting me with the state of things at present, and for keeping the estate in such good order." He rose, extending his hand. "Be sure I shall be consulting with you again before too long."

After leaving the agent, he made his way to the cottage occupied by Harrison. As he walked up a flagged path through a neat garden to the pleasant stone building with its thatched roof and trellised porch, he reflected that a man might pass the twilight of his days in many a worse place. The door was opened to him by Mrs. Harrison, who was Harrison's second wife and the mother of Bertram Durrant. She dropped a quick curtsey when she recognised her visitor, and whipped off the apron she was wearing. After exchanging a few civilities with her, Shaldon was shown into the parlour, where the pensioner was sitting with a large tabby cat at his feet on the hearthrug.

He started to rise at Shaldon's entrance, evidently quite overcome by the honour of this visit; but he was politely waved back into his chair. Mrs. Harrison, having offered refreshment which was civilly refused, withdrew, leaving the two alone in the room.

"And how are you keeping?" Shaldon asked, having shaken hands cordially and accepted a seat on the other side of the hearth. "Your quarters look snug enough, and evidently you've been busying yourself in the garden, for it looked quite a picture as I walked through."

The old man glowed with pleasure. "You're very good to say so, my lord. Yes, I'm out there most days when the weather's clement, though it don't help my rheumatics, or so Mrs. Harrison will have it. But a man must keep active, my lord, and mine was a very active life, when I was serving the Earl. Have you come down to see his lordship? No doubt you'll have been told he's away in Bath taking the waters just now." He shook his head dolefully. "His lordship suffers much with the gout, I fear."

"Yes, I did come hoping to see him. However,

that's no matter, and instead I've just passed a useful and instructive hour with Fowler, your successor."

"A good man, I can assure you, my lord, and has the interests of the estate at heart. I trained him myself, so I'm sure of that. I'm glad that your lordship has taken the opportunity of talking over some business affairs with him. It's time now that you should have some say in the management of the estate," he continued, with the freedom of an old servant which Fowler had lacked. "By rights, you should be taking over a little from the Earl, for the poor gentleman's health is not equal nowadays to the demands made upon him in that regard."

"Very true, and I hope to persuade him of it when next we meet."

Shaldon then went on for a time to discuss various points raised by Fowler. He listened with courteous attention to all the old man had to say, for he valued the opinion of one who was so expert on this subject.

"By the way," he said casually, when they had come to the end of this discourse, "do you know of any business affairs which my father has in Sussex?"

Harrison repeated the words slowly. "Odd that you should ask that, my lord. I was wondering about it myself. When Bertram was last here, he went posting down to Sussex on the Earl's behalf, though nothing would make him say what his errand was. There's something—I don't quite know what—"

He broke off, and Shaldon waited patiently.

"There's some maggot in that boy's head," Harrison went on, at last, sighing. "I don't understand him—never did, my lord; even as a boy he was too clever for me. His father was a lawyer, you know. Tricksy lot, lawyers, by and large." He hesitated again. "Seems he and the Earl have some secret together, though what it can be is more than I can fathom. Sussex, though. There's nothing I know of to connect your family affairs with that county."

"You don't chance to know the exact location of this errand?"

"No, my lord, though I did my utmost to discover

that and the nature of it, as you may suppose. But Bertram's as close as a clam when he chooses, and I daren't press him too hard for fear of upsetting his mother. Spoils him, of course, but what mother doesn't spoil her son? There's a friend a man may always depend upon, and precious little asked in return. What Bertram did disclose was that the Earl was to make some splendid recompense for his services—something to further his career beyond what he'd ever had any notion of, before."

"Indeed?"

"You may well sound surprised, my lord. So was I, for it puzzled me to think what the boy could possibly do that would cause his lordship to feel such gratitude. I only hope it may not be something that don't turn out well, for I think Bertram's building his hopes high, and often that's dangerous. He's a strange lad, my lord, and hasn't altogether turned out as I would have wished—but there, he's not my own flesh and blood, so perhaps I judge him too harshly. I've always tried to do my duty by him for his mother's sake, but I can't claim to have a natural father's feelings."

Shaldon could not help reflecting that Harrison had performed his parental role a good deal more satisfactorily than at least one natural father in the neighbourhood; but he kept this thought to himself, merely uttering reassurances to the old man, and recommending him to think no more of the journey to Sussex.

"Most likely it's all a hum," he said, rising to go. "And now I must be on my way. I shall look in on you again, if I may, when next I come down."

Harrison said he would be honoured, and insisted on accompanying Shaldon to the door, where he stood with his wife to bid a respectful farewell. Only the cat seemed unimpressed by the noble visitor; it yawned widely as the two men left the parlour, then settled back to sleep on the hearthrug.

Chapter XXIII

IT WAS SCARCELY to be supposed that Melissa would not demand a satisfactory explanation of her friend's extraordinary behaviour in Piccadilly. As soon as the two girls reached home and had gained the privacy of Melissa's bedchamber, Helen found herself called to account.

"It will be monstrous if you don't tell me what you meant by it!" declared Melissa, roundly. "And I confide *everything* to you—at least, almost everything," she concluded, on a weaker note.

"Oh, so you have a secret, have you?" laughed Helen. "Very well, Miss—a fair exchange, or nothing!"

"If that isn't just like you, to seize the advantage when I'm simply bursting with curiosity over your little escapade! But I do assure you that I've nothing to tell that can be half so intriguing as this mystery of yours, so you needn't think to fob me off so easily. You may as well begin at once."

She plumped herself down in a chair, folding her arms and looking very determined.

"Oh, very well," capitulated Helen, untying the strings of her bonnet and tossing it onto the bed to join Melissa's. "But doubtless you'll only laugh at me, as Lord Shaldon did, for perhaps it *is* all in my imagination. I warn you, Mel, this will take some time to explain, for the story really starts back in my childhood, so you'd best prepare for a long session if you're determined to hear the whole."

"Heavens!" squeaked Melissa, wide-eyed. "Never

say that you have been in the throes of a secret passion for all those years and have kept it tightly locked in your bosom, like the heroine of some delightful romance!"

This caused Helen to laugh so heartily that she soon infected her friend, and for a time neither could speak.

"Oh, Mel!" exclaimed Helen at last, as she wiped tears of mirth from her eyes, "I declare you're worse than I am for melodramatic imaginings! Now, pray be quiet if you really wish me to tell you anything, for I shall never begin at this rate."

Her friend having duly promised to attempt this difficult feat, Helen started by explaining the childhood relationship which involved Baron Lydney's secretary Bertram Durrant, of whom Melissa naturally knew nothing. She concluded her account by repeating the remarks made by Durrant which had caused her to feel some alarm for Viscount Shaldon.

"But when later I told Mama what he had said," continued Helen, "she thought it only spite, so I dismissed it from my mind. Especially as soon afterwards I came to London, and had other things to engage my attention. It was only when we went to Astley's that it all came back to me again."

"Astley's? Why, whatever can have occurred there?" demanded Melissa, incredulously.

"I didn't mention it to you at the time, but I saw Durrant there—and in the kind of company I knew well he would never keep in the normal course of things."

And Helen went on to explain more fully, finishing with an account of the recent escapade which had so startled her friend.

"You see, I felt I simply must dash after that man, whoever he is," she concluded. "And then what must I do but bump into Lord Shaldon, of all people, on my way back to you."

"Did you tell him about it?"

"I didn't intend to, at first, but he was prodigiously stuffy about my being in the street alone, so of course

262

it all came out. I wish it had not, for he only laughed at me and said I was letting my imagination run wild. Perhaps I am, too—but, Mel, I have the oddest feeling that there *is* something queer afoot, something that constitutes a threat to Lord Shaldon, if only he could be made to see it!"

Melissa nodded sympathetically, and was thoughtful for a moment.

"Why don't you consult with your brother?" she suggested at last, with a slightly self-conscious air that Helen was at present too preoccupied to notice. "He and Viscount Shaldon are close friends, and he will know what ought to be done, I am sure."

"I may perhaps do that," replied Helen, dubiously. "Only I'm not certain that James may not think me fanciful, too. As Lord Shaldon said, it does sound a farrago of nonsense."

"Did he say that?" asked Melissa, indignantly. "Well, I must say, Nell, I think it was vastly uncivil, after all your concern on his behalf!"

"Oh, well, we were almost one family as children, and I think perhaps he's beginning to slip back into the old familiar ways. Not that I mean to allow it!" she exclaimed, elevating her chin. "One brother is quite enough for any girl, and so I told him!"

"Quite right. And if you do want to confide in Mr. Somerby," said Melissa, pursuing her own line of thought, "could we not visit him at the hospital? We could perhaps find out at the same time how that poor woman goes on—the one who was knocked down in the street, you know."

Helen hesitated. "I doubt if your Mama would agree to that. She would almost certainly fear the risk of infection."

Melissa's face fell. "I daresay you are right. Well, then you must ask him to come and see you here. Mama said he was to come at any time, recollect, and not to stand on ceremony. He is invited to our ball, of course, but that is still more than a fortnight away, just after the Royal Drawing Room."

"The Drawing Room! The ball!" exclaimed Helen.

"Good heavens, as little as a fortnight away! I only hope I shall contrive to wear a hoop without falling over it. I know one should show respect to the Queen, but nothing could be more mortifying than positively to grovel on the floor before her Majesty!"

"Mama said we must practise," said Melissa, after they had laughed over this. "Her dresser, Travers, will soon put us in the way of it. She's so antiquated, poor dear, that I daresay everyone wore hoops in her youth! But do send a message to your brother asking him to call on us soon, for a come-out ball is not at all the occasion for serious conversation. Besides, you won't wish to leave it so long, I am positive, knowing you as I do."

This time Helen's attention was drawn by her friend's persistence in urging an early visit from James. She gave her a quizzical look.

"Pray tell me, Melissa, is it solely for my peace of mind that you wish me to summon James?"

Somewhat to her amusement, she saw Melissa redden.

"I can't think what you mean. He is the only member of your own family close at hand, so it's only naural for you to turn to him when there's anything vexing you," she said, defensively.

"Melissa!" exclaimed Helen, in stern tones. "Never say that this is Monsieur Falaise all over again!"

"Monsieur Falaise," repeated her friend, scornfully, while she pressed a hand to her telltale cheeks. "I wonder you can mention his name beside that of—of—"

"Of my brother James? Oh, Mel, you must not make *him* the object of one of your schoolgirl's fancies, as you termed them yourself not so long since! It will never do, my dear, you must see that."

brother go much deeper." Her voice dropped away,

"It's not like that—like the dancing master, I mean." Melissa's brown eyes were deep and serious. "I wanted to keep it from you, Nell, but since you've guessed, you may as well know that my—my feelings for your brother go much deeper." Her voice dropped away,

264

and she spoke the final words in a whisper. "I love him, Helen, indeed I do."

"Oh, no, how can you?" asked Helen, in a dismayed tone. "Why, you've met him only a few times, and then always in company with others. Depend upon it, the feeling will wear off presently just as the other did!"

"Why should you suppose that I can't truly be in love?" demanded Melissa, indignantly. "Other girls fall in love, don't they? Am I so vastly different from everyone else?"

"Well, dearest, you are rather inclined to be volatile," said Helen in an affectionate tone that robbed the words of any offence. "Also you're young yet to be certain of having formed a lasting attachment."

"I'm eight months younger than you, it's true, but I'm eighteen, after all! Besides, I don't think age has anything to do with falling in love, whatever you may say! But now that you know my secret," she went on, in a more subdued, almost humble tone, "do tell me, Nell—do you think I've the remotest hope of ever attaching your brother?"

"You've only to look in your mirror, love, to see that you're attractive enough to attach any man!" exclaimed Helen, in a rallying tone. "The only thing is," she went on, more doubtfully, "James cannot be thinking of marriage for some time yet. He's not in the same situation as your brother, or the other gentlemen of your acquaintance. He still has to make his way in the world."

"I would wait—for years and years, if need be! But I daresay he would never look my way," she continued, despondent again. "Tell me truly, Nell, without any hedging—is there anyone else?"

Helen shook her head decidedly. "No . . . I am quite confident of that, for he would have told me. We are very close. You see, I think he's always been too taken up with his vocation to have found time for those social occasions where he might have met suitable females."

Melissa's face brightened. "Then I can at least hope!"

"Yes, but—Mel, dearest, have you considered?" Helen spoke with some difficulty. "Your parents may not think a medical man an eligible match for you. Indeed, I must confess that it would surprise me if they did. All things considered—though I don't need to tell you that there's no one I would rather have for a sister!—I believe it would really be in your best interests to try to get the better of your partiality for James. And so I don't think I shall invite him to visit me here, after all, since the less you see of him, the easier it will be for you. Don't you agree, my love?"

A despondent shrug was the only answer. Helen placed an arm about her friend's shoulders.

"Come along. Let's go and practise walking in our hoops for a while. That should make you laugh again!"

Late afternoon was the fashionable time for riding or driving in Hyde Park, and as Lady Chetwode's smart landau turned through the gates, Helen's unaccustomed eyes widened at the sight before her. The traffic here was as dense as on any busy London street, but only the most elegant equipages were to be seen. The ladies, dressed in modish toilettes of every hue with fetching bonnets decked with plumes and ribbons, drove out in landaus, landaulets or barouches with a bewigged coachman on the box and sometimes a powdered footman resplendent in livery in attendance. The gentlemen drove their own curricles, tilburies or dashing high-perch phaetons, with what they termed 'prime bits of blood' between the shafts; or else they were mounted on stylish thoroughbreds like the one which Philip Chetwode was at present riding close by the vehicle which bore the ladies.

"Good Heavens!" exclaimed Helen to Melissa. "How on earth can we ever hope to see Catherine in all this crush?"

"There's no depending on it at all, my dear," replied Lady Chetwode, "but we shall see a great many other people. Look, there is the Duchess of Rutland—" She broke off to bow graciously in the direction of an elegant landau with a crest on its panels. "And there is Lady Jersey with the Countess of Lieven—I think they are stopping. I do hope so," she added in an undertone, "for I wish to present you both so that I can persuade them to give you vouchers for Almack's."

Her wish was granted, for the two ladies desired their coachman to halt the very slow progress possible in all that concourse, and brief greetings were exchanged. The introductions were made and received with a slight bow on the ladies' side and a more respectful one on that of the two girls, before the carriages moved away.

"That is very important, is it not, ma'am, to have vouchers for Almack's?" asked Helen.

"Oh, dear me, yes. One can almost say that it's as important to a young lady as being presented. You are not in the *ton,* you know, if you are not admitted there. Those are two of the patronesses, and their goodwill is essential to obtain an entrance."

"To as slow a place of entertainment as any in London!" exclaimed Philip, with a laugh, as he heard these remarks.

"Well, of course, gentlemen do not think much of Almack's, because the card games there are played for such low stakes," explained Lady Chetwode to her guest.

"Sixpenny points!" declared Philip, in disgust. "And the refreshments a disgrace, assure you, Miss Somerby."

Helen, whom he thought was looking particularly charming in a pale blue carriage dress and a high crowned bonnet trimmed with ruched ribbon of the same shade, turned towards him to smile at this remark, and caught the eye of a dark haired gentleman mounted on a handsome grey. Recognising Philip Chetwode with his second glance, the horseman hailed him; then managing his animal in all the press of vehicles and riders with an ease which drew forth Helen's admiration, he came close to the landau in order to pay his respects to Lady Chetwode. Something vaguely familiar in his face caused Helen to stare at him until she heard Lady Chetwode address him as Mr. Lydney; the next moment she found herself being presented to this playfellow of her youth.

"Miss Somerby, b'Gad!" he exclaimed, bowing for the third time. "We were very well acquainted at one time, ma'am, though I've no notion how many years it is since we last met! Permit me to tell you that I find you vastly changed, and most charmingly."

Helen accepted this tribute with a quiet smile which caused Lady Chetwode to give her an approving glance. It was only to be expected that young men would pay flowery compliments to a pretty girl, but it was pleasing to see these amiable nothings accepted without a parade of either maidenly flutterings or arch coquetry.

"How are your mother and sister?" Helen asked. "I haven't seen them since coming to Town, although we met shortly before I left Alvington."

"Oh, they go on famously! That's to say, Cynthia does, of course. But if Lady Chetwode will permit," turning deferentially to Helen's hostess, "I'll bring them round to call on you one day soon."

This made Philip Chetwode raise his brows. Lydney was not the man to squire the females of his family about the Town unless he had an ulterior motive for his devotion to them.

"That would be delightful," replied Lady Chetwode. "I have not yet made the acquaintance of your sister, and should like to do so before she attends the ball I am giving for my daughter and Helen. I trust we shall see you there, also? You will have had the invitation already."

"Indeed you will, my lady," he answered promptly, his eyes once again on Helen's countenance. "It is one engagement which I shall certainly do myself the honour of attending."

Shortly afterwards he was obliged to move away, owing to the difficulty of keeping abreast of the carriage among so many other vehicles and riders. Philip's face wore a frown after they had parted. He was well aware of his friend's reputation as a flirt, and had seen with misgiving how Lydney could scarcely keep his eyes away from Miss Somerby.

He fell silent as they moved slowly on around the Ring, taking himself to task for having too keen a concern in Miss Somerby's affairs. After all, he had known her only a week, and already he was allowing two of his closest friends to arouse the most unwelcome feelings in his breast on her behalf. What were their attentions to her, he asked himself, but those of friendship arising naturally enough out of an association in childhood?

His melancholy reverie was interrupted by the carriage halting yet again to enable its occupants to exchange delighted greetings with two ladies in a landaulet which had been attempting to pass at that moment. He recognised one of the ladies as his sister's visitor of the previous day, Miss Horwood, who had been so earnest in her defence of Miss Jane Austen's style of writing. There was little opportunity now for any such rational conversation, however; and when Lady Chetwode had issued a cordial invitation to the Horwoods to call in Cavendish Square on the following day, the carriages moved on once more.

After a further hour spent dawdling around the Park in this fashion, during which time they encountered several other acquaintances of Lady Chetwode's, the carriage returned to Cavendish Square. Philip Chetwode, resisting an impulse to spend the evening at home in Miss Somerby's company, took himself off instead to White's. Helen herself settled down to write a long letter to her parents full of lively descriptions of the London scene; but she omitted any mention of her encounters with Durrant. She felt it was only too probable that Mama would echo Shaldon's own words on that subject, and recommend her not to indulge in fantasy.

The following morning Mrs. Horwood and Catherine called as they had promised. Scarcely had they settled themselves in the morning parlour with the Chetwode family and Helen, than some other visitors were announced, and Henry Lydney walked in accompanied by his mother and sister. Lady Lydney had, as usual, little to say for herself. She was not well acquainted with Lady Chetwode, although the two ladies had met previously; Mrs. Horwood was a stranger to her, and judging from her manner, she was content that matters should rest there.

Cynthia naturally paid more attention to the gentlemen of the party than to the ladies, not scorning to practise her arts on Melissa's father, but devoting far more effort to Philip Chetwode, whom she saw at once was quite taken up with Helen. She was aided in this by her brother Henry, who was so determined in engaging Miss Somerby in conversation that no one else in the party had much opportunity to intrude. Somewhat to Cynthia's chagrin, Philip seemed able to resist her charms, talking quite as much to the shyer Catherine as to her dashing onetime schoolfellow, and seeming to enjoy their discourse, which was of a literary turn. Eventually, Cynthia privately dubbed him a slow-top not worthy of her efforts, and reminded her mother that they had another engagement. They rose to take leave, but not before Henry had obtained Lady Chetwode's permission to drive Miss Somerby out in the Park on the following morning, so that, as he phrased it, they might reminisce about their childhood days in Alvington.

"So she is to be your latest flirt," Cynthia said to him as they returned home. "I wonder at you, Henry. She is not near so striking as Diana Sawyer, your last. Indeed, I can't think what anyone can see in her. I find her insipid."

"Perhaps you're a better judge of a man, my dear sister."

"She's very fortunate in having someone to bring her out in Town," remarked Lady Lydney. "It's more than a country clergyman's daughter could hope for, I must say."

"But not more than she deserves," Henry retorted with spirit. "She's a dashed pretty girl, and with unaf-

270

fected manners that must recommend her to anyone of discrimination."

"I do trust, Henry, that you are not going to develop a tendre for the girl," reproved his mother. "I need scarcely tell you that it would be most unsuitable. Her birth is genteel of course, though scarcely in the first flight, but she has no fortune. She may inherit something from her grandparents later on, but doubtful expectations of that kind are no solid foundation for matrimony."

"For God's sake, Mother, who mentioned matrimony?" expostulated her son, disgusted. "May I not pass a few favourable comments on a girl I knew in childhood without your at once jumping to the conclusion that I intend to wed her? No such thing. I assure you, the bachelor life suits me too dashed well at present!"

He called for Helen on the following morning in a smart curricle drawn by a pair of well matched greys, with a young groom perched on the rear seat. Contrary to what he had suggested to Lady Chetwode, he and his passenger did not reminisce about the past, but found ample scope for conversation in the present. They laughed a good deal, for Henry could be an entertaining companion when he chose, and drew several amused glances from those they passed in other vehicles or on horseback, many of whom were known to Henry. When he returned Helen home at the end of a pleasant three quarters of an hour, she felt that Mr. Lydney had improved considerably since her early recollections of him, and that she would be quite ready to accept his invitation to drive out with him again before long. He would have liked to make a specific engagement, but she hedged a little, saying that she could not be certain what other arrangements Lady Chetwode might have made for her. This was partly true; for the rest, she was not so naive as to require Lady Chetwode to inform her that it would not be proper for her to appear too frequently in the company of any one gentleman. In such matters, observances in the country were quite as strict as in Town.

She had looked forward eagerly to the promised visit to the Opera that evening in the company of Lady Chetwode, Melissa and Philip. As they set off in the town carriage for the Haymarket, her delighted gaze took in the scene; tall houses ablaze with light, gold-laced footmen lining the steps where company was expected, and the crowd of gaping citizens watching for the arrival of elegant coaches bearing splendidly attired passengers. She watched a link boy on the pavement, bearing a flaming torch as he accompanied a sedan chair and its exquisite occupant. She listened to the rattle of the many carriage wheels over the cobbles, thinking with rapture that surely there was no place in the world that held half the splendour, the excitement, the glamour of London town. A mundane encounter with a loaded haywaggon bound for one of the markets did nothing to break the spell, even though the ungainly vehicle blocked their access to the Opera House for a time.

Once seated in their box, she found a fresh source of pleasure in the assembled audience. Never before had she seen so many beautiful gowns and glittering jewels displayed in one place. She looked eagerly about her, gazing into one box after another as she exclaimed in rapture to Melissa, to whom the scene was also new and who was quite as much overcome as her friend.

Presently her eyes lighted on a box almost opposite where four people were seated, two of each sex. The ladies wore extremely décolleté gowns, one of white satin ornamented with silver spangles and the other of pink silk with an overdress of gauze. Both had plumes in their hair and were liberally decked with jewels which scintillated in the light from the chandeliers.

Helen's gaze took in all this finery, then passed on to the less resplendent but still elegant gentlemen. She gave a start as she recognised one of them.

"Oh, look!" she exclaimed. "It's Lord Shaldon!"

The rest of her party at once glanced across to the other box. Philip Chetwode gave an apologetic cough on seeing the group sitting there, while his mother quickly averted her eyes. At that moment, Shaldon himself chanced to look in their direction and Helen impulsively raised her hand in greeting.

"Oh, *no,* my dear!" expostulated Lady Chetwode, seizing Helen's arm and forcing it down. "Pray do not —you mustn't!"

"Why not?" demanded Helen, as she watched the brief bow her gesture had drawn from Shaldon, who immediately drew farther back into the interior of his box. "Oh, I beg your pardon, ma'am. Is it not proper for me to wave to an acquaintance in the theatre? I didn't know."

Lady Chetwode looked embarrassed, and Philip gave another cough.

"Well, not precisely that, but—but—oh, dear, how very awkward it is to explain!"

Helen wrinkled her brow. "Nevertheless I wish you will explain it to me, for I must know how to go on."

"The thing is, you see, Helen," began her hostess, fluttering her fan before her face in an endeavour to hide a telltale blush, "the fact is that Viscount Shaldon may not wish you—or any of the ladies of our circle— to recognise him just at present."

"Not wish me—" Helen's eyes widened in astonishment, and she broke off for a moment. "Why, ma'am, whatever can you mean?"

Lady Chetwode sighed, redoubling her activity with the fan. "It's all most unfortunate, and I'm sure if I'd had the least notion that such creatures would be present, I would never have brought you and Melissa here tonight! But so it is—one may meet them everywhere, more's the pity!"

Had Helen been less curious, she would have seen that it was better now to let the subject drop. But any suggestion of a mystery was always a challenge that she found difficult to ignore; so she persisted in spite of a nudge from Melissa.

"Such creatures?" she repeated. "Do you mean the people who are with Lord Shaldon?"

"Certainly I do, and although it's not a subject on which I desire to dwell," replied Lady Chetwode, firmly, "I think you should know, my dear, that those

—females—whom Viscount Shaldon sees fit to honour with his company are not at all what they should be—indeed, are quite notorious! And now pray don't say any more about such a distasteful subject."

Helen, abashed, leaned back in her seat. Fortunately the curtain rose at that moment, so the awkwardness of starting on another, more acceptable topic of conversation, did not fall to anyone's lot.

She scarcely saw the scene that was unveiled before her, however, as a wave of indignation swept over her. So these were Lord Shaldon's Other Interests, were they? And she had been so concerned for his welfare as to try to discover what Durrant was plotting against him. Well, she had learnt her lesson! What did it matter to her now if he became positively *immersed* in troubles? she asked herself angrily. He evidently deserved all he was to get, and for her part she would not lift a finger to assist him!

Having reached this sensible decision, she bent a determined gaze on the stage; even though she found the view somewhat blurred by an unaccountable mist before her usually keen eyes.

Chapter XXIV

MRS. GERRIDGE'S LODGING HOUSE in Murphy Street was not far removed in distance from the tinselled splendour of Astley's Royal Amphitheatre, but to step from one to the other was to enter a totally different world. Mrs. Gerridge's establishment, if it might be dignified by that title, was respectable but seedy. She let single rooms to people with an insecure footing

in the humbler forms of entertainment. As her lodgers
rarely stayed with her for more than a few months at a
time, rent had to be paid in advance; anyone attempting to infringe this rule was at once shown the door, a
much chipped and scratched but reasonably solid
structure which had once been painted brown.

The rooms at No. 4 Murphy Street were all very
similar. They were cramped and gloomy, the one tiny
window being draped in a curtain of doubtful hue and
rarely cleaned. The furniture consisted of a bed with
a straw-filled mattress, a table more often than not
with one leg shorter than the others, a deal chair, an
iron washstand and bowl, and a small cupboard into
which all the occupant's personal possessions must be
crammed. Mrs. Gerridge provided neither meals nor
facilities for cooking, as her lodgers were absent all
evening and most of the day. There was no rule
against bringing food into the house, however, which
probably accounted for the prevalence of mice.

The landlady was a stringy female with sharp button eyes, an incipient moustache on her upper lip, and
sparse grey hair scraped back into a bun. She prided
herself on her respectability, was a regular member of
the congregation at one of the Nonconformist chapels,
and never permitted any "goings on," as she styled it,
in her household.

When pretty little Phyllis Stiggins had first arrived
at her door with a well set-up young man who called
himself Rowland Carlton, Mrs. Gerridge had scrutinised the female's left hand sharply and at once demanded to know if they were married or not. They
had hesitated for a moment, but under the influence of
those beady eyes, the girl had at last shaken her head.

"Ye'll be wanting two rooms, then," said Ma
Gerridge, briskly, and named her price. "Payment in
advance, of course," she added.

This appeared to disconcert the couple for a moment; but eventually they nodded reluctantly and by
a combined effort produced the required sum. They
were then shown to their rooms, which they looked
over bleakly from the door without comment; in-

formed of the house facilities and rules, they were left to settle in with the few possessions they had brought with them.

A few days' residence accustomed them to their new quarters, for indeed they had known many worse and few better. They had not been together long, having first met at St. Bartholomew's Fair last August, when Carlton had been lucky enough to be taken on as an extra in Richardson's travelling theatre booth. His life had mostly consisted of drifting from one fairground to another ever since he had attached himself to one at the age of twelve or thereabouts. He had been fortunate enough at one period to belong to a travelling company of third-rate actors—barnstormers as they were called, from the fact that most of their performances took place in village barns and taverns. Although this was an insecure enough livelihood, it had represented the most stable part of his existence, and one on which he looked back with nostalgia. But the company had been forced to disband from lack of funds after four or five years; and since then, he had drifted from place to place, picking up casual employment among showmen whenever he could, for this was the only life he understood.

After the Fair had ended, he and the girl were obliged to part. She went on the road with the small circus group to which she was attached at that time; while he, his services no longer required by Richardson, must seek employment elsewhere.

When they had met again a few weeks later, he was sadly down on his luck, but her star was for the moment in the ascendant. The circus group had eventually broken up, in the way that such associations often did; but she had managed to find temporary employment at no less a place of entertainment than the magnificent Astley's Amphitheatre. Although her act was of minor interest in the show, the engagement was for several months, and this in itself constituted a triumph. She related all this to him with glowing eyes which dimmed in sympathy when he told her of his own lack of success.

"I'll mebbe have a chance at Greenwich Whitsun Fair," he concluded, gloomily, "but there's naught I can see tell then, and that's more'n a month off, yet."

"D'ye reckon you could play a clown?" she demanded suddenly, eyes brightening. "One of ours had an accident last night—fell over in the ring and broke a leg. They'll be wanting someone in his place for to-day's performance, and no time to look around. Why don't ye try for it?"

He went off with her at once to see the manager, who seemed doubtful at first despite Carlton's rosy account of his experience in all forms of acting, but who eventually decided that no harm could come of trying the fellow out for one night to see how he did. Accordingly, Carlton was engaged on the understanding that either he gave complete satisfaction or was summarily dismissed, and that in any case he must go when the original performer was able to return. It was more than enough to put him on his mettle, and he did succeed in retaining his place for the time being.

Thus temporarily settled in employment, he and Phyllis sought lodgings close at hand, and so came to No. 4. Their relationship strengthened steadily; but they were obliged to exercise the greatest care over meeting in each other's rooms, because of the keen surveillance of Ma Gerridge.

On this particular day they were able to steal an hour or so together while the good lady was absent at one of her religious gatherings, and before it was time for them to depart for Astley's. They had for some time been lying closely entwined on the inhospitable mattress, lost to all sense of their drab surroundings, when Phyllis sat up, gently pushing her lover away.

"She'll be back soon, and we'll need to get ready to leave for the performance," she reminded him.

Rowland Carlton yawned and stretched lazily. He was a tall, lean man in his middle to late twenties with a strong-featured face and a thatch of auburn hair. The grandiloquent name was not his own, but one which had been suggested for his use in his barnstorming days by the proprietor of the company of strolling players.

"Looks well on the handbills, me lad," this enterprising showman had said. "Take my tip—if you want to get on in this business, you need a grand moniker, not something like Joe Bloggs or Will Smith."

One name had seemed as good as another to the recipient of this advice, so Rowland Carlton he had remained, though known more familiarly as Rowly to his associates. And though the necessity for a name that looked well on the handbills had never, alas, arisen since his time with the barnstormers, he still clung to the hope that someday it might.

"Reckon so," he said, in answer to Phyllis's reminder. "Old cow—pity we can't find another ken hereabouts."

Phyllis shook her tangled yellow curls. "No chance o' that," she answered gloomily. "Who else wants to take in show folk o' our sort? Reckon we're lucky to get this, which we wouldn't 'ave done if Betty 'adn't tipped me the wink."

Betty was one of the washerwomen responsible for the theatrical costumes at Astley's, a good-hearted creature who had taken a fancy to Phyllis.

Carlton rolled off the bed and began gathering up his scattered garments.

"Who was that swell you was talking to the other night?" asked Phyllis as she watched him.

"What swell?"

"A good-lookin', dark feller, dressed in fine clothes. 'E was with you in the passage outside the changing rooms—Wednesday, I think it was."

"Oh, that feller. Don't know 'is name; 'e didn't tell me."

"What did 'e want, then?" asked the girl curiously.

Carlton hesitated, pretending to be taken up with putting on his shoes. He was fond of Phyllis, a pretty little wench and obviously mad about him; but one could never trust females. He was not without experience of the sex, and knew well they were powerful gabsters. To tell one of them anything was to publish

278

it to the world. Besides, he himself knew little enough as yet of what this man's purpose with him might be, even if a promise of strict secrecy had not been exacted from him. The lure held out to him was a future free from want, an undreamt-of prosperity; but what he must do to attain this Eldorado was as yet unexplained. First he must undertake to place himself unreservedly in the stranger's hands; it had been explained to him carefully that this would mean that Rowland Carlton must vanish ovenight, never to be heard of again. Keen questioning on the stranger's part had established that there were no family ties to complicate this issue, and he had obviously been anxious to conclude the bargain on their second recent meeting in the Green Park. But tempting though the prospect was, Carlton had hedged. To break free from his present surroundings meant little to him, in spite of Phyllis. There would always be women elsewhere. What made him hesitate was the aura of mystery surrounding the stranger's proposition and the searching questions which had been put to him concerning his past life. A plain, straightforward offer of employment was one thing, and a very good thing, if it could be had; but this havey-cavey business frankly scared him. He asked for time to consider. The other man tried to press for an immediate answer, but capitulated when he saw that too much haste would only drive Carlton away altogether. Eventually, it was agreed that they were to meet again a month hence at Greenwich Fair, when Carlton would give his final decision.

Maybe he had acted like a fool, thought Carlton, uneasily, to turn down the offer of a job when his prospects were so uncertain. But let his luck at Greenwich decide matters. If he found someone there willing to take him on in any capacity, for however short a spell, then he would whistle this other offer down the wind, and be damned to it. If not—well, there was not much choice but to accept.

Aloud, he said to the girl, "Nothing much."

"Must have wanted something," she persisted.

"Didn't seek you out to pass the time o' day, not a swell like that. You're keeping something back," she added, displaying her feminine intuition.

"Well, I thought 'e might be offering me a job, see?" replied Carlton, goaded. "But naught came of it, anyways, so why waste breath?"

"What kind of job—on the road, or what?"

"Oh, Gawd, let me alone, will ye?" the now exasperated man shouted. "I've told you all there's to tell, wench—'ave done!"

"Hush! Ye'll bring Ma Gerridge up. She'll be back any minute."

She twined her arms about him, closing her mouth over his. He responded mechanically, shaking himself free in a moment, and making for the door.

She closed it behind him; but she stood looking into space thoughtfully for several minutes before eventually beginning to straighten up the room and make herself ready to leave for the next performance at Astley's.

When James Somerby began walking the wards, Mr. Guy's hospital in Southwark had been in existence for ninety years. Mr. Thomas Guy was a successful bookseller of charitable inclinations who late in life had become possessed of a considerable fortune through wise investments. Upon being appointed as a Governor of St. Thomas's Hospital in 1704 he began to give serious attention to this form of charity. He first created three new wards at St. Thomas's and donated one hundred pounds per year for the relief of indigent patients after their discharge from the hospital. It later occurred to him that a second hospital was needed, situated close to St. Thomas's, and accordingly he set about having one built.

The new hospital was surrounded by mean, tortuous streets and alleys crammed with old, tumbledown buildings where epidemics flourished. There was much work to be done, yet the training of medical men was still in its infancy. Gradually over the succeeding years medical and surgical training was taken in hand at the

United Hospitals of the Borough, as the two hospitals came to be designated. Lectures were given on medicine, anatomy and surgery; students walked the wards with physicians and surgeons, and were able to watch operations being performed in the hospitals.

There were three classes of students—apprentices, dressers and pupils. The apprentices served the whole of their time with one or other of the surgeons at the hospitals, and hoped eventually to succeed to their master's post. The dressers and pupils had already served their apprenticeship with a doctor elsewhere, and came to the hospital for six months or a year to study anatomy and learn something of surgery. Dressers held a superior position to pupils; they were attached personally to a particular surgeon to assist him in operations, and sometimes had patients and accident cases confided to their care. They were also responsible for all dressings in the wards. For these privileges they paid a higher fee than the pupils, who were not under the personal supervision of any surgeon and merely looked on and asked questions, pushing their way to the bedside or into the standings at the operating theatres in both hospitals as best they could.

At one o'clock on the day of his sister's coming out ball, James had been attending an operation in the small, airless theatre of the hospital. A semicircle of railed standings packed with students surrounded the central area where the operating table, made of wood with a movable headrest, was placed directly under a large skylight. The patient, a man of middle years whose left leg was to be amputated, had previously been dosed with the only anaesthetic available, a stiff shot of gin. Beside the table stood the surgeon, Mr. Astley Cooper, calm and confident, attended by his dressers and apprentices. James was carrying a dresser's receptacle containing plasters, bandages and other dressings, which besides being necessary to the business in hand, was a much valued symbol of his office.

The students in the standings kept jostling for position and calling out, "Heads! Heads!" every time those around the table impeded their view of the proceedings. The noise and confusion abated a little as the surgeon began his task. It was all over in a matter of minutes, for Mr. Cooper's skill in the business was famed. Afterwards it was for James and the others to play their part, and then the patient was removed to the wards. The surgeon washed his hands at a side table on which stood a china ewer and basin; removed his operating coat, which was hung on a hook in the wall; and resumed his street coat. Meanwhile, the students fought their way out of the theatre to rush down the stairs and across the street to St. Thomas's, where the jostling and pushing began all over again as they crowded into the lecture theatre.

James had accompanied the groaning patient into the ward, offering such solace as he was able, before making his own way to the lecture at St. Thomas's, one of a series on the bones of the skull. Striding purposefully along the central colonnade, which gave access under cover to the outlying buildings, he paused for a few minutes to speak a friendly word to a woman on crutches whom he was passing.

"Good day to you, Mrs. Dorston. You seem to be swinging along at a great rate on your crutches."

"Good day to you, doctor." She bobbed her head, the nearest approach she could make to a curtsey. "Yes, I'm getting about a bit now. I've been to the service in the Chapel the last few days."

"Good. You'll soon be home. I daresay you'll not be sorry for that."

She pursed her lips. "Many ways, I'm better off here, though there's no rules at home."

He frowned, knowing something of the neighbourhood from which she came. The hospital, rough though it seemed to anyone accustomed to a genteel background, must appear a haven to such as Mrs. Dorston. He was too much his parents' son not to feel compassion for the patients' sufferings, however much experience had taught him that an objective, practical approach generally served their interests best. He was always ready therefore to spare some of his time for listening to them, in the hope that easing the mind might contribute to ease of body.

"But you will be glad to rejoin your family," he suggested.

She snorted. "I've no family, sir, leastways only a grandson I've not set eyes on these eight years. Last time I did see him was at Bartholomew Fair—he was playacting in a booth there. He didn't know me at first, doctor, because it was five years since I'd left him with some fairground folk to get a living. He was twelve, then, or thereabouts." She sighed. "I didn't want to leave him, but it was the best I could do at the time. I'd a drunken husband, y' see, sir—my second: a bad mistake on my part, but how's a woman to know? He knocked the child about, so it was best to send him away. I kept my promise to my poor girl —she died giving birth to him. I said I'd look after the little lad, and I did my best," she repeated, dully. "No notion where he is now, but he's a man full grown and can look out for himself."

"I'm sorry," he replied, feeling the inadequacy of the words. "And your husband?"

"He's been gone these ten years. Killed in a street brawl, doctor, and nothing any of you medical gentlemen could have done for him. Someone split his head with a cleaver. I hope I'm a Christian woman, sir, but many's the time I'd been tempted to do the same myself. He brought me low, spent all my money, left me to scratch along as best I could. I should have had more sense than to take up with him, but a body gets lonely. Ah, well, no point in going back over the past," she concluded, shifting one of the crutches into a more comfortable position under her armpit. "You're very kind to listen to an old woman's mitherings, but I mustn't take up any more of your time, and Sister will be keeping a sharp look out for me in the Ward. A real Tartar, that one, though I don't mean to complain. Good day, doctor."

She made an awkward bob again, and swung away. James continued along the colonnade, reflecting, as he so often did, on the lot of these people who came under the care of the hospital. Sometimes their bodies could be healed; but who could do anything to improve their lives? If every wealthy man in the country turned philanthropist, the combined means would scarcely suffice to tear down every mean hovel and neglected tenement, to open up the foul alleys and courts to air and sunlight, to give the miserable inhabitants better sanitation, better food, and adequate clothing. He had often talked on this subject with other medical students from the Northern and Midland towns, where the growing requirements of mechanised industry for labour were producing mushroom housing of insanitary back-to-back dwellings, to add to the existing squalor of the overcrowded conditions already existing in the older parts of these towns.

He thought of Alvington, where the air was pure and sweet; and where, even if many of the cottages had the same lack of satisfactory sanitation, at least they had gardens and were not all huddled together in one vast block so that their occupants could breathe nothing but foul air. And from Alvington he passed on to thinking of the handsome town houses in Cavendish Square, spacious homes of elegance and taste, well appointed and run by servants whose lot was far superior to that of Mrs. Dorston and her like.

His abstraction was broken into as he ran down the steps leading from the colonnade into the front square, and saw a coach standing there with a familiar crest on its panels. A moment later its occupant alighted and came towards him with a cheery greeting. He recognised Shaldon with some surprise.

"James! How are you, old fellow?" Shaldon took his hand in a firm grip. "So this is where you torture your victims, you old bonesetter, is it? Not a bad place," he went on, looking appraisingly about him. "Quite a pleasant building, in fact—might almost be a gentleman's desirable residence, to employ the terms of the house agents. And is this your founder over here, perched up on this plinth—Mr. Thomas Guy himself, what? Looks a bit worried, don't he? But I daresay he's a good deal on his mind. Come to that," concluded Shaldon, with a change of tone as he looked shrewdly into his friend's face, "Come to that, James, so do you."

"I? No, I'm as right as a trivet," James assured him. "Might have been brooding a trifle over conditions prevailing in the slum quarters of the town. Hits one, sometimes."

Shaldon cocked an eyebrow at him. "Need to talk about it for a while, get it off your chest, what? I'm your man, James. But we can't talk here. What d'you say we adjourn to the George for a while? Can you spare the time?"

James hesitated. "I'm on my way to a lecture, in fact."

With a sudden flash of inspiration, he realised that it might be no bad thing to try to interest Shaldon in the matters over which he had just been brooding. Shaldon was already a wealthy man, and when he inherited the title and estate one day, he would be even wealthier. If conditions were ever to be improved for the poor either in London or elsewhere, more philanthropists like Thomas Guy were needed. Why should not Viscount Shaldon be one of them? James, who knew him well, realised that he was not simply the somewhat cynical man-about-Town he appeared. There was more to Tony than that; at Oxford and since he had shown himself receptive of new ideas, ready to listen to those who could expound them. Why should he not listen to James on this subject, perhaps with the most desirable results? One lost lecture, even to a conscientious student like James Somerby, seemed a small price to pay for the achievement of an ideal.

"But I daresay I could miss it, for once," he added, hastily. "I can get the notes from John Keats, who shares my lodging in St. Thomas's Street. He's a reliable student, for all he writes poetry in his spare time, and we're tolerably good friends."

"Poetry? That certainly seems a strange accompaniment to medical studies. But after all, you're of a literary turn of mind yourself. I don't wish to encourage you in a dereliction of duty, but if you're quite sure . . ."

James insisted that he was, so the two made their way on foot to the nearby George Inn, Shaldon having instructed his coachman to tool around for a bit and come back later. Once inside the bustling hostelry, Shaldon engaged a private room, and over some refreshment listened while his friend talked long and earnestly.

"You've only to walk around the poor quarters of the Borough," finished James, at last. "See the filth and squalor, the children's heads covered in ringworm, their faces with impetigo, the men suffering from glanders—"

"What the devil is that?" interrupted Shaldon.

"It's a disease contracted from horses—attacks people in the leather trade, too, and there are quite a few saddlers in the area."

"Well, you've convinced me, old chap. I'll make a donation to your hospital. Get my man of business to see to it at once. No, damn it," he amended, finishing his tankard of ale and standing up purposefully. "See to it myself. Take me to this Treasurer of yours whom you seem to think so much of. What d'you say his name is?"

"Harrison. Mr. Benjamin Harrison. He's a first rate administrator, even though some complain that he's too autocratic. But I think perhaps a good administrator needs to be autocratic at times."

"Well, I'll give him leave to be as autocratic as he wishes in administering my blunt—so long as it does some good. Come, let's be on our way."

Accordingly they returned to the hospital, where Shaldon sent in his card to Mr. Harrison, reflecting as he did so that it would do James no harm for the Treasurer to discover that one of the students under his authority possessed friends of rank. Knowing that such a thought was unlikely to cross the less worldly mind of James, he made no mention of it.

The business concluded, both young men stepped

286

out into the forecourt just as Shaldon's coach turned into the entrance gate.

"And now, can I drop you at your lodging?" asked Shaldon.

"No, I thank you, not yet. There are still matters awaiting my attention here. Besides, it's only a step away."

"You've not forgotten that we are both due at your sister's ball this evening? My original purpose in coming here was to offer to convey you to Cavendish Square."

"Very good of you, Tony. No, of course I'd not forgotten. In fact," added James, with a smile, "I've purchased a new coat for the occasion, and am to call for it at five o'clock."

Shaldon glanced quickly at the coat his friend was wearing at present, then looked away again.

"I know what you'd say. I could scarcely go in this. But it would never do to walk the hospital in a good coat."

"I suppose not. What time shall I call at your lodging, then? The ball begins at eight. Shall we say twenty minutes to the hour? One usually arrives late as a matter of principle, but in this case I don't think the usual rules apply. We would both wish to be prompt in our attentions to your sister—and the other young lady, of course."

James agreed to the hour, thanked him again, and they parted.

It was a little after five when James arrived at his tailor's, only to find that the coat was not quite ready, the pressing of it having been delayed to accommodate a more affluent and frequent customer. He waited as patiently as a young man might who was not only of a naturally active disposition but who was also feeling hungry, since his last meal had been several hours ago. When the garment was at last delivered into his hands, he raced from the shop with it so precipitately that the tailor began to entertain serious doubts as to whether or not the bank bills with which he had been paid were stolen.

Having reached his lodging just after six o'clock, James laid the coat reverently on the bed together with the rest of his evening attire, then went downstairs to request from his landlady the favour of a quick meal. She pulled a face.

"Having been h'informed, Mr. Somerby, sir," she said loftily, "that you was to be out this evening, naturally I didn't think to get in anything for dinner, Mr. Keats being to 'ave 'is at a tavern with some friends."

"Oh, yes, of course, I'm sorry. Could you manage any kind of sandwich, do you think, or"—seeing the adamant look on her face, he gave her one of his most charming smiles—"or even some bread and cheese? Anything will do."

Under the influence of those smiling, very blue eyes, even the unimpressionable landlady mellowed sufficiently to allow that bread and cheese might just be within the bounds of possibility.

"Splendid. I'll come and fetch it in a moment. You're very good, ma'am."

He left her and went to knock upon his neighbour's door. Upon being bidden to enter, he obeyed to find Mr. Keats engaged in tying a neckcloth before the mirror over the mantelshelf. He was a young man below middle height with very broad shoulders, which somewhat diminished the size of his face, the best feature of which was his intelligent, sensitive eyes.

"This cursed neckcloth!" Keats declared. "On my word, I believe it's invested with a life of its own!" He broke off, turning away from the mirror. "Is there anything I can do for you, my dear Somerby?"

"Oblige me by lending me your notes of today's osteology lecture, if you'll be so good. Unfortunately, I couldn't attend myself."

Mr. Keats picked up a notebook from the table and handed it to his fellow student with somewhat of a hangdog air. This was soon explained as James carefully turned over the pages until he came to the one he required, for the inner margin of it was embellished with small flower drawings.

"A trifle out of place, perhaps?" James said, smiling.

"No such thing. Can flowers ever be out of place anywhere? And are they not particularly suited to the subject of that lecture, which was on the bones of the nose?"

James laughed. "Your logic confounds me, old fellow, but I heartily agree with the principle that we shouldn't keep science and art in watertight compartments. Well, I shall leave you to your struggle with that cravat, which I'm sure will be resolved eventually. I'll return your book as soon as I've copied the notes from it. Once again, many thanks. I hope you enjoy a pleasant evening."

This civil wish being echoed, James returned to his room to place the notebook on his own table before going down to the kitchen again in order to collect his hasty meal.

When he had returned to his room with some bread and cheese which he had cut for himself, he consulted his watch. There was still three quarters of an hour before Shaldon was due to call for him, and he could be ready comfortably in almost half that time. He decided to begin on copying the notes.

This was a mistake. It is always difficult to disengage the attention from academic matters at a set time. He was still working assiduously away when he heard a firm step on the stair; and after a perfunctory knock, Shaldon entered the room, looking extremely impressive in a dark, well fitting coat, white satin waistcoat and black evening breeches.

James stared at him for a moment before giving a guilty start and jumping to his feet.

"Good God! Is it time already?"

Shaldon pulled out his watch to glance at it.

"It certainly is, you young jackanapes. In fact, a few minutes after the time we agreed. Don't tell me; I can hazard a guess. You've been so caught up in your work, you've forgotten all about your sister's ball."

"Not precisely." James pulled out a chair for his guest. "Events seemed to go against me. But I'll be ready in a trice. Make yourself easy."

He retired to the adjoining bedchamber and could be heard casting off his shoes and generally bustling about. Shortly after eight had chimed by the clock on the mantelshelf, he appeared in the doorway.

"Will I do?" he asked.

Shaldon looked him over critically.

"No," he replied, with the bluntness of an old friend. "One of your stockings is twisted. And pray what do you call that manner of tying your cravat—the Medico?"

James reddened a trifle. "Oh, damn it all, I'd no time to stand on points, Tony! If you can do any better, tie the confounded thing yourself."

"If I couldn't do any better, I'd wear a made-up stock, old fellow. But I'll allow something for the fact that you were short of time. All the same, we can't grace Miss Somerby's ball looking less than our best. Owe it to her, don't you agree? Come here, and we'll see what can be done. How do you fancy an à la Byron?"

"Not at all—can't stand the fellow."

"Oh, very well, we'll make it an Orientale," said Shaldon, accommodatingly, as he deftly arranged the folds of the neckcloth. "Stand still, damn you, if you want the thing done respectably."

"Sorry. Oh, Helen, what I'm prepared to suffer for your sake!"

"Yes, indeed. But I rather fancy the lady's worth it, you know."

Chapter XXV

A GRATIFYING NUMBER of gilt-edged invitation
cards had lately been arriving at the Chetwodes' house
in Cavendish Square, among them one from Baron
Lydney and his lady for the coming out ball of their
daughter Cynthia.

"And it's to be a few days later than ours!" exclaimed Melissa, gleefully. "I'm monstrous glad of
that, Helen, for Cynthia has a way of being first with
everything and making everyone else's concerns appear insipid by contrast. And see, here is one from
Catherine, too, in the following week," she added,
skimming through the pile of correspondence which
lay on her mother's escritoire. "Gracious, we are bidden to rout parties, musical parties, a masquerade—
oh, Helen, a water party! I must say, that does sound
the most delightful thing! But, Mama, how in the world
shall we contrive to attend them all?"

"You may well ask, my dear, and I can only feel
thankful for my health's sake that your two sisters are
safely married. But what pleases me most is that your
vouchers for Almack's are promised. Once you have
both been presented, you can begin to attend the balls
there."

The Royal Drawing Room had loomed large in the
girls' minds; but in the end it proved to be, as eagerly
awaited events often are, something of an anticlimax.
The room was so crowded with young ladies waiting to
be presented and their attendant sponsors, that the
actual ceremony was for each no more than the mat-

291

-ter of a few moments. The old Queen seemed stiff, and her heavily accented voice came as quite a surprise. The Prince Regent, his ample figure swelling beneath the blue coat adorned with orders, spoke a gracious word to everyone, and pressed the hands of all the prettiest young ladies with a winning smile. Helen, casting up her hazel eyes timidly to his face, thought that she could detect in it some lingering trace of the gentleman who had in his youth been called Prince Florizel. It was true that nowadays he had run to fat, that his extravagance and loose living had alienated him from the London populace; but in spite of this, some of that early charm and graciousness remained. She remembered, too, how her father had often said that literature and the arts owed much to the Prince, whose excellent cultural taste had prompted him to extend his patronage wherever possible in this direction.

The Court presentation did nothing to diminish the excitement attendant upon Helen and Melissa's first and most important ball of the season. There had been anxious conferences in Alvington Rectory between Amanda Somerby and her daughter as to the kind of gown to be worn on this occasion; the final decision had rested on one of white silk, low necked and with puff sleeves, embroidered round the flared hem with a pretty motif of pink rosebuds. Helen's honey coloured hair was dressed high with a cluster of curls at the back, secured by a pink ribbon, and her only jewellery was a gold locket set with pearls. Melissa's pale yellow gown, trimmed at the hem with gold ruched ribbon, set off admirably her chestnut hair dressed in small ringlets framing her face. As Sir George Chetwode was quick to comment, they made a very charming picture as they stood beside himself and his wife to receive their guests; and, judging by the look on Philip's countenance as the remark was made, it seemed that his son agreed with this point of view.

The ballroom began to fill up quickly, much to Lady Chetwode's relief; for with so many other engagements now that the season was in full swing, one could never be certain of a full attendance. Among the early arrivals were the Lydneys, Cynthia looking ravishing in a very décolleté gown of aquamarine silk under silver spangled gauze. Henry Lydney at once attached himself firmly to Helen's side, soliciting her hand for the first dance.

"I fear you are come too late," she replied, smiling. "Mr. Chetwode bespoke that yesterday."

"Now I must say that's a great deal too bad," he complained. "And he's not nearly such an old friend of yours as I am—but there, he possesses an unfair advantage in living under the same roof, lucky fellow! I wish I had his chances. Dear lady, I implore you to grant me at least the favour of the succeeding dance. If you are so hardhearted as to refuse, I assure you I shall do something quite desperate!"

Helen gave him a quizzical glance. "I'm almost tempted to refuse in order to see what manner of desperate deed you intend, sir. You pique my curiosity."

"Ah, fair cruelty!" he exclaimed, striking an attitude. "But I'll willingly gratify your lightest whim, so your curiosity shall be satisfied. What would you have me do? Go out into the grounds and shoot myself?"

"No, indeed," she protested, laughing. "Or at least, not until my brother James arrives, for he's the only person present who could render medical assistance, I daresay. But since you ask," she went on, in a severe tone, "I must tell you that the only thing I'd have you do is to behave in a less extravagant way."

"Your word is law, and henceforth I'll be a model of propriety, if only you will consent to stand up with me for the second dance."

"I'm not at all sure that I'd recognise you if you were a model of propriety, Mr. Lydney."

"Unkind! And you look such an angel in that white dress, too. But tell me, do you prefer men who are? Models of propriety, I would say?"

"I don't know. It sounds prodigiously dull, don't you think?" Her laughing eyes clouded for a moment, as a sober thought intruded on the nonsense they were both talking. "And yet one would not care for a friend to go to the other extreme," she added, slowly.

He sensed her change of mood, though without understanding its cause, and swiftly adjusted his own manner to it.

"Never fear, I shan't do that, ma'am. And may I consider myself accepted as your partner for the second dance?"

She bowed assent as she turned away to play her part in welcoming some newcomers. By now, most of the invited guests had already arrived, and she noticed that Melissa was giving a strained attention to the names announced by the footman at the door. It was not difficult for Helen to guess the reason that lay behind this.

"I fear James may be a little late," she said. "He sometimes finds it difficult to get away, as you'll readily understand. But I know he'll come if it's at all possible, for he's never yet failed me in anything important, and he quite realises that it is important to me for him to be present here tonight."

Melissa wanted to say that it was important to her, also; but remembering her talk with Helen a few weeks since, she restrained herself, although she continued to listen carefully as the later guests were announced. Presently the last of them seemed to have arrived, as there had been a hiatus during the past ten minutes or so. Lady Chetwode and Sir George pronounced that the dancing could now begin. Helen was led on to the floor by Philip Chetwode, while Melissa, her face a trifle downcast for such a memorable occasion, was partnered by one of her brothers-in-law, Lord Calcot.

Helen herself felt unaccountably subdued as she and her partner took their places in the set that was forming. It was disappointing that James had so far not put in an appearance, although perhaps she need not quite give up hope that he would eventually arrive. There was someone else, too, who had certainly received an invitation, yet was missing. But what did it matter to her whether Viscount Shaldon attended

294

her ball or not? Doubtless he had other, more interesting, engagements to keep with his companions of that evening at the Opera.

She reminded herself that this was an occasion for enjoyment rather than the indulgence of gloomy thoughts, and proceeded to devote all her attention to her partner and the dance. When it was over and she returned to Lady Chetwode's side, she found several prospective partners already lined up for her. Henry Lydney again insinuated himself close enough to remind her that she was promised to him for the next dance.

"I warn you," he said in a confidential tone which nevertheless reached the ears of several bystanders, "if you break faith with me, Miss Somerby, I shall feel myself obliged to challenge the usurper."

She saw that the other gentlemen exchanged amused glances at this remark, and she felt a trifle foolish. It was all very well for Mr. Lydney to talk nonsense to her in private, but she did not intend to permit it in public. That was going beyond the line of what was pleasing; she determined to give him a sharp setdown.

She delivered this when they were dancing together. He pretended to be most contrite, but there was a contradictory twinkle in his eye.

"It's too bad of you," she concluded, in tones of reproach. "You will have people saying I am fast."

"Only let them say it to me!"

"That's all very well, but of course they wouldn't do so. Nevertheless, you must know that I should soon feel the effects of acquiring such a reputation."

"You mean it might scare off your other admirers?" he asked audaciously. "I can't pretend I'd be sorry for that, ma'am!"

She gave him a half-laughing, half-exasperated look. "Oh, you're incorrigible, sir! What is to be done with you, I wonder?"

Her hand was resting lightly on his as they danced. He pressed it and looked into her eyes.

"Do you wish me to answer that?" he asked softly.

Their shared glance held some kind of magnetism; Helen quickly averted her eyes. She looked towards the door and espied James, who had that minute entered the room. Forgetting immediately both her partner and their share in the dance, she quitted his side to make her way towards her brother. One or two of the dancers and several onlookers stared at this lack of decorum, but Helen was quite oblivious of them.

"James!" she cried, flinging her arms about him. "Oh, so you have come! I had almost given you up, you're so late!"

"Steady on, Nell," he replied, kissing her warmly but detaching himself gently from her grasp. "We must take care of this coat, y'know, for I'm not likely to be able to afford another of this quality for some time."

She stood back, appraising him lovingly. The dark blue tail coat he was wearing looked, even to her inexperienced eye, to be both elegant and expensive. It fitted snugly over his broad shoulders and enhanced his deep blue eyes and blond hair. His knee breeches and snowy, intricately tied cravat completed the picture of a well turned-out gentleman in evening attire. Her sisterly heart swelled with pride.

"Oh, Jamie! I've never seen you look so well!" she exclaimed.

"Had to do you credit, didn't I? Must say, love, you look as fine as fivepence yourself. I'm sorry to be late —would have been later still had it not been for Tony here, who was good enough to call for me and bring me in his carriage."

He stepped aside to reveal Shaldon, who had been standing behind him and had altogether escaped Helen's notice in her delight at seeing her brother.

"I daresay I may scarcely hope for such a rapturous welcome," remarked Shaldon, smiling as he extended his hand. "May I say, ma'am, how very charmingly you look?"

She put her hand in his and he carried it briefly to his lips. Unaccountably, she suddenly felt shy.

"Thank you. I am so glad you could manage to come," she said, awkwardly.

"Perhaps we should present ourselves to our hostess to make our apologies, James," suggested Shaldon. "Ah, yes, there is Lady Chetwode."

Sir George and his wife had now noticed the late-comers and were approaching them, but before they arrived on the scene Henry Lydney had joined the group. He had remained at his place in the set for a few moments after his partner's abrupt desertion of him; then, seeing the cause of this, he had neatly extricated himself from the other dancers. He greeted the newcomers affably, in particular James Somerby, whom he had seen only rarely since Alvington days.

"Do you wish to resume dancing, Miss Somerby?" he asked presently. "Or would you prefer to sit the rest out? I must say, though, ma'am, that I shall consider myself prodigiously ill-used if you don't grant me another dance to replace the one I've just lost!"

James frowned at the intimate tone in which this was said; but he had no opportunity just then to comment on it, as both he and Shaldon were occupied in apologising for their tardy appearance to their host and hostess. Helen disclaimed any intention of returning immediately to the floor, so Henry Lydney stayed chatting with the group until the dance was over.

The arrival of Mr. Somerby had certainly not escaped Melissa's notice. She wished fervently that she, too, could escape from her present partner—a pleasant enough gentleman who seemed as if he admired her—and rush across to greet the one person whom she most wished to see. But it was not to be thought of; she had no valid excuse for behaving in the way that her feelings dictated. She was obliged to finish the dance, though all her attention was now centred on the group near the door. When they moved away to sit down, her eyes followed them, and her replies to her partner's efforts at conversation became increasingly absentminded. At the conclusion of the dance, she sketched him a hurried curtsey which certainly did not conform to the rules of etiquette so carefully taught her; then moved purposefully across the room before he was able even to begin on his civil speech of thanks for the honour. The unfortunate young gentleman could only conclude that Miss Chetwode, whom he had previously considered such a pretty-behaved young lady, must suddenly be feeling unwell. And so in a way she was, but the malady was one which might easily enough be cured by a certain young doctor.

It was some time before her previous commitments allowed her to accept James as a partner. In the interval, she tried not to allow her eyes to follow him round the room. Her thoughts, however, were not so easily disciplined; and more than one of her partners wondered why it was so difficult to interest her in even the most trivial of polite conversational exchanges, and reflected what a pity it was that such a pretty girl should be so stupid.

She scarcely managed any better with James Somerby at first. He decided that she must be shy, and determined to break through the barrier by shock tactics.

"And how have you been amusing yourself lately, Miss Chetwode?" he asked, smiling down at her. "I suppose you must have quite given up your old trick of tumbling off high walls?"

The ruse succeeded, for a spark of mischief came into her eyes.

"Ungenerous, Mr. Somerby! I only wish I knew of some youthful escapade with which to taunt you!"

"Ah, but you see I must find some device for making you talk to me—unless you prefer to dance in silence, that is. Possibly you think that more dignified?"

"Well, I daresay it may be, but your sister will tell you that I don't often study for dignity," she replied, flashing a quick smile at him. "I'm sorry if you find me a poor conversationalist, sir."

He shook his head. "No such thing—now you are started, you go on charmingly. Which is just what I would have expected."

At this point they parted to follow the movements of the dance down the room, and the brief interval allowed Melissa an opportunity to take a firmer hold on her emotions. If one wished to captivate a gentleman, she reminded herself, the way to do it certainly did not lie in downcast looks and shy responses. And she did wish—oh, so much!—to make him think of her, to find her way into his heart. So for the remainder of the dance she made a strong effort to appear her normal lively self; and if her brown eyes at times held a deeper message than her carefree words conveyed. this only served her purpose better. When James Somerby parted from her at the conclusion of the dance. his reluctance was evident, and he begged for the favour to be repeated later on in the evening. Melissa. knowing it would be more proper to refuse yet unable to do so, replied demurely that perhaps she could spare him a dance after supper.

"And who's the lucky fellow who will take you in to supper?" asked James, never slow to seize an opportunity.

"I believe Mama has arranged for my brother to do that."

"And doubtless for me to partner my own sister?"

Melissa nodded.

"A poor notion, if you'll forgive my saying so. Who wishes to converse with his own sister when he might enjoy the company of someone else's? I'm sure that Chetwode would agree with me. Shall I ask him?"

Melissa felt helpless before this masterful onslaught. "Oh, dear." she said, weakly. "I'm not at all sure that Mama will like it."

"Then we must rely on your brother to persuade her." He glanced across the room to where Philip Chetwode was standing with a group of young people surrounding Helen. "I don't think he will be altogether averse to the change."

"Oh, no! He admires Helen extremely," replied Melissa, impulsively.

James looked at the group again, frowning as he noticed Henry Lydney's close proximity to his sister.

"And not the only one, seemingly. It appears Nell is becoming a flirt."

"She is not!" Melissa's quick temper took wing, stung by loyalty. "How can you say so? Just because she is admired by several gentlemen—and she doesn't make the least push to secure their interest!—She is just her own sweet, unaffected self!"

He smiled at her, the warmth spreading to his eyes.

"Here's a termagant," he teased. "But your loyalty does you credit, ma'am. Be easy. I know my own sister. And perhaps I am beginning to know you, though not as well as I could wish. Say I'm forgiven?"

He put out his hand and she placed hers within it. For a moment they stood thus, looking into each other's eyes.

"Quite affecting," said a voice close beside them. "But do you realise, Melissa, that the floor is clearing, and you must soon provide a vastly amusing peep show if you do not move on?"

They turned sharply to see Cynthia Lydney standing there. She had just turned away from her previous partner and was walking across the room to rejoin her party.

James released Melissa's hand and bowed curtly.

" 'Servant, Miss Lydney."

"Oh, Mr. Somerby—or should I call you *Doctor* Somerby?" Cynthia replied, in a careless tone. "I'm never sure of the etiquette in such matters, as I number so few medical men among my acquaintance." She looked him over with a bold, arrogant glance. "Dear me, you are vastly changed since last we met, but I knew you instantly."

He bowed again. "Whereas I find you little changed, ma'am."

"I scarce know whether to be flattered or displeased at that remark, sir," she said, archly.

"Oh, you must know I'm a poor hand at flattery." he returned coolly. "But permit me to find you ladies a chair."

During this interchange, Melissa had said nothing. At first she had been too overcome with embarrass-

300

ment at Cynthia's opening remark; but the subsequent jibe at Mr. Somerby's profession had so roused her that now she dared not trust herself to open her lips. She closed them firmly, directing such an unloving look on Cynthia that Helen, seeing the three approaching, guessed at once that Cynthia must have let fly one of her poisonous barbs.

Fortunately Cynthia declined the offer of a seat next to Helen and Melissa, returning instead to her mother's side, where a hopeful group of young gentlemen still lingered. Characteristically, James wasted no time in setting his plans into motion, and everything was soon arranged to his and Philip Chetwode's satisfaction.

Soon after his arrival Shaldon has approached Helen during one of the intervals between dances. She was sitting with Lady Chetwode, Melissa and Catherine, but several gentlemen were standing beside them, among these Philip Chetwode and Henry Lydney.

"Dear me," began Shaldon, leaning towards her with a smile "how difficult it is to secure an audience with you, ma'am. And I daresay it's quite useless to beg for the honour of standing up with you for the next dance?"

She had not previously seen him since the evening at the Opera, and she was still feeling a trifle out of charity with him; but when he smiled down at her so engagingly, she found it hard to resist an answering smile.

"I fear it is, sir. I am promised until supper."

"And if you're thinking of asking to take Miss Somerby to supper, Shaldon," put in Philip, grinning, "let me warn you that I've been before you there."

"So I'm thoroughly dished, am I? Well, ma'am, I shall consider it uncommonly shabby if you don't save one dance for me afterwards—for old times' sake, shall we say?"

She promised; and seeing that private conversation between them was impossible at present, he moved on to do his duty by Melissa. She, too, was engaged for the moment, so he left the group to seek a partner elsewhere.

His eye was caught by Cynthia Lydney, flaunting herself among the group of dazzled admirers a little distance away. He would have passed by; but she hailed him in a commanding tone, so he approached her, and soon was leading her out to dance.

"I noticed you came late," she said to him, as they moved down the line of dancers. "I really cannot blame you. An insipid affair, is it not? But one must attend, I suppose, when one's been so long acquainted with people."

"Why do you think it insipid?"

She shrugged, the movement displaying an intriguing glimpse of cleavage which was not intended to escape his notice.

"Oh, it's so slow! Nothing but country dances and the cotillion. I intend to have the waltz at my ball."

He raised his eyebrows. "The deuce you do! And Lady Lydney will permit that?"

"I've no notion, as I haven't yet mentioned it. I dare say Mama may not quite like the notion, but I usually get my way in the end. I can always twist Papa round my little finger, at all events."

"I recall that you could do so as a child," he replied, drily.

"A grown woman has even more influence, Lord Shaldon, wouldn't you say?"

"That would depend on the woman."

She gave him one of her provocative glances.

"Am I to understand by that, sir, that you don't consider me to be the kind of woman to influence men?"

"Since you ask, I consider you're the kind of woman who is very well aware of her powers, ma'am."

"I see you don't intend to flatter," she replied, making full use of her dark eyes again. "Possibly you reserve that for certain other females of your acquaintance."

She had the satisfaction of seeing him frown before they were parted by the movements of the dance.

When they came together again, he determinedly steered the conversation away from any personal topics in spite of all her efforts in the contrary direction. Nevertheless, he found himself responding instinctively to her feminine allure, as on that evening when he had dined with her family in Berkeley Street.

Something of this must have shown in his manner; for Cynthia looked complacent, and Helen, watching them from time to time as she herself danced with Lord Calcot, felt a slight lowering of spirits. At their first meeting in Alvington, Lord Shaldon had told her quite firmly that he did not wish to marry Cynthia Lydney, yet now it began to look very much as though he was changing his mind. Well, that was scarcely surprising, thought Helen. With both families in favour of the match, which would be a brilliant one for Cynthia, it was only to be expected that the girl would do her best to bring on Viscount Shaldon's addresses. And Cynthia's best would almost certainly fascinate any man, even though he did start by feeling reluctant to respond.

Once again Helen had to remind herself that she took no interest in Viscount Shaldon's affairs. He might disport himself with those bold females at the Opera, or else wed Cynthia Lydney—or both. It was of no consequence to her. Accordingly, she threw herself wholeheartedly into the evening's enjoyment, and was so vivacious when dancing later on with Henry Lydney, that afterwards she brought James frowning to her side.

"What does that fellow Lydney mean by hanging about you so much?" he asked, fiercely.

"How do I know, stupid?" she replied, laughing. "Why don't you ask him yourself?"

"I might do that," he said, with a resolute air.

She put her hand urgently on his arm. "Oh, no, pray don't James! It's nothing—we have known him for ever, recollect!"

"I daresay, but he should know better than to make you the subject of gossip by paying you such marked attentions," answered James, in severe tones. "You've

303

known Shaldon for ever—as you put it—but *he* don't hang on your arm."

"No, because he's too busy hanging on Cynthia's," retorted Helen.

"Cynthia? Absurd! He don't like her above half."

"But Lord Alvington wishes him to marry her."

"Does he? I daresay he might, but if I know Tony, he'll choose for himself—if he does choose."

"You mean you don't think he'll marry at all?"

James nodded. "Wouldn't be surprised. You can't wonder at it, if you consider his parents' marriage. Hardly a recommendation, you must say."

"I only know what Mama has told me, but, yes, I suppose you are right. Only I think perhaps Cynthia is changing his mind for him."

"Voluptuous female," remarked James, not mincing matters. "In another walk of life, she'd have been —but never mind that," he added, hastily. "Do you remember that woman who was knocked down in the street when we were on our way to Astley's?" he asked, deliberately changing the subject. "Her name's Mrs. Dorston. I was talking to her today. Told me the story of her life, pretty near."

"Oh, how does the poor soul go on, James? You said her injuries weren't too serious—she had concussion, and what you called a simple fracture of the— oh, dear, I've forgotten! What was it, James? Something to do with cats," she finished, vaguely.

"Cats?" He was puzzled for a moment, then chuckled. "Oh, you mean the tibia—front bone of the lower leg. Yes, we set it and it's coming along nicely. She's been supplied with crutches now, and is able to move around a bit. She was fortunate it wasn't a compound fracture, for that would have meant losing the leg. I expect she'll be discharged soon."

Helen shuddered at the thought of amputation. "I suppose the poor creature's had a very sad life?"

He repeated Mrs. Dorston's story to her.

"Is there nothing we can do to help her?" Helen asked, when he had finished. "Could we not attempt to find her lost grandson?"

He shook his head. "Daresay he don't wish to be found—at any rate, not for the purpose of being re-united to his grandmother. He could have sought her out for himself without a doubt, had he been of a mind to do so."

"I suppose you're right," Helen reluctantly conceded. "You'll let me know when she leaves the hospital, won't you? And then perhaps we can take some comforts to her home."

"To *Tothill Fields?* You'll do no such thing, my girl, though possibly I may visit her myself."

"Why not? I have often accompanied Mama to the poorest homes in Alvington."

"The poorest homes there don't compare to Star Court, my girl! It's a hotbed of disease, and the in-habitants can be unpleasantly violent towards strangers, I warn you. No, leave all that to me." He broke off. "And now we won't speak of such matters any-more, for here comes Chetwode to take you in to supper. Smile, Nell!" He tapped her cheek. "This is your evening for smiles, you know."

Supper was a success from almost everyone's point of view. Surveying the well-spread board with its deli-cacies, Lady Chetwode congratulated herself on hav-ing once again secured the services of Gunter's, the foremost caterer in Town. But the majority of her guests, while fully enjoying the food and drink pro-vided, found their chief satisfaction in the company.

Melissa, sitting beside Mr. Somerby, thought that she had never felt half so happy in her life. As for her companion, he wondered for a moment if the champagne was going to his head, for he felt an al-most irresistible urge to sweep his attractive compan-ion into his arms. But it did not take him long to arrive at a more accurate diagnosis of his condition and to realise that it was not the champagne. but Miss Chetwode herself who was affecting his state of mind. Tomorrow might bring reflection about this and more sober thoughts in its train; tonight, he determined to enjoy the heady sensation, even if he might not obey its promptings.

Helen, seated between Philip Chetwode and Lydney, who had somehow contrived to place himself on her other side, found herself talking a great deal of airy nonsense to both and not at all disliking the fact that from time to time Shaldon glanced her way with a slight frown on his brows. She knew that she was flirting a little, but so were many other young ladies at the table. It was reprehensible, of course, but quite surprising how enjoyable it could be. One must not make a habit of it, certainly, but tonight *was* a special occasion. . . .

Cynthia was permitting herself the same indulgence with the Honourable Cedric Partridge on her left hand and Shaldon on her right. Both played up to her delightfully, but she noticed with slight chagrin that now and then Shaldon's attention wandered from her bold eyes and the provocative neckline of her gown to Helen, tossing gold brown curls in laughter on the opposite side of the table.

Only one young lady seemed a little subdued for such a gay, lively assembly, and that was Catherine Horwood. She was sitting on Philip Chetwode's other side, between him and a young gentleman whose acquaintance she had made for the first time that evening, and who had previously partnered her in one of the country dances. He was attentive enough towards her, but her response, though civil, was not encouraging; and whenever Mr. Chetwode chanced to be at liberty to turn in her direction to address some remark to her, there was a noticeable difference in her manner. A modest girl, she thought too little of her own claims to attention to feel at all slighted because Mr. Chetwode obviously preferred to talk to her friend Helen. All the same, she did feel a little wistful.

When Shaldon came shortly after supper to claim his promised dance with Helen, there was a slight constraint in his manner at first. Finding a reserve, too, on her part—which he wrongly attributed to this present attitude of his—he quickly threw it aside and did his best to resume their former friendly relationship. After all, why should not a pretty girl flirt a little?

And she was undeniably pretty—those gold-flecked eyes, now serious, now laughing; the fine-boned, mobile face framed in honey brown hair; the warm, soft lips. No, pretty was too tame a word to describe her fresh, unstudied charm. She had a regal look at times tonight, in her elegant gown of white silk; yet he preferred his memory of her in the wood at Alvington, dishevelled and breathless, her hair tumbled about her face. She had been more approachable then.

He exerted himself to break through her reserve, but without success. She kept up a ready enough flow of polite small talk, but her manner towards him bordered on formality, as though he had been a newly introduced partner. The dance was nearly over when he decided to tax her directly with this treatment.

"I collect," he said, as he took her hand when they came together again after one of the movements, "that you've still not forgiven me for adopting too brotherly a concern towards you when we encountered each other in Piccadilly some three weeks since."

She opened her eyes wide, an ingenuous expression in them. "Why, pray what can you mean, Lord Shaldon?"

"It's of no use to try and gammon me, ma'am. The very air surrounding you is frosty. I wish I had thought to bring my overcoat."

She laughed at this, relaxing a little. "I am sorry if you find anything lacking in my conduct."

"Not a whit. I seldom danced with a better conducted young lady. But I was looking for more than politeness from you, Miss Somerby. I had hoped for the friendship we seemed to have renewed at Alvington."

"It is still yours, if you desire it," she flashed at him quickly, as they parted momentarily again.

As he mechanically performed the movements of the dance apart from her, he pondered over what exactly this could mean. And then he suddenly recalled the evening at the Opera, saw in his mind's eye her hand raised in a friendly greeting and the way in which Lady Chetwode had leaned forward to restrain her. He cursed softly. So that was it. Her chaperone, though doubtless reluctant to enter upon such a subject with a young girl, must have offered Helen a sufficient explanation to give her a disgust of him.

She could not know, and he could not tell her, that the sight of her sitting in the opposite box had quite ruined that evening for him. Why he did not know, but from that moment he had taken no further pleasure in the society of his Cyprian companions. Moreover, since then, there had been no more assignations with the bewitching Harriette Wilson. Perhaps the reason might be that he had always regarded Helen Somerby as a sister, and a man would not wish his sister to see him in such company. But what was to be done? The subject was taboo; he could not venture one word to her on it. And yet the one thing he most wished for now was to regain her good opinion.

When they came together again, he was silent for a while. She looked up at him enquiringly.

"You may perhaps recall," he said presently, breaking the silence, "giving me a warning about something Durrant had said to you?"

He could not have hit upon a more successful way of combating her reserve, and perhaps it was not entirely chance that suggested it.

"Why, yes," she replied, quickly, in a more friendly manner. "Only you laughed at me and thought me fanciful!"

"True, and I beg your pardon, for I've come to think better of that; or at least, to wonder if there may not be something in it. Lord Lydney seemed to be hinting at something amiss when I dined with him. He recommended me to make my peace with my father, and used some deuced odd words—said he feared the outcome for us both, if I did not."

"Oh!"

Helen almost stopped dancing, so intrigued was she by this communication.

"Did you not ask him exactly what he meant?"

He guided her onwards. "Of course, but he shut up like a clam. Told me to ask my father, which I was unable to do, in the event. When I went down to Alvington on the following day, the old gentleman had left for Bath."

"And did you not follow him there?" she demanded eagerly.

"To Bath? Of all places, the one I most detest! Besides, he'll return in a few weeks, and I can ask him then. I daresay it's all a hum," he added, carelessly.

"Oh, but no! I don't think so! If Lord Lydney said so much, he must feel that the matter is serious. I believe you were mistaken in not going at once to Bath," said Helen, vehemently.

He smiled at her earnestness. "You do, do you? Well, madam, perhaps I should have consulted you in the matter before this."

She reddened slightly. "Of course, I don't mean to interfere. It's no concern of mine—"

"That's a whisker! Confess, now—you are all agog to get to the bottom of this little mystery. Well, so you shall, for when I've seen my father, I promise to acquaint you with the whole. There, will that do?"

She said that it would, and they finished the dance on much better terms than when they had begun.

But Helen could not help feeling that he was taking the matter too lightly. Somewhere at the back of her mind a sense of uneasiness sprang once more to life, a foreboding of trouble in store for Viscount Shaldon.

Chapter XXVI

BERTRAM DURRANT FOUND IT DIFFICULT TO concentrate on his work nowadays. He was in a mood of uncertainty. Sometimes the future looked bright for him, with all his plans dovetailing neatly into place; at others, it seemed that he had built only a structure of cards that would collapse at a touch.

Cynthia was lost to him. At Alvington he had at least seen her occasionally, whenever it had pleased her to look in on him at his work in the book room of Askett House. He had realised quite well at that time that this had been only because she lacked other, more interesting diversions. Here in London, all that was changed. She was seldom at home for more than a few hours at a stretch, and then there was a constant stream of callers for her—mostly eligible young men, he reflected bitterly. She was for ever dashing off to some entertainment or another; balls, routs, the play, Almack's, musical soirées, excursions to well known beauty spots, riding or driving in the Park, with one or other of the young men of the *ton* who had rapidly formed a court around her. It was small consolation to him to observe that Shaldon was not often in her company. He had been aware for long enough that both the Earl of Alvington and Baron Lydney were firmly decided on a family alliance, and could not doubt that eventually both Cynthia and Shaldon would fall in with the arrangement. He lived in daily expectation of hearing their engagement announced, and could not quite fathom what Shaldon's game was in not coming to the point at once. All the better for his own plans if no formal betrothal existed, though; Baron Lydney would certainly wish to hedge off once Shaldon was no longer heir to the title and estate, and it might be more difficult for him to do so if the pair had already become betrothed. As for Cynthia, it was simple to understand why she did not trouble to bring matters to a head between herself and Shaldon. Obsessed as he was by her, Durrant suffered from no illusions. She was making the most of her first season, revelling in the heady delights of being the centre of a crowd of adoring suitors. To be engaged would spoil all this, and restrict her to the attentions of one man alone. He wondered if that would ever satisfy her; and swore to himself that, if he were the man, he would make sure that it did.

She would have been surprised, not to say amused, to discover how much he knew of her comings and goings. As most of the family correspondence passed through his hands, he was often required to answer cards of invitation on her behalf, so was naturally well informed about her social engagements. When the family dined at home alone, which was seldom, he had an insignificant place at table and could glean further information from the conversation. Apart from these sources, he relied a good deal on Cynthia's personal maid, Pinker, an elderly female who had a secret admiration for the handsome secretary and was always ready to chat with him about her mistress's concerns. He often told himself that Pinker might come in even more useful to him some day.

He had a certain amount of free time from his secretarial duties, and would often pass this in frequenting the neighbourhood of houses where Cynthia was bound on one or other of her engagements. He had often watched her from a safe distance riding or driving in the Park; or sometimes he had joined the crowd standing about in the street to watch the arrivals at some brilliant function to which she had accepted an invitation. His heart would lift as he saw her, exquisitely gowned, alight from her carriage to mount the carpeted steps where the flunkeys were waiting to admit her. He was always very careful never to be observed on these occasions. It was folly, he knew; but it was like some powerful drug on which he had come to depend.

On the night of Cynthia's come-out ball, he had intended to leave the house and seek consolation in a tavern; but in the end, he could not bring himself to go. Instead, he settled down with a book of travels in his own apartments, a sitting room and bedchamber removed by a short flight of stairs from the family bedchambers.

He attempted to concentrate on his book, which concerned a subject usually of interest to him; but even at this distance he could hear faint strains of music wafting up from the ballroom, and the thought of Cynthia floating round the floor with some other man came between him and the text. After a while, he could stand it no longer. Thrusting the book away from him with an oath, he left his room and made his way cautiously downstairs, using the servants' staircase.

There was a small gallery attached to the ballroom for the use of the musicians, and this was approached by a short flight of steps behind the service door. There were no servants about in the passage as he reached the foot of the staircase, so he quietly mounted the steps to the gallery. One or two of the musicians looked up as he made his appearance there; but he waved his hand in a gesture indicating that he had no wish to interrupt, so they ignored him and continued to play.

Telling himself that, if noticed by his employer, he could always claim that he was anxious to see if everything was going smoothly with the arrangements, he walked over to the edge of the balcony and looked down.

His questing eyes soon found Cynthia. She was whirling round the room with a swish of silken draperies, tightly clasped in Shaldon's left arm, with her one hand on his shoulder and the other locked palm to

312

palm with his free hand. They were dancing the waltz! Even as his shocked gaze took in this fact, she raised her dark eyes to her partner's with the provocative look that Durrant knew so well.

With a muttered imprecation, he turned on his heel and left the balcony. So fierce was his anger at what he had seen that he remained stock still at the top of the balcony steps, scarcely aware of his surroundings.

Presently he realised dimly that the music had ceased and there was a shuffling of feet in the gallery behind him. It must be an interval. In another moment the musicians would be pushing past him down the stairs, in quest of some quick refreshment before their next performance. Not wanting to be noticed by them, he quickly descended the steps and started on his way back to his apartment. But now he went slowly, nursing his sense of outrage.

Cynthia, his Cynthia, the girl he worshipped and longed for, to be clasped in another man's arms, and that man Shaldon! To be dancing the scandalous waltz with him in the sight of all those people! It was not to be endured. He *could not* endure it. But what was to be done?

His mind was still confused as he reached the top of the servants' staircase and walked slowly along the passage. Without knowing it, he passed his own door and went on towards the family bedchambers. And as he loitered along, he almost bumped into the one person who had so disordered his normally orderly mind.

They both gave a start. Cynthia recovered first.

"Why, Mr. Durrant!" she exclaimed. "Did I not catch sight of you a little while ago, in the musicians' gallery?"

He gabbled an incoherent assent. She looked at him coyly.

"Was it you who directed them to take an interval? If so, it was a great deal too bad of you, for I was enjoying myself prodigiously!"

He had some control of himself now.

"So I observed," he said, woodenly. "But no, I did

not order them to cease playing. I fancy it was all arranged beforehand."

"Then why were you there?"

"To watch for a moment."

"Ah, what a pity!" She laid a hand on his arm, looking up at him with mocking compassion. "Do you feel very like Cinderella in the fairy tale? Would you, too, have liked to be on the floor, whirling some young lady around in your arms?"

"Yes," he said, hoarsely, "indeed I would."

"Poor man," she murmured. "And who is she, the young lady whom you would desire as a partner? Will you perhaps be taking her some evening to a ball where you may dance with her to your heart's content?"

In the subdued lighting of the passage, her eyes appeared darker, more inviting than ever. He clenched his hands at his sides to prevent himself from springing forward to seize her in his arms.

"No." His voice was harsh now. "No, I may never dance with her. There's no hope for such as me—"

"Oh, dear, a hopeless passion! And you told me once that you were not romantical! I would give much to know who this fair cruelty is, so that I might give her a piece of my mind."

He shook his head, unable to answer.

"Well, I see you don't mean to confide in me, so I won't press you. But she must be very stupid not to return your feelings. Who could wish for a more personable young man—"

He was unable to contain himself at this.

"For God's sake, don't patronise me!"

The cry was almost one of physical pain. She removed her hand from his arm, looking up at him with an expression first of surprise, then of satisfaction.

"Well, if she won't dance with you, perhaps *I* will. There, would that do?"

"You—you don't mean it—you—couldn't," he stammered, thrown completely off balance.

"Could I not?" she responded to the implicit challenge. "We'll see that."

At the start of their conversation she had intended to bait Bertram Durrant as usual for sport. He so patently admired her, and the social inhibitions which prevented him from in any way showing his admiration only added spice to the game. But now some unknown, unexpected element had crept in, something which aroused the hidden devilment in her own nature and prompted her to outrageous behaviour.

"I'm to attend a masquerade the day after tomorrow," she whispered, "at Lady Plummet's in Richmond. She's young, a thought wild, and not at all stuffy. Guests are to keep secret their identity until midnight, when masks will be removed. There's to be no announcing of names at the door; one simply shows one's card to gain admittance. You may go, and leave before midnight with none the wiser, if you wear a mask and domino like the rest. And then you may dance with me—if you can recognise me, that is, in my disguise!—or with anyone else who takes your fancy, for that matter."

She reached forward and placed a finger momentarily on his lips.

"Say no more. I'll procure you a card—in an assumed name, of course—and leave it on your desk tomorrow. And now I must return to the ballroom."

She flitted away before he could recover from his astonishment sufficiently to make any reply.

He spent the rest of that evening shut up in his room in a state of confusion unlike anything he had ever known. At times he wondered if he could have been delirious and conjured up the whole incident out of a fevered imagination. But when on the following afternoon he returned to his desk, after a short interval for nuncheon, to find a gilt-edged invitation card lying there requesting the pleasure of Mr. D. Bertram's company at Lady Plummet's Moonlight Masquerade, he knew that this was no dream.

D. Bertram. That had been a clever notion, to transpose his names, he thought; his Cynthia was a lady of resource, as well as being the most desirable creature in the world. He saw that the masquerade was due to begin at half past nine—a Moonlight Masquerade, so the card stated. It sounded vastly romantic, and by God! he would make it so. He found his confusion vanishing, to be replaced by a mood of wild elation which could not entirely obscure his cooler, more calculating side. There were plans to be made if this escapade were to be brought off safely. It would not do to depart in a vehicle from Berkeley Street at the same hour as the daughter of the house; better take a room for the night at an inn in the City and take a post chaise from there. It would be expensive, but what did he care for that when his reward would be so great? Besides, he could always charge the amount to the expense account to be submitted to the Earl of Alvington for outgoings in connection with his affairs. He thought with a bitter smile what a nice touch of irony it would be that the Earl should foot the bill for his private investigator's assignation with Shaldon's bride elect.

There was not the slightest hitch in his plans. When he arrived at the mansion in Richmond on the appointed evening, he was one of a crowd of masked ladies and gentlemen all anxious to preserve their anonymity for the present. They were led to the ballroom, where an illusion of moonlight had been created by a large yellow disk suspended from the ceiling, from which only a faint glow emerged. The only other light in the vast, dim room came from a few coloured lanterns hung along the walls at infrequent intervals. Even the musicians, who required a good light to read their scores, were screened off so that only the faintest gleams were visible at their end of the room.

Durrant's tension eased. Even without the concealing masks, it would have been difficult in this subdued lighting for one guest to identify another with any certainty. And he was unknown.

He looked about him. Dominoes of all colours, bright as rainbows, encircled him. Masked faces, looking more than usually mysterious in the dim light, came and went, their owners laughing and talking in animated, high-pitched accents. A footman suddenly appeared beside him out of the gloom, proffering a tray on which stood glasses of wine. Durrant accepted one, tossed it off hurriedly and took another. This was not a night for half measures, he told himself. But how in the world was he ever to find Cynthia in such a poor light, amid so many people?

Groping his way to one of the small tables set in the alcoves of the room, he put down his glass. Just then, the orchestra struck up with the music for a quadrille. Immediately, he was seized on by a lively young lady with a head of yellow curls, who gathered another lady and gentleman from those around her to make a foursome. In a similar scrambling way other sets of four were formed, and everyone took to the floor amid much laughter and chatter.

"This is famous fun!" gasped his partner, as she threw herself enthusiastically into the dance. "Do you not think so? Oh, what shall I call you?"

"My name is Bertram, madam," he replied, formally.

"Oh, Lud, you mustn't call me madam! My name is Lydia, but I prefer Lyddy."

He raised his eyebrows over this; but his partner's extremely informal manners were not isolated in that assembly, as he was soon to discover. When the quadrille ended, a Scottish reel was started. He at once found himself unceremoniously pressed into a set by several pairs of urgent female hands. The pace of the evening was fast and furious. Dance succeeded dance, with brief intervals occasionally for refreshment, and though he changed partners many times, he did not succeed in finding the one for whom he had come here.

After a cotillion and another quadrille, danced with partners who obligingly supplied their forenames and whose behaviour was decidedly fast, he made up his mind to search the room for her. Accordingly, he eluded all those who would have urged him again onto the floor, and began a systematic quartering of the ballroom.

His task was made difficult by the fact that most of the females were constantly in motion and in that dim light it was almost impossible to identify anyone. Once or twice he thought he had seen her, only to realise on a closer inspection that it was some other female with hair of the same colour or of a similar height. None of the ladies appeared to object when he drew nearer to peer intently into their faces.

"Fie, sir, are you trying to discover who I am?" laughed one. "You must wait until the time comes for unmasking!"

After he had traversed the length of the ballroom without succeeding in tracking down his quarry, he began to be assailed by doubts. A masquerade was always a slightly more informal affair than a ball, but surely this one was informal to the point of being positively improper? The ladies were behaving like sad romps and the men taking liberties far beyond the line of generally acceptable behaviour. Cynthia had said that the hostess, Lady Plummet, whom so far he had not had the honour—if such it was—of meeting, was young and a thought wild. Wild indeed, since she was the originator of a party such as this! And from this thought he passed to another. Would Lady Lydney really have given her daughter permission to attend a gathering of this kind?

He halted suddenly, seized with shock as a most unpleasant realisation came to him.

He had been duped.

Cynthia had never intended to be present tonight. She had been playing relentlessly on his hopeless passion, pretending that she would actually permit him to dance with her, and all the time laughing at his credulity. How she must have enjoyed the joke! It was the very kind of thing to appeal to her malicious sense of humour. And the final bitterness was that no doubt she considered it a just punishment for his presumption in daring to lift his eyes to her.

From chagrin he passed to furious anger. Come what might, someday he would even the score with her, would show her that he was not a man to take meekly such a hoyden's trick!

Evading the grasping hands which sought to detain

him, he strode purposefully towards the exit. He had almost reached it when the musicians broke into the opening bars of a waltz.

And then from behind him a soft arm entwined his neck and a low voice spoke in his ear.

"Going so soon? And before our waltz?"

He turned abruptly, almost knocking over the lady whose arm had captured him, and whose voice he could not fail to recognise.

"Miss Lydney! I thought—"

She placed a finger over his lips.

"Hush, no names. Did you think I had deserted you? Foolish creature, I've been here all the time—but come! Waltz with me."

He needed no second invitation, but placed his arm about her waist. She removed hers from his neck and allowed the hand to rest on his shoulder; and away they went, twirling down the room, locked together more closely than was the practice in more polite assemblies, such as Almack's.

They did not speak. The anger which had swept over him had changed now to an equally fierce emotion which found its expression in his increasingly tightening embrace. She did not attempt to slacken his hold, but strained towards him in a way which inflamed his desire. For Cynthia Lydney was making the discovery that, although it was pleasant enough to flirt with gentlemen of the *ton* who knew just how far they ought to go, to yield to this unbridled passion was more enjoyable still. And for a few hours, what could it matter?

The waltz had almost come to an end when she spoke again in his ear.

"Let us go out into the garden. It's a warm night, and there's a little temple there."

As one in a dream, he allowed himself to be led out under the stars. His arm still encircled her waist, and her head rested on his shoulder.

The garden ran down to the Thames, silvered in the moonlight. The temple was set at the extreme end, its windows looking out on the river. It was very quiet

319

there, for so far no one else had come into the garden; they felt as if they had the whole world to themselves.

They sat down upon a velvet-cushioned bench against the wall. For a moment, he gazed into her dark eyes without either moving or speaking. Then he whipped off his mask, flinging it down on the seat beside him. He put up a trembling hand to hers, but she forestalled him, removing it herself. She unfastened her lilac domino, letting it fall to the ground to reveal beneath it a gown in a deeper shade, with a décolleté neckline which exposed her white shoulders.

He caught his breath.

She looked up at him with one of her bold, provocative glances; but this time there was something of curiosity in the look, as of one who sought knowledge.

He took her into his arms, kissing her again and again, ruthlessly, demandingly. Far from resisting, she responded eagerly, and did not draw away when his lips moved from her mouth to the white neck and shoulders, so irresistible in the moonlight.

At last, his impatient hands pulled at the neckline of her gown to lower it, to open to his caresses the sweetness that lay concealed there. And Cynthia gave a low moan, surrendering completely to his importunity and to her own hot blood.

It was some time later that they stirred, feeling cramped. Cynthia stood up, rearranged her dress, fastened the domino around her and began to resume her mask. He watched her, silent for the moment, then came to with a start and looked at his watch.

"A quarter to midnight—I suppose I must go," he said, reluctantly. "But what are we going to do?"

"Do?" Her tone was casual, her manner calm.

"About us. About what has happened tonight."

"Why, nothing. What should we do?"

"But suppose you should chance to find yourself—"
She interrupted him with a laugh.

"Oh, never worry your head over that! There are ways and means, you know."

He did know, of course, but it shocked him to think

that she did. He was still more shaken as he gradually realised the implications of her remark.

"Do you mean," he asked, slowly, "that you did not come unprepared to this Masquerade?"

"Of course not—that would be stupid, and I hope I am never stupid. I have married friends, you know, who are willing to give me the benefit of their experience and knowledge in such matters. All my friends are not innocent young ladies like Helen Somerby and Melissa Chetwode."

Calculating as he was himself, he did not quite relish the thought of this degree of calculation in her.

"But what of the future? Now that you are mine, I want to keep you, to marry you."

Her tone took on a sharper note. "You must see for yourself that cannot possibly be. My father would never consent to such a match. I shall marry Shaldon, as Papa wishes, but you and I can still be lovers."

"No!" He rose and gripped her by the elbows so that she winced. "No, I shall never let you do that!"

She tried to disengage herself. "But why not? Lots of fashionable women take lovers. It is almost de rigueur. Besides, I must marry to have an establishment of my own, and since I cannot marry you, Shaldon will do as well as any."

"Shaldon! You fix on him because he is heir to an Earldom and a large estate—or so you think!" he exclaimed, wildly.

"Of course." She eyed him sharply. "But what do you mean by that last remark?"

"Another few weeks, and I may be able to enlighten you," he said, in a more guarded way. "When Greenwich Fair comes round at Whitsuntide. And then you'll consign Shaldon to the devil, if things go as I hope they will."

"What can you mean? Greenwich Fair? What has that to say to anything, pray? Be plain with me, Bertram. What is this mystery about Shaldon?"

"I can tell you nothing now. I should not have spoken at all, but I'm maddened by the thought of you as his bride—or as any man's, except myself! Cynthia, my darling"—he drew her towards him—"can we not brave your father's displeasure and seek his permission to wed? He thinks the world of you and would grant you anything, and I may not always be in as humble a sphere as now. If things go well with me, I may in time enter Parliament and hold up my head with the best of them."

She disengaged herself with an air of finality.

"You are talking wildly. I can only suppose that all this has gone to your head. But if you don't wish to be discovered when the unmasking takes place, you'd best go at once. There's a side door leading from the garden. I'll show you."

He resumed his mask and domino and followed her out of the temple and back towards the house.

"Can I leave you safely in this place?" he asked, as they turned along a narrow path leading to a side gate which gave access to the mews.

"Of course. I came with a party of friends. Mama believed I was to spend the entire evening at their house. They will conduct me home."

"And when shall I see you alone again?" he asked eagerly, as they reached the gate.

"I cannot say. We must be discreet, as you will realise. There'll be few, if any, opportunities such as this. You must leave all to me. On no account must you attempt to come to me in my room, or even betray by one word or look that we are more to each other than we should be. It won't be easy, but it must be done."

"You'll find it easy enough, I dare swear," he muttered, bitterly.

"And so will you. Don't tell me that you've never yet acted a part, for I shouldn't believe you. And now I must go, for my friends will be looking for me at the unmasking."

He gathered her roughly into his arms to kiss her once more, lingeringly, desperately. She yielded for a moment, then thrust him resolutely away and ran back along the path as he stepped through the gate. The masquerade was over.

Chapter XXVII

THE MORNING AFTER Cynthia's ball, Helen and Melissa were sitting together in the morning room dealing with some of their correspondence. The season was now in full swing, and every day brought a batch of fresh invitations, some of which they were obliged to decline owing to previous engagements.

"It's a pity your Mama did not wish us to attend that Moonlight Masquerade," remarked Helen, pausing in her task. "Of course, Lady Chetwode knows best, but it *did* sound so prodigiously romantic, and more fun than the musical party which we're to attend instead."

"Yes, indeed it did, Nell, but when Mama says that anyone is bad *ton,* as she did of this Lady Plummet, there's no arguing with her, you know. Besides, I mentioned it to Philip, and he said he wouldn't like any sister of his to attend such a ramshackle affair, and he wondered how it was that we ever came to be invited, as Mama is not even acquainted with the lady."

"Oh, I know the answer to that, for Cynthia Lydney told me yesterday evening that she had put forward our names to Lady Plummet. And come to think of it, Mel, she had that gleam in her eye as she mentioned it. You know very well the look I mean, when she's planning to play off a jest on somebody! I might have guessed then that there was something smoky about the business. Well, if Cynthia's sense of humour was tickled at the thought of our going, I'm glad after all that your Mama did prevent it."

"Do you suppose Cynthia means to go? I wonder that Lady Lydney should permit it, for she places herself on a very high form."

"Oh, Cynthia can always find ways of doing just as she pleases. You notice she managed to persuade Lady Lydney to allow the waltz to be danced at her ball."

"Did I not?" replied Melissa, with emphasis. "Mama was horridly shocked, and I could see she would have liked to persuade us not to take part in it, but for seeming to cast a reflection on the good taste of our hostess. I know she was glad that I decided for myself to sit it out."

"Perhaps I should have done so, too," confessed Helen, "because I did notice your mother's qualms. But I was so eager to try it out for the first time. I don't count our attempts to learn it at the seminary, with only other girls as partners. And I must say I did enjoy it, Mel! That twirling motion is so exhilarating, like being bowled along at speed in a curricle, or putting a horse to the gallop! I'm sure you would love it."

Melissa said nothing for a moment. She had failed to enjoy Cynthia's ball, but hesitated to confess the reason for this to Helen. Had James Somerby been present, she would have risked her Mama's disapprobation for the pleasure of waltzing with him; but the young doctor had not been invited, and there was no one else present with whom she had the smallest wish to dance in such intimate proximity.

"Philip offered, and Mama wouldn't have minded that, but I wasn't in the mood for dancing with my brother. Besides. he only asked me because Mr. Lydney had already secured you as a partner. I fancy Viscount Shaldon was disappointed over that, too."

"Disappointed?" Helen repeated, in a careless tone. "Oh, no, I don't think so. He asks me as a duty, you know, because we've been acquainted for so long and he is fond of my parents. He seemed to go on very well with Cynthia, don't you think? Everyone was saying what a handsome couple they made."

"And so did you and Mr. Lydney. You're to go driving with him this morning aren't you? Don't you think, Nell, he's becoming a trifle particular in his attentions?"

Helen's cheeks showed a faint pink. "Cynthia's already warned me that her brother's a shameless flirt, so it would be foolish in me to attach the least significance to his behaviour, don't you agree?"

Melissa leaned eagerly towards her. "But do you like him, Nell—really like him, I mean? You can tell me, for you know I would never betray a secret of yours for anything!"

"Of course I know that, and I would tell you if there were anything to tell! But the truth is that at present I believe him to be flirting with me—in the nicest possible way, so that I cannot take exception to it—so I am returning the compliment." She broke off, laughing. "There! Is not that shameless?"

Melissa joined in the laugh. "It's just like your nonsense," she said. "But be careful that you don't find yourself taking it more seriously than you bargained for, and falling in love with him in earnest."

"Oh, Mel, you sound for all the world like my dear Mama! Before I came to Town, she warned me that I mustn't be too ready to give my affections to the first gentleman who paid me attentions, as men of fashion were sadly addicted to flirting. Don't worry, I've quite decided to profit from her advice and not take any of them seriously."

"But you *can't* decide that. What I mean is, that one doesn't choose the moment when one falls in love, or even the person, in a way. It just *happens,* Nell, like—like night and day, or the seasons—"

"Oh, dear, now you're becoming poetic!"

She dissolved into helpless laughter. Melissa, after looking offended for a moment, was obliged to join in, and the conversation was suspended for a time.

They had just resumed their writing when they were interrupted by a summons to the small drawing room, where they found that Mrs. Horwood and Catherine had arrived to pay a call.

They had all been chatting together for some mo-

325

ments when Mrs. Horwood turned to Helen with a request for her brother's direction.

"I should like to send Mr. Somerby an invitation to Catherine's ball," she said. "It would have been done before this, but that scatterbrained daughter of mine kept forgetting to ask you."

To describe Catherine as a scatterbrain was scarcely just; but Helen lost sight of this in her delight that James was to receive this attention from the Horwoods, who were barely acquainted with him, after all. Although she had said nothing to Melissa at the time, she had felt it as a slight when he had been passed over by the Lydneys, who had known him and his family since childhood. Melissa's countenance, too, glowed with satisfaction; and she at once embarked on quite an animated conversation with Catherine on another subject, in an attempt to conceal her feelings. This, however, did not succeed with her friends, who knew her too well to be deceived.

Presently Henry Lydney arrived to keep his appointment with Helen. He stayed just long enough to do what was civil towards the other ladies, before bearing Helen off to the waiting curricle.

"Ah, at last I have you to myself!" he said, as he took up the reins to give his horses the office to start.

"Yes, together with all the dozens of other people who'll be in the Park this morning," she answered, with a laugh.

"Don't remind me of that! I heartily wish them all at Jericho."

"Where exactly is Jericho, sir? I must confess that geography was never my strong point."

"Nor mine, assure you! But in any case, Jericho is only an euphemism—in reality, I wish them much farther away than that."

"Unkind!" She made a reproving face. "Besides, you must know I like being greeted by sundry acquaintances, and admiring the splendid horses that go by, not to mention quizzing the absurd bonnets worn by some of the females!"

"You yourself have the most delightful taste in bonnets, ma'am," he replied, studying the yellow straw trimmed with green ribbons which she was wearing.

"No, you can't flatter me on that account!" she protested, laughing. "I possess as many absurd hats as the next female! I wore something simple today, you see, so as not to put you to the blush."

"You're very good to study my sensibilities to the extent of suspending your own pleasure, Miss Somerby, but I assure you such excessive caution is needless," he replied, with a solemn face. "My sister has long since inured me to the worst extravagances of female attire. I have seen it all!"

"Why, how unhandsome of you, and so like a brother! I'm sure Cynthia always looks charmingly."

He did not answer for a moment, as he was occupied in turning the curricle through the gates into the Park.

"Perhaps another man may think so," he said, when this was accomplished, "but you can't expect that I should notice. Especially not," with an openly admiring look from his dark eyes, "when I have you beside me."

She thought that she knew to a nicety just how to keep his flirting on the light side, but now and then she would find herself momentarily discomposed. This was one of those occasions. Her eyes fell before his, and to her annoyance she felt a blush starting.

"Good morning, Lydney. 'Servant, Miss Somerby."

They turned their heads to see Shaldon beside the curricle, mounted on a sleek chestnut. His tone was cold and the look he directed at them severe. It had the unfortunate effect of deepening the red in Helen's cheek.

Lydney reined in his horses.

" 'Morning, Shaldon. That's a prime bit of blood," he said, running his eye over the chestnut's points. "Don't fancy I've seen it before. A recent acquisition?"

"Took a fancy to it at Tattersall's," replied Shaldon, briefly. "And pray how did you enjoy yesterday's ball,

Miss Somerby?" he continued, directing an unsmiling look at Helen.

"Oh, vastly! I did so like the waltz!" she exclaimed, rapturously.

"So I observed." His tone was dry. "Lydney's a very accomplished performer, of course—one of the many evidences of a misspent youth."

Lydney grinned. "While you have chiefly employed your time in reading improving works?" he demanded, mockingly. "Come off it, Shaldon! If you think to impress Miss Somerby with such stuff, you're faint and far off. Isn't he, ma'am?"

"Pray don't bring me into it, if you two are determined to quiz each other," she laughed. "But in case you may feel that I'm becoming too rackety, let me inform you that I'm to spend an improving evening myself for once, at Mrs. Somerton's musical soirée. Do either of you chance to be going?"

"A musical soirée? Lud, no—" began Lydney, then stopped. "Now I recollect," he continued, avoiding Shaldon's eye, "I rather fancy I did have a card."

"And if you didn't, I shouldn't put it past your powers of persuasion to obtain one," said Shaldon, with a mocking smile. "Well, I mustn't make you keep your horses standing any longer. Doubtless we'll be meeting again before long, Miss Somerby."

He bowed and rode on; Helen's eyes followed him for a moment. She reflected that, although he always looked well, he appeared to even better advantage than usual on horseback.

They met one or two other acquaintances during the remainder of their drive through the Park, and the time passed so pleasantly that when Lydney finally set Helen down at the house in Cavendish Square, she was conscious of a regretful feeling. All the same, she would not promise to drive out with him at any other time during the next few days, in spite of his earnest requests. Although she very much enjoyed his company and was not averse, as she had admitted to Melissa, to indulging him in a discreetly mild flirtation, she had no wish to flout the proprieties to the extent of causing everyone to couple their names together. She knew that he was only flirting, however serious he might sometimes appear. Cynthia had told her so; and moreover Mama had prepared her adequately for guarding her heart against such frivolous assaults. But she could not help thinking that in a way it was a pity; he was such an agreeable young man, and she was sure he would make a charming husband. She did not wish for a husband, she reminded herself—at least, not yet. Someday, perhaps, when all the dizzy excitements of a London season were behind her and she was home once more among the green meadows and woodlands of her beloved countryside, she might settle down with some amiable young man. Someone like Papa, she thought, with a sudden lump in her throat; kind and loving, yet with a strong sense of humour, too, so that he and she could have fun together in the way that Mama and Papa had always done. And they would have laughing, happy children scrambling all over the place, and puppies and kittens and a pony for the children to ride. It would be a real home, an abode of affection such as her own parents had created about them. She could not quite visualise Mr. Lydney in such a role. Now that she came to consider the matter as she walked slowly upstairs to her room, she could think of no other gentleman of those admirers whom she had left behind her in Alvington who seemed better suited to it, either. She suddenly recalled what Melissa had said earlier, that one could not choose the moment for falling in love nor even the person concerned. She smiled; dear, romantic Melissa, who at present fancied herself in love with James. Melissa was only too ready to meet love halfway, but she, Helen, was more wary. There was time enough for such matters, and she certainly did not intend that they should interfere with her wholehearted enjoyment of the novel, exhilarating experience of a London season.

She was not surprised to meet Mr. Lydney later at Mrs. Somerton's soirée. With his usual adroitness, he managed to secure a seat with her party, which consisted of Lady Chetwode, Melissa and Philip. The first item on the evening's programme was provided by a plump lady in a purple gown and a turban ornamented with three large feathers. Before she sang, she inflated her generous bosom to such an alarming extent that Helen had to suppress a ridiculous thought that it might burst like a balloon. She dared not look at Melissa for fear the same notion had entered her friend's head, in which case she knew that they would be bound to disgrace themselves by a giggle, at the very least. As the song progressed, the feathers kept nodding in response to the singer's impassioned rendering, and this again almost led to Helen's undoing. Altogether, she felt relieved when that item came to an end and the audience broke into applause.

"Oh, dear!" whispered Melissa to her, under cover of the noise. "I had to keep my handkerchief pressed to my mouth, for fear I should laugh!"

They were safe enough from this hazard during the next item, which was a brilliantly executed pianoforte solo. After it was concluded, there was an interval for refreshments, during which most people left their seats. Helen had seen Catherine and her parents seated not far away, and before Henry Lydney could rise to follow, she had jumped up and was moving towards them. A crowd of other loiterers soon intervened between her and her objective, however; and while she was threading her way through, someone touched her lightly on the arm. She turned to see Shaldon beside her.

"You here?" she asked, in some surprise. "I had a notion you didn't care for music above half."

"I don't," he replied, "although not for anything would I have missed the Purple Peril."

Helen laughed. "Oh, no! Melissa and I were hard put to it to keep a straight face!"

"We can't talk here," he said taking her arm and steering her purposefully through the crowd to a less congested spot. "And since I came especially to talk to you, perhaps you will not object to giving me a moment of your company."

"You came to talk to me?" she repeated, puzzled. "What in the world about?" Then, with a sudden change of tone, "Oh, have you seen the Earl and discovered what is afoot? You promised to acquaint me with it, when you had any news."

"Oh, that. No, I've not given that matter a second thought, for I'm convinced it's a mare's nest," he said, dismissively.

"I disagree! And I think you are very foolish not to try and get to the bottom of it. Though, of course," she added, belatedly, "it is none of my business, and *I* don't mean to be uncivil, telling you you're foolish. I beg your pardon."

"You needn't, for I am about to say the same thing to you in another connection," he said, fixing his grey eyes upon her in a serious look which reminded her of the one he had been wearing that morning in Hyde Park.

She had some inkling then of what he meant to say, and she coloured faintly, between embarrassment and annoyance.

"If it's what I suppose—"

"I expect it is, and I'm quite sure you won't wish to hear it." His tone was stern. "If your brother were at hand, this would come more properly from him; but since he's not, as an old friend of your family, I must speak in his stead. What the devil do you mean by encouraging Lydney to hang about you? Do you want to set the Town talking?"

Her eyes flashed. *"Encourage* him? How dare you say that!"

He gave her back look for look. "How else would you describe that touching little scene I chanced upon in the Park this morning?"

"You misunderstood!" she said defiantly. "It was all nonsense—"

"There were a good many others passing at that time, and you may be sure they all misunderstood, too," he interrupted, grimly. "Do you positively wish to acquire a reputation for flirting? If so, permit me to tell you that you're going the quickest way about it."

331

"Oh, this is intolerable!" Just in time, she prevented herself from stamping her foot. "What right have *you* to bring me to book? As I've said before, you are *not* my brother! If there's anything amiss with my conduct, I have Lady Chetwode at hand to tell me of it."

"That's all very well, but doubtless she, too, misunderstands the situation."

This puzzled her; for a moment she forgot her anger.

"What do you mean by that?"

"Simply that Lady Chetwode most likely considers Lydney's intentions to be serious, and would be reluctant to throw any rub in the way. In such cases, a little encouragement on the lady's side does not come amiss."

"And pray how do you know that she is mistaken in that?" she challenged him, once more firing up.

For the first time, a look of anxiety came into his face.

"Is that what you suppose, N——Miss Somerby? Have I perhaps really misunderstood your part in the affair?"

"No——that is to say, it's none of your business!" she exclaimed in exasperation. "I wish you will stop trying to watch over me. I am very well able to look out for myself!"

"I sincerely trust that events may prove that," he replied, soberly. "I can only beg your pardon for my intrusion into your personal affairs. Like most of what is termed interference, it was well meant——but the road to Hades is paved with good intentions, so they say."

He bowed and left her, only a moment before Henry Lydney appeared at her side.

"Where's Shaldon off to in such a hurry?" he asked. "Gone to get you a glass of lemonade?"

She attempted to make a quick recover. "No, but I would like one of all things! It has become so very close in here."

"Yes, you do appear a trifle flushed," he answered,

studying her. "Shall we go into the refreshment room, or would you prefer me to fetch something out for you?"

She allowed him to guide her into the anteroom, where they were presently joined by the rest of her party, together with Catherine Horwood and her parents. She took little part in the conversation, however; and whenever she was addressed directly, she answered more or less at random. Melissa noticed that she was out of spirits, and determined to discover the cause later, when they should be alone. For the moment, she loyally did her best to talk volubly enough for both of them.

As they all strolled back to resume their seats, Helen, now somewhat recovered, looked about her covertly for Shaldon, but could not see him anywhere. This was scarcely surprising, as he had left immediately after their conversation.

Repeating it to Melissa later in the seclusion of her bedchamber, her indignation revived.

"I think him odiously interfering! What right has he to tell me how I should go on, I'd like to know? I wish I had given him a sharper setdown, now I come to think of it. Why, we've been strangers for *years,* until he came to Alvington in March and visited my parents!"

"I'm sure he meant well," said Melissa, in a conciliatory tone. "No doubt he was persuaded that your brother would have spoken to you in that way, had Mr. Somerby himself been by."

"I doubt very much that James would be so—stuffy! And, anyway, who is he to discharge the office of a brother on my behalf? I tell you, Mel, I will not endure it! And so I told him!"

"Then you need have no fear that he'll err again," pointed out Melissa soothingly. "And, after all, Nell, you yourself have behaved in exactly the same way towards Viscount Shaldon, come to think of it."

"Behaved in the same way? Oh, you mean when I tried to warn him against Durrant? But that was different—I was not criticising his conduct!"

"No, but you were warning him against what you believed to be a hazard. It appears to me," went on Melissa, with a light laugh, "that you're both concerned with trying to protect each other! You must share more family feeling than you suspect!"

Helen gazed indignantly at her friend for a moment; but it was not in her nature to persist in feelings of rancour, and she had to acknowledge the truth of Melissa's statement. She began to laugh, too, and at once felt better.

Chapter XXVIII

"REALLY," REMARKED LADY LYDNEY, to her husband wearily, as she sat before her quilted dressing table at the end of another exhausting day, "children are a mixed blessing! Chaperoning Cynthia through the Season—if Cynthia can ever be said to allow one to chaperone her—is just the kind of fatiguing, tedious business that I thought it would be, Lydney. It will be a relief when the girl is married and set up in her own establishment. I have had more than enough of this, I promise you! Have you any notion when Shaldon is likely to make his offer?"

Lord Lydney shook his head. He was in no mood to listen to his wife's complaints, and intended to beat a retreat to the peace of his own bedchamber as soon as he could do so without annoying her. It was a pity that he had ever entered the room in the first place; but she had said earlier on at their dinner party that she wished to speak to him as soon as they could be private together, and this had been the first opportunity.

"For my own part, I cannot think why he hasn't done so already!" she exclaimed, petulantly. "You told me months ago that Alvington was to broach the matter."

"We must give Cynthia and Shaldon sufficient time to become a little better acquainted, Sophia. Recollect that until we brought Cynthia to Town, they had not met since childhood."

"What's that to say to anything? Many good matches are made between couples who know far less of each other. Do you suppose Shaldon to be hedging off?"

"Good God, no. Why should he? Cynthia's not only a good catch, she's a devilish attractive girl—beats all the others into fits, I'd say. Moreover, from what I've observed myself when I've seen them together, he seems quite alive to her charms." He paused. "The fact is, Sophia, I've reasons of my own for not pushing the business on at present. In a way, I'm relieved that he hasn't yet come to the point."

"Reasons . . . what reasons?" Her voice sharpened.

Again he hesitated. "I am not prepared to communicate them to you at this present time," he said at last, in what she thought of as his Parliamentary voice.

"Oh, well, I suppose you know what you're about, but I only hope you don't let Shaldon slip through your fingers! There are plenty of others in the running for her, but none with an Earldom in view."

"I'm quite aware of that, and you may trust me to play my cards carefully, I believe," he answered in a quelling tone.

"Oh, well! I suppose we must allow matters to take their own course," she said, resignedly. "But I must confess that I'll be relieved to get the girl off my hands. She's so monstrous self-willed that I am no match for her! She would insist on dancing the waltz at our ball, and I could see that people considered it bad *ton* to do so at a come-out ball."

"H'm." Lord Lydney cleared his throat judicially. "Well, Prinny has danced it at Carlton House, and even at Almack's it's not frowned upon, if done with permission. Times change, you know, and one must advance with them."

"And then she has some most undesirable friends," continued his wife, abandoning the former theme in favour of another. "I'm sure I don't like above half the females she's been dining with this evening, nor any of that set."

"Then you must put your foot down, my dear, and refuse to let her associate with them."

"Refuse to let Cynthia do anything on which she is determined?" asked Lady Lydney, incredulously. "I wish I may see that! It is impossible to deny her anything, since you have indulged her beyond permission!"

"I? Her upbringing has been entirely in your own hands, as is only fitting with a daughter."

"And whenever I've tried to check her in anything, she has at once wheedled you into persuading me to permit it," retorted his wife. "I tell you what it is—she can always bring you around her thumb, and well she knows it."

"This is a fruitless discussion," said Lord Lydney, taking out his watch and glancing at it. "At this hour, I think it would best be abandoned. Was there anything further you wished to say to me before we retire?"

"Yes, indeed there was. What is to be done about Henry?"

"Henry?" Lord Lydney raised his eyebrows. "I'm afraid I don't follow you."

"You surely must have noticed that he's been dangling after the Somerby girl for the past month?"

"My dear Sophia," replied Lydney, wearily, "I cannot be expected to endure the tedium of keeping under observation all the females whom my son chooses to honour with his transitory attentions."

"That's just it. They always have been transitory up to now, but I'm not at all sure that this one is in the same category. He's for ever at her side—driving in the Park, dancing at private balls and at Almack's—"

"Oh, my God! The boy's five and twenty, and must go on in his own way."

"But not if it's to lead him into marriage with Helen Somerby! I sincerely hope he can do better for himself than that!"

"Marriage? I shall own myself surprised if he has any such thought in his head," said Lord Lydney, scornfully.

"But *she* may have, and it's not difficult for a determined girl to attach a young man who begins only by flirting."

"There I think you do the chit an injustice," said her husband, thoughtfully. "I've seen nothing in her behaviour to suggest that she's at all a calculating female, out for a good catch. If that were the case, you know, she would surely set her cap at Shaldon."

"Oh, no! I believe they've been too much used to regard each other as brother and sister. I have no fears on that score."

"And, believe me, you need have none on Henry's account. Moreover"—his tone was dismissive—"I refuse positively to meddle in my son's amatory concerns, and I advise you strongly to avoid falling into that error yourself. Good night, Sophia."

And with a chilly kiss on her cheek, he quitted his lady's bedchamber.

Thursday was admissions day at Guy's Hospital. James Somerby watched as the sad specimens of suffering humanity filed into the Steward's room to present their petitions for admission, usually signed by the Parish Overseer. After this formality was over, those applicants who were accepted would be directed into the male or female admission room for examination by either the Physician or Surgeon. As the Physician was concerned with internal complaints, his examination of a patient took longer than the Surgeon's, requiring a close enquiry into symptoms and case history, answers to all of which were set out fully in Latin on a record card. The Surgeon, presented with more obvious evidence of the complaint, made a cur-

337

sory examination to establish the degree of urgency of each case and to mark the record cards accordingly. Acting on this information, the Steward would then allocate the available beds.

Mrs. Dorston's bed was now vacant, for she had been discharged a few days since. James himself had paid her subsistence of fourpence a day, and the sum due to the Ward Sister for the washing of body linen. He had also given her some money to help her out until such time as she could resume her normal employment. Mindful of what Helen had said, he asked her if she would like him to try to trace her grandson.

"Lor' bless you, no, Mr. Somerby, sir," she replied. "He'll be too taken up with his own concerns to bother with me. Besides, he went by another name than his own when last I set eyes on him—something grand it was, that the owner of the play booth had chosen for him." She frowned for a moment, trying to concentrate on this elusive memory. "There, I disremember what t'was. So it is when we grow old, doctor. We forget everything. But thank you kindly, sir, for all you've done for an old woman."

And yet it was little enough, thought James, as he watched the influx of new patients before setting about his duties in the wards.

On that particular day, he was a trifle abstracted because in the evening he was to take yet another excursion into the very different world that his sister had entered for a time. The invitation to Miss Horwood's ball had come as a surprise; he was himself very little acquainted with the family, and knew it was given because of Helen's friendship with the young lady. It had stirred up again those feelings which Melissa Chetwode had inspired in him at their last meeting, and the effect was unsettling. Her piquant face with the liquid brown eyes and rich chestnut curls kept coming between himself and his work in a way that was so far novel in his experience, and not entirely welcome. It would not do at all for a man in his position to begin daydreaming over a female. One day he would wish to marry; that went without saying—one

338

day some time ahead, when he had obtained a firm footing in his chosen occupation. He had first to complete his training and then present himself before the examiners of the Society of Apothecaries to obtain their licence to practise medicine; afterwards, if successful, he was to be taken into partnership with Dr. Gillies, and might expect to acquire the practice himself when the older man retired. But all this was in the future; what had he to offer any young lady at present?

Not that an offer from a medical man, however well qualified, would be looked upon with much favour by the parents of any young lady of *ton*. A realist by occupation even if an idealist by temperament, James Somerby had no illusions on this score. A medical practitioner was still considered by persons of Quality more in the light of a tradesman rather than a professional gentleman, with the exception of those select few who were Fellows of the Royal College of Physicians.

The time might come when this attitude would change. The recent Apothecaries Act had brought about a better organisation of medical education in order to satisfy the more stringent requirements of the Society of Apothecarites' examinations. Higher standards for students must eventually bring greater prestige to the profession as a whole. But such changes took years, not months, thought James impatiently; in the meantime, what Society Mama would consider him to be an eligible match for her daughter, even granted a long-standing friendship between the two families?

True, he was of good birth and in possession of a small private income to add to his professional earnings. He might perhaps look to marry someone such as a country squire's daughter. But Miss Melissa Chetwode of Cavendish Square, daughter of a Baronet? No, damme, he reflected bitterly; that was too high a flight!

When his hospital duties were over for the day and he returned to his lodging, his thoughts were somewhat diverted by his fellow lodger, John Keats. With a touching mixture of shyness and pride, Mr. Keats showed James a recent copy of Leigh Hunt's journal, *The Examiner,* in which one of his poems had been published.

"I wrote it last autumn," he said, "when I first took up residence here. The contrast between the sweet, rural calm of the village of Edmonton, where I served my apprenticeship, and this beastly place, full of dirt, dark turnings and murky buildings, so obsessed me that I simply had to write about it. You may think it a poor enough thing, Somerby, and indeed I hope to do better in time—but I am pleased to see it in print and venture to hope that you may share in my pleasure."

James read the sonnet carefully twice through before making any comment. His intelligent praise, when it came, evidently afforded Mr. Keats much gratification.

"You must find your medical studies somewhat of an encumbrance," he finished, "when you're in the grip of an urge to compose poetry?"

"I must admit to a feeling of conflict. The other day, for instance, during a lecture, a sunbeam came into the room and I was wafted away to Oberon and Fairyland! I find little emotional commitment to my medical work, and begin to wonder if poetry is not the proper business of my life."

James nodded. "I'm more fortunate, then, than you, in that I'm certain where my true vocation lies. Ever since I can remember, I've wished to be a doctor. My father is a clergyman, so it might have been supposed that I would follow him into the Church. But my inclination was for curing bodies rather than caring for souls. I may not be much good at the one, but I'm convinced that I should fail miserably at the other."

"You're become very elusive," said Henry Lydney accusingly to Helen as he presented himself at her side soon after the dancing commenced at Catherine Horwood's ball. "I've called on you three times this week, and without success."

"Oh, one is so caught up in engagements, you know," she replied vaguely.

This was not strictly true, because she had been at home on two of those occasions, but had requested Lady Chetwode to deny her to the caller. It was not that she had the slightest intention of paying any heed to what Shaldon had said, she told herself; but perhaps after all she had been seeing too much of Mr. Lydney. She found his attentions flattering and admitted to herself reluctantly that she might be in some danger of taking them too seriously.

"Oh, quite so. But now that I have been fortunate enough to find you at liberty, may I crave the favour of this dance?"

She had no excuse for refusing, so allowed him to lead her on to the floor; and as she always enjoyed his company, it was not long before they were laughing and chatting away together in a very animated style. This was the sight that met James Somerby's eyes when he entered the ballroom and began to look about for his sister. It brought a thoughtful frown to his brow, which deepened when he saw how, at the conclusion of the dance, Lydney placed a proprietorial hand under Helen's gloved elbow to guide her back to her seat. It took some time for James to shake Lydney off so that he could have a few moments in private conversation with his sister. When he at last managed this, he came to the point at once.

"You seem very confidential with that fellow," he began.

"Mr. Lydney? Oh, we're on quite easy terms now. After all, I've been in Town for over a month, and one meets the same people everywhere, you know.'

"All the same, I don't care to see him making you the object of his attentions quite so blatantly," replied James severely. "Perhaps you may not know it, but he has the reputation of being a compulsive flirt."

"Oh, James, not you as well!" she exclaimed in exasperation.

"What do you mean? Who else has been warning you off—Lady Chetwode?"

"No. I shouldn't object if she were to say anything, for she has the right to do so. But, of all people, Lord Shaldon has taken it upon himself to read me a lecture!"

"Tony? Well, I'm indebted to him for that."

"And so am *not* I! What possible concern can it be of his?"

"Don't like to see you making a cake of yourself, for old times' sake, I daresay."

"*Making a cake!* Really, James, if you've come here only to be insulting and—and beastly to me, I shall wish that Catherine had not persuaded her Mama to ask you!"

"No need to get in a miff," said her brother, placatingly. "You're a sensible girl and don't need to be told anything twice, so I'll say no more." He looked about him. "Where is your friend, Miss Chetwode? I was hoping to dance with her."

"I can't see her in all this crush, but she won't be far away. If we return to Lady Chetwode's side, I daresay she'll appear there in a moment."

"I don't see Tony here," remarked James, as they strolled towards the alcove where Lady Chetwode was sitting with some of the other chaperones.

"Don't you? I haven't had time to notice," she replied carelessly.

"I can believe that." There was a hint of acerbity in his tone.

He remembered his promise, though, and quickly changed the subject to an account of his recent doings at the hospital. He told her what had passed between himself and Mrs. Dorston on her discharge, and finished by describing the delight of John Keats on having his first poem published. She listened with interest; but the conversation came to an abrupt end when they reached Lady Chetwode to find a group gathered about her comprising Melissa and her brother, Catherine Horwood, and—yet again—Henry Lydney.

This time, James darted no indignant glances in the latter's direction. His eyes found Melissa's and rarely strayed, even though he joined pleasantly enough in the general conversation. It was Helen's turn to feel a slight pang of concern; she had never seen her brother look at any young lady quite in that way. He solicited for and was granted the pleasure of the next dance with Melissa; while Helen accepted Philip Chetwode as a partner, and Lydney dutifully offered for Miss Horwood.

Melissa and James talked very little as they danced together, perhaps less than any couple on the floor; but an unseen, unheard dialogue was being conducted between them, with only the expression in their eyes to give evidence of it.

By the time the dance was ended, Melissa's heart was beating so that she thought it must choke her.

"I—I feel faint," she whispered.

Most young men would have at once hastened to conduct her to her Mama; instead, James drew her arm into his and guided her towards a conservatory which led off the ballroom.

"Come out into the air for a while," he said.

The air in the conservatory was certainly much cooler, as the doors leading into the garden beyond had been set wide on this warm May evening. One or two couples were already strolling up and down here, away from the heat of the overcrowded ballroom.

"Sit down for a moment," he suggested, finding her a suitable chair facing the open doors and tenderly placing her in it. "There! Take two or three deep breaths, and it will pass off."

She did as she was bid, while he sat silent beside her, watching. After a few moments, the thudding heart steadied and she began to feel foolish. He would think her a poor creature indeed, to be overcome by an exercise to which she was so well accustomed. How could she know that it was not the dancing, nor the heat of the ballroom, but suppressed emotion?

"Better now?" He smiled as he asked the question.

She nodded, looking a trifle embarrassed. How gentle he was, she thought, and yet how masterful—and how much she loved him.

"Then shall I take you back to Lady Chetwode?"

He truly intended to do so; but when they both rose and stood for a moment facing each other with the secret of their hearts made plain in their eyes, he acted on instinct. No longer gentle, he crushed her in his arms; and she came willingly, eagerly lifting her face for his kiss.

"Melissa!" he murmured, when at last he drew back to stroke tenderly first her soft cheek and then her hair. "Oh, Melissa—my adorable, lovely girl!"

She wanted much more of this, and offered her lips again. He could not resist. But presently other considerations began to enter his whirling senses, and he gently set a distance between them, still retaining a hold on her hands.

"I shouldn't have done that—though God knows I wanted to!"

"Why should you not? I wanted it, too," declared Melissa, brazenly.

"Oh, my love! Then you *do* love me—you do wish to be my wife?"

"More than anything!" she exclaimed, rapturously, attempting to draw nearer to him again.

Making a strong effort, he still kept her at a distance.

"I'll not treat you lightly, Melissa, even if my feelings did get the better of me just now. I must first speak to your parents and obtain their consent to our betrothal—if that can be had," he finished, on a sober note.

A shadow came over the bright glow of happiness in her eyes.

"Do you suppose there'll be any difficulty?" she asked, haltingly.

"I hope not, with all my heart," he replied, earnestly. "But there's no denying that there may be objections to my suit. I'm not what is termed a good catch, my love. You could do much better for yourself."

"That I could *not!* There's no one in all the world whom I wish to marry but you!"

He weakened sufficiently to kiss her again, this time gently and more briefly.

"They will say you are very young," he persisted. "And I haven't yet completed my training. Even when I have, we shall never be wealthy, my own love. I cannot hope to support you in the style to which you're accustomed. We shall be tolerably comfortable, of course, but it won't be the affluence of a town house, an army of servants, carriages, horses, expensive gowns—" He broke off and groaned. "No, I can't ask you to do it! You would be giving up too much."

"Nothing I can't do without!" declared Melissa, valiantly. "But I can't and I won't give up *you!*"

They clung together again for a moment, two young people who saw shoals ahead and felt uncertain of a safe passage. Presently he disengaged himself, placing her hand decorously on his arm.

"We must return now, dearest. Our absence will be remarked, and I'll not have scandalous tongues maligning your name! I will call and see your father on Saturday—I can't get away from the hospital before. Tomorrow is operations day and always very busy. Only two more days, then, and we shall know our fate. God willing, it will match our hearts' desire."

They exchanged a long, loving look before he escorted her back into the ballroom to her mother's side.

He came on Saturday, as he had promised, and was closeted for more than an hour with Sir George Chetwode. At the end of this period, Melissa and her mother were summoned to the conference in the library, while Helen waited hopefully in the small drawing room, wondering how matters were proceeding.

She was to be kept in suspense for some time longer, however. She heard the library door opening as someone emerged, and presently James appeared alone in the drawing room, his face rather set.

"I can't stay now Nell," he said, hurriedly, as he bade her good-bye. "I'll see you again soon, and we'll have a long talk then."

"But what has happened?" she demanded. "Are you

and Melissa to be engaged? Can I wish you happy?"

"Not yet awhile. She'll tell you," he said, through tightened lips.

Before Helen could stop him, he had dashed away.

She followed him out into the hall, but seeing the front door close upon him, she climbed the stairs to her friend's bedchamber.

Sounds of distress were audible outside the door, so she dispensed with the formality of a knock and burst into the room.

Melissa was lying on the bed with her face buried in the pillow, sobbing as if she could never stop. It was not a moment for speech, so Helen sat down beside her and gently stroked the tumbled curls.

Presently Melissa raised her face, blindly accepting a handkerchief which was held out to her.

"It's no use!" she gasped between sobs. "They say we must wait—wait—wait! For ever, most like! Oh, what can I do, Helen?"

Murmuring soothing endearments, Helen drew the distracted girl into her arms and helped to dry her tears.

"Well, the first thing you can do," she said, when presently this treatment produced a lull in the storm, "is to tell me the whole."

Melissa obeyed, with many minor outbursts of grief by the way. It seemed that the interview had gone very much as James had anticipated. Sir George had been kind and understanding; he had not rejected out of hand the son of an old and valued friend, a young man, moreover, of exemplary character and well liked by all the family. The objections he had raised, gently but firmly, were Melissa's youth and the uncertainty of James's future prospects.

"And I'm only a few weeks short of nineteen!" wailed Melissa. "Dozens of girls are married even younger! But you'd have supposed, Nell, that your brother was on Papa's side, for he agreed with every word that Papa said about its being desirable to wait until I was sure of my own mind, and he—Mr. Somerby—could establish me comfortably! I *know* my own mind now, and so I told him, but it made no difference! As for the other matter, your brother must be aware that Papa will make me a generous settlement, whomsoever I should marry—not that I'd so much as *look* at anyone else!"

"But James wouldn't wish to live on your fortune, Mel—you must see that. He'll want to provide for you adequately himself."

"Yes, so he said, and Papa thought it very proper, but I think it a great piece of nonsense! How stupid gentlemen are in such matters! As though it's of any consequence who has the fortune, husband or wife. Are they not one? Besides, Mama says that both you and your brother will be wealthy one day, as you are heirs to your grandparents' estate. Not that I care for that! I'm sure we may live very comfortably on Mr. Somerby's present income added to his professional earnings. He says he can't give me a town house, carriages, horses, armies of servants, expensive gowns and the like; but what do I care? So long as we may be together, I would live in a far more modest style than we should be called upon to do, given what we already have!"

Helen nodded sympathetically. "Of course I know you would! But what exactly has been decided, my love?"

Melissa's tears began again. "Papa says we must wait for at least six months, by which time your brother will be established in partnership with Dr. Gillies and his affairs more settled. And if by then we are still of the same mind, Mr. Somerby may apply to Papa again. The same mind, Nell! As if either of us could ever change! It means waiting for almost *a year* to be married, even if Papa does give his consent in the end. I daresay I shall be *twenty* and dead of a broken heart besides!"

"No, love, you couldn't be both, you know," Helen pointed out, with an attempt to make her friend smile.

"Oh, Nell, you can't be so heartless as to joke when I feel so monstrous unhappy!" protested Melissa, now between laughing and crying. "I'm mistaken in you. I'd no notion you could be so odiously unfeeling!"

"Perhaps you may be, but only try to cheer up a little. After all, things might have turned out a great deal worse. Your parents might have forbidden the match altogether. As it is, you've a long time to wait, it's true, but at least you may hope to become bethrothed to James at the end of it. Did they forbid you to see each other in the meantime?" she added as an afterthought.

"Not precisely, but Papa said he thought it would be as well if we didn't meet too often," replied Melissa dolefully. "He thinks I shall forget your brother and turn to someone else, no doubt, but I shan't, I shan't! And so I told him!"

"What did your father say to that?"

"He said, 'If that is so, my dear child, and your affections do indeed stand the test of time, then I shall place no further obstacle in the way of your engagement to Mr. Somerby.' And instead of opposing his dreadful proposition, James agreed to it! That was the worst blow of all!"

"What else could he do, dearest Melissa?" pleaded Helen. "He knows that your parents are acting with your best interests at heart, and himself sees the wisdom of what they propose."

"I don't want him to be calm and rational about it! I'd like him to seize me and carry me off to Gretna Green, or something desperate and romantic!"

"Then you've mistaken your man. James would never behave in so shabby a fashion! He has by far too much respect for you, for your parents, and—yes—for the institution of marriage," retorted Helen, warmly. "And I tell you what, Mel—if he did act like that, I'm sure you wouldn't like it above half!"

"I should like it of all things!" declared Melissa, defiantly. "And I don't intend to wait another year to marry him, what's more, so there!"

Chapter XXIX

FOR SEVERAL DAYS Melissa was very low in spirits. She would have preferred to excuse herself from all her engagements in order to stay at home nursing her disappointment, but this Lady Chetwode wisely refused to permit.

"Only consider how singular it must appear to be shutting yourself away in that fashion," she said, reprovingly. "Tongues are always ready to wag, and you won't wish to wear your heart on your sleeve! Besides, it will do you good to be obliged to exert yourself for civility's sake. I myself have always found it a most efficacious corrective when I have anything on my mind."

"But you are not my age and in love, Mama!" protested Melissa, the tears starting in her eyes.

"No, my dear." Lady Chetwode patted her daughter's cheek. "But I have been, you know. You must not be supposing that, because a woman is well on into her middle years and has a grown up family, she hasn't experienced any of the heartaches of youth. Why, I recall a time——"

She broke off, a faraway look in her eyes.

"But all that is gone by now," she resumed, briskly, "just as your troubles will resolve themselves, if you will only be patient for a while."

Melissa was unconvinced, but knew that she must do as she was bid. So she continued to appear as usual wherever she was invited; and though she could no longer find any delight in a ball, she was too young not

349

to enjoy in some measure the other entertainments that offered. She talked long and earnestly to Helen about her hopes and fears. Had their friendship been slighter, it must have felt the strain; but Helen was always ready to lend a sympathetic ear, bearing in mind her own mother's adage that a trouble shared is a trouble halved. It took her back to the days when Melissa was newly arrived at Mrs. Cassington's seminary, homesick and desperate for comfort, as an eleven-year-old child often is when torn up from its childhood roots and transplanted to an alien place. Helen, being eight months older, had already settled down at school. She at once took the new arrival under her wing until the time came when Melissa was happily integrated into the new community. She trusted now that history would be repeated and that she would soon see her friend reconciled to the present situation.

In the following week the London drawing rooms were buzzing once more with scandal about Lord Byron's love affairs, resurrected by the recent publication of a book entitled *Glenarvon,* which had become an instant best seller.

"What is this book, ma'am, that everyone is talking about?" Helen asked Lady Chetwode, curiously. "Have you read it?"

Lady Chetwode pursed her lips. "No, indeed, I haven't, nor do I intend to do so! And I think Caroline Lamb will live to regret writing such a piece of scurrilous nonsense! Lady Holland says that some of the characters can be clearly identified as leading members of the *ton*—the Duchess of Devonshire, Lady Jersey, Lady Granville and Lady Oxford, to name only a few. As for Lord Byron himself—well, no matter! The last furore forced him to leave the country, and great poet or not, one cannot be sorry for it. A most unsavoury business, and certainly not fit for a young girl's ears."

Not surprisingly, this speech served only to heighten Helen's curiosity about the Byron scandals, of which she had heard many hints before. Accordingly, the next time she was in company with Cynthia Lydney at a rout party, Helen applied to her for information, certain that she would prove a good source.

"Oh, don't you know?" asked Cynthia, lifting an incredulous eyebrow. "Why, it was all over Town when first you arrived. Lord Byron and Caroline Lamb were quite wild for each other at one time. She said that he was 'bad, mad and dangerous to know,' but by all accounts she was more than a little mad herself. She's married, of course, but that didn't prevent her from going her length and setting all the Town talking. Such things can be, and usually are, managed discreetly, but she seemed determined to draw attention to herself by all the wildest starts imaginable."

"I have heard that Lord Byron's marriage did not turn out well, and that he has recently been legally separated from his wife," put in Helen.

"Yes, but the Caroline Lamb affair was not responsible for that, as it occurred before his marriage." Cynthia dropped her voice and looked knowing. "He's a determined womaniser, and among several others has been involved in an illicit liaison with his *own half-sister,* Mrs. Augusta Leigh."

Helen gave a gasp.

"You may well be shocked," continued Cynthia, with relish. "And now all this has been stirred up again by Caroline Lamb's outrageous book. Do you know, she's had the audacity to publish in it some of the actual love letters she received from Byron? No wonder the Town can talk of little else at present! But of course," she added, in a cynical tone, "it will all be forgotten again when the next scandal rears its head. The way of the world, my dear. And what's amiss with Melissa?" she demanded, dismissing the former topic. "She has quite lost her bloom, don't you think? No one could possibly think of her as plump, nowadays."

"Oh, you know very well that schoolgirl plumpness vanished long since," replied Helen, a shade tartly. "There's nothing whatever amiss with her, except I think she may be feeling a trifle tired this evening. So, too, am I—we were at Mrs. Wilmot's ball last night, and did not get to bed until the small hours.".

"Well, I still think she looks hagged—more as if she'd been crossed in love, or something of that kind," persisted Cynthia, with uncanny shrewdness. "Is there some hopeless passion? You would know, naturally, better than anyone."

Although quite ready to discuss with Cynthia the affairs of a famous poet with whom she was not acquainted, Helen was certainly not prepared to speak of Melissa's private concerns; so it was with more eagerness than usual that she welcomed Henry Lydney, who came upon them at that moment.

Cynthia watched their meeting with a cynical eye. Henry really did the thing extremely well, she reflected; anyone looking on would suppose that he was head over heels in love with this insipid chit. He would get little joy there, however, other than a mild flirtation. He would scarcely be such a fool as to offer marriage, and a carte blanche was not for young ladies of Helen Somerby's quality.

Bored, she let her eyes range around in search of diversion and noticed Viscount Shaldon standing in conversation with a group of people not far away. Their glances met for a moment; hers signalled an invitation which presently he accepted, strolling across in a leisurely way to join her and her two companions.

Helen had not met him since their encounter at Mrs. Somerton's soirée. When he greeted them all in his usual easy style, she was quite surprised to discover how glad she was to see him again. Accordingly she responded with an especially warm smile, deciding at once to forgive him for the untimely lecture he had favoured her with on that occasion. His grey eyes twinkled, and he looked as if he would have liked the oportunity of a few words in private with her, perhaps to ask her pardon yet again for that second transgression; but Cynthia had summoned him for her own entertainment and quickly proceeded to monopolise his conversation.

"I haven't set eyes on you this age!" she began. "Pray, where have you been hiding yourself away?"

Helen did not hear his reply, as just then they were joined by some more of their friends, among them Melissa, Catherine, and Philip Chetwode. Although Shaldon paused for long enough to greet the new-comers civilly, Cynthia determinedly kept him in conversation with herself while the rest chatted together. To her shame, Helen found herself attempting to over-hear what was passing between these two, instead of concentrating on the general conversation. She took herself sharply to task; but try as she would to disengage her attention from them, it kept slipping back like a wandering sheep. The temptation was all the stronger because she was standing next to them in the group, in a much better position for overhearing than anyone else.

She told herself that their conversation could scarcely be considered truly private, as it was taking place among a group of other people; nevertheless she felt annoyed with herself for wishing to eavesdrop at all. She had almost conquered her weakness and was at last paying attention to the general discourse, when a question of Cynthia's carried clearly to her ears and riveted her attention again.

"Have you some particular interest in the Whitsun Fair at Greenwich?" Cynthia demanded of Shaldon.

"Not a particle," he replied, laughing. "Why do you suppose that I should, ma'am?"

"Oh, something that I heard recently." Her tone was careless. "Something that made me suppose you might be going there—or perhaps it was more that something concerning you might be taking place there," she corrected herself.

"Indeed? Your information sounds delightfully vague, not to say improbable. May I enquire as to its source?"

"Oh, I forget. No, come to think of it," she went on, in what Helen recognised as a malicious tone, "it was something said by my father's secretary. Most likely he meant nothing by it, but my curiosity was stirred sufficiently to put the question to you."

"Durrant, eh?" He sounded alert.

"Why, yes, he's my father's secretary. You know that, sir."

"H'm. Intriguing. What precisely did he say?"

"Oh, if you want me to be precise, I'm quite unable to satisfy your curiosity, I fear. I wasn't paying much attention at the time."

"Perhaps I should ask him about it myself."

"No, I beg you will not!" Cynthia sounded alarmed. "You see, I overheard the remark quite by chance, and possibly I ought not to have been listening. It sounded odd, and you must know how I'm always intrigued by oddities! Promise me you won't say anything to him. That would be to betray me, and I'm sure you could never be so unfeeling!"

He promised readily enough, though sounding a trifle surprised at her concern, which was somewhat out of character. Although Helen listened unashamedly now, the topic was not mentioned again and the two soon joined in the general conversation.

Helen's share in this was only spasmodic. Her mind kept going over what she had just heard. Durrant again! And still some hint of a sword of Damocles hanging over Viscount Shaldon. This time, even Shaldon himself had seemed to be taking some interest. Indeed, had not Cynthia put him off with her plea of betrayal, he sounded as if he might have approached Durrant for an explanation. But how in the world, she wondered, did *Greenwich Fair* come into this?

At intervals throughout the evening she kept revolving the puzzle in her mind, but without arriving at any kind of solution. Henry Lydney, who as usual kept close to her side, at last commented on her abstraction.

"Do you find this party tiresome, Miss Somerby? Or is it—I can only hope it is not!—my company which bores you?"

He posed the question in a half-jesting, half-serious way.

354

"Oh, no, certainly not!" She tried to infuse a little more animation into her manner. "I am enjoying myself prodigiously! If I seem a trifle thoughtful, it's only because"—she looked about her, improvising swiftly—"I've noticed another young lady in the room wearing almost the exact counterpart of this gown I have on. It's too provoking!"

"Where is she, ma'am?"

Helen inclined her head in the direction of a nearby group. His glance found the offender, a plain girl who lacked Helen's trim figure, but who was nevertheless wearing a very similar gown of blue silk, low necked and with the full skirt finished in a flounce.

His eyes came back to his companion, studying appreciatively the effect of pale blue against a fair skin and the honey-coloured hair, which tonight she wore piled high on her head with curls hanging loosely at the back. Those warm hazel eyes were bewitching, he thought, with a sudden leap of his pulse. Of late, he had found them more and more disturbing.

"Since you say it is similar, ma'am, I must take your word for it, yet I defy anyone else to notice that. You look quite differently in it—you look enchanting."

Under his intent gaze, she blushed a little.

"Thank you," she said, in an embarrassed tone, "but I did not mean to fish for compliments."

"There's no need. I cannot help but pay you due homage."

"You know to a nicety, sir, how to turn a pretty speech," she said, attempting to introduce a lighter note. "Shall we join Miss Chetwode and her brother? I think supper is about to be served."

He acquiesced, realising quite well that although she was ready to join him in a little light nonsense, she had no intention of allowing their relationship to take on a more serious tone. Was not this exactly what he himself wanted? And yet there were times when that sweet face haunted him . . .

Supper was an informal affair, with all the guests seating themselves more or less at random. Both Helen and Henry Lydney felt that a brief separation might

355

be of mutual benefit at present, so for once they sat apart. Helen took a chair next to Melissa; when she glanced round to see who her other neighbour might be, she was somewhat surprised to see Shaldon there. For some time his attention was claimed by those seated on his other side, but eventually he turned to her and some general remarks passed between them.

"I was with James the other day," he said presently, in a lowered tone, "and he confided to me his aspirations concerning your friend. Not surprisingly, he was a trifle cast down. I only wish I could see some way to assist him, but there seems little hope of that at present. Later on, when he has set up in practice, his friends may be able to put some wealthy patients in his way—though I needn't tell you that it would have to be done with the utmost address!"

"Yes, it certainly would, but you are very good to think of it. My friend is cast down, too. They must wait six months at least, and that seems an age to poor Melissa—as indeed, it would to me."

"Is that a hypothetical statement, or are you in fact seriously thinking of becoming engaged yourself?"

His drawling tone belied the sharpness of his glance. She met it steadily, laughing.

"Goodness, no! I do not think seriously of anything for two minutes together here in London. No doubt it's monstrous of me, but I seem wholly given over to pleasure and the vanities of the world!"

"That I don't believe. I fancy I know you too well."

"How should you? Our acquaintance is very recent."

"Nonsense! It goes back to our childhood."

"There is a great deal of difference, Lord Shaldon, between a child and a woman," she said, with assumed dignity.

"A most gratifying difference," he replied, with a frankly admiring glance that made her look away for a moment. "But, you know, I think it is mostly on the outside."

"That's to say you consider me still immature," she protested, smiling.

"It's to say that I find you unspoilt," he amended. "There, even you can't quarrel with that."

"No, indeed. Mama always said that you have considerable address," she retorted.

"Your game, I think, ma'am," he said, laughing. "But I'll concede it gladly if we're to be friends again. We are, I trust?"

"Of course, if you promise to refrain from acting as my mentor," she said, warningly. Then, in a more sober manner, "May I ask you a question?"

He looked at her searchingly, but his tone was bland as he replied, "Of course."

"Well, I'm not perfectly certain if I should have listened while you and Cynthia were talking together just now, before supper," she began, apologetically, "but it was difficult to avoid hearing what was said, as I was standing so close to you both."

"I absolve you," he answered quickly, a twinkle in his eye. "But what is the question?"

"I heard her say that Durrant had mentioned your name in some connection with Greenwich Fair, of all things. Do you mean to go there on Whitsun Monday to see what it is all about?"

"Dear me"—the twinkle spread to an amused smile—"you do take a keen interest in that man's sayings and doings, don't you?"

"You know very well why! I believe he means you some harm, one way or another. I couldn't manage to persuade you to persevere in discovering the truth from your father, but at least you must see that a visit to the Fair might throw some light on the matter!"

"Did you chance to hear all that Miss Lydney had to say on that subject?"

"Most of it, I think."

"Then you'll realise how nebulous it was. Although," he added, frowning, "I must admit that I'm becoming somewhat intrigued by the subject myself. The obvious course would be to tackle Durrant—but again you may have heard that I was obliged to promise Miss Lydney not to do that."

She nodded. "But you will go?" she persisted, eagerly.

He pondered for a moment. "I think perhaps I may, if only to satisfy you," he replied at last, laughing.

"Oh, how I wish I could go with you!"

"I daresay, but you could not," he said decidedly.

"I suppose it would not be considered proper for you to escort me there," she said, thoughtfully. "Although you might drive me in the Park without occasioning remark—Mr. Lydney has often done so."

"So I have observed."

"I don't perceive any difference, but I suppose one must conform to the conventions. But what if James were to take me?"

"He wouldn't. Really, ma'am, you do have the most ramshackle notions! A fairground is no fit place for any gently reared female."

"Is it so bad? I thought it might be fun, with swings and merry-go-rounds and all manner of colourful sideshows—"

"And a vulgar, jostling crowd milling about, with pickpockets and other malefactors mingling among 'em," he interrupted ruthlessly. "No, you can put that notion right out of your head!"

Helen straightway determined that she would not, but she was wiser than to say so.

"Well, if you do go—and I hope you will, for I'm certain it will be in your interest—perhaps you'll be good enough to remember your promise to me and tell me afterwards what you have discovered there?"

"Of course I'll do that, but I must warn you that I haven't any great expectation of discovering anything to the purpose. All these rumours which reach me of Durrant's sayings and doings seem to point only one way—that the fellow has windmills in his head!"

"You think perhaps he may have become unhinged?" she asked, doubtfully.

He was rather amused to see that she had taken his remark seriously for the moment.

"Let us say that I can think of no other rational explanation for his behaviour. At first, I must admit that I thought you were indulging your fancy, building a romance worthy of Mrs. Radcliffe—"

"I know that, and it was too bad of you!" she interrupted indignantly.

"But later," he continued, ignoring this, "when Lord Lydney dropped me a hint of trouble, I was disposed to think there must be something in it. And now it seems that friend Durrant has been uttering further mysterious pronouncements, the very content of which can only suggest an unbalanced mind. Greenwich Fair, indeed! Good God, what on earth can the activities of a fairground have to do with me? I shall certainly go, but only in the expectation of seeing Durrant carried off in a strait jacket, if in fact he does attend!"

"Oh, dear!" Helen seemed much struck by this. "Do you really suppose that could be the explanation? Perhaps he's suffering from the same malady that afflicts our poor King! James tells me the doctors are puzzled to account for the Royal disorder and have tried everything to cure it, but without success. I've never really liked Durrant, you know, but I wouldn't care to see him so stricken down."

She glanced at his face, and saw that he was hard put to it not to laugh.

"Oh, you are roasting me!" she exclaimed indignantly. "You are the most odious person!"

"Well, if he ain't mad," he said, laughing, "you may depend he has some crafty scheme afoot."

"Why, so I told you from the first, and you only laughed at me!"

"That was very reprehensible, and I do sincerely beg your pardon. I can only urge in my defence that it did appear to be a laughing matter at that time. Now, however, with hints and hearsay buzzing about me like gnats, I intend to make some attempt to get to the bottom of it, once for all. Whit Monday is next week. I'll go to this Fair, and if I draw a blank there, I'll see what light my father can throw on the business. He should have returned from Bath by this. There, does that satisfy you?"

"Oh, yes, but you will tell me all about it, won't you, should you discover anything?"

He laughed. "Yes, Miss Curiosity, I promise you that. I wouldn't put it past you to come prying yourself, should I fail you!"

She joined in his laughter, but made no other answer for fear of betraying herself. For she had now quite decided that by hook or by crook she was going to Greenwich Fair herself.

Chapter XXX

FOR SEVERAL DAYS, it seemed an insoluble problem. Since she could look for no assistance from either Shaldon or her own brother—for she knew perfectly well that Shaldon had judged James's reactions to the scheme correctly—who was left to escort her to the Fair? The impropriety of asking either Mr. Lydney or Mr. Chetwode to perform this office struck her more forcibly than when she had begged Shaldon to take her; besides, she was certain they would never agree to the proposition either.

Then she must go alone.

This important decision failed to solve her problem. She could think of no way to secure a whole day away from Lady Chetwode's protection that did not involve her in the telling of elaborate lies to one who had shown her so much kindness. Helen's straightforward nature revolted from such a course, and she almost gave up the scheme.

It was then that she remembered Uncle Charles.

Captain Charles Paxton was the elder brother of Helen's mother, a Naval Captain on half pay since the cessation of the war with France. He was a bachelor of a lively disposition, and had always been particularly fond of Helen, whom he declared was exactly like her mother had been at the same age.

"Do try and find time to visit him with James," Amanda Somerby had urged her daughter on parting. "He lives in Blackheath, on the other side of the Thames. Papa will show you the place on the map, and I'll give you his precise direction. I've written to tell him when you'll be in Town, but he's not a man for making social calls. Moreover, he isn't acquainted with the Chetwodes, so I daresay the first move will have to come from you."

Helen had promised readily, for Uncle Charlie was a firm favourite; but in the rush of engagements which awaited her in Town, there had been no time yet to pay the visit. She hastened to consult a map in the library, and confirmed that Uncle Charlie's house in Blackheath was no distance at all from Greenwich Park, where she had learnt the Fair was held. Delighted, she at once sought Lady Chetwode's permission to make the visit on Whit Monday, it then being Sunday.

Lady Chetwode could not object, but she did demur. It was very proper that Helen should pay a visit to her Uncle, but would it not be wiser to write first and find out which day was convenient to him?

"And it would be so much nicer, too, if you could arrange for your brother to accompany you," she added.

Helen felt crestfallen, but did not allow this to appear.

"Oh, no, Uncle Charlie is very easy, ma'am. Besides, tomorrow is the only day for ages when we have no other engagements. I don't know when I can promise otherwise."

361

Her persistence won the argument, and it was arranged that Helen should go on the following day in the Chetwodes' coach, accompanied by her maid. Only Melissa said darkly, when they were in private, that she was sure Helen was up to something; an accusation that was laughed off a trifle self-consciously.

Captain Paxton occupied a house in the Paragon, an elegant crescent of moderate sized houses linked by Doric arcades which unified the design. The crescent had originally been built to provide suitable accommodation for either serving or retired naval officers, and there were still many such among the Captain's neighbours. Helen trembled a little as she raised her hand to the knocker, for so much depended upon finding Uncle Charles at home.

Her fears soon subsided as a manservant admitted her and showed her into the drawing room, while her maid was offered a seat in the hall. A quick step on the threshold, a "God bless my soul!" and Uncle Charles had enveloped her in a bearlike hug.

"God bless my soul!" he exclaimed again, a wide grin spreading over his tanned, lively face. "Little Nelly! And where's that rascal of a brother of yours, eh?"

"At the hospital, as far as I know, Uncle," she said, kissing him on both cheeks.

"Couldn't get away from duty, what? He'll be finished there soon, though—six months, wasn't it? Went there in October, as I recall, so he should've finished at the end of last month. What's keeping him on, eh?"

"He's waiting for his examination by the Board of the Society of Apothecaries. I think it's to be in a few weeks' time."

"Anchor's aweigh then, what?"

Helen considered this for a moment. "If that means he'll be ready to begin on his partnership with Dr. Gillies at Paddington, I suppose so," she conceded.

"Should have gone into the Navy as a sawbones— quicker to get on there. Told y'father so at the time, but he preferred his own road. Quite right. A man should make his own decisions. Well, and how many beaux have you got dangling on a string, young lady? Sit down, sit down, and I'll get some wine. No, of course, not wine—what is it you females take? Ratafia? Pernicious stuff—don't think we've any in the house, but soon remedy that. Davey!"

The final word was uttered in a bellow and brought the manservant into the room at the double. He stood to attention as if on the quarterdeck.

"Ratafia for the lady," snapped the Captain.

"I don't think, sir—"

"Not paid to think, are you? If there ain't any, get some. Understood?"

"Ay, ay, Cap'n."

Helen interrupted just as the man turned smartly on his heel to leave.

"No, no, not for me—I detest it, too. Well, if you insist, I'll take a glass of lemonade instead."

As this seemed to pose no problems in the household, Helen was soon supplied with it. She chatted vivaciously away for the next quarter of an hour on family matters, until she chanced to notice the Captain glancing surreptitiously at the clock on the mantelshelf.

"Oh, I beg your pardon, Uncle, I had not thought. Do you happen to be doing anything particular today?"

"Matter of fact," he admitted, "I had arranged to go and see a mill—prize fight, boxing, y'know—with a neighbour of mine. He was to call for me presently —but that's no matter, I'll send a signal to say I'm not available. Not every day a pretty girl calls on me, what?"

"Pray don't put off your engagement on my account, because I can't stay long myself. There's just one thing, though, Uncle Charlie—a favour I've to ask of you—"

"Ask away."

"Well, it's this."

She hesitated, not quite knowing how to proceed. It was useless to suppose that Uncle Charles, even though he did happen to be the least stuffy man in the world, would look with favour on her intended project; yet she could not bring herself to deceive him.

"I'm waiting to hear, child," he prompted her.

"Oh, dear! Will you try to be most angelically understanding?" Her soft hazel eyes looked pleadingly into his. "Lady Chetwode supposed that I would be spending the whole day with you, and doesn't expect me back before five o'clock. But in fact—in fact—"

She faltered and broke down before his shrewd look.

"In fact you're off somewhere you've no business to be, eh, my girl? And you want to use me as a smoke screen, that it?"

She nodded, blushing.

"Is there a man in this?" he demanded, fiercely.

"No! It's nothing of that kind, I assure you—only —only a—a prank of which she wouldn't approve. But I *must* go. It's very important. I can't tell you now, but I will later—truly!"

"A prank, eh? A bit old for that, ain't you? And what would your Mama say to it, I wonder? D'you suppose she'd allow you to do whatever it is?"

"Well—well, no, I don't suppose she'd like it," Helen admitted, honestly. "But I think she'd do it herself, in my place, all the same."

He gave a short laugh. "Very likely! Amanda was always a resty piece, full of larks. Well, I'm not the man to spoil anyone's fun, but see here, Niece, I must be sure that you'll come to no harm in this. Why, your Ma would have my blood if I let anything happen to you, make no mistake." He took her by the shoulders, looking long and earnestly into her face. "D'you swear there's no man at the bottom of this? No clandestine meetings, or anything of that kind? Answer truthfully, now!"

She gave him back look for look as she assured him of his. He appeared satisfied, for he nodded.

"Ay, well, no doubt I'm a fool, but I'll trust you. Always found you a truthful child, and folks don't change in that way. One thing, though, you must be back here by three o'clock from wherever it is you're

364

going. That's an order. It gives you three and a half hours, and that's quite long enough. If you're not here by then, b'God, I'll send out a search party. Don't care to tell me whereabouts you'll be, I suppose?" She shook her head apologetically. "Very well, I won't press you, but just have a care. Bring your maid, did you?"

Helen nodded.

"You won't want her, so I'll give her sailing orders back to Cavendish Square. I'll be back here before three o'clock, and when you turn up—and you'd better not be late, my girl!—I'll drive you home myself. Understood?"

Helen flung herself into his arms. "Oh, Uncle Charlie, you are the dearest, best, most understanding of uncles in the whole, wide world!"

"Ay, and the greatest fool," he retorted, trying not to look pleased. "Now, can I drop you off anywhere, or am I to leave you to your own devices? I hear my neighbour's knock at the door, so I must be off in a minute."

Helen insisted that she would take her own way when she had tidied herself up a little, and with a final admonition to take care, the Captain left her alone.

"Roll up now, roll up now!" bawled the showman. "Come on, ladies and gents, where else can ye see lovely ladies like them?" He indicated a trio of females clad in off-white garments decorated with tarnished spangles and with their faces set in the performer's fixed smile. "Lovely ladies a-dancin' for ye, followed by a play so full o' horrors that ye'll all be clingin' to yer seats, an' all for a penny! Only a penny! Where else, I say, can ye get such good value for money? Roll up, now. Step inside. Only a few seats left, but a good view from every one! Roll up."

"Now, 'ere's a game as'll make ye laugh," shouted a man in charge of a round board on which stood three thimbles and a pea. He manipulated the thimbles dexterously until the pea was covered. "Now, sir, what d'ye say, sir?" addressing a member of the gaping crowd which stood about him. "Would ye like to make a guess which o' them thimbles covers the pea? I'll wager ye anything from sixpence to a 'alf sovereign as ye can't guess right. C'mon, sir, it's a bit o' sport, an' by the look o' ye, ye're a sportin' cove. What d'ye say?"

The young man being addressed felt himself nudged in the ribs by a pretty girl at his side.

"Go on, then, Jack," she said, encouragingly. "Show a bit o' holiday spirit!"

Thus adjured, the young man sheepishly proffered sixpence to the showman, then bent over the board trying to decide which thimble to choose. After listening to several shouts from the crowd offering conflicting advice, he finally picked one up, as gingerly as if he expected it to bite. Predictably, it was the wrong thimble.

"Oh, 'ard luck, sir!" commiserated the showman, who had long since pocketed the loser's sixpence. "Care to 'ave another try? The luck can't always desert ye. Ye only need to watch, see? One, two, three, three, two, one, an' it's gorn! Now where is it? C'mon, sir, never day die. 'Ave another go!"

Rowland Carlton, watching apathetically from the fringes of the crowd, placed an arm about Phyllis to steer her onwards.

"Might have a go at that lay," he said, dubiously. "What d' you reckon, Phyl? I daresay I could learn to do it after a bit. Trouble is, there's not much to be made out o' it—doubt if it's a living."

"Ye couldn't set up 'ere, anyways," she reminded him, "not against 'im." She indicated the glib showman with a movement of her head. "They'd all be out for yer blood, if ye tried that on."

"Gawd knows what I'm to do, then," he said, gloomily. "Astley's finished weeks agone, and all I've got 'ere so far was two shillings for playing the back legs o' a bleedin' 'orse. And naught in view whatsoever. Leastways—"

"What?" She uttered the word sharply, perceiving that he was weighing some possibility in his mind.

366

"Oh, naught," he answered, after a lengthy pause. "Anyways, you're all right for the moment, fixed up with that circus troupe for the rest o' the summer. No tellin' where it might lead, either. That feller's taken a shine to ye, an' if ye plays your cards right—"

She clung to him, rubbing her face against his sleeve. "I want naught to do with 'im. You're my man, Rowly. Come with me. At a pinch we can make the money stretch for both o' us, and mebbe ye'll find something while we're on tour. There's Bartholomew Fair in August, too—"

"Three months off," he scoffed. "Living 'and to mouth until then, just on the off chance. Besides, that feller Pollock wouldn't 'ave me around to spoil 'is chances with you, don't ye think it. 'E'd soon give me the push. Don't 'ardly blame 'im. I'd do the same in 'is shoes. Wish I was in 'is shoes, all the same," he added regretfully.

"If only we'd some money," sighed Phyllis, as they made their way with some difficulty through the excited, jostling crowd. "We could set up our own troupe, with you in the lead, Rowly, an' me doin' my act on horseback!"

"Ay, if only pigs could fly," he answered sardonically. "Look, Phyl, ye'd best get back to the caravan now to get changed for yer act. I'll just take a turn or two in the Park, an' see ye later."

Helen had never seen anything like Greenwich Fair. A hackney hired outside her Uncle's house had dropped her right in the thick of it, and the noise was deafening. Girls screamed; boys shouted in excitement; vendors bellowed their wares or rang strident bells to save overstrained voices; monkeys jabbered as they swung from chains tethered to their owners' wrists; a mangy lion in a cage gave vent to the occasional half-hearted roar; while dogs barked and scampered about, adding yet another hazard to the difficulty of negotiating a safe passage through the dense crowd, all pushing in contrary directions with

367

the fixed determination not to yield an inch to those who wished to go another way.

She tried hard to keep on the edges of the crowds about the various stalls and sideshows, hoping by this means to make some progress along the road; but her lively curiosity kept getting caught by first one spectacle and then another, so that she soon found herself jammed tight among a mass of people, unable to budge.

Fortunately she was not at present dressed in a style to stand out from the rest of the crowd. She had prudently borrowed a plain gown of cheap material and a bonnet to match from the young housemaid whose duty it was to clean her bedchamber. Martha had a great admiration for Helen, and had been only too eager to make the loan, promising secrecy for what she understood was some kind of harmless prank. Helen had taken the borrowed clothes with her to her Uncle's house and changed into them after he had left her alone. Thus equipped, she felt certain of escaping unwelcome notice.

She almost forgot her real purpose in coming, so entranced was she by the lively scenes about her. She would have liked to try her luck at the pea and thimble game, even though she realised it was a take-in; but she soon observed that no other females were taking part in this sport, so judged it wiser to refrain. Instead, she watched the others at it until the spectacle began to pall for those members of the crowd who were blocking her exit, and then she moved away with them to find some fresh entertainment.

She found herself standing before the play booth, and before long she yielded to the impulse to tender her penny and go inside the stuffy tent to sit upon a narrow wooden bench crammed tightly with London's humbler, but on the whole respectable, citizens. Nobody took the slightest notice of her; the fact that she was an unescorted, unchaperoned young female did not seem to matter here in the slightest. She drew in her breath with excitement, feeling an unaccustomed sense of freedom. How pleasant it was to be accountable to no one for her actions, to be able to come and go as she chose and to share in the delights and diversions of these simple, unsophisticated people! At this point in her thoughts, one of the men seated alongside her wiped his nose on his sleeve. She grimaced. Well, perhaps they were something lacking in social graces; but, after all, they had never been taught any better. She fixed her attention on the stage.

The spangled ladies danced for a while amid suitable encouragement from the male section of the audience and indignant protests from their female escorts of "For shame, Ted!" or "Hold your tongue, do!" Then the play began, a melodrama in which a wicked baron—whose costume and social manners were quite unlike those of any of his Society counterparts with whom Helen was acquainted, although she would not have cared to vouch for any difference in character—gave an extremely bad time to a deserving poor family, one member of which was a beautiful young girl. The lovely creature was within only a moment of being ravished by the villain amid the jeers, catcalls, and cascade of orange peel and banana skin contributed by the excited audience, when she was saved in the nick of time by the hero of the piece, a well set-up young man who kept a lion as a pet. This noble beast of the jungle might have appeared unconvincing to more critical eyes than those of the present audience, for it sagged in the middle, and its front and back legs did not move in unison; but they had paid their pennies and by this time were well into the spirit of the piece. They cheered loudly as the lion fell upon the wicked baron and the curtain closed waveringly upon the doubtless bloody scene which ensued.

With one accord, they all rose and began pushing towards the exit, Helen helplessly crushed in among them. She grabbed at her bonnet just in time to prevent it from being swept off into the crowd, and felt her hair sliding down onto her neck as the pins became loosened. Her feelings of enjoyment began to be replaced by slight panic; at that moment she would have been glad of a strong male arm to protect her

369

from the buffeting of the mob about her. Borne along helplessly in this way, she presently found herself outside the booth and being steered in the direction of the Park.

Once inside the Park the crowd was able to disperse a little to permit her some breathing space; although here, too, masses of people were congregated. All kinds of sports and games were in progress among the various groups scattered about the grass. One in particular seemed to be causing great merriment; and as soon as she could move about freely, Helen walked over to watch it. There were three steep slopes in the Park, one of these leading up to the Royal Observatory building, which had been constructed in the seventeenth century on the foundations of a much older castle. The sport was for all the young men to drag their protesting female friends almost to the top of this hill; then when all the participants were lined up ready, a signal was given for them to make the descent, each male hurrying his lady down at breakneck pace. It was all very rowdy and improper, for frequently the girls fell and finished the descent by rolling over and over with a most immodest display of undergarments. Helen smiled as she watched, however; in spite of the tumbles, they all seemed to be enjoying themselves like small children at play.

"Like to have a go? Come on!"

Absorbed in watching, she had failed to notice anyone approach her. She now felt her hand seized as she was dragged forward towards the hill at an unseemly rate.

"Oh, no, no!"

She dug her heels into the soft turf, attempting to withstand the sudden onward rush. Her captor paused for a moment as she looked up into his face with frantic appeal.

Her expression changed momentarily as she stared hard at him. He was a tall, well built man in his mid twenties, with auburn hair and a face which she recognised instantly. He was the man whom she had seen on two previous occasions with Durrant.

"Why d' ye stare so? Ain't afeard of me, are ye? I'll do ye no 'arm. C'mon, now. I've seen ye watchin' the others and I can tell ye're longin' to have a go. Come on, it's rare sport, I promise ye!"

So saying, he took a fresh grip on Helen's hand and began to drag her onwards, laughing loudly at all her indignant protests. She did her best to oppose him, but her strength was no match for his.

The panic which she had begun to feel in the crowded play booth now overtook her more strongly. She had enjoyed watching the populace at play, but she was of no mind to take part in a romp such as this. Shaldon had been right in saying that it was a ramshackle notion to consider setting aside the proprieties to the extent of coming to such a place, and especially unattended. And what had she hoped to learn from it, in any event? True, this man was here, and he was connected in some way with Durrant; but at the moment, her only desire was to get away from him as far as she could. If only she had been wise enough to curb her wretched curiosity! She might well have left it to Shaldon to investigate whatever there was in his interest to discover at the Fair—if, indeed, there was anything—and herself remained safely at home. Shaldon had assured her that he intended to come here today. Hot on the heels of this thought followed a yet more unnerving one; what if either Shaldon or Durrant were to appear now, and see her in this undignified fix?

While these incoherent thoughts rushed through her mind, her captor continued to pull her relentlessly, laughingly, up the first gentle rise of the hill, although she opposed him every step of the way with all the strength at her command.

All at once, their progress was halted by a flying female form which flung itself upon the man and dealt him a stinging slap across the face.

"Let this 'ussy be, ye blackguard, will ye?" bawled the newcomer, a pretty girl whose hostile face seemed to Helen vaguely familiar. "As for ye, wench, keep off

371

my man and get one o' yer own, or I'll scratch yer eyes out, an' so I warns ye!"

Helen backed a pace, fearing attack.

"I—I don't want him," she said, breathlessly. "He seized upon me, and I'd no choice but to go with him. Pray believe me, do!"

To her relief, the girl seemed ready to credit this. Ignoring Helen, she turned on the man with a flood of angry words. Helen at once seized her opportunity and ran off, leaving them to their lovers' quarrel.

Because of the crowds thronging the Park, she did not get very far towards the gates before she felt her arm seized and turned to find the girl once more confronting her. Her heart sank; was she now to become involved in a vulgar brawl?

But to her surprise, the girl spoke propitiatingly.

"I'm sorry if I was sharp, Miss. I could see it weren't nohow yer fault. Ye was truly doin' yer best to get away from 'im, not shammin' it fer fun, like the other wenches. But Rowly's my man, see, an' it fair makes me mad to see 'im goin' after other wenches, which 'e does soon enough if 'e gets the chance, worse luck!"

Helen gave her a wavering smile. "I'm sorry it occurred, but it was all a misunderstanding. I don't think your—your friend meant any harm, either. He truly thought I wished to take part in the game. I trust you've forgiven him and made up your quarrel."

She nodded and was about to turn away, but the girl addressed her.

"Ye talk like ye was gentle born, Miss. Ye don't seem to belong 'ere. Be ye abigail to some lady, belike?"

"Something of that nature," hedged Helen. "Well, good-bye—er—"

"Phyllis is me name," supplied the other, helpfully.

"Oh. And is the—that is to say, was that your husband?" asked Helen, curiosity once more getting the better of discretion, which urged a speedy retreat from the scene.

Phyllis laughed and shook her head. "Not yet. One day, p'raps, if I can keep 'im long enough."

"I see. Well, I hope matters will turn out to your advantage, Phyllis."

She was about to go, when a sudden realisation of her extremely dishevelled condition made her pause to ask if Phyllis knew of any respectable place where she might go to make herself more presentable.

"Ye can come to my caravan and welcome," offered the girl, generously. " 'Bain't much o' a place, but it'll be better nor the taverns on a Fair day for the likes o' ye."

Judging by what she had seen of the tipsy crowds frequenting the taverns in the vicinity of the Fair, Helen was bound to agree. She followed Phyllis out of the Park. With difficulty they made their way along the crowded streets beyond until they reached an open space where several caravans stood. Phyllis led the way to one of these, gaily painted in red and green but somewhat spattered with mud. The place was deserted at present.

The interior of the caravan was dingy and depressing. Two narrow shelves a few feet from the floor extended the full length on either side; these evidently served as beds, for there were rugs and pillows flung down upon them amid a jumble of clothing and other personal possessions. A cupboard on one wall and a spotted mirror hung askew on the other comprised the rest of the furnishings. A small window beside the door was covered by a grimy curtain and afforded little light.

Helen could not repress a grimace of distaste as she climbed into this unprepossessing shelter, but fortunately she altered her expression quickly so that it escaped Phyllis's notice.

"Mebbe ye'd like to wash yer 'ands," suggested her hostess, reaching under one of the shelves for a tin bowl.

"Oh—no, thank you," said Helen, hastily. "If I might just put up my hair again before your mirror and replace my bonnet, that will do very nicely."

She produced a comb from her reticule. Phyllis watched incuriously for a few moments, then moved to the window and drew aside the curtain a fraction to look out.

Helen had just finished pinning up her hair neatly again when Phyllis uttered an exclamation which made her turn away from the mirror.

"What is it?" Helen asked.

"Rowly's with that swell cove again. I saw 'im at Astley's. Mebbe 'e's come with a job for Rowly this time."

This information brought Helen in a flash to the other girl's side. Two men were standing in earnest conversation only a short distance away, beside one of the now deserted caravans. The man whom Phyllis called Rowly was one; the other, as Helen had suspected, was Durrant.

"What kind of job?" she asked, brusquely.

"I dunno, though it'd be somethink in Rowly's line, I reckon, somethink to do wi' fairground work. But 'e was cagey when I asked 'im about it afore—said 'e was mistook and the cove 'ad nothink for 'im. I knew 'e was lyin', though—got the feelin' somethink 'ad scared 'im, and 'e didn't want to talk about it. I knows Rowly."

Helen watched the men for a few moments longer while she digested this information in silence.

"Your friend isn't likely to bring that man in here, is he?" she asked in sudden alarm, moving away from the window and snatching up her bonnet.

"Wot's yer worry?" replied Phyllis, still watching. "Anyways, they're movin' off now towards the Park."

She released the curtain and turned to face Helen.

"Ye knew that cove, didn't ye?" she accused. "I could tell from the way ye looked at 'im."

Helen nodded. "Yes, and he must not see me here!"

"Why not?"

"Because—oh, because I'm not supposed to be here, and—and he would tell—"

"Peach on yer, would 'e?" said Phyllis, knowingly. "Come out on the sly, 'ave ye? Well, it's none o' my

374

business, and I'm not one to give the game away, specially when I takes a fancy to a body, as I 'ave to ye. Who is 'e, though?"

Helen thought rapidly. It was possible that this girl might be in a better position to unravel the mystery of Durrant's actions than either Shaldon or herself; but obviously it would be unwise to tell her too much.

"His name doesn't matter, but he's employed by —by someone of influence. Now, listen. Will you do something for me, something that may be of benefit to us both? If you do chance to learn what the business may be between him and your friend, would you acquaint me with it?"

"Think I'd spy on Rowly, do ye? What d'ye take me for?" Phyllis said, fiercely. "What's yer game?"

"You'd be doing him a service. I have reason to believe that this man may be trying to involve him in something which could have unpleasant consequences for your friend."

Helen threw all the conviction she could muster into this statement, which was mere intuition on her part. She saw that Phyllis was struck by it, and hastened to press home her advantage.

"You said yourself that your friend seemed afraid of something. You would not wish him to get into serious trouble."

"Gawd, no!" Phyllis was alarmed now. "If that's the way o' it, yon cove can go to the devil with 'is job! Tell me where to find ye, and if I do get anythink out o' Rowly, I'll let ye know. But mind this"—she wagged a menacing finger in Helen's face—"if any 'arm comes to 'im, I'll make ye suffer, if I 'angs for it!"

Helen repeated her assurances before directing Phyllis to the house in Cavendish Square and bidding her ask first for Martha. There would be less difficulty for a girl like Phyllis to obtain access to one of the housemaids, and Helen intended to prepare Martha for the visit.

This business concluded, the two parted with mutual goodwill, Phyllis remaining in the caravan to change for her act, while Helen left cautiously, alert for any sign of Bertram Durrant.

When she managed to gain the crowded Park without encountering him, she breathed more easily. Her one thought now was to return to her Uncle's house unrecognised, for she could see no useful purpose in remaining. Although she had learnt very little by her hazardous visit, at least she had gained an ally who might help her to the required information. Shaldon himself could have achieved no more, she thought triumphantly, unless he had encountered Durrant and interrogated him. And this seemed scarcely likely, since he would feel bound to honour his promise to Cynthia. Really, a gentleman's sense of honour was an extremely difficult matter for a mere female mind to comprehend! It was more probable that he had decided against coming here at all, and intended to seek a solution to the mystery from the Earl, as she had urged him to do all along.

With these thoughts in her mind, she made her way as quickly as possible through the throng, avoiding the worst crushes wherever she could, but frequently finding herself at a standstill for several minutes. She had almost won past the last of the stalls lining the road, beyond which there was a hackney carriage stand, when she inadvertently collided with a small boy carrying a balloon. There was a loud pop, followed by an even louder howl from the child, and all eyes were at once turned in her direction.

"Oh, dear, I'm so sorry," she said, in her clear voice. "You must allow me to buy you another."

She unfastened her reticule and was about to proffer some money to the child under the approving gaze of everyone thereabouts, when a familiar voice spoke close beside her.

"No," said Shaldon, in a grim tone. "You must allow me."

He gave the child a coin, then took her arm in a relentless grasp, steering her out into the open road, away from the crowds.

"Where is your brother?" he demanded, once they stood alone.

She shook her head timidly. "He's—not here."

"I'm not surprised. I scarcely thought he would bring you on such an outing. Who has been so misguided as to escort you here?"

His tone was now even harsher, and she quailed slightly.

"No—no one, sir. You see, I—"

"You came *alone?*" he asked, incredulously. "Upon my word, ma'am, if you're to get up to such wild starts, it's high time you were returned to the protection of your own family! And what tale did you concoct for Lady Chetwode's benefit, pray? She cannot have been a willing party to this."

She fired up at that. "I did *not* lie to her! She gave permission for me to visit Mama's brother, my Uncle Charles, who lives not far from here in Blackheath. She sent me in the carriage, with my maid. I had hoped to persuade Uncle to bring me to the Fair, for he's not in the least stuffy, like some people"—here she glared at him—"but he mentioned another engagement, before I could ask. So I remained with him until he was obliged to leave for his engagement, and then afterwards I came here."

"He must be a dashed loose screw if he didn't make sure you were safely installed in Lady Chetwode's carriage before he parted from you," Shaldon remarked, with more frankness than civility. "How did you get over that difficulty, what?"

She explained the matter, albeit resentfully.

"So you see, he is *not* a—what did you say?—a loose screw at all, but as anxious to protect me as anybody, and with more right than some!" she concluded, with another meaning glance. "Only he's more understanding!"

"More easily brought around your thumb, you mean," retorted Shaldon, with another access of frankness. "Well, I suppose I'd better restore you to his care, since you say he intends to escort you himself to Cavendish Square. We must take a hackney, I fear, as

I did not bring my own vehicle this far. Like you, I decided to preserve my incognito. Tell me, where did you acquire those modest garments? You are truly a young lady of infinite resource."

He sounded more amused than angry now, and Helen's indignation subsided as he handed her up inside the hackney which had come instantly at his signal.

"Phaugh!" he exclaimed, waving a handkerchief before his nose. "These vehicles always have the most unpleasant odour, but we shan't be obliged to endure it for long, thank Heavens! And pray what do you intend to tell Captain Paxton in order to redeem your promise to him?"

"Why, I shall tell him all about it. That is, if you've no objection?"

"Not the least in the world, but I hope you won't object to being laughed at. He is certain to think the tale a great piece of nonsense," he warned her.

"But *you* don't think that any longer, do you?" she asked, shrewdly. "And I may as well tell you that I saw Durrant while I was at the Fair. He was with that man again, and what's more, I know now who the man is."

She could see that this information interested him, so she went on to give a carefully expurgated account of her meeting with Phyllis, leaving out the part where Rowland Carlton had attempted to drag her up the hill.

"Certainly Durrant's behaving deuced oddly," he admitted, frowning. "And if that girl's to be believed, he's evidently making some proposition to the man Carlton which scares the fellow. But there's still no evidence to show how all this in any way concerns myself. Unless," he added, with a short laugh, "Durrant is planning to have me assassinated!"

"Oh, no, why should he?" asked Helen, in a shocked tone. "It could not in any way benefit him— but you aren't serious, of course," she added, realising this belatedly.

He laughed again. "No, but you have put your finger on a fact for our possible guidance. Whatever Durrant is about, it will be something to benefit himself. Some shady deal, perhaps? What motives do people have for dubious undertakings? Money, most often—power, perhaps. Durrant would like both, I daresay. But where do I come into the picture? I tell you, N— Miss Somerby, it must be a nonsense!"

They argued the matter back and forth until they reached Captain Paxton's house, but without arriving at any conclusion other than that Shaldon should visit the Earl and see if he could glean any information in that quarter.

Chapter XXXI

TWO DAYS LATER, Shaldon arrived at Alvington Hall. He had delayed going because he was still more than half-convinced that he would be making a fool of himself. The only matter on which his father might be expected to throw any light was Durrant's mysterious errand to Sussex some two months ago. If this had any connection with the Alvington estate, the Earl could not question his son's right to be informed of it. As for the rest of Durrant's activities, curious as these were, Shaldon could not credit that they bore any relevance to family affairs, and therefore did not intend to mention them.

He found his father's health little improved by the visit to Bath. The gouty leg still troubled him, and moreoever he looked frailer than he had done in March; he had shrunk a little in his clothes, and his once handsome face was now that of a man much older than his years. In spite of the lack of family feeling between them Shaldon felt a pang of compassion, and spoke in a gentle tone as he asked after the older man's health.

"I feel devilish, and no better for seeing you," was the unconciliating reply. "But it's as well you've come, for I was about to summon you, anyway."

"Indeed, sir?" Shaldon raised an enquiring eyebrow.

"I've something to tell you," went on the Earl, uncertainly. "The devil of it is, I don't quite know how to make a start. Damned uncomfortable business all round!" he continued, in an aggrieved tone. "And I wish to God I'd never meddled with it in the first place! Can't let it rest now, though—it'll all have to come out, I suppose, and you'll need to know before anyone."

By now, Shaldon was on the alert. So there *was* something amiss with family concerns? He said nothing, but gestured to his father to continue.

"Told you last time you were here not to be so cocksure of yourself, didn't I?" went on the Earl, with a hostile glare. "Well, now you'll see what I meant, my fine fellow! Let me inform you that you are not my heir—nor Viscount Shaldon, come to that!"

For a moment Shaldon sat in stunned silence, staring.

"Good God, are you out of your senses?" he demanded, at last.

"Ay, you'd like to think so, wouldn't you? But when you hear what I have to say, you'll find it's true enough, and your goose is properly cooked, damn you! You've never been aught but trouble to me, Anthony—even your damned name caused trouble with my father, and all because that mother of yours must have her own way."

Shaldon, his face set in grim lines, abruptly halted this flood of recrimination.

"A plain tale, if you please. You say I am neither Viscount Shaldon nor your heir. How so?"

"Because you've an elder half-brother. I married a girl secretly the year before your mother and I were wed. She died giving birth to this child."

Shaldon jumped to his feet. "My God, are you saying that you made a bigamous marriage with my mother?"

The Earl flinched before his son's threatening aspect. "No, no, it's not as bad as that." His tone was now more propitiatory. "Dorinda was dead by then —had been dead for some months. But I'd best tell you the whole."

He began upon the story, making the most of the difficulties of his situation and glossing over his selfishness and moral cowardice in dealing with them. Shaldon, listening for the most part in silence, was easily able to read between the lines. He knew his father well enough. Now and again, he shot out a brief question.

"How did you avoid telling them where you lived?"

"Dorinda was a trusting girl who never asked awkward questions and was content with what I chose to tell her. The mother, Mrs. Lathom, tried to get it out of me, but she was afraid to insist, lest she cause trouble between us."

Shaldon nodded. "But you must have given a domicile for the marriage licence?"

"A false one, yes. No use thinking that invalidates the marriage, for it don't. There was a legal case a few years back—'09, I think it was—where the fellow not only gave a false domicile, but even a false name. The judge declared that marriage legal, and mine was made in my own name. I'll allow it was sometimes tricky to keep the secret, but then I'd a far worse task at home in Alvington, keeping the marriage from my father. A damnable business! When I think what I went through at that time!"

Shaldon made no reply to this; but the contempt in his eyes deepened as the Earl went on to the conclusion of the story.

"I can't tell you what a relief it was to learn that the woman Mrs. Lathom had vanished," he finished. "For some years afterwards I lived in constant dread that she would turn up again, but she never did, thank God! At last I was able to wash my hands of the whole devilish business. Yes, and if you hadn't goaded me into it, I'd never have been such a fool as to stir it all up again now!"

"*I* goad you into it?"

"Yes, damn you! You came here and quarrelled with me two months ago, though you might have known with my poor health I was in no mood to be crossed! Only natural I should fly off the handle and think to teach you a lesson, put you in your place, once for all! So I set about tracing the child of my first marriage. Mind you," he concluded, defensively, "I was pretty well certain the brat was dead. Looked almost gone when I saw it, and that woman said she didn't expect it to survive more than a few days."

"So that's it," said Shaldon. "Sussex—yes, I heard that Durrant had made journeys there on your behalf. And why Durrant, may I ask? Why not the family lawyers?"

"Ned Lydney's idea—thought to keep the business quiet since the child was most likely dead in any case. Too many fingers in the pie when lawyers handle matters—things leak out. Durrant would see to it discreetly, Ned said."

"For a consideration, of course?"

The Earl nodded. "Seat in Parliament, with my influence. Money, too, naturally."

"And paying off an old score," said Shaldon, drily. "Doing well out of it, ain't he? I collect that the child did not die, after all, but is very much alive, and that Durrant has traced him? You'd better tell me about that."

"My God, you take it damned coolly!" exploded the Earl.

"What would you have me do—go into a fit of the vapours? Get on with the story."

"Devilish clever chap, Durrant," continued the Earl, thus prompted. "He wanted to advertise for Mrs. Lathom, but I wouldn't have that; so he went off to Rye to see if he could discover anyone who might know where she'd been bound for when she left there. Took a bit of doing, after six and twenty years, and he drew a blank at first. But he went there a second time and managed to trace the maid who used to help at the cottage. Found out from her that the woman had intended to go to London—to Southwark, in fact."

"But I daresay this female was unable to say precisely whereabouts in Southwark?"

"No. Durrant returned and quartered the area, questioning tradesmen, innkeepers and the like, but without result. Thought he was at a stand. Then he had a brilliant notion. He remembered the ring—"

"What ring?"

"Oh, my gold signet ring with the Stratton poppy and my initial engraved on it. I gave it to Dorinda."

"Surely you showed less than your usual caution over that? They might have traced you by its means."

The Earl flushed at his son's ironic tone. "That's what Ned said, but in fact they never attempted anything of the kind—not sufficiently up to snuff. Naturally, I wouldn't have handed it over voluntarily, though. I was obliged to make use of it for the wedding ceremony, owing to an oversight on my part, and afterwards the poor girl begged to keep it, even though I gave her another wedding ring."

"So how did Durrant make use of this fact in his quest?"

"He had a notice posted in the shop windows of all the pawnbrokers in Southwark and the immediate vicinity, to the effect that a collector would pay highest prices for gold signet rings over twenty years old engraved with the letter *N*. The notices made no mention of the crest, but he informed the pawnbrokers exactly what to look out for. He paid them well for inserting the notice, in addition to offering good commission on any transactions. I tell you, this affair has cost me a pretty penny, all told! Of course, several other rings were brought in, too, and I had to pay for the lot. But it worked. He got the one he was after. The pawnbroker concerned took the name and direction of the man who brought it in, and Durrant interviewed him."

"Ingenious," remarked Shaldon, drily. "But I'm sure

it wouldn't escape Durrant's notice that the man at present in possession of your ring need not necessarily be your long lost offspring?"

"No more it did! Durrant interrogated the fellow thoroughly and the story he told, together with the other proofs in his possession, made his identity certain. He said he was brought up by his grandmother in Southwark, his mother having died at his birth. The grandmother made a second marriage to some drunken brute who knocked the boy about. In order to get him away from this villain, she let the lad go to some fairground people, and he's been making a living up and down the country in that kind of employment ever since—not too successfully either, it seems."

"Ah!" Shaldon drew a quick breath. "Fairground, eh?"

The Earl looked at him curiously. "Yes, why does that interest you in particular?"

His son shrugged. "No matter. But what of this grandmother? Did Durrant talk to her, too?"

"No. She's dead. The last this fellow Carlton saw of her—"

"Carlton," murmured Shaldon. "Yes, I see. But never mind that. Continue with what you were saying, sir."

"You put me out," complained the Earl. "Damned if I know what you're talking about. Where was I? Oh, yes, I was telling you that Carlton said the last time he saw his grandmother was about eight years since, when she met him at some Fair and handed him a box that had belonged to his dead mother, telling him to take good care of it. Some years later, he went round to the place where she used to live in Southwark and was told she was dead. Anyway, he showed Durrant this box, and that clinched the matter. Besides the ring, it contained the only letter I ever wrote to my first wife. Moreover, this fellow has the Stratton hair, even if there's no such strong physical likeness as exists between you and myself. But that's nothing— daresay he favours poor Dorinda's family in features. He's my son, right enough. I've seen the proofs. The ring and the letter are both mine, and I recognised the box as one Dorinda once showed me which had been given to her by her father. I've no doubts whatever."

Shaldon was silent for some minutes. He was turning these astounding revelations over in his mind.

"A pity the grandmother's dead," he said at last. "She was the one certain proof. Presumably you would have known her again, even after a lapse of so many years, since you once spent so much time under the same roof together."

"Who's to say?" growled the Earl. "I don't scruple to admit that I'm so altered myself that anyone who knew me in those days might be hard put to it to recognise me now! But no other proof is needed than my ring and the letter, together with this fellow Carlton's story. Durrant is convinced, and so am I. Though in a way," he added, in a petulant tone, "I can't help wishing it had turned out as Ned Lydney expected, and the child had died. God knows what's to be done to make this fellow presentable, for one thing. You'll have to lend a hand there."

"Will I, indeed? You'd do well not to count on that," Shaldon warned him grimly. "Since you obviously find him somewhat lacking in certain respects, I collect that you've already met him?"

"Of course I've met him. Durrant brought him here two days since."

"And where is he now, may I ask?"

"Why, here, of course. Where else should the fellow be? This is his rightful place, ain't it?"

"Possibly," replied Anthony, cautiously. "Have you informed the domestic staff of his identity?"

"Not so far. They know him as Mr. Carlton, at present staying here as a guest. It's all devilish awkward," complained the Earl.

"But not perhaps so awkward for you as for myself," Anthony reminded him drily. "Perhaps you will introduce him to me. I should very much like to have a talk with Mr. Rowland Carlton."

Anthony arrived back in Town that same evening, and having dined alone and somewhat more hurriedly than was his custom, set out for Cavendish Square. Now that he had at last discovered the solution to the mystery which Helen had first scented, he intended to lose no time in redeeming his promise to place her in possession of the facts.

He was disappointed to be informed at the house that the ladies were not at home, having gone to spend the evening at Almack's. Although this was not a favourite haunt of his, he decided to follow them there. He could scarcely hope to find a suitable opportunity at the fashionable Assembly rooms to enjoy a lengthy private conversation with Miss Somerby; but at least he might make an appointment to see her on the following day. He was somewhat put out at having to return to Clarges Street in order to change into knee breeches, but the strict rules obtaining at Almack's made this delay essential.

He finally arrived at his destination just before eleven o'clock, the hour at which subscribers ceased to be admitted. The dancing was in full swing. Having first civilly greeted the patronesses and one or two other acquaintances, he looked round for his quarry, and saw her enjoying the intimacy of a waltz with Henry Lydney.

The sight did not please him. He almost made up his mind to leave the ballroom at once; but Helen, glancing down the room in an interval between her animated conversation with Lydney, had seen him and raised a hand in greeting, so he remained. He watched the rest of the waltz with a jaundiced eye, however, then joined Lady Chetwode's party just as Helen and her partner returned to it.

"I don't often see you here," she remarked, after general greetings had been exchanged.

"I don't often attend," he replied, shortly.

"Finds it too slow," explained Lydney, with a grin at his friend. "Don't know what he's missing, though."

Shaldon attempted some light reply, though at that moment he was wishing Lydney at the devil. Helen, perceptive as always, detached herself a little from her late partner's side.

"Have you been to Alvington?" she asked, in a low tone.

He nodded, but was unable to say any more because Lydney moved towards them at that moment. The best he could do was to solicit Helen's hand as a partner for the next dance, a favour which she readily granted.

"Did you succeed in finding out anything?" she asked eagerly, as they moved down the set.

"The whole," he answered. "But it's not a story to be told in snatches, as it must be if I attempt to recount it here. When can I see you alone? Will you drive out with me in the Park tomorrow?"

Her face clouded. "Oh, dear, how unfortunate! We are engaged on an expedition to Middlesex tomorrow to visit Lady Calcot—Melissa's married sister, you know, who lives in Harrow. Melissa has been quite looking forward to it, and since she's been so sadly out of spirits lately, I wouldn't care to disappoint her. Besides, what possible excuse could I make to Lady Calcot?"

"Why, you couldn't, of course." His tone was disappointed. "Are you and Miss Chetwode to go alone?"

He was thinking that, if so, he might ride part of the way with them and possibly contrive some private conversation with Helen; but her answer put an end to this scheme.

"No, we're to go in a party. Melissa, Catherine Horwood, and I will be in the coach, while Mr. Chetwode and Mr. Lydney are to ride."

"Lydney; so he's accompanying you, is he?"

"Yes, Lady Calcot said her brother might bring a friend, if he chose, and she had already made Mr. Lydney's acquaintance at our ball. Oh, it is so vexing that we cannot meet tomorrow! I am dying to hear what you have to tell me! Are you sure you cannot tell me now?"

"I am positive. We are about to be separated now for the figures of the dance. Any sustained conversation of a serious nature is impossible in these circumstances."

She was bound to agree, though her patience was sorely tried by the abstinence.

"Then when can you see me in private?" she demanded, as soon as they came together again.

"Whenever you contrive to shake off that fellow Lydney," he replied, somewhat tartly. "I daresay if I call in tomorrow evening, after you've returned from your outing, I shall still find him with you."

"Oh, you do sound cross!"

"Not at all—merely baffled for the moment. I don't care to make clandestine assignations with you, yet if I call on you in the normal way, I can scarcely hope to see you alone."

She sighed. "If only we were at Alvington, you might easily enough snatch a few moments' private conversation with me in the Rectory garden or the wood. But a female is so protected in London."

"And then not sufficiently," he replied, drily. "You contrived to go to the Fair alone, in spite of all Lady Chetwode's care—not to mention my own warning."

She wrinkled her nose at him. "You shouldn't warn me against things—it gives me an overwhelming desire to do them!"

"You are the most incorrigible madcap," he said, severely.

His eyes gave a different message, however; for he was thinking at that moment how young and fresh she looked, how unspoilt in spite of having been subjected to the sophisticating influence of a London season and the attentions of at least two eligible men. She caught the glance and felt to her dismay the slight tingle of excitement which sometimes came to her when Mr. Lydney looked at her in that way. Oh, no, no! Shaldon must not flirt with her, nor she with him; she valued his friendship too much for that.

They danced in silence for a while, separating and coming together again once more before Shaldon finally spoke.

"I have it," he said, triumphantly. "I'll write you a letter. It will be best in many ways, for you'll then have time to think over what I have to tell you."

"Oh, but that will take so long!" she complained. "I shan't receive it until the day after tomorrow."

"You will. I'll write it tonight and have it delivered by hand in Cavendish Square first thing in the morning. And I can only hope," he added, "that it won't spoil your day's outing for you."

"Oh, dear," she said, looking doubtfully at him, "is the news so very bad?"

"It certainly appears to be, but I'm not yet convinced," he answered, with forced cheerfulness. "And now, let us talk of something else, for if anyone is watching our performance, we must appear a very dull couple."

"There's only one thing," she persisted. "Am I at liberty to communicate anything of what you tell me to Melissa? She already knows all about my suspicions, you see. She was with me that time when I saw the man Rowland Carlton in Piccadilly and jumped out of the coach to follow him—naturally, I was obliged to explain it later to her. But I won't divulge another word, if you'd rather I didn't."

"There's little purpose in concealing it from anyone, I suppose, since it may all have to come out in time," he said, wryly. "All the same, for the moment I would prefer your confidences to be restricted to Miss Chetwode—and your brother, of course. I shall inform James myself, in any case, when next I see him."

"Oh, dear, you sound sadly out of spirits." Her hand was resting formally on his arm at the time, and she gave it a sympathetic squeeze. "If only there were anything I could do to help—anything in the world!"

"You can," he replied, with a twisted smile. "Make me laugh with some of your absurdities."

And under the influence of her lively countenance and the light-hearted chatter which she obediently produced for him, he did succeed in forgetting his troubles for a while.

Chapter XXXII

HELEN SLEPT FITFULLY that night, too full of combined curiosity and apprehension to relax. She was down to breakfast before anyone else, and sure enough the letter had arrived, in the flowing hand which she had come to recognise as Shaldon's.

She hastily broke the seal and read avidly. It was as well that no one else was present, for as she devoured the contents of the letter—her breakfast, on the other hand, remaining untouched—a look of deepening dismay spread over her face.

She had imagined many things, but never anything as bad as this. How could the Earl have behaved in so cruel a way? Cruel to his first wife, and to the child of that marriage; cruel to poor Aunt Maria, whom she still vaguely remembered; and, worst of all, cruel to Anthony himself. It seemed hard to believe that any father could have treated his son so—allowing him to be brought up in the belief that he was the undisputed heir to Alvington, only to shatter his expectations when he had reached manhood. At that moment she felt she hated the Earl, little though she was usually given to violent antipathies.

After the first storm of dismay and anger had somewhat abated, she read the letter through again. This time she noticed that Anthony—she supposed she could no longer think of him as Viscount Shaldon— was fighting back. The evidence appeared conclusive, but he meant to examine it carefully for himself. He had already spoken to Rowland Carlton, and allowing for the fact that the man was understandably uneasy in his new and totally unexpected situation, his story seemed straightforward enough. Anthony announced that he next intended to question Durrant to see if there should be any discrepancies in their separate accounts.

I am not very sanguine on this head. Durrant is the last man to make any kind of slip. But the matter is too serious to be accepted without question. At some stage, of course, the lawyers will have to come into it, but at present I wish to make some investigations myself. I may even go down to Rye, though it's doubtful if anything fresh can be learnt there after so long. I must be doing something, however.

So don't look to hear from me for several days—perhaps a week—though you may be assured that you'll be the first person I shall seek out on my return. That much I owe you, dear Nell—may I for once assume a brother's right to your name?—in return for all the affectionate interest you have taken in my concerns.

If Carlton is in truth my father's heir, I shall accept the fact philosophically, even though I have a fondness for Alvington and would have liked to think that it would be mine someday. But my case is far from desperate, whatever the outcome. I already possess an estate, if much smaller, and an adequate income.

From this you'll see that I am counting my blessings in the approved fashion, and not succumbing to flat despair!

Until our next meeting, then,

    I remain,

The letter was signed with the single initial *A* instead of the usual *S*.

Melissa had been eagerly looking forward to this visit to her sister's home in Middlesex, because she intended to seize the opportunity of a heart-to-heart talk with Julia. In spite of the difference of five years in age and their varying temperaments, the two sisters had at one time been very close, sharing their little feminine secrets until Julia's marriage to Baron Calcot four years ago. Since then Helen Somerby had replaced Julia as Melissa's chief confidante; in family matters, however, Melissa still turned to her sister for guidance. She had written a frantic appeal for help after James Somerby's proposal of marriage had been so cautiously received by her parents, and the invitation to Harrow had resulted.

Lord Calcot had evidently had his instructions on the way in which a tête-à-tête between the two sisters was to be contrived. Shortly after an excellent nuncheon, he proposed that the visitors should accompany him on a tour of the grounds. Julia, who was shortly expecting her second confinement, chose instead to sit on a shady bench on the terrace in her sister's company, an arrangement which seemed agreeable to everyone.

As soon as the others had walked away out of earshot, Melissa began her tale of woe, while Julia listened in a sympathetic silence.

"Are you perfectly certain, dearest," she ventured to say at last, "that what you at present feel for Mr. Somerby will stand the test of time? You are still young, you know, and haven't met many gentlemen so far."

"I shall be nineteen next week," protested Melissa. "You weren't much older than that when you were married, and Mama herself was wed at eighteen! Besides, I don't see what age has to do with it. One can be quite as desperately in love at my age as at—oh, any age you care to mention! I know what it is, Julia. Just because I am the youngest, you all persist in thinking of me as being still a child! But I'm *not*. I'm a woman, with a woman's feelings, and I *am* truly in love with Mr. Somerby! If I wait until I'm thirty, I shall never meet anyone to whom I'll be more passionately attached. I've met some other perfectly amiable gentlemen already, but to my way of thinking—

and feeling—not one of them could ever have the power to attach me! They are all such—such *statues* compared to James Somerby! I shall never change, I tell you! And I would rather die an old maid than marry anyone else!"

Julia smiled gently. "Well, love, I hope you won't do that, nor wait until you're thirty to get married."

"I shall if Mama and Papa have anything to say to it," replied Melissa despondently.

"Try to understand their point of view." Julia's tone was quietly persuasive. "They only want what is best for you. I have a little girl of my own, and I know just how they feel."

"Then they must surely see that it's best for me to follow the dictates of my own heart!"

"Perhaps. Yet love sometimes blinds us to disadvantages which might later disrupt a marriage." She hesitated for a moment, feeling her way over what she realised was difficult ground. "James Somerby is an excellent young man, I know. His character leaves nothing to be desired. He has many advantages—good looks and address, genteel parentage—"

"Now I know you're going to say *but!*" interrupted Melissa, hotly. "And I know what your objection will be, too! It's because he's a doctor and must practise a profession, instead of being simply a gentleman of leisure!"

"We have to live in the world, Mel, and sometimes must accept its judgments. There can be no doubt that our world regards a medical man as being very little removed in social degree from a tradesman."

"Yes, but all that is changing! If you could but talk to Mr. Somerby, you would learn how much the Apothecaries' Act, which was passed last year, has done to ensure the raising of standards in medical education. Before the Society will issue its Diploma, candidates are required to produce certificates of attendance upon courses of lectures in medicine and the medical sciences, and also upon medical practice in the wards. It will not be long before a fully qualified medical practitioner stands in as high social regard as a clergyman, whom everyone respects! Why, students come from all over the country to attend the medical courses at Guy's Hospital. Mr. Somerby told me there was even one from America there at present, a Mr. John Wagner, from New York."

Julia smiled at her sister's enthusiasm. "Well, you are certainly well informed on the subject, at all events. But have you considered, Melissa, what a change in your material circumstances marriage to Mr. Somerby would mean? You will be obliged—at first, at any rate—to live in a much smaller house than any to which you've been accustomed, with only a few servants. And I don't suppose you'll be able to keep a carriage or have any of the luxuries to which you've been used all your life."

"I shall be no worse off than Helen's Mama," said Melissa, stoutly. "And she is one of the happiest ladies I know!"

"So you have already considered all these objections thoroughly?" asked Julia.

"Of course I have! I've been obliged to do so, for Mr. Somerby himself was the first person to point them out to me. And all I can say is exactly what I said to him—that to be deprived of these material advantages will be nothing compared to the misery of being separated from *him,* and perhaps obliged to marry some odious nobleman who can give me everything but what I most desire!"

She seized her sister's hand, looking imploringly up into her face with tear-dimmed eyes.

"Oh, dearest Julia, surely you can understand? You loved Calcot to distraction. I know you did! Would it have mattered to you? Would it have made any difference to your decision to marry him had he been in the same situation as Mr. Somerby?"

Julia needed no time to answer this. "No," she said, decisively. "No, it would not. And I do believe, Melissa, that with your strength of purpose, you could be happy in spite of all the worldly disadvantages to the match. Besides," she added, thinking aloud, "it would be for only a short time. I know that both the Somerbys stand to inherit a comfortable competence from their grandparents, since they are the sole grandchildren. And then, of course, James Somerby has some influential friends—Viscount Shaldon, for one."

"Well, we care nothing for that!" exclaimed Melissa, impatiently. "But if you think it will persuade Mama and Papa to sanction our engagement at once, then by all means mention it to them. And you will do your best to persuade them will you not, dear, *dear* Julia? You can't wish me to die of a broken heart, or at best go into a decline! Pray say you'll intercede on my behalf. It will be the most welcome birthday present you could possibly give me!"

Julia gave her promise, and was rewarded by seeing the animation return to her sister's somewhat pale face.

Melissa was able to communicate this good news to both her friends on their way home, for Catherine was in her confidence as well as Helen. The less happy tidings which were burdening Helen's mind, however, had to wait until later, as they must be for Melissa's ear alone.

When they were back in Cavendish Square and she was at last able to speak of it, she was heard with astonishment.

"Well!" exclaimed Melissa, once the contents of Anthony's letter had been explained and discussed thoroughly. "So you were right all along, Nell, and there really was something odd going on! I half thought you were imagining the whole, you know! Poor Viscount Shaldon," she added, reflectively. "I suppose he cannot be called by that title any longer. How shall we style him now, I wonder?"

"I suppose he will be the Honourable Anthony Stratton."

"Do you think Cynthia will still wish to wed him now that he's no longer the heir to an Earldom?" asked Melissa, curiously.

"I'm sure I can't say." Helen's tone was curt.

"I don't believe he'll be too downcast if she doesn't, for I've never seen him give any sign of wishing to attach her seriously. Of course, he's flirted with her a little, but everyone does flirt with Cynthia. She expects it."

Helen made no reply to this, so Melissa continued in another strain.

"You say Lord—Mr. Stratton, I should say—told you that you might inform your brother. Do you mean to do so?"

Helen nodded. "Oh, yes, it would be a great relief to talk the matter over with James, for I don't mind admitting that it occupies my thoughts to the exclusion of all else, just at present! I suppose I can't very well ask him to come here, though," she added, doubtfully, "in view of your parents' wishes that you and he should not meet too often. I must therefore go to him at his lodging. His term at the hospital finished at the end of last month, and he's waiting to appear before the Board of Examiners. I wonder if I might go tomorrow? We have no engagement until the evening."

"I only wish I could accompany you," said Melissa wistfully.

"Well, that's not to be thought of, but you've no occasion to look so gloomy, Mel. I shall certainly tell him that you have high hopes of your sister's intercession with your parents."

This undertaking did much to restore her friend's newfound cheerfulness.

No difficulties were raised to Helen's proposal; and it was arranged that the coach should convey her to St. Thomas's Street on the following morning and call there for her again later in the day.

When his sister arrived at his lodging, James was sitting in his room poring over a copy of William Babington's *Chemical Lectures*. He looked up as the little maid-of-all-work tapped on his door, frowning at the interruption.

"Helen, what brings you here?" The frown vanished, to be replaced by a smile. "You're the last person I expected to see—well, nearly the last, at all events."

"The last being Melissa, I suppose? Never mind,

Jamie, I'm the bearer of some news from her which may turn out to your advantage—now, don't expect too much," she added hastily, seeing his face light up at once. "It may come to nothing, but at least it's a ray of hope."

She proceeded to tell him of Lady Calcot's promise. They talked of this for some time; James was not inclined to be overoptimistic about the outcome, but could not help feeling encouraged that one member of Melissa's family, at any rate, was prepared to approve the match.

"And did you come all this way to tell me of that, Nell?" he asked, presently. "It was deuced good of you."

"Well, no," she answered, slowly. "That wasn't all—there's another matter. . . ."

He scrutinised her sharply. "What is it? You're in some kind of distress, I can see! If that fellow Lydney—"

"No, no! It's nothing to do with him. My distress is not for myself, but for a very dear friend of us both. James, I've something of the utmost seriousness to tell you, so pray be quiet while I attempt it."

He subsided at her tone, listening with the keen attention he had always given to his medical lectures, and interrupting only when some point needed clarification. At the end, she handed him Anthony's letter; like herself, he read it through twice before making any comment.

"What a damnable business, Nell! But in a way, I'm not surprised that the Earl had a secret in his life. Our father always said there was something preying on the man's mind. Very astute, our Papa. It seems to me that Tony's not satisfied about this claimant. What's the fellow's name? Rowland Carlton, that's it. Yet his story seems to fit the facts as related by the Earl, and is substantiated by the proofs in his possession. That story of his, though—"

He broke off, brooding for a moment. Then suddenly he slapped his fist down upon Samuel Sharp's

Operations in Surgery, which was one of the several textbooks lying about on the table.

"Damme, Nell, I thought something about it sounded familiar! Remember what that woman Mrs. Dorston told me about her grandson? Why, it's almost the same tale!"

Helen caught her breath. "Oh, do you suppose there *can* be any connection? But, no, James, the man Carlton says his grandmother is dead."

"Wrong, Helen. You must state your facts correctly. He only said that he was *told* she was dead. He went to the place where she used to live to make his enquiries—somewhere in the Borough, though we don't know quite where. Now, Mrs. Dorston also used to live in the Borough, though she says she moved away ten years ago, on her husband's death. Suppose for a moment that Mrs. Dorston is indeed Carlton's grandmother? Anyone enquiring for her some years afterwards, as Carlton says he did, might well be misinformed. Things do become confused in people's minds after a lapse of time, especially in those overcrowded areas, where life is a hand-to-mouth business."

"Oh, yes, you could indeed be right, Jamie!" said Helen excitedly. "And what Mrs. Dorston told you does seem to fit with Carlton's own account of his life! If that is so—if she is the man's grandmother—then she must be this Mrs. Lathom of whom the Earl spoke. And then," she concluded, her face falling, "finding her would provide the final proof that Carlton is truly the Earl's heir. It wouldn't serve Anthony at all."

"Nell, dear, Tony will best be served by finding out the truth," he said, gently. "While he feels there is the slightest shadow of doubt about the business, he naturally intends to question it. But to produce this female Mrs. Lathom and confront the Earl with her must settle things once for all. I think we should be wrong not to attempt it."

Helen nodded, a lump in her throat.

"Of course, you are right," she managed to say at last. "And it may be that Mrs. Dorston will turn out to have no connection at all with Carlton. Shall we go there now, Jamie—to Mrs. Dorston's home, I mean? I feel I cannot wait to know the outcome, whatever it may be."

He nodded. "The sooner we know the answer to this puzzle, the better. I'll go. You may await me here. There's plenty of light reading for you." He indicated the pile of medical textbooks.

"Oh, no, that's too shabby of you! Why should I not come, too? I've been too much involved in this affair to be excluded from it now!"

They argued the point for several minutes; at last James gave way to the extent of saying that she might accompany him to Star Court, but that she must sit in the hackney while he visited Mrs. Dorston alone. No amount of persuasion on her part could move him from this position, so she was obliged to agree at last.

James summoned a hackney, and after threading their way through streets crowded with traffic, they at last reached their objective, a narrow alley sadly miscalled Orchard Lane, which led to Star Court.

"I can't take this 'ack down there, gov'," warned the driver, "nor I don't mean to try, not nohow."

Recognising the validity of this objection, James instructed the driver to await his return; and bidding Helen remain inside the vehicle, he dismounted and set off along the uneven, worn cobbles of Orchard Lane.

It was not more than a few minutes before the vehicle was surrounded by dirty, ragged children who pressed white, thin faces against the windows, peering in on Helen.

"Ger outa it!" bawled the hackney driver, flourishing his whip. "Clear off, or I'll tan yer 'ides!"

A few of the children stood back at once, but the majority paid no heed. Beatings were no novelty to the young of this district; whereas a vehicle was, and particularly a vehicle with a pretty lady in fine clothes seated inside.

"Damn ye, will ye clear off?" demanded the driver, reaching down to lay the whip about him.

Several piercing screams showed that he had made contact with some of the offenders. These drew back against the wall, while the others moved out of reach of the punishing whip, but remained clustered around the rear of the vehicle.

Incensed by their defiance, the driver jumped down from his seat, whip in hand, and rushed towards them. But before he could vent the full force of his wrath upon them, Helen had wrenched open the door of the coach and leapt into the road.

"No, you shall not!" she said, fiercely, seizing his arm. "That's no way to treat children! They mean no harm. They're only curious!"

"Children, lady? D'ye call them monsters children? Prigs and no-goods, the lot on 'em, and born to be 'anged. Ye'd best get back in the 'ack, or they'll 'ave yer val'ables, as easy as skin a rabbit! Do as the gennelman bid ye, and stay inside."

"Thank you, I am the best judge of my actions," she replied, coldly. Then, with a change of tone, "Oh, look what you've done! That poor little mite. You've lacerated his cheek!"

She went over to a small boy of about seven years old who was crying lustily and fingering his cheek, where a few drops of blood were oozing from a superficial cut.

"Serve the little perisher right," said the driver, defensively. "Only way to deal with 'em—only thing they understands. As fer ye, Miss, ye'd best get in sharp, afore ye comes to mischief."

But Helen was paying no heed. Hastily untying the strings of her reticule, she produced a handkerchief with which she began gently to wipe away the blood and surrounding dirt from the child's face.

"Where do you live, little fellow?" she asked the boy, who had now stopped crying and was regarding her openmouthed. "I will take you home."

He was too overawed to reply to this himself, but several bolder spirits shouted that he was Jem and lived in Star Court. Bidding the driver await her return, without more ado she took the small boy's hand and started down the alley.

The children at once crowded round her, jumping about, shouting excitedly and fingering her gown. In spite of her compassion for them, she did not altogether relish their proximity; for most of them had disfiguring sores of one kind or another, and they smelt abominably. She was under no illusions about their behaviour, moreover, and kept a firm grasp on her reticule, although it contained little of value beyond Anthony's letter.

After a short distance, the alley led into Star Court. Helen looked about her in horror, for it was one of the foulest dwelling places she had ever seen. Tall, decaying tenements with boarded-up windows, peeling paint, and rickety doors crowded round the small central area, which was littered with piles of evil-smelling rubbish, among which lean, mangy cats and dogs rummaged.

The noise made by the children had attracted some attention, for heads popped from behind doors, and one or two slatternly women came out to stare at the visitor. One of these, seeing that Helen was holding young Jem by the hand, approached threateningly. The children parted to admit her to the centre of the group.

Making a sudden swoop, she snatched the boy from Helen's grasp, dealing him a sound box on the ear which set him howling again.

"What's the little varmint bin up to, lady?" she demanded, in such a thick Cockney accent that Helen found it difficult to understand her. "Prigged somefink off ye, 'as 'e? No need ter fetch the Watch. We don't want no trouble, see. I'll soon get it back—see if I don't!"

She started to belabour the child again, but Helen caught at her ragged, filthy shift and pulled her back.

"No, no, he's done nothing!" she protested. "He was hurt."

The woman did not wait for her to finish, but turned

on her with a snarl that suggested an animal rather than a human being.

"Done nothink, eh? Then what d' ye mean, comin' 'ere makin' trouble, eh? Clear out, or I'll soon spoil them fancy togs o' yourn!"

She seized the skirt of Helen's gown and reached out to claw her face. Putting up an arm to protect herself, Helen desperately wrenched her skirt free from the woman's grasp, at the same time emitting a loud cry for help.

She heard the crash of a door being flung open hurriedly, and the next moment James was at her side. At his appearance, the court cleared as if by magic. The children slunk away into whatever holes afforded them shelter; while the onlookers, who had been enjoying the prospect of watching one of their number put a gentry mort to flight, discreetly withdrew to their sleazy quarters.

The woman's aggressive stance changed instantly; it was one thing to intimidate a soft young moll, but only a fool would have a go at a man, and him with plenty of muscle under those fine clothes. So with a few sharp words, James sent her shuffling off, whining as she retreated.

"Really, Nell!" he exclaimed, in exasperation, once they were alone. "You're the most devilish girl! Didn't I tell you to stay in the coach? You're not hurt, are you?"

She was trembling, but she managed to shake her head. "No, but I fear my gown is torn a little. I felt it rip."

She looked down to ascertain the extent of the damage, and saw that a small piece of material was hanging loose.

"It's nothing. Oh, but, James, I'm so thankful you came! They're just like animals!"

"So would you be, if you lived in like conditions," he replied, grimly. "Well, since you *are* here, you'd best come with me into Mrs. Dorston's quarters— they're clean enough, or I wouldn't allow it."

Putting his arm supportively about her, he led her

through a half-open door on the ground floor of one of the appalling dwellings in the Court. She was received commiseratingly by Mrs. Dorston, who apologised for the roughness of her neighbours, but said philosophically that one got used to it in time.

The room, though dark, cheerless, and containing the minimum of plain deal furniture, was nevertheless clean, and as neat as any room can be when it must necessarily contain everything that its owner possesses. Mrs. Dorston invited Helen to sit down, offered her some water which James quietly signalled to her to refuse, and produced some pins with which to fasten the rent in her gown until it could be mended.

By this time, Helen was once more feeling sufficiently mistress of herself to take an active part in the conversation which followed. Skilfully steering it in the desired direction, James persuaded Mrs. Dorston to repeat the details of her past life which she had previously recounted to him. They learnt nothing new until she suddenly exclaimed that she had now remembered the name by which her grandson had been known in his barnstorming days.

"At least, I remember part of it," she said, dubiously. "The last name was Carlton, I'll take my oath. But the first—now was it Robert?—or Roger?—it began with *R*, that I'm sure. It was a very grand sounding name—"

"Would it by any chance have been Rowland?" suggested James.

"Rowland!" she exclaimed, triumphantly. "Yes, that's it—Rowland Carlton!"

They looked at each other with mixed feelings. James had been right, then, and Mrs. Dorston was Rowland Carlton's grandmother. Her history fitted, too, with the account given by the Earl of his first marriage; her daughter had died in childbed, leaving her with an infant to rear, an infant who was now Rowland Carlton, an unemployed fairground player. And also heir to the title and estate of Alvington?

Helen's heart sank. It looked as though Anthony had indeed lost his inheritance, for in finding this woman they had discovered the final, irrefutable proof of Rowland Carlton's claim. There remained one more question to be asked, but Helen voiced it without hope.

"Who was your first husband, Mrs. Dorston? What was your name before your second marriage?"

Chapter XXXIII

AT MUCH THE SAME TIME that Helen and James were visiting Star Court, Anthony had started out on a journey to Rye.

The interview with Durrant had yielded nothing beyond a conviction that the secretary was finding a malicious pleasure in the situation. He had evidently expected a confrontation with Anthony before long, and possibly would not have been surprised had it been an acrimonious one; but Anthony's cool head kept their brief but pertinent conversation on a calm, objective note, thus denying Durrant the satisfaction of seeing his adversary at a disadvantage.

The secretary repeated the story much as Anthony had heard it from his father and Carlton. The only additions he made, at Anthony's request, were the present name and abode in Rye of Mrs. Lathom's ex-housemaid, together with the exact location of the pawnbroker's shop where the ring had come to light. Anthony watched the other closely while he put these questions, but could find no trace of reluctance in giving the information. Durrant seemed to take it for granted that the family lawyers would be set on to check his own findings, and the notion appeared not to disturb him at all.

When Anthony parted from him, it was in a less sanguine frame of mind than before. Both Carlton's and Durrant's accounts tallied; and if Durrant could contemplate with equanimity a legal inquiry, he must be certain of his ground.

There seemed no purpose, therefore, in a visit to Rye. What could he hope to learn there? The ex-housemaid would merely repeat the little she had already told Durrant. Apart from that, he might visit the church and see for himself the entries in the parish register of his father's marriage and the subsequent burial of the unfortunate bride. If the child had been baptised before leaving Rye, the date of the baptism would also appear. Most parishes kept a conscientious record of the religious rites performed within their boundaries, as they were required to do. But there seemed little point in this, as these facts had been supplied by the Earl, and therefore their accuracy was unquestionable. It was only Durrant's testimony which Anthony persisted, in spite of so much corroborative evidence, in thinking suspect.

It was this uneasy feeling which finally persuaded him to make the journey into Sussex, after all. He encountered a good deal of delaying traffic on the road to Sevenoaks; this decided him to stay overnight at the Chequers Inn at Lamberhurst, where he was known and could be certain of finding a good dinner.

He left soon after breakfast on the following day and well before noon was entering Rye by the Land-gate, one of the fourteenth-century town gates with two massive towers on either side of its archway. He had never before been in the little town, and was much struck by its charm, in spite of his preoccupation with personal matters. He soon found the George Inn, where he stabled his curricle and set out to make his calls on foot, glad of the opportunity to stretch his legs for a while.

An inquiry at the inn furnished him with the direction he must take to find the home of Mrs. Fremlin, and before long he was knocking at the door of a small neat cottage in a passage running between two of the streets. It was a few minutes before his knock was answered; then a plump little woman with greying hair tucked tidily under a cap poked her head round the door.

"Mrs. Fremlin?" he asked, with one of his disarming smiles.

She acknowledged this, staring at him curiously.

"I wonder if I might have the favour of a few moments' conversation with you?" he went on, persuasively. "There is a matter in which I believe you may be of assistance to me."

"And what might that be, sir?" she asked, doubtfully.

He glanced up and down the passage before replying.

"It's difficult to explain in the street," he said, sustaining the smile. "If you would permit me to step inside for a moment, where we can be private, I would deem it an inestimable favour."

Reassured by his air of gentility, she opened the door to admit him into a tiny parlour, sparsely furnished but spotlessly kept. Asking him to be seated, she herself took a chair, then waited expectantly for him to speak.

"I believe that recently you were visited by a gentleman who asked you some questions concerning a Mrs. Lathom who used at one time to live in Watchbell Street?" he began.

Her expression, which had been puzzled, now cleared.

"Oh, yes, sir, so I was. I told 'im all I could, though t'were little enough. 'Tis a long time since, and I only worked for the lady less than a couple o' years. I used to do for 'er in the mornings."

"And during that time, the lady's daughter was married, later dying in childbed, as I understand?"

Mrs. Fremlin nodded. "Ay, poor young soul! Her 'usband wasn't with 'er, neither—'e was often away. I only set eyes on 'im a few times, but—but—"

She stared at Anthony again.

"It's a mortal long time, but 'e was a 'andsome gen-nelman, and as I recall somethink favoured yourself. Be ye any relation, sir?"

He dismissed the question with a brief nod. "Can you recall exactly what Mrs. Lathom said to you before she quitted Rye?"

"Why, just what I told the other gennelman. Didn't 'e tell ye 'imself, sir?"

"He did, but I prefer to hear it again from your own lips, if you'll be so good as to repeat it."

"I don't mind, but there's naught to tell, sir. She said as 'ow she wouldn't be needin' me again, but would give me a character an' a month's wages, an' I was to go to the Vicar to find me another place. Which I did, an' the Reverend sent me to Mrs. 'Olyoake's, where I stayed till I was wed."

"I am glad that you so quickly found employment," replied Anthony, admirably masking his impatience at being supplied with detail irrelevant to his inquiry. "But I understand that the lady told you where she intended to go when she left this town?"

"That she did, sir. She said as she was goin' some-where close to Lunnon." A vague expression came into her eyes, and she clicked her tongue with impatience. "There, now, if I 'aven't been an' gone an' forgotten it, again!"

"Forgotten what again?" asked Anthony, sharply.

"The name o' the place. She let it drop, like, an' I remember thinking at the time she 'adn't meant to tell me at all. Girls is sharper at fifteen than women is at my age, for danged if I can bring that name to my tongue! No more I could for the other gennelman, until 'e chanced to say it."

"You mean," said Anthony, with an inner feeling of excitement, "that the other gentleman prompted your memory by suggesting a name?"

She nodded. "Ay, that's it, sir."

"Was the name he suggested Southwark?"

"Southwark!" she repeated, triumphantly. "To be sure, that was it, an' I knowed it as soon as ever I 'eard it again! But it's a long time . . ."

He stayed chatting with her for a few minutes longer, but learned nothing of consequence beyond the exact situation of Mrs. Lathom's onetime dwelling in Watchbell Street. Nevertheless, he thought, as he turned his steps in the direction of the Parish church of St. Mary the Virgin, he had made one discovery. It had been Durrant, and not Mrs. Fremlin herself, who had first mentioned Southwark. Why had he done so? His enquiries in Rye had been the first stage of his search for Mrs. Lathom, and it was acting on the information gleaned from Mrs. Fremlin that he had later traced Carlton. Had Durrant perhaps run through a whole list of villages close to London, coming at last to a name which Mrs. Fremlin recognised? Perhaps it would have been wiser to check that point with the woman; but it had occurred to him only now when he had the necessary solitude for thought. He turned on his heel with the intention of returning to put the question, but changed his mind. As he was so close to the church, he might as well go there first.

He glanced up at the clock as he approached the building, and read the inscription which so long ago had brought a shiver of apprehension to Dorinda Lathom. Entering, he was struck by the vastness of the interior; he walked about it, admiring the evidences of Norman workmanship, his boots on the stone floor breaking the unearthly silence. Something in the solitary atmosphere of the place at length played on his senses, making him reconstruct in fancy the scene of that clandestine marriage which had brought so much trouble to everyone concerned, born and unborn, living and dead.

He squared his shoulders. The registers would be under lock and key. If he wished to see them, he would need to apply at the Vicarage; but was there any point in doing so? He left the church to stroll around the graveyard, inspecting the tombs. And presently he came upon the one he sought, a simple granite stone as simply inscribed.

To the beloved memory of
DORINDA STRATTON
born 1772, died 1790
R.I.P.

It must have been erected after Mrs. Lathom had
left Rye, he mused; either she had placed an order for
it before leaving, or else despatched one from her new
abode. He wondered if an inquiry at the local stone-
mason's would throw any light on this. But after
twenty-six years, it was doubtful if a small craftsman
would have kept a record. In any event, Durrant would
not have overlooked that avenue of research; and had
he succeeded in finding the woman's precise direction,
he would not have had recourse to his later attempts
to trace her through the signet ring.

Anthony's mood was sombre as he paced the paths
crossing the churchyard, the weight of bygone events
settling upon his spirits. He was stirred by pity for the
young girl who had given her life so trustingly into his
father's keeping, and by contempt for the moral cowardice which had prompted the Earl to betray that
trust.

Finally—but this came after half an hour's solitary
reflection—by the beginnings of compassion for the
Earl himself, enmeshed in the classic tragedy situation
of adverse circumstances and weakness of character.

The path along which he was now walking took him
out of the churchyard and into Watchbell Street. Still
thoughtful, he strolled along until he came to the cottage which had once been inhabited by the Lathoms.
He had formed no intention of doing more than look
at the place out of a curiosity inspired by his present
mood. It was unlikely that anything could be learned
there of Mrs. Lathom after all these years, for several
other tenants had probably succeeded her. But when
his idle loitering outside caused a face to appear at
the window, on a sudden impulse he knocked.

Doors were opened warily in Rye, he thought, as
this one, too, was eased back a few inches. Behind it

stood a shrunken old man with bald head and toothless gums. He gave a half-witted stare at the visitor.

"Pray forgive me for troubling you," began Anthony. "I wonder if you could tell me whether you had a call from a gentleman some seven or eight weeks since? He would have been making inquiries about a former tenant here, one Mrs. Lathom."

The man's face showed no change of expression, and it was obvious that he had not understood. Anthony silently cursed his luck, but determined to try again.

"Is there anyone else at home to whom I could speak?" he asked, gently.

The unwinking stare remained. Anthony decided that there was nothing else for it but to abandon the enquiry; Durrant had not mentioned calling here, so the odds were against his having done so. He thanked the old man, though it was not clear for what, and turned on his heel.

As he did so, he almost bumped into an angular female of uncertain age with a basket over her arm. She was evidently intending to enter the cottage, for she sharply instructed the old man to open the door. As he obeyed, she eyed Anthony shrewdly, taking in the elegance of his attire and his air of Quality.

"Be ye wantin' somethink, sir?" she asked, in the same sharp tones.

Anthony repeated his enquiry, with more hope now of receiving an answer, but little expectation of its turning out to be helpful.

"'Tis a long time agone," she said, "and I'm busy —can't stand 'ere all day answerin' questions."

"I would be more than willing to recompense you for your time," replied Anthony, making a move towards his pocketbook.

Her mean little eyes sharpened and she glanced quickly up and down the street.

"Well, ye'd best come in," she capitulated. "Get along now, do, Father, or ye'll get trodden on!"

She pushed the old man aside to make way for the visitor to enter. He did so, and she slammed the door behind him, then went over to the window to pull the curtain closer.

"Folk can be curious," she said. "Sit down, sir, and I'll be with ye in a trice—must put the marketin' away."

Anthony seated himself in a wooden armchair, while the old man shuffled to a bench in the chimney corner and proceeded to nod off to sleep.

"Touched in the nob," said the woman, indicating him as she came back into the room. "Ye was sayin', sir, somethink about—what was the word?"

"Recompense," supplied Anthony, promptly, and drawing out a banknote, pressed it into her ready hand.

She looked at it thoughtfully, then said slowly, "Well, now, mem'ry's a funny thing. It plays tricks. Some folks pays ye to remember, an' some pays ye to forget. It depends which pays best, see?"

"Perfectly," he replied, pausing in the act of restoring the pocketbook to its secure resting place. "In matters of business, a direct approach is best, don't you agree, my good woman? How much?"

She shook her head. "Ah, now, that's askin'. Depends what it's worth to ye to know."

"From all of which I collect that the gentleman I mentioned did come here, and did ask you the same question?"

She looked blank. He passed another two banknotes over, pausing interrogatively between each one.

"Well, now, I'll tell ye what I telled 'im," she said, tucking the notes away in the pocket of her apron. "I never 'eard of no Mrs. Lathom—don't know nothink about 'er, an' that's Gospel."

His disappointment showed in his face. He rose and stood over her menacingly.

"And you have the effrontery to take money for passing on that information! Have a care, woman!"

She cowered away from him. "There's more, isn't there?" he continued, relentlessly. "He didn't pay you to keep silent about that! Very well, out with it. What was it?"

It was evident that she was scared of him; but her

411

cupidity was stronger than the fear and urged her to persist in the hope of a larger reward. She shook her head, compressing her lips tightly.

Anthony surveyed her for a moment in frustration, wishing she had been a man so that he could have dealt with her as she deserved.

"Very well," he said, at last. "How much did he pay you?"

"Ten pound," she replied promptly, with a sly look.

She wondered for a moment if she had put the figure too high when he continued to glare at her; but at last he drew two ten-pound banknotes from his pocketbook, placing them out of her reach on the table.

"Yours—if I find the rest of your information more worth the price than the first part," he said grimly.

She argued for a time, attempting to snatch the money; but he easily restrained her without doing her any harm, though she cursed volubly.

Defeated at last, she subsided in her chair and reluctantly passed on to him the information he desired.

Since that ecstatic evening at the Moonlight Masquerade almost a month since, Durrant had scarcely set eyes on Cynthia. He would occasionally catch a glimpse of her as she set out for an evening engagement exquisitely gowned and with jewels glinting on her white neck; or he might chance to be crossing the hall as she left the breakfast parlour in the mornings, ready to begin on the day's hectic social round. Always there were others about at these times, and the only recognition she would give him was a distant smile and a cool, formal greeting. He chafed under this neglect, finding it hard to reconcile with the memory of that passionate night of shared delight.

After he returned from escorting Carlton to Alvington, he determined that he would somehow contrive to see her privately and inform her how matters stood for the displaced Viscount Shaldon. She would soon be hearing rumours, for he had left nothing undone to spread the tale abroad. Only a few days since he had been closeted with a journalist whose speciality it was to obtain spicy items of news for one of London's scandal-sheets; he had also sent anonymous letters to those quarters where he judged they would be received gleefully and promptly broadcast in malicious whispers to anyone who could be induced to listen. And who could not, in the scandal-hungry hothouse of the London salons?

In the event, he was saved the trouble of contriving a meeting, for Cynthia sought him out herself one morning some days later when her father was out of the house. She walked coolly into the library where he was working alone, just as she had been used to do in the old days at Alvington.

He sprang up as soon as the door was closed behind her and made as if to take her in his arms. She waved him back imperiously.

"Not now—too dangerous," she said, rapidly. "Anyone might come in. I must not stay a minute, but I came to ask if you know what all this is about Shaldon. I was shown something in a journal yesterday evening by a lady of my acquaintance. Oh, it was cautiously written, with all the names in initials—you know the kind of thing—but quite obvious to anyone acquainted with the persons concerned! Moreover, this lady has recently received a letter, not quite so cautious. Your work, I suspect? You've dropped more than one hint to me on this subject from time to time, so I believe I've come to the best source for information."

"I would have told you the whole before this, but I can never get near you," he replied, in disgruntled tones.

"Of course not. That would be the height of folly, as I've said often. But tell me, is there any truth in these extravagant rumours? They credit Alvington with making a secret marriage before his union to Maria Cottesford and with abandoning the child of that first marriage! And it seems the child has now appeared to lay claim to Shaldon's place as Alvington's heir! Can it be true? And what has been your part in all this?"

He speedily recounted the full history of the affair

413

and of how he had set about tracing Alvington's other son at the Earl's request. She could see that he was enjoying the recital, and she commented on this when he told her triumphantly what the reward for his services would be.

"Oh, it's vastly gratifying, no doubt, to contemplate the enlargement of your own consequence," she said, with a cynical smile. "But I believe you'd have relished your task almost equally had you been offered no other reward than that of humbling Shaldon."

"He no longer holds that title," he reminded her, harshly. "Well, yes, I'll admit that it's pleased me to be able to depress his pretensions somewhat. You'll not wish to marry him now that there's no Earldom in prospect, since you've never pretended to any passion for the man himself."

"Oh, no, he is nothing to me," she answered, thoughtfully.

"But I am!" he insisted, drawing her into his arms. She yielded to his kiss, but detached herself immediately afterwards, thrusting him away.

"What kind of man is this? What did you say he was known as?"

"Rowland Carlton—a stage name," he explained. "He's unpolished, boorish—but I daresay they'll go to work on him, turn him out in the correct rig, give him lessons in elocution and deportment and so forth. Clothes and a good address make the gentleman, after all," he finished, with a sneer.

"But what is he like to look at?" Cynthia persisted.

"Why do you ask? Feminine curiosity, I suppose. Oh, he's tall, well built—not much like the Strattons in features, but has their particular shade of red hair."

She considered this for a moment.

"And you say the Earl's keeping him secluded at Alvington for the present?"

He nodded, watching her uneasily as he tried to follow the workings of her mind.

"Well," she said, at last, "I might take a trip to Alvington and see this new heir to the estates. After

414

all, one Viscount is very like another, when the title is the sole matter of interest."

"Cynthia! You're saying that to torment me!" he cried, reaching out for her again. "You can't mean it. You're mine, mine, I tell you!"

But she evaded him and whisked out of the door before he could prevent her.

Chapter XXXIV

HELEN, too, had heard the rumours. She and Melissa had attended a ball on the previous evening and had chanced to overhear two dowagers discussing the affair with the zest generally accorded to a juicy titbit of scandal.

"I recall the fifth Earl," tittered the first lady. "The most fascinating man, and an outrageous rake! I had quite a tendre for him in my first season, but he was already married, alas! The present Earl never appeared as dashing as his sire, but who can tell, my dear? Not just a mistress, which is common enough, goodness knows—but a secret marriage! And the offspring of it lost for all these years, so they say, and now discovered, to displace that handsome boy, Shaldon! Though, of course, he is not Viscount Shaldon, any longer. A pity—he can't now be considered near such a good catch."

"No, indeed, and I collect that Lydney's gal was intended for him," replied her companion. "I suppose they will call off the match, though I don't know where there's another quite as highly eligible at present. She will have to make do with someone rather lower in the scale. But do you really think there's any truth in these rumours?"

Her friend looked at her scornfully. "Oh, my dear, of course! There's no smoke without fire, you know! Besides, it would almost be a pity if it turned out to be nothing but a hum. I haven't been so diverted since the Byron affair!"

"And that," remarked Helen to Melissa, in disgust, as they passed out of earshot, "is all that they care about! Inhuman monsters, waiting to pounce on the misfortunes of others to provide for their entertainment!"

"I daresay when one is as old as that," replied Melissa, with the indulgence of eighteen for those three times her age, "one is glad of almost anything to talk about! But how do you suppose these rumours got about, Helen? There are so few people in the secret and none of them likely to spread the tale abroad."

"There is one who wouldn't scruple to do so!" said Helen, fiercely. "And I only wish Shaldon were here, so that I might tell him what I know! If only James hadn't been expecting to be called soon before the Board of Examiners, he would have posted off to Sussex at once with the news. Oh, I do hope Shaldon returns before long, for I can't bear the suspense, especially not with all this malicious gossip flying about!"

Her fervent wish was to be granted on the following day. She went riding in the Park with Melissa and Catherine, escorted as usual by Philip Chetwode and Henry Lydney. The latest gossip was by now circulating in all the Clubs as well as the drawing rooms; but though both young men had heard it and were concerned for their friend, they did not consider it a suitable topic of conversation to introduce before the ladies.

Philip Chetwode had gradually come to realise that his admiration for Miss Somerby was unlikely to spark off any reciprocal emotion in her, and for some time now he had been leaving Lydney in undisputed possession of the field. More and more he was consoling himself with the company of the shyer, gentle Catherine, whose disposition was more suited to his own. Catherine herself was very content with this state of affairs. It was many weeks since she had first thought of Mr. Chetwode as the beau ideal of her dreams; but she was too loyal and high-principled to make any attempt to attach him while she was still uncertain of Helen's feelings towards him. Now, however, she could see that her friend was much more attracted to Mr. Lydney, whose interest in Helen was evident. Catherine had often watched them laughing and joking together in the way which usually denoted a strong, unspoken attraction between two young people. She wondered when it would come to a head. Melissa had told her that Helen believed Mr. Lydney merely to be flirting, and that moreover his family would never approve of such a match. Although Catherine had little experience of flirtations, she had noticed the light in Mr. Lydney's eyes at times when they rested on Helen, and she judged his feelings to go far deeper than this. As for Helen—well, perhaps her friend might not altogether understand her own emotions.

They had been together in the Park for more than an hour and were about to return to Cavendish Square when they saw a horseman approaching them at a brisk canter. Helen's heart gave a leap; it was Shaldon, looking as cool and immaculate as ever in his well cut riding coat, buckskins, and highly polished boots.

He greeted them in his usual style, but the other two gentlemen seemed a trifle constrained. It did not take him a moment to realise that his friends wished to make some reference to his misfortunes, but judged this unsuitable in the presence of the young ladies. He solved their predicament by inviting them both round to his rooms that evening. Before he turned to go, he contrived to have a private word with Helen.

"I've something of the utmost importance to tell you," he said, in a quick undertone, "but it's useless to attempt it now. Can you possibly drive out with me this afternoon?"

"And so have I something to tell you!" she whispered. "Yes, I can come. Will two o'clock suit you? I've been awaiting your return in a positive fever of impatience!"

He nodded, then took his leave, civilly declining Philip Chetwode's invitation to accompany them back to the house.

Helen scarcely knew how she managed to live through the time that must elapse before the fingers of the clock reached the hour of two. The fever she had spoken of metaphorically almost became a physical reality as she first toyed with a cold nuncheon, then changed into an attractive cherry coloured carriage dress, and afterwards sat fidgeting in the small salon with her eyes constantly on the clock. Melissa understood, for she knew all about it; but Lady Chetwode looked surprised and asked if her visitor was feeling quite the thing. Helen managed to reassure her, and afterwards tried her best to appear calm, but it imposed a great strain on her nerves.

Punctually on the stroke of two, Shaldon was announced. The usual civilities had to be endured before the impatient pair could at last find themselves alone together in Shaldon's curricle.

They said little while he negotiated the busy traffic; but soon they turned for the second time that day into the Park, which at this unfashionable hour was comparatively peaceful. Shaldon heaved a sigh and slackened the reins, allowing his horses to amble along at an easy pace.

"At last we can talk," he began. "And when you hear what I have to tell you, Miss—oh, confound it, I mean to call you Nell when we're alone, if you shouldn't dislike it?"

She shook her head. "Of course not, but pray do go on! You see, I've something to tell you, too, and I can't bear the suspense!"

"Then I'll put it in a nutshell and explain afterwards. Nell, that claim of Durrant's to have found Carlton through the signet ring was nothing but a bag of moonshine! Durrant himself had the box containing the ring and letter in his possession right from the start—from his first visit to Rye, that's to say!"

She turned towards him, her eyes wide in surprise. "Truly—oh, truly? How did he obtain it, and from whom?"

"From the present tenants of the cottage where Mrs. Lathom once lived. Durrant made no mention to me of having visited them, so I scarce thought it worthwhile to go there myself. But I did, acting on an impulse, and I'm devilish glad of it, I can tell you! Because it turned out that he did go there, after all, and bribed the woman—a tough harridan, I promise you—to keep her mouth shut about his visit. It seems he first asked if they knew anything of Mrs. Lathom, and drew a blank. Then he went on to ask if by any chance they'd ever found anything which had been left behind by her. No doubt he was hoping at best for an old letter or paper which might offer some clue to her destination. People leaving in a hurry often forget to destroy such things, though he must have known it was highly unlikely that the present tenants would trouble to preserve any documents they came upon. He certainly couldn't possibly have anticipated the windfall he did get!"

"The box!" breathed Helen in excitement. "But how did such an important thing come to be left behind at all?"

"I think I can guess. The woman at the cottage told me that there'd been a violent storm in Rye last winter, and it had brought down the cottage chimney. There was a frightful mess in one of the bedrooms—rubble and so forth—and among it she and her husband found that box. Now, in view of the contents, it seems to me that my father's—his first bride, that is to say—might at some time have concealed the box somewhere inside the chimney. She was very young—my father said she'd begged to be allowed to keep the signet ring with which she'd been married—and the letter was the only one he ever wrote to her. He was frequently absent. Oh, confound it all!" concluded Shaldon, fiercely.

419

Tears stood in Helen's eyes. "She wanted to have the box where she could brood over these things without her mother knowing. Oh, yes, I understand. Poor, unhappy girl!"

Shaldon stared ahead unseeingly for a moment before continuing with his tale.

"The woman and her husband thought of selling the ring, but they were scared of questions as to how they'd obtained it. So they did nothing until Durrant came along with his queries. They showed him the box and its contents, then made him pay through the nose for it. So you see what that means? Durrant had in his own possession the very proofs of identity which make Carlton's claim valid! As for the rest, I don't know yet how he really contrived to trace Carlton, or on what authority he declares the man to be my father's son—but I soon will do, never fear! I shall see Mr. Bertram Durrant as soon as I've taken you home."

"But that's what *I* want to tell *you!*" cried Helen, jolted abruptly out of her wistful mood. "Carlton can't be the Earl's son, for he's certainly *not* the grandson of Mrs. Lathom! James and I discovered his grandmother, and she's a Mrs. Dorston now, but her name was formerly Baker. So was Carlton's—Joe Baker. That's why the show people changed it. You see, Mrs. Dorston's daughter was"—she hesitated—"was unwed when she had the child, so he was given her maiden surname."

Shaldon was so shaken by this news that he inadvertently jerked on the reins and had to spend a few minutes bringing his horses back to an easy pace. Once he had done so he pressed Helen for details, and she eagerly told him the whole story.

When it was concluded, he placed his hand over hers and looked earnestly into her face.

"I owe a great deal to you, Nell," he said, simply.

She caught her breath as an unexpected quiver of excitement ran through her at his touch. Defensively, she looked away from the grey eyes which suddenly she found so compelling.

"Don't forget James," she amended, trying to speak

lightly. "But for his interest in Mrs. Dorston when she was a patient in the hospital, the true identity of Carlton might never have come to light! His part in the affair was by far more important than mine."

"Believe me, I don't underrate James's service to me," he replied, still keeping her hand in a light clasp. "But it was you, my dear Nell, who first scented some danger ahead and did your best to warn me of it— and all I did was to make game of you. Can you ever forgive me? When I consider your constant vigilance, the way you unhesitatingly put yourself into situations of the utmost embarrassment, and all for my sake— for the sake of our childhood relationship—"

"Oh, but you are forgetting my insatiable curiosity!" she exclaimed, a trifle unsteadily, but with a desperate determination to introduce a lighter note before underlying emotions should gain the upper hand. "You may recall you have frequently quizzed me over that!"

He removed his hand and looked ahead. "So I have," he answered in a more casual tone. "It was a great deal too bad of me. But I see you will not be thanked, so I won't embarrass you further by persisting in the attempt."

"So what will you do now?" she asked, feeling an odd mixture of relief and disappointment that the tense atmosphere between them had been dispelled.

"Bring Durrant to account, first of all, then inform my father."

"Bring him to account? Yes, for it must surely be a criminal offence to act as he has done? I suppose the man Carlton, too, will be punished by the law?"

"Pooh! That poor devil's merely a cat's-paw! If I have my way with my father, there'll be no charges brought against the fellow. The lawyers ain't concerned in this so far, so we may as well keep 'em out for the present, at any rate. Carlton will be glad enough to undertake to say nothing about the business, in return for getting off scot-free, I'll wager. He'll know it means transportation, else."

"I'm relieved to hear that, for Phyllis's sake," said Helen.

"Phyllis? Oh, the equestrienne you mentioned, who's sweet on the fellow."

"And Durrant? Will he be transported?"

"I don't know what I may ultimately decide, but at the moment I mean to deal with him myself. I require some further explanations from him."

She glanced at his rigid countenance and blazing eyes, and a shiver of fear shook her.

"You don't mean—a duel?" she whispered.

He laughed, mirthlessly. "Good God, no! That's not in my style! What I had in mind was a physical and vastly more satisfying form of combat—though that's no subject for a lady."

"Oh, no, Tony!" she exclaimed, involuntarily. "You might get hurt!"

His face momentarily relaxed into a smile.

"I appreciate your concern, but we'll see that!"

She was silent for a moment.

"At any rate, it is all over now," she said, presently. "You are in truth Viscount Shaldon and heir to Alvington."

He shook his head. "No, Nell, that is still uncertain. There is only one person who can enlighten us, and she may be dead, for all we know. This must be cleared up once for all now, though, so we must make a genuine attempt to trace her. I refer, of course, to Mrs. Lathom."

When Anthony arrived at the Lydneys' house in Berkeley Street, he was relieved to be informed that all the members of the family were out.

"If I might perhaps deliver a message, my lord?" the butler suggested, deferentially.

"No, thanks, my business is in fact with Lord Lydney's secretary," replied Anthony, handing over his hat, cane, and gloves. "I take it I shall find him in the library? I know my way, so you need not trouble to announce me."

"Very good, my lord." The butler bowed and went about his business.

Anthony strode purposefully across the hall to the library, gave a perfunctory knock and entered.

Durrant was working at his desk. He looked up in surprise at the unexpected interruption, then leapt to his feet as he saw who his visitor was. For a moment his face betrayed the smallest flicker of alarm, soon suppressed as he forced a frigid smile.

"Good afternoon. I was not expecting you."

"Daresay not," replied Anthony, brusquely. "I've been making a few enquiries of my own since last I had the doubtful pleasure of seeing you, Durrant, and I've discovered you're a damned liar. Ay, and a scheming rogue!"

Durrant passed his tongue over his lips, which had suddenly gone dry; but his voice was calm enough as he answered with a sneer.

"You'd like to think so, doubtless."

"I know so! I went to the cottage in Rye where the Lathoms once lived. Ah!" he exclaimed, as he saw the other man start involuntarily. "Thought you were safe there, didn't you? No one would consider an enquiry worthwhile after a lapse of so many years? Thought you'd bought 'em off in any case, I daresay. You'd do well to remember that what can be sold once can be sold again, especially when rogues make the bargain! You had the box with its contents from the start, you damned villain! And then you set about manufacturing the rest of the evidence!"

Durrant was now as white as the papers on his desk, but he stood his ground and answered defiantly.

"Very well. I used the box to make Carlton's claim more certain. It simplifies matters, that's all. He is still your father's son. He was told by his grandmother—"

"His grandmother!"

Anthony's temper, under control until now, at last burst forth. Seizing the secretary, he shook him like a terrier with a rat.

"His grandmother's alive, Durrant," he said, between clenched teeth, "and she's *not* Mrs. Lathom! Ay, that's set you back, hasn't it?" he demanded, as he had the satisfaction of seeing the other man give a start of surprise. "Somerby found her at that hospital of his, and she gave him the whole true history of Rowland Carlton, otherwise Joe Baker! And now, b'God, I'm going to give you the thrashing you deserve, so look to yourself!"

Flinging Durrant away from him, he quickly peeled off his coat, then strode to the door and turned the key in the lock.

"You're welcome to try, Shaldon, damn you!"

Durrant's voice was still defiant as he, too, rapidly discarded his jacket.

For a moment the years rolled back as they faced each other grimly. They were two schoolboys again, fighting as they had done in the wood at Alvington. Then it had been over a little girl's toy, but now it was because of a man's inheritance. In those days they had been evenly matched and their struggle had been inconclusive. But now, although still of an equal height and weight, Shaldon had something the advantage. During the years that his opponent had spent sitting at a desk, he himself had been active in outdoor sports and a frequenter of Gentleman Jackson's boxing academy in Bond Street.

This was no friendly sparring match, though, but deadly earnest. As blow after blow was exchanged, each fought with the impetus of his own particular fury—Durrant's the venom of years of envy mixed with rage at his thwarted schemes, Anthony's the wrath of an avenger.

"One satisfaction!" panted Durrant, as he dodged a powerful right. "There's a pretty scandal!"

"Think I care for that?" retorted Anthony, scoring a bull's eye this time on the other's chin.

Durrant staggered, but remained upright, and was soon pressing in again with renewed vigour.

"Soon forgotten when the next gossip does the rounds," finished Anthony, successfully parrying a series of blows aimed at his head.

He was less successful a moment later, when a glancing blow of Durrant's caught him on the mouth, cutting his lip. Blood started, but he brushed it impatiently away with his left hand while his right went out with all the force of his weight behind it. The blow landed on Durrant's temple and felled him.

He lay still.

Panting a little, Anthony bent over him for a moment. Then, reaching for a chair, he sat down until he had recovered his breath.

Presently Durrant stirred, looked vaguely about him, then sat up.

"A lucky hit," he said, thickly.

"Perhaps."

Anthony mopped his lip, which was still bleeding.

"The game's up, now, Durrant, so you may as well tell me the part I don't yet know. How did you come to choose this fellow Carlton for the imposture?"

"Saw him at Bartholomew Fair last August, in a play booth. Put me in mind of you because of his red thatch, although he don't otherwise resemble you. Same age and height, though, which I recalled later."

"I collect that when you gained possession of the box, you decided to abandon a genuine search for Mrs. Lathom?"

Durrant nodded incautiously, then winced, uttering an oath.

"The Earl's account gave me little hope of finding your half-brother alive, even if I did succeed in tracing the woman after all those years. Why should I go to that trouble, when I could set up a claimant of my own, with any luck? I had the proofs already."

"And you then thought of Carlton?"

"Tracked him down to Astley's, where he was standing in for an injured clown. It was a devil of a job to persuade him, though. I daren't reveal too much at first—concentrated on finding out his history. No living relatives, no ties, reared in Southwark by a grandmother—it was just what I wanted."

"And having discovered he was brought up in Southwark, you suggested that place to Mrs. Fremlin as being the destination mentioned by her mistress when she quitted Rye? Afterwards, you set up the elaborate deception with the pawnbrokers, I collect?"

Durrant smiled, though the effect was strained. "Ingenious, don't you think? I actually sent Carlton into the shop with the ring, you know, so that if the pawnbroker were questioned later, it would appear genuine."

"Your ingenuity is certainly in the first flight," said Anthony, coldly. "It's a pity you didn't confine it to a legitimate enterprise."

Durrant struggled to his feet.

"What do you mean to do? Will you bring charges against me?"

Anthony shrugged. "That's for the Earl to say."

"I shall lose everything—my livelihood, my expectations—what in God's name is to become of me? You can't do it. For old times' sake—"

Anthony gave him a contemptuous look.

"For old times' sake, Durrant, you were ready to trick me out of my patrimony."

"Yes, and you can't be certain of it yet!" Durrant flung back at him. "I may not have found your half-brother, but who's to say he doesn't exist somewhere? I'll tell you this, too—you won't get Cynthia, damn you to hell!"

"Are you referring to Miss Lydney?" demanded Anthony, at his most frigid.

"Yes, Cynthia. She's mine, mine, I tell you!"

"I think even Miss Lydney might aspire to a better fate," said Anthony, as he turned on his heel.

"It wasn't only that I hated you!" shouted Durrant after him. "Though I always did—that was no secret! But when they decided she was to marry you, I knew I must do something to stop it! And she's mine, now, finally and irrevocably mine. She has already come to me willingly, gladly! And I shall never let her go again. Never, do you hear?"

"I should think all the house must do so. All I can say is that you evidently deserve each other."

He closed the door, almost colliding with the butler who, drawn by the noise, had been loitering outside.

Chapter XXXV

AFTER returning from her drive with Anthony, Helen went up to her bedchamber to remove her bonnet. She found the housemaid Martha hovering on the landing, and the girl greeted her with relief.

"I was hopin' you'd come soon, Miss Helen. I've been waitin' about here thinkin' I might see you without anyone else bein' by."

"Why, what is it, Martha? Is something amiss? Perhaps we'd better step inside my room while you tell me what it is."

"Not exactly amiss, ma'am," replied Martha, once the door was safely shut behind them. "But that girl you told me to look out for is downstairs askin' to see you."

"Oh, yes, I see. Well, can you conduct her up here by the servants' staircase without attracting undue attention, do you suppose?"

Martha undertook to do this, and presently Phyllis Stiggins was shown into the room. Dismissing Martha with instructions to return in a quarter of an hour or so to show the visitor out, Helen turned enquiringly to the girl.

Phyllis, who looked pale and anxious, fixed an incredulous stare on Helen, taking in every detail of her modish attire.

"Crikey!" she exclaimed, momentarily forgetting her errand in her astonishment at seeing this transformation of the dishevelled female she had rescued at Greenwich Fair only a week since. "I knew ye wasn't what ye seemed that day, but I never guessed the 'arf on it!"

"No, but never mind that now. Tell me why you

came to see me. Won't you be seated for a moment?"

Phyllis obediently sat down gingerly on the extreme edge of a brocaded chair.

"Now," said Helen, encouragingly, as she herself took a chair.

"It's Rowly, Miss," began Phyllis, with a gulp. " 'E's gorn—vanished, an' no one seems to know where! Not even a word left be'ind fer me. 'E went that same day you was there, an' to my way of thinkin' with that same chap we seen 'im talkin' to. I've lost 'im, Miss, fer sure! Worse nor that, 'ow do I know 'e b'ain't in some kind o' trouble? I tell ye, 'e was dead scared o' whatever it was that swell wanted 'im to do, an' wouldn't never 'ave listened to 'im, but 'e needed the money so bad. I said as I'd come to tell ye if I found out what 'twas, but I still don't know nothin'; I swear it on me Bible oath! I was meanin' to ask 'im, see, that same night—but 'e never come back to me. And no one knows where 'e went, though I tried ever so to find out!"

She paused for a very necessary breath, then burst into tears.

"Oh, what'll I do, Miss, what'll I do? I come to ye 'cos I don't know where else to turn, an' that's the truth, Gawd 'elp me!"

Helen rose and went over to put an arm about her shoulders.

"There, there, don't cry. I know where Carlton is."

"Ye do?" The girl grasped her hand fervently. "Oh, tell me quickly, so's I can go to 'im!"

"I'm not sure about that," said Helen, slowly. "The situation's a trifle awkward."

"What d'ye mean, awkward? Oh, Gawd, is Rowly in trouble, then, as I feared 'e was?"

"Now don't be alarmed, Phyllis. In a way—yes, he is in trouble, but I don't believe that any serious harm will result to him, in the end. Perhaps I should explain a little, though I'm not at liberty to divulge the whole."

She hesitated, seeking for words that would accomplish this purpose, while Phyllis gazed eagerly into her face, waiting.

428

"The man we saw with your friend," she began, at last, "was persuading him to take part in a serious fraud. Doubtless that's why Carlton had the misgivings that you noticed."

"I knowed it. I told ye so! Oh, Gawd, Miss, what will become of poor Rowly? It was the money, see, an' not bein' able to find work. 'E'd never 'ave done it else. 'E's not a bad cove, not one to go agin' the Law, leastways! Ye'll 'elp 'im, Miss, if ye can, won't ye? Please —please—I'll do anythin' for ye. I'll serve ye all the rest o' my days."

She broke down again, and Helen soothed her for a while, thinking what was best to be done. Anthony had assured her that he intended to persuade the Earl not to bring any charges against the man. Should he succeed, Carlton would be free to return to his old way of life; but would he return to Phyllis? It was evident that the girl loved him to distraction. There could be no certainty, however, that he returned her love, as Phyllis herself had expressed doubts about being able to keep him long enough to make him her husband. It was melancholy, reflected Helen, to see a female so deeply in the toils of love. She thought about Melissa, who was just as desperately enamoured of James; and she wondered why it was that she herself seemed to have escaped this intense passion. Did she feel like this about Mr. Lydney? There was no doubt that she was somewhat attracted to him. She enjoyed his courtship, often felt the magnetism of hand on hand and eye meeting eye when they danced together. Believing him only to be flirting, she had not allowed herself to go beyond that. But if he went away, would she experience the heartbreak that poor Phyllis now felt? If he were in serious trouble, would she be prepared, like Phyllis, to go to any lengths to rescue him from it?

For a moment, she turned cold as a sudden realisation swept over her.

But this was no moment to be thinking of herself. She must do something for Phyllis, and now she knew what she intended to do.

"Listen to me, Phyllis," she said, urgently, as the

girl's sobs began to subside. "Where are you living at present?"

"I'm back at Mrs. Gerridge's place, No. 4, Murphy Street. I went there so's Rowly could find me, if 'e do come back."

"Then go back there now, and wait for a few days—no longer, I promise you," said Helen, recklessly. "I think it's most likely that your friend will return by then, but if he does not, I myself will come to give you news of him. There is someone working on his behalf to see that no harm shall come to him for his part in this affair. I truly believe that this—this person—will succeed, and that Carlton will be none the worse for his venture. But remember this"—Helen infused as much gravity as she could muster into her tone—"if he does return without having incurred any penalty for his wrongdoing, you must both of you keep as silent as the grave about it all. An unguarded word might lead to the most *serious* consequences for him. Do you understand?"

Phyllis said that she did, and promised fervently that no word about the affair should pass the lips of either. Her gratitude was touching; and Helen could only hope as they parted that Anthony had not overestimated his influence with the Earl on Rowland Carlton's behalf.

On the following morning Anthony arose early, conscious of a full day ahead. It was imperative that he should go at once to Alvington to inform his father that Carlton was an impostor and Durrant a fraud; but first he considered it only right to acquaint Lord Lydney with these facts, and to consult him about what action should be taken. He himself felt an odd reluctance to bring charges against Durrant. Physical combat had brought him all the satisfaction he required for the injury done to him; but Baron Lydney was Durrant's employer, after all, and could fairly be considered to have some say in the matter.

He was sitting at his breakfast in an elegant dressing gown of blue brocade when his man brought him a brief note from Helen telling him of the visit she had received from Phyllis Stiggins. She also gave the girl's direction, in the hope that Carlton might eventually be at liberty to return there. The note concluded with the writer's good wishes and a plea to be kept informed of events.

He smiled over this last, started to crumple the note, then changed his mind and, smoothing out the creases, inserted it instead in his pocketbook.

Presently he stepped round to Berkeley Street. Lord Lydney seemed a trifle surprised at receiving a call at such an early hour of the morning; but understanding that the matter was both urgent and private, conducted his visitor to a small parlour next to the library, explaining that Durrant would be at work in the latter.

"It's about Durrant that I've come, sir," began Anthony. "I fear you must be prepared for some unpleasant tidings."

"If you mean news of your damnable situation, my boy, I know of it already; and, believe me, you have my heartfelt sympathy. If only your father could have been persuaded to let well alone. But, there, talking pays no toll. I collect that the news is spreading about the Town, and I am grieved for you both."

"Thank you, sir, but I supposed you to be already informed on that head. That is not why I came. My purpose—I don't particularly relish it, but it must be done—is to apprise you of Durrant's infamous conduct in the affair."

Lord Lydney's eyebrows shot up as he repeated these final words. Anthony then went on to explain everything, ending with the encounter between himself and Durrant on the previous day. At the conclusion of the recital, Lord Lydney leapt to his feet, his face dark with fury.

"Good God, we'll see the fellow straightaway!"

He charged out of the room and into the adjoining library, Anthony at his heels.

The library was empty. The desk where Durrant

431

normally worked was clear of documents and had obviously not been used at all that morning.

"Where the devil is he?" demanded Lord Lydney, stepping over to the bellrope and tugging it violently.

He repeated the question to the butler, who came himself in answer to the summons.

"I can't rightly say, m'lord, but I have reason to believe that Mr. Durrant is no longer on the premises."

"No longer—What in thunder d'you mean?"

"Mr. Durrant appears to have departed for good, m'lord," replied the butler, woodenly. "The housekeeper informs me that his bed has not been slept in and all his personal possessions have been cleared from his room. He summoned a hackney last night and had a quantity of baggage transferred to it before leaving in it himself, m'lord."

"Then why the devil was I not informed of this before?"

The butler coughed. "I believed that Mr. Durrant must be acting under your orders, m'lord. Of late, he has frequently gone away on your lordship's business. It was only when I was informed by the housekeeper half an hour ago that he had left nothing at all behind, that it occurred to me to wonder if he had—to use a vulgar phrase, m'lord, if you'll forgive me—done a flit."

"Yes, yes!" said Lord Lydney, impatiently. "Did any of the servants chance to hear him give a direction to the jarvey as he got into the hackney?"

The butler admitted regretfully that they had not, although he left his audience with the impression that it had not been for lack of trying.

"I rather think your man may have overheard most of our quarrel yesterday afternoon," remarked Anthony, when they were once more alone. "Durrant was shouting, towards the end. And I almost fell over the butler when I opened this door to leave."

"Servants always know most of what goes on," said Lord Lydney, disparagingly. "No use trying to hide anything from 'em! Now what's to be done? Shall I set the Runners onto the damned fellow? He was al-

432

ways an excellent secretary—discreet, reliable—must be dicked in his nob, to risk his career on a foolhardy ploy like this!"

"The rewards were tempting, though," replied Anthony, reflectively, "and the risk wasn't so great, when one considers the matter, sir. It was a well thought-out plan that would have stood up to legal investigation, as far as he could tell. The one weak spot was the tenant of Mrs. Lathom's old cottage at Rye—and why should the lawyers make enquiries there, when Mrs. Fremlin would have already told them where her mistress was bound for when she left the town? I myself only went there on impulse, not supposing for a moment that there could be anything to be learnt by doing so. As for the rest, he had planted all the necessary evidence by inserting advertisements in the pawnbrokers' shops, and making sure that the one to whom Carlton took the ring would see enough of the fellow to recognise him again. No, as far as Durrant *knew,* he was safe enough. What he didn't know, of course, was that Carlton's grandmother was still alive. Carlton himself believed her to be dead."

"The damned clever, scheming devil!" exploded Lord Lydney. "I feel responsible, my boy. It was I who suggested Durrant, though I give you my word I could never have supposed he would act in such a way! One good thing, though—your inheritance is safe. You have nothing to fear on that head, now."

"No such thing, sir. For all I know, there may exist a genuine claimant."

"Good God, boy, never trouble your head over that," replied Lord Lydney smoothly. "You may depend that if the child had survived, we should have heard of him long since. There's only one point to be considered, though," he added thoughtfully. "If we do bring charges against Durrant, a deal of unwelcome publicity is bound to attend the business! Assuming that this female Mrs. Lathom is still alive, it may result in making her come forward to start the whole damnable affair up again, just when it's comfortably settled. I don't know how you feel—"

"It must come to that, in any event," Anthony interrupted. "I intend to instruct my lawyers to advertise for her."

Lord Lydney stared in astonishment. "But why the devil? Why not let matters rest as they are, my dear boy?"

"No. I want it settled, once for all."

"Well, no doubt you know your own business best," said the older man, in the tone of one who did not believe this. "So as regards Durrant—"

"Can we leave that, sir, until I've seen my father? I'm off there at once, because he's in ignorance of all this at present, and there's the man Carlton to be dealt with. Perhaps I might look in when I return, and we can discuss it further? I hope to be back in Town tomorrow, and one day's delay can't signify."

Lord Lydney agreed.

After parting from his visitor, he went at once to pass on the astounding news to his wife and daughter, who were sitting together in the morning room. Cynthia, who looked somewhat pale already, turned even paler as the tale unfolded; while Lady Lydney frequently had recourse to her vinaigrette as she uttered exclamations of horror.

At length, Cynthia rose, apparently tiring of the discussion.

"I am going to visit Lady Plummet at Richmond, Mama, but I shall return soon after two o'clock."

"Oh, I wish you will not go to that female!" exclaimed Lady Lydney, pettishly. "You know quite well that I do not approve of her as a companion for you. Still, if you have already engaged yourself to go, I suppose you can't very well back out. Your maid will go with you, of course, since I cannot—all this has quite overset my nerves, even if I could relish the notion of a visit to Lady Plummet at any time! Pray do not overstay your time, for we are to attend Mrs. Winstanley's rout this evening, you may recall—though I never felt less like a party in my life!"

Cynthia reassured her on this point before thankfully quitting the room.

434

"And what is now to become of the match between her and Shaldon?" Lady Lydney asked her husband plaintively.

He frowned. "I see no reason for it to be abandoned. The only thing is, the foolish fellow insists on proceeding with the quest that Durrant was supposed to be undertaking. While the issue is in doubt, perhaps it would be best to wait. What are Cynthia's views, I wonder? Has she said anything to you since the rumours were noised abroad? She seemed very anxious to make her escape just now. I would have expected her to remain and talk the matter over with us, since it so nearly concerns her."

"Oh, there's no accounting for your daughter's behaviour!" Cynthia was always referred to as Lord Lydney's daughter whenever her mother happened to be displeased with her, which was not infrequently. "If you imagine that she ever talks her personal concerns over with me, you're vastly mistaken. I daresay that dreadful Plummet female knows more about Cynthia than her own mother does!"

This was true. Cynthia's visit to Lady Plummet that morning had not been prearranged, as she had allowed her mother to think. It was the outcome of a desperate realisation that she knew of no one else to whom she might turn in a situation such as faced her at present.

She was in a fever of impatience during the journey to Richmond, and kept snapping at her maid until that inoffensive individual was almost afraid to stir in her seat. They arrived at last, however; and the maid thankfully watched her mistress being shown into the drawing room, while she herself remained in blessed solitude on a chair in the hall.

Fortunately for Cynthia, Lady Plummet was at home. She entered the room in a gown of violet silk embellished with countless knots of ribbon and a double row of flouncing at the hem. She greeted Cynthia effusively, but her expression changed gradually as her visitor explained the reason for this unexpected call.

"Lud, my dear, how could you be so monstrous

careless?" she demanded, presently. "Did you not follow the instructions I gave you?"

Cynthia nodded despondently.

"Well, I never knew those precautions to fail before. But then, a first time, and the man no doubt ardent"—here the lady tittered salaciously—"and you, I'll be bound, not backward in returning his ardour! Unfortunate, yes, prodigiously. But are you quite, quite certain? There can be no mistake?"

"None!" Cynthia snapped. Her nerves were understandably on edge. "It should have happened two days later. I'm a month overdue."

"Tut, tut! Two days before—the very worst time, believe me. But sometimes, you know, some little upset—nerves, for instance—may disturb the rhythm."

"Not in my case. I assure you I may set the clock by it—regular not only to the day, but even the hour, almost the minute! And always so, ever since I first started. Don't let us waste time over that, but tell me at once what I can do to right matters!"

Thereupon Lady Plummet suggested a number of homely remedies, most of which Cynthia had already tried without success. At last she mentioned a more drastic one.

"Of course, it will be prodigiously expensive," she warned, "but I daresay you'll find a way to obtain the fee. This man's reliable and discreet. Don't be put off by the unsavoury neighbourhood or the fact that he's somewhat lacking in social graces."

Cynthia shivered. She was not ordinarily an imaginative girl; but now a vivid picture crossed her mind of a dingy back room and a slovenly quack bending over her, most likely gin-sodden and with black fingernails.

"No, not that!" she said, fiercely. "There must be some other way!"

Lady Plummet surveyed her with amused contempt. "Well, I must confess, I'm hard put to it to think of another. I suppose you couldn't arrange for an early marriage to one of your suitors? You must have several, I imagine."

"No one whom I've encouraged sufficiently for a wedding to be imminent. You must know how I've been placed, more or less promised to Shaldon. There was no need to look around for others."

"Oh, yes, and now it seems he's no longer heir to Alvington—a pretty titbit of scandal! But in the circumstances, my dear, why not bring him speedily to the point? It scarce matters that he's no longer a Viscount. All you require at present is a husband of any degree."

"Those rumours are all nonsense, Louisa, as I've just learned this morning, so you'd do well not to spread them. But never mind that. Even if I did succeed in bringing on a declaration from Shaldon—and I don't mind admitting that I'm by no means sure of him—it would be a matter of months before a wedding could be arranged, as you must realise for yourself. And by then, my secret would be plain to all!"

Lady Plummet shrugged. "Well, there may be something in what you say. Since you reject all my other suggestions for one reason or another, have you considered marrying this man Durrant himself? At least that match could be arranged with sufficient speed, since he would know of your fix."

"Marry Durrant?" shrieked Cynthia, beside herself. "What kind of future could I look forward to, then? Besides, he's in disgrace! He's made off somewhere, Lord knows where—and when he is found, he'll most likely be handed over to the Law!"

"I must say, you both seem to have behaved most improvidently," replied Lady Plummet, with another shrug. "However, if you don't know where he is, I quite see that you can't very well marry him. All the same, remember that beggars can't be choosers. I'll give you the direction of this quack, in any event, for you may change your mind later about making use of his services."

She crossed over to a writing table, scribbled a few lines on a piece of paper and handed it to Cynthia.

The interview was at an end.

A dullness of spirit settled over Cynthia as she trod

437

slowly down the staircase to the hall. Oh, Lord, what a mess everything was! She would have given anything now to undo that fateful night at the Moonlight Masquerade which at the time had brought her such ecstatic sensual delight. This was what happened, she thought bitterly, when one took a gambler's chance. If only she had waited until she was safely married to some unsuspecting nobleman, she might with impunity have taken what lovers she chose.

Not that there were any she fancied at present to the same degree as Durrant. In spite of her dejected mood, for a moment she conjured up again the memory of their intense passion on that night—his ruthless kisses, his questing hands, his urgent body pressed closer and ever closer by her own eager embrace. He was the man for her, not a doubt of it, in everything but rank. And now she had lost him along with everything else, because she had been an impatient fool.

She came out of her reverie as Lady Plummet's front door closed behind herself and the subdued maid, and looked expectantly up and down the street for her carriage. It was nowhere in sight; but a post chaise with four horses was drawn up before the house. In a moment, someone emerged from this vehicle and came towards her.

She almost fainted from shock as she recognised Durrant.

"What—what are you doing here?" she gasped.

"Waiting for you," he answered, calmly. "Won't you get into the chaise? I've dismissed your coachman, telling him I mean to drive you home myself, so you have no other conveyance at hand."

"You've had the effrontery to do that? And what kind of reception, pray, do you imagine you'll find after all your recent exploits? I should advise you to keep well away from my father!"

"I need to talk to you," he said, persuasively, "and this was the only way I could think of. Won't you please come with me? We must be private, so if you should not object, I propose to send the maid back in a hackney."

She hesitated for a moment, turning over in her mind the recent interview with Lady Plummet. She shivered as she thought of the piece of paper in her reticule and her image of that dingy room and the repellent abortionist. Perhaps she, too, needed to talk with Durrant. She nodded.

He spoke briefly to the maid, who had waited respectfully on one side during their conversation, and handed her some money. The girl turned away with a backward glance at her mistress, who was being tenderly assisted into the post chaise. She watched Durrant climb in after Miss Lydney and shut the door. Then the postillion started up his horses with a flourish of his whip, and the vehicle disappeared down the street in a cloud of dust.

With an uneasy feeling that all was not well and that she might later get into trouble over it, the maid went in search of a hackney.

Chapter XXXVI

IT HAD BEEN decided some time since, that Melissa's birthday should be celebrated quietly with a small evening party for her available relatives and a few chosen friends. In the beginning, it had been taken for granted that James Somerby should figure among the latter; but since his proposal of marriage, Melissa had heard nothing more of an invitation for him.

"And I don't care to ask," she confided to Helen, a few days before the event, "because I couldn't bear to hear Mama say that it would be wiser for him not to come! I know Julia has written. Mama was perusing a long letter from her this morning, but she didn't pass it over to me afterwards, as she generally does. That indicates Julia's kept her promise, don't you agree?" She sighed heavily. "Oh, if only it will make Mama and Papa see matters differently! Sometimes I am hopeful, then at others I'm plunged into despair! I suppose your brother said nothing to you, Helen, about having been invited?"

Helen did not have the heart to remind her friend that when she had last seen James her mind had been occupied with other matters, so she merely replied that he had made no mention of it. Melissa sighed and remained downcast for some time afterwards.

On the morning of her birthday she was in a more sanguine frame of mind, however, and was all smiles as she received gifts and loving wishes from her family. She was particularly pleased with Helen's gift of a small cameo pendant in Wedgwood's jasperware, which both girls had admired when they had visited Wedgwood and Byerley's warehouse in York Street on their first shopping expedition.

It was a little later that the butler came into the room with a fragrant bouquet of deep red, velvety roses and handed them to her.

"How very pretty!" exclaimed Lady Chetwode. "Who has sent them, my dear? See, there's a card attached by that piece of ribbon. Do look."

Melissa looked, blushed, looked again, then silently handed the card to her mother. There was no need to read the brief, understated message; everyone present knew who had sent the flowers. And later, when she was dressed for her party in a gown of peach satin overlaid with gauze, she wore one of the roses pinned to the ribbon which bound up her glossy chestnut curls.

During the interval before dinner, visitors were constantly arriving, among them Catherine Horwood. The Lydneys had not been invited, as Melissa had stated categorically that she did not count Cynthia as one of her most intimate friends.

"It's a trifle awkward about her brother, though,"

440

Lady Chetwode had demurred. "We can't very well invite him without Cynthia, yet in the circumstances, Helen may feel the omission, don't you think?"

In truth, Helen's mind was very little on Melissa's party, though she contributed her fair share of polite chatter. She kept wondering how Anthony had fared at Alvington and what the outcome would be of his revelations to the Earl. He had promised to let her know developments as soon as possible after he returned to Town; but in the meantime, she could not concentrate fully on any other matter.

She was standing beside Melissa in conversation with several other guests when she heard her friend draw a quick, excited breath. Turning, she saw with surprise that James had just entered the room. Sir George and Lady Chetwode at once went over to him and greeted him with welcoming faces before bringing him to join Melissa and herself. They then tactfully detached the remainder of the group so that the newcomer was left alone for a time with the two girls.

"Well, this is a surprise!" said Helen. "You said nothing of being here this evening when last we met."

"I received an invitation a few days later," he replied, his eyes all the time on Melissa, whose face was radiant. "I have some good news for you, too. I have obtained my Diploma."

This matter-of-fact statement was received by both his auditors with enthusiastic congratulation.

"So you will soon be returning to Dr. Gillies to take up your new duties?" asked Helen.

He nodded. "Yes, it is all arranged, and I am to move out to Paddington in a day or two. By the way, there is something else you'll be interested to hear, Nell. I have fixed up our friend, Mrs. Dorston with somewhat more congenial quarters than Star Court. It's a small place in Southwark—not grand, you know, but quite comfortable. And since so much of her life was spent in the Borough, she is very content to make the move."

"Oh, that is famous! But," said Helen, as a doubt occurred to her, "will it be within her means?"

"As to that, her means are to be a trifle enlarged by a small annuity from Tony. He called in to see me the day before yesterday to seek my aid in the matter of finding accommodation for her, and he told me then that he meant to instruct his lawyers about the annuity as soon as he could find a minute to visit them. He was off to Alvington on the following day—that is yesterday—but expected to return today. He said life was a confounded rush at present."

"Oh, how good he is! James, had he already seen Durrant when he visited you?"

James grinned. "Indeed he had. And since I know you'll be wondering, Nell, how matters went between them, I collected that our old friend Durrant got the worst of it. But this is Miss Chetwode's birthday party, so we mustn't bore her with our selfish concerns. Forgive us, ma'am."

"But I am not bored at all!" insisted Melissa, who indeed could have listened to James talking on any topic just so long as she could have him beside her. "I know all about this, you see, for Helen had permission from Viscount Shaldon to divulge it to me."

His very blue eyes looked into Melissa's with an intensity of expression that told Helen she had now lost his attention completely. She wondered if she might venture to leave them alone together for a little while without offending Lady Chetwode's sense of what was proper. It seemed hard that they should not be allowed any private conversation when they could meet so seldom. She glanced about her and saw to her relief that both Sir George and his lady were at present engrossed in conversation with some of their guests. She slipped quietly away to join a nearby group; neither James nor Melissa even noticed her departure.

The evening wore pleasantly away until it was time for the guests to take their leave. Most of them had already gone before James reluctantly decided that he must part from Melissa.

"When shall I see you again, I wonder?" he asked her in a subdued tone.

She shook her head wordlessly, not far from tears.

"At least we've had this one evening together," he said, in a rallying tone, "and on your birthday, too. We must try to exist on memories for a while." Then, dropping his voice, "Oh, my dear, my dearest dear!"

Her emotions threatened to overcome her; but at that moment she felt an arm about her shoulders and looked up tearfully into her father's face. He was smiling at her tenderly, then raised his head to address James.

"Will you do me the favour, Mr. Somerby, of waiting behind a while after the other guests have left?" he asked, quietly. "I rather want to have a little chat with you—with you both, in fact. Melissa, my dear, your Mama wishes you to join us now in bidding our guests good-bye."

He guided his daughter away; and James was left to speculate with Helen, who soon joined him, on what the request might portend.

"There's only one thing I'd like to know," said Helen, when this topic had been thoroughly aired without producing any conclusions. "Not about that, but about Shaldon—Anthony. Was he—was he at all hurt in the encounter with Durrant?"

He grinned. "Devil a bit of it! Oh, there was a piece of sticking plaster needed for a cut lip, but nothing to require the expert attention of your newly qualified medico brother. A pity, really—I'd have liked a stronger challenge for my skill."

"Wretch! But what is to be done about Durrant?"

"He was to consider that matter with Lord Lydney and the Earl. As far as Tony's concerned, I think he's satisfied with the bout of fisticuffs. There was one thing, Nell, he said Durrant had told him—though I'm not at all sure that I should repeat it to you," he added, doubtfully.

He should have known that this could only serve to stir her curiosity. After some moments of urging on her part, he at last confided to her as delicately as he could Durrant's claim that Cynthia had become his mistress.

The shock of this silenced her for a while; then she

suggested that it might possibly be just one more fabrication on Durrant's part.

"I don't know about that," he replied, thoughtfully. "Of course, he may have said it maliciously to Tony, in the hope of inflicting a hurt on him. On the other hand, from my own observation of Cynthia Lydney I don't find it at all difficult to believe that he was speaking the truth, whatever may have been his motives."

Once more Helen relapsed into silence. Did Anthony really care for Cynthia, as Durrant had evidently supposed when he made his taunt? When the Earl had first proposed a match between them, Anthony had certainly not shown any interest in her; but that had been before he had met Cynthia in Town. Helen recalled the times she had watched them dancing together, and was forced to admit to herself that Anthony had seemed far from unresponsive to Cynthia's charms on those occasions. Perhaps he had changed his mind about her. In any case, she thought with a heavy heart, he regarded Helen Somerby merely as a sister. All his conduct towards her had made that plain.

At that moment Sir George Chetwode beckoned to James, and he left her side to accompany his host out of the room, leaving her alone. Tired after the evening's entertainment and preoccupied with her own thoughts, Helen scarcely noticed how long they were absent.

She was abruptly startled from her reverie when the door burst open and Melissa flew into the room to fling herself upon her friend.

"Nell, oh, Nell, dearest! The most wonderful news—you'll never guess! Your brother and I are to become engaged at once. Papa and Mama have consented! And we may be wed at Christmas. Oh, Nell, I'm so very, very happy!"

Anthony returned to Town two days later than he had intended, as he had spent some of his time visiting both his grandparents and the Somerbys in order to inform them of recent events. They were all very much shocked at Durrant's perfidy, and more concerned for Anthony's situation than he appeared to be himself.

"Your father must be sadly grieved at having been so taken in," commented Amanda Somerby. "And indeed, when I recall all of you playing together as innocent children, I can scarce credit that Bertram Durrant should have turned out so badly! Helen was convinced from the first that he intended you some harm, you know, but I tried to persuade her that it was only the figment of a dramatic imagination. But what does the Earl say? Does he intend to see Durrant punished? And what of this other man, the impostor?"

"I've persuaded him otherwise about Durrant, ma'am. You know how it is with Father. He wants no more trouble in the business. As for Carlton, as he's called, no action will be taken against him. I packed him off on the stagecoach for London yesterday, with a stern warning that unless he held his tongue about the affair, he might find himself charged and transported. I believe he's taken it thoroughly to heart."

"And you say that you now intend to pursue a genuine search for this missing lady, Mrs. Lathom?" asked the Rector. "I think you do right, my boy."

"Yes, but she may be dead," protested his wife, "and then poor Anthony will never know for certain whether he's the true heir to Alvington, or not! To be sure, it's the most wretched situation to be in! I think the Earl greatly to blame, not to have made enquiries many years since. But there, I suppose I ought not to criticise a parent to his son," she added, belatedly, in a contrite tone. "I beg your pardon, Anthony—my tongue, like my daughter's, frequently runs away with me, I fear, in spite of my husband's beneficent influence."

She bent over to pat the Rector's hand, and he smiled up at her with so much affection in his glance that for a moment Anthony felt a pang of envy. He found himself thinking unexpectedly that after all, some marriages were made in Heaven.

He forced a laugh to cover these feelings. "Miss

Somerby has been of the greatest assistance to me in uncovering this plot of Durrant's, ma'am. Her methods are somewhat unusual, to say the least—but I won't go into details," he added, realising the inadvisability of disclosing some of Helen's less conventional exploits. "I'm sure she will prefer to tell you the story herself. This much is certain, though—but for the efforts she and James made, Durrant's fraud might well have succeeded."

He parted from them with the reluctance he always felt at quitting that family.

Arrived in Town on the following day, he went first to his rooms in order to freshen up a little and then presented himself at the Lydneys' house in Berkeley Street. He was surprised to be received by Henry, who was seldom to be found under the parental roof, more especially not in the early afternoon of a fine day.

"Pull up a chair," invited Lydney, once they were alone. "I've a good deal to tell you. Devil of a kick-up we've had here, this last few days! Father's absent and m'mother's totally prostrated, so I've been called in to hold the fort until the old man's return. Least I can do, I suppose, though I don't exactly relish it. Never mind that. Will you take a glass of wine?"

Anthony accepted the offer, and once they were served, Lydney plunged into his tale. He had received an urgent summons to the house on the evening of the day Anthony had departed for Alvington, and found a state of panic prevailing. Durrant had packed up and gone, no one knew where, on the previous evening; and now Cynthia seemed to be missing, too. She had left in the morning on a visit to Lady Plummet in Richmond, promising to return by early afternoon. Later, the maid who had accompanied her came back alone, saying that she had been sent home in a hackney by Durrant, of all people, and that he intended to bring Miss Cynthia home himself.

"In a post chaise and four, so the girl said, and that sounded devilish smoky, what? They waited for a time after the maid arrived, then when Cynthia failed to turn up, my mother threw a fit and my father

446

dashed off to Richmond to see this Plummet female—a prime bit of muslin, know her?" Anthony nodded with a grimace. "Yes, well, seems Cynthia would've done better to have steered clear of that set. Not to wrap it up in clean linen, Shaldon, m'sister played the fool at some masquerade given by that harpy, and let Durrant seduce her—worse, she caught cold at it, and she's breeding! My father forced the whole story out of the Plummet bitch."

Anthony drew an audible breath.

"My father guessed then that Durrant must have made off with her, though the maid insisted she went willingly enough. Without more ado, he set off to follow 'em. It wasn't too difficult to discover where the chaise had been hired and whither it was bound. To cut a long story short, he traced them to the posting inn at St. Albans, where they'd broken their journey overnight. Marched in on 'em, found 'em in bed together as snug as you please, and Cynthia as brazen about it as be damned! Said they were off to Gretna to get hitched, and told my father he'd be forced to do something for them. Tried to cut a wheedle in her usual way, but the old man had reached his limit."

"What did he do?" asked Anthony.

"Gave them his blessing with a horseshoe tied to it," Henry replied, grimly. "Said they needn't go to Gretna—he'd seen them wed at once in St. Albans by special licence. As for what he'd do to provide for a daughter whom he'd so much reason to be proud of, he'd ship the pair of 'em off to the West Indies—he's some property there, y'know—and Durrant could exercise his talents on the plantation. Cynthia went into hysterics over that, but my father didn't relent."

"Damnable business," said Anthony, awkwardly.

"Understatement, my dear chap. My father came back here yesterday to set matters in train, and then returned to the happy couple. He's there still, and I undertook to stay here until he gets back. Pretty story, ain't it?"

Anthony nodded. "I'm sorry," he said, soberly. "She's your sister, after all. You must be feeling it."

Henry looked fierce. "Not as much as I should do, I daresay. Never any love lost between Cynthia and myself—you know that. But thanks, all the same." He hesitated. "Not sure if I oughtn't to offer *you* sympathy. You and Cynthia were to make a match of it, after all."

"An arrangement which found favour with our respective sires, but not, I believe, with either your sister or myself. We should not have suited. All this upheaval concerning the Alvington estates arose in the first place because I informed my father of that fact."

"Ay, I can see how that would be. Well, that's settled now with the downfall of Durrant's damnable scheme. I sincerely hope, Shaldon, that you gave the swine a good drubbing! Wish I could have done it myself—still would, if I could lay hands on him."

"I must admit few things have afforded me so much satisfaction. But you're out when you say my affairs are settled, Lydney. I've now to set about tracing this female, Mrs. Lathom, who holds the solution to the puzzle."

"Good God, why not let matters rest, man? My father lays any odds both she and the child are long since dead, and he's no gambler, assure you!"

"That may be, but I don't choose to assume it. Either I am the rightful heir to Alvington or not—that must be finally settled, one way or the other."

"Well, if you will insist on making life difficult for yourself! Once you'd taken a notion into that addle pate of yours, there never was any use attempting to turn you from it," replied Henry, with the candour of an old friend.

"Precisely. How long must you remain here?"

"Until my father returns, which I hope will be soon. There's a matter of some importance which I wish to settle on my own behalf. And it may well cause yet another stir in the family," he added. "But much I care for that!"

Anthony raised an enquiring eyebrow, but tactfully refrained from a direct question. If Lydney wished to

448

say more, no doubt he would do so. After some hesitation, he did.

"I mean to make a declaration to Helen Somerby," he said, in an unusually diffident tone. "Do you suppose I shall have any chance with her?"

Anthony felt as though he had been delivered a powerful punch in the solar plexus. For a moment he could make no reply.

"You know her as well as anybody—any man of her acquaintance, that is," continued Henry. "What d'you say?"

"Can anyone venture to pronounce on a female's emotions?" Anthony replied, quietly. "But you seem to deal extremely well together."

Chapter XXXVII

AMANDA SOMERBY FLEW into the study where her husband was working, excitedly waving a letter in her hand.

"Oh, Theo! Oh, you'll never believe—what do you think? Oh, the most exciting news—you'll never guess!"

He smiled and, laying down his pen, rose to his feet.

"Will I not, love? Then why not tell me? Or better still, let me read your letter for myself."

He reached out to detach it from her grasp and let his eyes travel swiftly over the contents. She stood by, meantime, hopping about from one foot to the other in a manner more suited to an excited schoolgirl than a woman of mature years with two adult offspring.

"Is it not famous news? Jamie has gained his Di-

ploma! Clever boy, I knew he would! And he's betrothed! To that sweet little friend of Helen's who used
to spend some of the holidays here when they were
still at school—Melissa! Oh, I'm so happy for them,
Theo. I know they'll make the most delightful couple!"

So saying, she suddenly burst into tears.

"My love!" The Rector gathered her into his arms.
"Is this your way of showing happiness? I am only
thankful you're not distressed—or would you break
into laughter on that account?"

She gave a little gurgle, half-laugh, half-sob. "I
know I'm foolish, Theo, and truly I am happy! But it
suddenly came over me that now Jamie really and
truly has left us, and will be making a family life of
his own. Yet only a short time ago he was a little boy
running in and out of the house, his pockets stuffed
full of conkers or marbles or some such boyish tro-
phies—"

She stopped and swallowed. The Rector kissed her
gently and dabbed her eyes with his handkerchief.

"They grow up so fast!" she said, defensively. "It
seems they are only lent to us for such a little while."

"That's very true, my love, but there are some com-
pensations. Only think how delightful it will be to
have a new daughter and a sister for Helen. A young
lady, moreover, well-known to us and of whom you've
always been fond. And later, perhaps, if God wills,
we may see their little ones playing in the Rectory
Garden. Now, dry those foolish tears before they
cause my coat to shrink. I don't wish to incur the expense of a new one until the wedding is at hand."

She was obliged to laugh at this, just as her husband
had intended.

"I see that James has formed the intention of coming home for a few weeks before he finally settles in
with Dr. Gillies," he continued, "and he asks our permission to bring Miss Chetwode with him for a part of
the time. It seems her parents are agreeable, and I'm
sure we can have no possible objection. Why do you
not at once compose a letter of welcome to Miss Chet-

wode, my love, in your own inimitable, warm-hearted style?"

The letter arrived in Cavendish Square on the following day and was read with much appreciation by Melissa and her parents. Some consultation with James was necessary as to the day of departure, so a servant was despatched with a message requesting him to call at the house at his earliest convenience. His reply was prompt, for he returned with the messenger; and it was soon settled that they should set out for Alvington on the day after tomorrow, taking Helen with them.

To Melissa's delight, her parents invited James to pass the rest of the day in Cavendish Square, and he was not slow to accept. After nuncheon the three young people found themselves left to their own devices for a time. Sir George, as was his custom at that time of day, retired to his library, while Lady Chetwode had an appointment with her dressmaker.

At first, all three chatted animatedly together, but presently Melissa and James could not help betraying an absorption in each other usual in engaged couples. Helen began to feel somewhat in the way, and was considering a strategic removal to another room, when a visitor was announced.

It was Anthony. Having spent the morning with his lawyers, he had called in at Cavendish Square in the hope of finding an opportunity for a private word with Helen. On seeing James there, he at once guessed that the young couple's fortunes had taken a turn for the better, and would say nothing of his own affairs until he had heard their news and given them his most sincere felicitations. Afterwards, he told them how he had settled matters with the Earl and sent Carlton back to London with some modest funds to provide for the future.

"What he makes of it, of course, depends upon himself," he concluded.

"And upon Phyllis," put in Helen. "He did return to the poor girl, I trust?"

451

"That I cannot say. I furnished him with the direction you had provided, however."

"Then I expect he would have returned to her. Oh, I do so hope he did! She is most devoted to him, poor Phyllis!"

"You're tolerably satisfied, Tony, that he'll keep mum about the affair?" asked James.

Anthony nodded. "I pressed well home the lesson that he had everything to lose by doing otherwise. My impression was that he felt mightily relieved to be out of it with a whole skin. No, I think there's nothing to fear on that head. By the way, I called in on your parents and acquainted them with the whole."

On learning this, both the Somerbys pressed eager questions as to how Mama and Papa had taken his news. After he had satisfied these queries, Helen had one more to add.

"And how was Patch? Did you see him?"

"Indeed I did. He seemed in excellent form, and had to be deterred from treating one of my gloves as a rat or some other hostile invader," replied Anthony with a smile.

"Oh, dear, I did hope his manners might have improved by now! Perhaps he needs my sobering influence."

"Is that what you call it?" he asked, with a twinkle.

"Lord, yes, Nell, the little beast pays no heed to you at all," put in James. "But what did the Earl decide concerning Durrant, Tony?"

Anthony shrugged. "You know my father. He dislikes making decisions. It was to be all left to myself and Lord Lydney. In the event, however, it's been taken out of our hands."

"How so?" asked James.

Anthony then went on to give them a carefully expurgated account of Durrant's elopement with Cynthia. Once or twice, he contrived to catch James's eye in order to convey meanings which he was unable to make plain before the young ladies; but Helen, forewarned by her brother of Cynthia's exploits, had little difficulty in interpreting these cryptic messages.

"Phew!" exclaimed James, when the recital was concluded. "So by now they will be married—Lord Lydney intends to send them overseas? Transportation, in effect. D'you think he'll stick to it?"

"Undoubtedly. I saw Henry yesterday, and he was confident that his father meant to send them on their way as soon as the knot was tied. Not a man who'd relish being hoodwinked, Lydney."

"But he was always prodigiously fond of Cynthia," put in Melissa. "I remember her telling us once that she could do anything with her Papa."

"She'd gone her length," replied Anthony, brusquely. "Even the most doting parent must eventually reach point non plus."

Helen looked at him, troubled. Apart from the brief reference to her puppy Patch, which had seemed to cheer him up momentarily, his mood had been sombre throughout. Perhaps this was understandable, for although many of his difficulties were now cleared away, he was still left in doubt about his right to Alvington. But how much was it due to the loss of Cynthia? His eyes met hers, and she saw that they were clouded with doubt—it might be pain. She thought sadly that she could read her answer in them.

"You've had a wretched time of it," she said, in a sympathetic tone, "and now you are faced with a further period of uncertainty. We must all hope that it will soon be resolved."

"Thank you. You are very good." His manner was unusually formal, thought Helen. "My lawyers are to see that the first of the advertisements for Mrs. Lathom appears in tomorrow's newspapers, and they'll be inserted every day until further notice. If she is still alive, one would suppose that eventually they must come to her notice. Should she be dead, however—"

He broke off and shrugged.

"I tell you what it is, Tony," said James, who had also noticed that his friend was not in spirits, "you could do with a diversion at present. I am to escort Nell and Miss Chetwode to Alvington for a short stay with my parents on the day after tomorrow, but tomorrow I'll be kicking my heels and wishing for something to fill the time. Why do we not spend the day together, you and I, at Lord's cricket ground, watching the MCC play against Hampshire? I haven't seen a single game this season, and I shall most likely be too occupied hereafter. What d'you say?"

Anthony's expression at once took on life. Cricket had always been a major interest of his, ever since his days at Eton, as James very well knew. And it was true that at present he felt the need of something to relieve a weight on his spirits that in fact was due in only some small part to his equivocal situation.

"Famous—my dear doctor, you seem to have an infallible remedy for most maladies. Shall I call at your lodging to take you up?"

"Deuced good of you, Tony, but I've some books and other gear to convey to Paddington first, since I'm to take up residence with Dr. Gillies as soon as I return from Alvington. I thought I might get a hackney and meet you afterwards at the ground."

"And waste half the day's play?" demanded Shaldon, scandalised. "No, let me call for you and take you and your traps straight to the match. Would there be any objection to your looking in on Dr. Gillies later in the day, when stumps have been drawn?"

James gave it as his opinion that these arrangements would be suitable, and soon afterwards Anthony took his leave. He appeared in a more sanguine frame of mind as he repeated his good wishes to the betrothed pair. When he said good-bye to Helen, he not only took her hand, which was in itself unusual, but carried it briefly to his lips.

This unexpected gallantry brought a warm rush of colour to her cheeks; but he had gone before he could notice it.

After leaving Cavendish Square, he looked in at White's, where he encountered several of his acquaintances, among them Sir Jeremy Linslade, who could talk of nothing but a pair of matched greys which he had just purchased. Although everyone present had heard rumours concerning the Alvington scandal, naturally the subject was not mentioned before Shaldon. Indeed, his presence there, looking his usual insouciant self, inclined most people to the view that, as far as his own position was concerned, there could be nothing in it.

Besides, already a fresh scandal was going the rounds.

"Heard the latest on-dit?" Anthony overheard someone say, when presently he was on his way out of the Club. "They say that dashing filly of Lydney's has eloped with her father's secretary! Care to hazard a wager on whether Lydney will catch 'em up before they reach Gretna?"

There was no keeping anything a secret in the small, select circle of London society, he reflected cynically. How long would it be before the whole, unelevating story of Cynthia's folly was being avidly circulated?

James Somerby had been right in saying that his friend needed some diversion at present. As he strolled away from the Club with spirits that showed a tendency to sink again, it occurred to Anthony that he might seek just such a diversion in a quarter which for some time he had neglected. Accordingly, after reaching his rooms he changed into evening dress and in due course presented himself at the house of Harriette Wilson.

When he was admitted, he found it crammed to overflowing with guests. Couples stood about in the hall and passageways or sat on the stairs, most of them in various stages of inebriated lovemaking. He pushed himself past these with scant ceremony, coming at length to the drawing room. As he thrust open the door, a babble of high-pitched voices and immoderate laughter burst upon his ears, making him grimace. It seemed as if all the demireps in Town must be gathered here tonight, their gowns in all colours of the rainbow, their persons bedecked with glittering jewels generously supplied by the various gentlemen who had them in protection. There was no shortage of these gentlemen, either, many of them known to Anthony, but too amorously occupied at present to spare him more than a passing nod.

He stood still for a moment taking in the scene before Harriette herself noticed him and, shaking off an admirer who appeared somewhat unsteady on his legs, made her way through the crowd to his side.

"Shaldon!" she exclaimed, in tones of rapture which perforce were loud, so that she might make herself heard. "I haven't set eyes on you this age!"

"Been out of Town," he shouted back.

She moved nearer so that he caught a whiff of the heady perfume she wore, and was afforded an excellent view of her extremely low decolletage. She stood on tiptoe to whisper in his ear, pressing her half unveiled bosom to his chest.

"Do you not find it too noisy and crowded in here? Shall we seek a more secluded spot?"

Unaccountably, his senses for once failed to respond to her blandishments, and he stepped back a pace. Her face changed; but he was providentially saved from having to deliver the rebuff which was forming in his mind, and which might well have precipitated an emotional storm. One of the nearby gentlemen suddenly seized her around the waist and whirled her, laughing and protesting, into the midst of a group of revellers. Before she could shake herself free, Anthony had closed the door firmly upon the scene and pushed his way out of the house.

As he walked briskly away, he drew several deep breaths of the cool night air. So much for Harriette Wilson, he thought, and so much for the lust that drove a man to females of her kind. Lust was an uncomplicated matter, soon satisfied and as soon forgotten. That deeper emotion which could be inspired by a woman was altogether a more complex affair. Physical desire had a part in it, but only a part; it also brought respect, friendship, a desire to protect and cherish, a longing to share all one's life with the beloved. There was all the difference in the world between lust and love; and now he knew without any

456

doubt that he was in love, and with no hope of a return.

When Helen looked in at Melissa's bedchamber on her way downstairs to breakfast the following morning, she found the room in disorder. Carriage dresses, walking dresses, evening gowns, and their various accessories were laid out on every available space; and Melissa was snatching up first one, then another, only to discard each in turn while her abigail stood helplessly by, doing her best to keep pace with her young mistress's constantly changing decisions.

"Oh, Nell, I'm so thankful to see you, for now you can help me decide what to pack for my visit to your parents! I'm near distracted with making a choice, and am almost persuaded that nothing I possess will quite do, and I shall be obliged to purchase something new, after all!"

Helen laughed. "Well, you certainly can't take the half of this, my dear! We should require a second coach to accommodate it. Besides, you will quite dazzle Mama and Papa with so much splendour, not to speak of the villagers, who are used to see me in an old muslin gown and a straw bonnet, as often as not. We shall be there only four or five days at most, so unless you wish to pass all your time prinking in your room instead of spending it in my brother's company, you'd best limit your selection, don't you think?"

"Why, yes, of course, but I do so want to make a good impression!"

"On James?" teased Helen. "Or on my parents?"

"On all of them, you wretch." She turned to the maid. "Very well, Foster, you need not wait, for Miss Somerby will help me."

The abigail thankfully departed to regale belowstairs with the laughing tale of how Miss Melissa was in a proper state over packing for a visit to her prospective parents-in-law.

"You just wait until it's your turn," Melissa said balefully, when the maid had gone. "See if I don't roast you, too!"

457

"You may have to wait a long time for that."

"I don't think so. There's a gentleman known to us both whose attentions to you are becoming more and more particular, and whom I for one feel sure will be popping the question any day now!"

Helen made no answer, but held up a gown in jonquil muslin with a white ruff round the neck.

"Take this, for one, Mel. It becomes you extremely and James has never seen it."

"Oh, yes, thank you, I will. I knew you would find something suitable! But, Helen, tell me, are you not just the tiniest bit in love? I know you've said often that you intend to take no one seriously, and only to flirt a little, but sometimes I wonder if you understand yourself as well as you think. Are you quite, quite sure that your heart isn't melting a little? Can you positively *swear* it?"

"You are like all girls in love, Mel—you cannot wait to see your friends in a similarly happy state," replied Helen evasively, as she directed her attention to the matter in hand. "Why not take the blue silk and the white with gold gauze for evening, and this green walking dress?"

With her assistance, the selection was soon made and they went down to breakfast together. Melissa did not mention the other subject again, for which Helen was grateful, for she would scarcely have known how to answer. It was only recently that she had realised how greatly she had been deluding herself about her own emotions.

Melissa was still not completely satisfied that one or two purchases were not desirable; so when her mother suggested that they might make a visit to Bond Street to choose suitable gifts for taking to the Rector and his wife, she at once fell in eagerly with the scheme. Helen for once had no particular desire to accompany them. She recollected that Catherine Horwood might be expected to call, as Catherine had made some mention of this at Melissa's birthday party; and with this excuse, she remained at home.

It was as well that she did, for Catherine put in an

appearance soon after the others had left. She was decidedly not a girl for gossip, but she had heard the rumours of Cynthia's elopement and mentioned the subject diffidently to Helen.

"Do you suppose there can be any truth in it?" she asked. "There are always so many wicked scandals in circulation about the Town, and I daresay most of them grossly exaggerated! I should not pay any heed in the ordinary way, but as we were at school with Cynthia, I did wonder. . . . Not that it sounds in the least like her, I must say."

Without feeling it necessary to impart the full details of the unsavoury story to her innocent friend, Helen acknowledged the truth of it. Catherine was very much shocked, and relieved when Helen turned the talk into other channels. This was made easier when Philip Chetwode walked in accompanied by Henry Lydney, and the four sat chatting together until the butler announced that Miss Horwood's carriage had called for her.

Philip at once rose to accompany Catherine to the carriage, leaving Lydney and Helen alone.

"I suppose you know of this devilish business with my sister?" Lydney asked, suddenly. "It all ties in with the scandal about Alvington, and Shaldon tells me you are informed of that. Indeed, he said that he is grateful for the help given him by your brother and yourself, in clearing it all up."

Helen replied quietly that she did know.

"God knows it's not a subject I wish to dwell upon with you, least of anyone, only insofar as it touches upon another which I am most desirous of discussing —have been for some time, as a matter of fact. Only now that my confounded sister has brought the family name into notoriety, you may not care to hear. In short, I could scarcely blame you if you wished to sever all connection with anyone of my name," he ended, on a despondent note.

"Why should I do that?" demanded Helen, indignantly. "You must think me a despicable creature if you suppose that I would abandon a friend only because there's a scandal connected with his name—and that not of his own making! No such thing, I assure you!"

"Think *you* a despicable creature?" he repeated, softly, his dark eyes subdued by emotion. "Do you really want to know what I think of you, Miss Somerby—Helen—I think you the most adorable, the most bewitching, the sweetest, dearest girl in the world—"

She put out a hand in a delaying gesture, but he seized it and carried it to his lips. Her cheeks were red now, and the hand trembled in his grasp. He looked at her keenly, taking these for signs of encouragement.

"Don't mistake me, Helen. I want you for my wife. Will you marry me, dearest?"

He pulled her gently to her feet and would have taken her in his arms, but she held back and shook her head, evidently in some distress.

"I can't, Mr. Lydney," she said hurriedly, in a low voice. "I like you prodigiously, and—and we go on famously together—and I am very much honoured," she continued, remembering the formula all young ladies were taught for such moments, "by your declaration—"

"No, don't give me such conventional stuff, Helen," he said, imploringly. "Since you say you like me and admit that we deal well together, surely that means that you could care for me well enough to be my wife? Or that, given a little time, you could come round to it? I've been too hasty—that's it—you need more time."

She shook her head again, more decidedly now.

"It would be unkind to allow you to hope," she said, giving him a look in which firmness and compassion were oddly mixed. "I shall always value our friendship, but believe me when I say it can never be anything more."

"How can you be so sure?" he persisted. "Many a good marriage has been made where the lady's feelings were far less favourable than those to which you freely admit! Only give me time to change them to something warmer! I know what it is," he continued, in the tone

460

of one who has arrived at a satisfactory explanation. "You haven't thought me serious until now! Plenty of tattlemongers to tell you I'm a flirt, I'll be bound. Believing that, it's only natural that you'd be very wary of permitting yourself to consider me as anything closer than a friend."

"It's true that I believed you to be merely indulging in a light flirtation—"

"Just as I said! And now that you know how deeply I love you, admire and respect you, your own feelings towards me will change," he said, confidently.

"It grieves me to give you pain, but the hurt would only be greater in the end if I allowed you to hope," she replied, gently. "You see, there is a good reason why I cannot expect any change in my feelings towards you."

"A good reason. You mean someone else? Of course, I know you have many admirers, but I had not noticed."

He looked at her keenly, but she said nothing.

"I will not importune you further now," he went on, making an obvious effort to speak calmly. "But do not think that I shall ever despair until I hear of your betrothal to some other man! I shall approach you again, Helen, if that event does not transpire within a few months, and see if I cannot persuade you next time to give me another answer. You shall not discourage me so easily!"

Chapter XXXVIII

As HE SETTLED DOWN with James to watch Hampshire play the Marylebone Cricket Club at Lord's ground in St. John's Wood, Anthony reflected that few sights could afford so much aesthetic pleasure as a game of cricket. The green turf with white garbed figures moving across it in the sunlight made an attractive setting for the skill and artistry of the players; while there was something particularly satisfying in hearing the crack of bat on ball.

This game, which had originally been played by Kentish and Hampshire boys and yeomen on village greens and rural meadows, had by now developed into one of the favourite sporting pastimes of the fashionable world. It was necessary, therefore, to find a location for it near London; and in 1787, Thomas Lord, a Yorkshireman with the enterprise for which natives of his county were well-known, had opened a cricket ground in Dorset Square. Circumstances had unfortunately made two removals necessary since then; and enthusiasts for the game hoped that the present ground in St. John's Wood, comfortably provided with a pavilion, a tavern, and stabling for the horses and carriages of the gentry, might remain a fixture.

"They're betting five to four on Hampshire," remarked Anthony. "I'm not so sure, are you? Carter's the opening batsman, I see, and Beauclerk's bowling. Trust him to bowl first, of course!"

Lord Frederick Beauclerk was known to be somewhat autocratic in his dealings with the MCC; but this was only to be expected from the son of a Duke and one, moreover, who was a very fine cricketer.

"Odd thing about cricket, though," replied James. "Unites men in very different walks of life. There's Beauclerk, son of a Duke, playing against Holloway, who used to be an ostler, so I'm told!"

"Both sportsmen, that's what matters," returned his friend. "B'God, he's done it! Bowled Carter for a duck!"

Thereafter the game occupied all their attention as they watched Lambert, a renowned all-rounder, punishing the Hampshire side. At the end of the first innings, he had stumped three, caught out three and bowled one for a duck. When the MCC came in for their first innings, he acquitted himself equally well with his bat, and had knocked up the highest score of the game, not out, when stumps were drawn.

"Magnificent!" exclaimed James, as they made their way through the crowd to the stables. "Pity about Osbaldeston, though—didn't get a look in this time, did he?"

"Bad luck," agreed Anthony. "But when he's in good form, now there's a hitter! He was at Eton, a bit before my time—a splendid man to hounds, first-rate shot, and with a handy bunch of fives, into the bargain. Only a little chap, but plenty of bottom—good-humoured fellow, too. You were quite right, James," he added, as they climbed into the curricle and spent several tedious minutes getting it clear of the other traffic and onto the highway. "I did need diverting, and cricket was just the thing— capital notion of yours."

As they proceeded on their way to Paddington, they gave themselves up to that delight of all cricket enthusiasts, the talking over of past matches they had watched and the personalities who had played in these events. It seemed no time at all before they drew up outside the grey stone house where Dr. Gillies lived. Roses were blooming in the small, white-fenced garden, and many-hued pansies lined the flagged path which led to the door.

"What a capital place!" exclaimed Anthony, involuntarily. "It looks so neat and trim, just the right setting for a country doctor. But I daresay you'll be looking out for a house of your own hereabouts before long, since you're soon to become leg-shackled, poor devil! Heigh-ho! Friends are never the same when once they've quitted their carefree bachelor existence for the bonds of holy matrimony. I daresay it will be long enough before we watch cricket together again."

James grinned. "Doing it too brown, Tony. I can tell you're envious."

"I, my dear fellow? No such thing—I don't aspire to matrimony, assure you."

"I might suppose it to be sour grapes on Cynthia Lydney's account, were I not pretty certain that you never had the slightest tendre for her."

"How well you interpret my state of mind. In fact, she was the last female I should ever have wished to have as a wife. No, our mutual friend Durrant is very welcome to her, and I believe no couple could be better suited."

"Cynical devil, ain't you?" retorted James as he sprang down from the vehicle, hauling two parcels after him on to the pavement. "Look, I've a better notion than your awaiting me at the Red Lion. Why not stable your equipage there and come back to join me here? Dr. Gillies and his sister are hospitable people, and won't care to hear that I've left my friend at the inn. Besides, I may be a little while with them, since they're sure to wish to drink my health over the betrothal. You know how it is."

Anthony demurred a little, but was eventually persuaded that it would be putting the doctor and his sister to no inconvenience.

"Good," said James. "I'll go on in, then, and prepare them for the signal honour awaiting them."

With these words, he pushed open the white gate and, picking up one of the parcels, started up the path to the house. Anthony meanwhile turned his curricle expertly in the narrow road and drove it into the yard of the neighbouring inn, where an ostler received it deferentially.

He then strolled back to the house. There was no sign of James or of the second parcel, so evidently both were now within doors. He raised the knocker.

James himself answered the door and ushered his friend into a neat parlour bright with the evening sunlight. Two elderly people were sitting there, and both came to their feet as Anthony entered.

"This is my friend Shaldon, of whom you've often heard me speak," began James, presenting Anthony first to the lady. "Tony, this is Mistress Betty."

Anthony bowed. "How d'you do, ma'am?"

Oddly, Mistress Betty made no reply. She was staring at him as if thunderstruck.

In a moment, all traces of colour left her cheeks, leaving them white and pinched. She moved forward a step, staggered, and would have fallen, had not James promptly leapt forward to support her.

She uttered a choking cry and gasped out a name. "Neville Stratton!"

Mistress Betty had never been in such a luxurious room as the small salon at Alvington Hall. For a moment she felt overawed by the evidences of wealth —the thick Aubusson carpet, the claret coloured velvet curtains caught back in bands of gold braid, the highly polished mahogany furniture, and the elegant ormolu clock on the mantelshelf. Then her eyes came to rest on the man in the wing chair, his leg swathed in bandages and supported on a footstool.

Two people much changed by time and circumstance, they faced each other as they had often done in the past in the humbler setting of the cottage at Rye.

Anthony placed a chair for her, and silence fell on the room for a while.

"Do you recognise this lady?" asked Anthony presently, in a quiet tone.

The Earl stared without speaking at the woman seated opposite. Her once bright hair was now grey and her face creased by the wrinkles of time; but

465

her features and expression struck an instant chord of memory within him.

He nodded. "Ay, she's Mrs. Lathom, right enough."

Anthony released a suspended breath.

"Should you be in any doubt," said Mistress Betty, "you will surely recognise this."

She unfastened from her neck the locket which she always wore and passed it to Anthony, who rose to hand it to his father. With trembling fingers, the Earl opened it.

The bright countenance of Dorinda smiled out at him across the years.

A spasm of pain contorted the Earl's face. He closed the locket with a snap and handed it back.

"I should scarce have recognised you again, Mr. Stratton." Unconsciously, she gave him the name by which she had always known him. "You are greatly changed—and not, I fear, in the best of health. But I knew your son at once. It was as if a ghost had stepped out of the past. He is very like you once were."

Her eyes studied Anthony again, noting now a firmness and resolution in his countenance which had been lacking in that of Mr. Stratton.

"And yet unlike," she murmured, almost to herself.

"I did come back to see you, y'know, after that last time," said the Earl, defensively. "You may suppose that I totally abandoned you and the child, but it was no such thing. There was a devilish old hag living next door, and I questioned her; but beyond admitting that she'd seen you go off in a chaise with the child, she kept mum. I couldn't find anyone who knew where you'd gone."

"That was because I didn't wish anyone to know. At that time, my heart was filled with hate towards you, and the last thing I wanted was to have you follow me."

"You let slip something to your maid, though, did you not, ma'am?" asked Anthony.

She nodded. "I worried over that afterwards, though I hoped an ignorant country girl such as she was

466

would most likely forget what I'd said. I told her I was going to Paddington, a village near London."

"She recalled that it was London," replied Anthony. "I suppose to a country girl London would appear invested with glamour, and therefore it stuck in her memory. But she forgot the name of the actual village."

"As I've already explained to you, sir, I took the child there thinking that my brother, Dr. Gillies, might be able to save it."

"And had you been known under your formal title of Mrs. Lathom, we must have discovered you before this. My friend Somerby often spoke of his mentor Dr. Gillies and of Mistress Betty, both of whom had been so kind to him during his years as a medical apprentice. But of course there was no reason to suspect any connection between Mistress Betty and Mrs. Lathom."

"My brother never found it natural to refer to me as Mrs. Lathom. We had met so rarely after my marriage, you see, until I went to live with him as a widow. In the old days it had been Betty, in the family—my full name is Elizabeth—and he had spoken of me to others as Mistress Betty. He did make an attempt at first to call me by my proper title, but soon gave it up and reverted to the ways of our childhood. I suppose no one has called me Mrs. Lathom for close on five and twenty years."

The Earl had been paying no attention to their conversation for some time now, immersed in his own thoughts.

"Daresay you did hate me," he said, at last, returning to an earlier remark Mrs. Lathom had made. "Don't think I relished the part I had to play, but what could I do? I couldn't afford to alienate my father, dependent as I was upon him financially. *De mortuis nil nisi bonum,* and all that, but everyone knows he was a tyrant, especially with his own family! It's easy for others to say they'd act in this way or that, but in the end it's he who pays the fiddler who calls the tune. Damn it all, my hand was forced, choose how!"

The final words came out in a burst of angry self-justification.

Mrs. Lathom's eyes rested on him with a hint of compassion.

"All that has long since gone by, Mr. Stratton—my lord," she said quietly. "Time has laid healing fingers on my wounds. As for you, your health is not good, and dwelling on past sorrows will not benefit you. I should not have come here at all, but that I needed to do so, in justice to your son." She sighed. "The sins of the fathers have been visited on the children, as the Good Book says. But now at last your surviving son has his own again. As for the little mite who expired soon after I brought him to my brother, he is at peace. May God rest him and my beloved daughter."

Patch was delighted to see his mistress at home once more. None of the other humans seemed to understand so exactly what a dog liked, or to have the time to provide it; a sedate walk on a lead through the village, for instance, could not compare with a wild scamper through the wood such as he was enjoying at the present moment.

Helen had been glad of the excuse to escape for a time from the Rectory drawing room where James and Melissa were sitting with her parents. She wished to be alone with her thoughts. James had given his family a full account of the events of the past few days: how Mrs. Lathom had been found and brought to Alvington to inform the Earl that the child of his first marriage had died in infancy, and that therefore Anthony was the rightful heir to Alvington.

She was thankful, as they all were, to know that Anthony's uncertainties were now over; but she still could not rid herself of a lingering suspicion that he might be suffering some pangs over the loss of Cynthia. James had laughed this off when she had voiced it, repeating to her the words which Anthony himself had used.

"He said she was the last woman he'd have wished for as a wife. No getting beyond that, is there?"

468

Helen's common sense told her that there was not; but in the present state of her emotions, common sense counted for little. She could not entirely dismiss the notion that Anthony might have been making an attempt to conceal his chagrin from James. At times she was still haunted by the mental image of Cynthia and Shaldon dancing together in all the intimacy of the waltz at Cynthia's come-out ball. The look he had bestowed then on his partner had certainly not been cold and indifferent.

Her reverie was interrupted by an outburst of barking from Patch at a little distance away, and she moved quickly towards the sound. She found the dog standing at the base of an elm tree hurling defiance at some creature perched high among the foliage.

"Silly boy!" she scolded, peering up to try to see what was the cause of all this commotion. "Stop that odious noise at once!"

The dog obeyed for a moment, but broke out into protest again when the unseen creature leapt in a flash to another branch.

"It's only a squirrel, stupid. Now stop it, do! Do you hear me?"

"It seems he doesn't," remarked an amused voice behind her. "Patch, you young fool, ycu can't climb trees, so you'd best abandon the hunt."

Helen turned quickly and saw Anthony. The dog whisked round, too, a low growl in its throat; but seeing its mistress give a smiling greeting to the newcomer, it changed its tactics, bounding joyously towards him.

"Down, sir! No, I shall not permit you to sully my garments with those doubtless filthy paws!" chided Anthony, bending to pat the dog. "Try to be more worthy of the company in which you find yourself."

Helen laughed. "Mine or yours, sir?"

"Can you doubt I meant yours?" he asked, with a smile. "Do you mean to walk with him much farther? If so, perhaps you'll not object if I accompany you? I was on my way to call at the Rectory, but there's no hurry for that."

Helen replied that she herself was just about to turn

back, and for several moments they strolled along together in a leisurely way, saying nothing. Presently she felt the silence becoming oppressive and nerved herself to speak.

"I am so glad that at last all your difficulties are resolved, sir," she said, a trifle awkwardly.

"You are very good, but why all the formality?" he asked, giving her a keen glance. "I thought we had agreed on using first names when we were alone together?"

"I—well, yes, but that was before—" He raised an enquiring eyebrow, and she continued, "Before we knew for certain that you were indeed Viscount Shaldon. It was so difficult to call you by any other name —Mr. Stratton would have made you seem a stranger!"

"You are making me feel a stranger now, Helen," he said, gravely.

"Oh, I beg your pardon. I don't mean to do so."

"Is it because," he asked, with another searching glance, "you've any particular reason for setting me at a distance?"

The unexpected question brought a rush of colour to her cheeks which she tried to conceal by turning her head away to watch the dog cavorting ahead of them.

"How absurd you are," she reproved him, in a light tone. "Why should I have?"

"Only you can know. Yet there is something different in your manner towards me, Helen."

She caught her breath. Had she betrayed herself?

"What nonsense!" She forced a laugh. "Of course there's not!"

"No? Well, maybe I imagine it," he replied, in the tone of one who was far from convinced. "It occurs to me that possibly there may be something on your mind. Have you any news to give me?"

"News?" she repeated in astonishment.

"Yes. You would tell me, surely, since we've recently shared so many exploits together? Besides, everyone must know soon enough, when the notice appears."

She was staring at him now in frank bewilderment.

"I fear I don't in the least understand you, Tony," she said in a more natural manner. "What notice are you expecting—what do you mean?"

"Do you wish to keep it a secret for some reason? I refer, of course, to the notice of your betrothal."

"My betrothal—oh!"

Now she understood, and to her annoyance she was blushing again.

"May I wish you happy?" He made a strong effort to infuse the right degree of congratulation into his tone. "Lydney's a lucky dog. He don't deserve you, but who could? All the same, you've known each other a long time, and seem to deal extremely well together. I wish you the best of everything, my dear Nell"—there was no mistaking the sincerity of this—"now and forever. And if at any time you should need a friend—"

He could manage no more, and fell silent, looking away from her.

"But—but you're mistaken, Tony!" she cried. "I'm not betrothed—to Mr. Lydney or anyone!"

He turned quickly with a sudden exultant light in his eyes which made her pulses leap. It died away in a moment, leaving his face sombre.

"Unpardonable of me—I seem to have anticipated events. I was quite certain that Lydney must have seen you before you quitted Town."

She nodded. "So he did."

"And did he not speak?" asked Anthony, incredulously. "He confided in me that he certainly meant to do so. Oh, Lud, I beg your pardon, Nell! I have no right to question you in this way. You must be wishing me at the devil! I am once again trying to act the part of a brother, and you've told me often enough how much you dislike that. Pray forgive me."

She smiled at him a little tremulously, for some very chaotic feelings were stirring within her.

"I'll forgive you this once, provided you promise not to repeat the offence. But even though you are not my brother, Tony, I haven't the least objection in the world to answering your question. Mr. Lydney did

471

make me a declaration before I left Cavendish Square."

"So you refused him."

It was a statement, not a question; but she nodded, taking care to avoid his eyes, which were now fixed intently upon her.

"And yet I could have sworn that you were attracted to him," he said, almost in an accusing tone.

"Well, so I was, in a way," she replied, with her usual candour. "In the way that most girls will find themselves attracted to any personable gentleman who sets out to flatter and please. That's human nature, isn't it? But there must be a deeper feeling involved before one thinks of marriage."

"Yes, you would realise that from the start, having before you the example of your own parents' happy marriage." There was bitterness in his tone. "I was not so fortunate."

She looked up at him with softened eyes.

"I am sorry. I fear you must be feeling the loss of Cynthia," she said gently.

"Cynthia?" He laughed cynically. "I feel nothing for Cynthia but that she has come by her just deserts! What in the world makes you suppose that I ever gave her one serious thought, or can spare a single regret for a female whom I was determined not to marry in the first place? Did not all this trouble over my father's secret marriage arise because I'd refused to fall in with his wishes in that regard? Cynthia may go to the devil, for all I care!"

All at once her heart felt so light that she wanted to dance for joy. She turned a mocking face upon him.

"And yet I was certain that you must have changed your mind about that, seeing how attracted by her you appeared to be when you were waltzing together at her come-out ball," she said, outrageously.

"Nell, you little wretch!" He stopped abruptly, advancing on her in a threatening manner that recalled their childhood days. "So you think to pay me out in my own coin, do you, you saucy madam!"

Laughing, she put out her arms to ward off the

threatened attack. And in a moment, he had gathered her unresisting to him, pressing his lips against her bright hair.

"Nell—oh, Nell!" he murmured, incoherently. "My darling—my lovely girl!"

She snuggled closer. "But, Tony," she said plaintively, into his chest, "why do you not kiss me properly? I've been wanting you to—oh, for ages and ages!"

Her words set his pulses leaping, but he told himself he must be careful not to alarm her by too much ardour. She was young, innocent, and infinitely precious to him. So he tilted up her face and kissed her gently on the lips. That fleeting contact, though soft and tender, was so charged with emotion that it left their senses swimming.

He would have released her then, not quite trusting himself to sustain his gentleness if she remained any longer in his arms. But Helen, looking for something more masterful from her childhood hero, tightened her own arms about him and freely offered her lips again. This time he could no longer resist the urge to crush her to him and kiss her in quite another style; far from being dismayed, she responded eagerly.

After an interval, he held her a little way from him, smiling down at her tenderly.

"Dearest Nell, how could I ever be such a fool as to suppose I thought of you as a sister?"

"I always knew I didn't want you as a brother," she answered, somewhat breathlessly. "But it was a long time before I really understood why. You see"—she gave a little laugh—"I thought it was because you tried to interfere too much in my affairs!"

"A husband has the right to interfere even more than a brother," he warned her, but there was a twinkle in his eye.

"Well, I *will* try my best to be a dutiful, obedient wife," she said, blushing a little. "But pray don't positively *forbid* me to do things, will you, Tony? I fear it brings out all the contrariness of my nature!"

"Not much chance of that," he replied, putting on

a glum expression. "You'll have me eating out of your hand, I daresay."

"I'd like to see that! Why, when we were children it was always the other way about, and I was your slavish disciple!"

"Ah, but you're a woman now, Nell, and a very lovely one. Tell me, dearest, how will you like to be a Viscountess?"

"Oh, that's of no account to me—but I shall like extremely to be Anthony Stratton's wife," she replied shyly, burying her face in his chest.

He clasped her once more in a strong embrace.

In this very wood, thought Helen, a little girl once dreamt that her Prince would come; and now he holds her in his arms, and they will nevermore part. But even that thought vanished in the next moment, as all but the intoxication of their love was forgotten.

Patch had wandered off long since, but now he returned in search of his mistress. Seeing her held captive, he leapt forward with a growl to her defence.

The pair moved apart, laughing.

"Down, old fellow!" ordered Anthony. "You'd best accustom yourself now to this kind of thing."

Helen bent down to pat the dog. "Silly boy," she whispered, in his cocked ear. "Can't you see I *like* it?"

Patch settled himself down beside them with an air of resignation. He might as well make himself comfortable, for it looked as though they would be here for some time. There was no accounting for humans, even the best of them.